Times Like These

Other Books by Rachel Ingalls

Times Like These

Stories by

RACHEL INGALLS

Graywolf Press
Saint Paul, Minnesota

"Last Act: The Madhouse," "The Archaeologist's Daughter," and "Somewhere Else" were first published in Great Britain in 1992 by Faber and Faber Limited, in the collection *Black Diamond*.

"Correspondent," "Fertility," "Veterans," "The Icon," and "No Love Lost" were first published in Great Britain in 2002 by Faber and Faber Limited, in the collection *Days Like Today*.

Publication of this volume is made possible in part by a grant provided by the Minnesota State Arts Board, through an appropriation by the Minnesota State Legislature; a grant from the Wells Fargo Foundation Minnesota; and a grant from the National Endowment for the Arts, which believes that a great nation deserves great art. Significant support has also been provided by the Bush Foundation; Target, with support from the Target Foundation; the McKnight Foundation; and other generous contributions from foundations, corporations, and individuals. To these organizations and individuals we offer our heartfelt thanks.

MINNESOTA
STATE ARTS BOARD

NATIONAL
ENDOWMENT
FOR THE ARTS

Published by Graywolf Press
2402 University Avenue, Suite 203
Saint Paul, Minnesota 55114
All rights reserved.

www.graywolfpress.org

Published in the United States of America

Printed in Canada

ISBN 1-55597-431-7

2 4 6 8 9 7 5 3 1
First Graywolf Printing, 2005

Library of Congress Control Number: 2005925169

Cover art and design: Scott Sorenson

Contents

Times Like These

LAST ACT: THE MADHOUSE

Four other boys in William's class shared his name. At home he was Will. At school someone else was called Will, two were Bill, and one went under a middle name. Only William was given the full, formal version.

His family had money. They owned a large house in town and a summer place at the beach. He was closer to his cousins—until they moved away—than to any of the boys and girls in his class. Everyone liked him, but he had no special companions. He had pets: as a child he'd kept mice, frogs, goldfish, and a dog his parents had bought for him when he was two. The dog lived to be almost thirteen and died of kidney disease. After that, William didn't want another pet. His energy went into the car he was learning to drive.

When he wasn't out on the road he'd spend his time playing phonograph records. He had hundreds, most of them highlights from Italian opera, though there were a few albums of Dixieland in his collection, and some blues and early jazz. He got interested in opera by listening to the radio. He liked the tunes. For years he knew nothing about the stories that were meant to accompany the music—in fact, he had no idea that the songs were intended to be played in any definite order. One day he decided to write down the name of a composer as it was announced at the end of a broadcast. He went to the library to find out more. He started to buy the records and to read about music in general.

Every once in a while his parents would take him along to a concert in the capital. They were glad to see that he wasn't completely brainwashed by the rock and roll everybody his age was dancing to, but they considered opera to be going a little too far. They drew the line at foreign languages, even the kind of French used in restaurants. The waiter could always tell you what things meant.

He began to pick up a few phrases in Italian. At school he was offered French, and Latin if he wanted it; he didn't want Latin because he thought he'd never need it. He did well in French. He even bought a couple of records of French opera, and some in German, but they failed to hold his attention. Already he was a specialist: it was the Italians or nothing.

He studied the stories from booklets that came with his boxed sets. The text included pictures of the singers in costume. And, on the back covers, photographs showed him how each scene would look to an audience. He read reviews in the papers. He subscribed to an opera magazine. As in many other matters, his acquaintance with opera was theoretical: imagined. He'd heard a lot, but seen nothing firsthand.

He knew the characters' names; he was familiar with their lives. The young men who sang the hero's part were soldiers or scholars, dukes and princes. Sometimes they were in disguise: that was the way life was then, apparently. And they loved. That hadn't changed. They were like real people to him. They were like himself. Of course they were also melodramatic and silly, but however inane the people and the plot, the music always won out. The music persuaded him so far that he even began to like the faults as well as the virtues of opera. He was captivated by the ludicrous misunderstandings, the eccentric motives and contrived emotions, the coincidences that could never happen.

The stories were usually, as anyone could see, ridiculous. That wasn't important. You had to realize that certain conventions and situations were constant because they set the scene for a particular kind of music. There were arias of anger, forgiveness, longing, supplication; if you wanted to cram them all into one work, the story had to make room for them. Occasionally things got to the point where—because of the need to fit in all the songs—the plot no longer made sense. William didn't mind too much about that. He preferred an overcrowding of drama to a lack of excitement.

He also understood that sometimes the kind of voice a composer was writing for would determine the style of the music. In quite a few of these operas, for instance, there was a mad scene. When a coloratura soprano was in the cast, you could be fairly sure that before the last act she'd be crazy, although still able to hit a high E. Almost always the reason for her mental collapse was desertion or betrayal by her lover, whose black cloak (dark, anyway, according to the photographs) she would press to her heart as she trilled away at the high bits. The traditions of stage madness demanded that the more crazed a girl became, the higher she sang. Purity of tone would indicate the intensity of her love and pain. Another custom governed the color of her dress: it had to be white, and of a simple, shiftlike design. You were supposed to think it was her nightgown, and that she'd be too distracted to want to change her clothes, or perhaps to remember how to. Occasionally the nightdress resembled some sort of tattered bridal garment she'd put on under the impression that the hero would call for her in just a minute, to take her to church and make her his wife. Her complaint might not have been insanity as the twentieth century knew it, but more a kind of madness peculiar to the dictates of Romanticism.

As his knowledge and appreciation grew, William no longer felt that his greatest wish was to see an opera staged. What he longed for was the world the operas described: the emotions of other people, given to him by the music; the place where grand events took place, usually in the distant past or at the time when the music had been composed. That time too was gone. But all times in opera were equal; fictional and historical past occupied the same world. It was the world where William wanted to live. The time of Romance seemed more real to him than Korea, the Second World War, the Depression, the First World War, the Founding Fathers, and all the rest of it. A century or so made no difference to him, nor did the setting. People still felt the same, no matter where they were; love, hate, jealousy, the urge to kill, to die, to sacrifice, to capture beauty: emotions didn't change. But a small American town in 1958 wasn't an ideal stage on which to express emotion. You could get into trouble just trying to park at the side of the road with a girl.

He'd been out in his new car one night with a girl from the class above his, when a policeman had sneaked up and shone a flashlight at them through the window. William came home raving, asking his parents what kind of man would take a job like that—what kind of pervert? His father laughed. William said, "Somebody old and ugly and envious; some slob that hates anyone young. He wanted to see my license and know all about the car, and—I bet he wasn't even on duty. He was probably one of those Peeping Toms. I'm going to report him."

"Don't do that," his father told him. "He can say he was checking the car. To see if it was stolen, or if you'd had the brakes tested. Anything like that."

"He wasn't checking the car. He was checking on us, to see if we were making out."

"You wouldn't be able to prove that."

William's mother said, "It's part of their job, dear." She was a generation younger than her husband. She'd been brought up primly and had always been cautious with younger men.

William shouted, "How could that be anybody's job? It isn't anybody else's business what I want to do."

"They just have to make sure you're not doing anything wrong," she said.

William thought he was going to choke. He threw out his arms and stamped on the floor. "Wrong?" he said. "Jesus Christ!"

"Will, I don't want to have to keep asking you to watch your language."

He marched up to the sideboard, back to the table, and out of the room. His father called after him, "That'll teach you to park a little farther out of town."

He went down to the basement room his parents had let him make into a music studio. He put a record on the turntable. His anger and frustration flooded away on a tide of music. He couldn't understand how other people could hear the notes and not realize that opera was more beautiful, and better, than the kind of stuff they normally listened to. The music said everything. It told you, without words, everything that was going on, and what it meant: what the people in the story felt. Even the plots, even the silly ones filled with coincidences, were marvelous: the violence, intimacy, and commitment of the emotions they dealt with, the exaltation they allowed you; it was all wonderful. Small towns in American didn't leave any margin for that kind of uplifting experience. They didn't even let you try it out in your car.

He was in his third year of high school when he started going out with Jean. She was two years younger than he was. His mother didn't approve of that. She didn't trust Jean's parents, either, who were ordinary people no one had ever heard of. William's mother didn't associate with such families. She had sound instincts about that sort of thing; his father thought so, at any rate. Once William knew what his parents' attitude was going to be, he spent a lot of time in crowds: playing tennis, going to the movies, going out with seven or nine other people in his class. And he met Jean in secret.

Secrecy speeded up the affair, as did the knowledge that there were hindrances against them. They met and embraced in an isolation as charged with expectancy as any midnight assignation between soprano and tenor. All they needed to heighten their passion was an appreciation of danger. But the dangers were so obvious that they overlooked them.

Their conversation was all of abstract things. First of all they agreed on how wrong most people—especially the older generation—were about everything. Then they talked about love and about art. And poetry. They both wrote poems; they had written poetry long before they had anyone to write it to.

He'd have liked to listen to his records with her, but she was shy about coming to the house. She knew his parents still thought she wasn't the kind of girl he should be seeing: they didn't go out of their way to discourage the friendship—that might persuade their son to commit himself to the girl. They said instead that they felt sorry for her.

As for taking his records to her place: that wouldn't work, either. Her parents were definitely not the kind of people who listened to opera. If he'd brought it into their house, they'd have thought he was showing off, or worse—that he considered them in need of extra education.

He played the records after seeing Jean, and before. He had Callas, he had Gobbi; he had everybody. He also had a car and good clothes and enough money to take a girl out dancing, to the movies, to restaurants. That should have been in his favor. What it actually meant was that Jean's parents suspected him of being unreliable: financial freedom leads to other freedoms. And although it might be possible in their town to conceal an aberrant or extravagant mind, any generosity or transgression of the body was found out immediately. Even when it wasn't true, illicit intercourse could be presumed: by the way people behaved, what they said, how they looked at each other. Hints, supposition, inference, couldn't harm a man; they hurt women and girls. There were many reasons for the parents of a daughter to feel mistrust. They would want her to refuse all physical advances in any case; but if she didn't, she'd have no control over what happened to her. Any power she had over her future would pass to the man she was with. A man, married or not, could buy contraceptives at the drugstore, whereas no unmarried woman of any age could legally ask a doctor to fit her with a diaphragm; a young girl who tried such a thing would be reported to her parents, or possibly to the police. That would be considered a question of morality. Jean was fifteen, William seventeen, which would have made it immorality. They thought it was love.

They made love outdoors at night and then in the daytime, too. As his father had advised, William parked the car far enough from the center of town not to attract attention. The fact that neither of them had sisters or brothers made it easy to keep their secret, although later it would mean that they'd have no allies against their parents' generation. And at school they hadn't found anyone to take the place of brothers and sisters. It seemed that all their lives they had been waiting for each other. William had his gang of pals, none of them very important to him. Jean was temporarily without anyone she wanted to confide in. She'd had two good friends, but both of them had left school. Her best friend had moved to another town the year before. She'd written letters

for the first few months of their separation. After that, the correspondence became sporadic. She never mentioned William to the girl. She
felt it would be a betrayal to talk about him behind his back, to share
with anyone else the secret understanding they had; and as soon as
they were lovers, there was no need for emotional corroboration from
a third person: William had taken the place of best friend.

They wrote poems to each other and also letters. Sometimes they'd
mail their poems, sometimes one of them would just slip a piece of
paper to the other between classes. To exchange a look among a group
of people, to brush by each other so that their hands touched, set them
alight: to know, when nobody else knew.

They lost interest in schoolwork. When they weren't falling asleep
over their books during the day, they'd want to laugh and joke. They
liked sneaking into the back row of movie theaters to watch B-features
while they fed each other popcorn and tried to see how much they
could do with each other before anyone noticed.

At night he'd stand outside her house while she shinnied down the
tree that grew in front of her bedroom window. Later on, he'd take
up his post again as she climbed back. They blew kisses to each other.
He'd take long walks or drive around for a while before returning to
his parents' house. When he got back, he'd turn the volume down on
the phonograph and play his records. He'd sink into the harmony—his
breathing, his skin, his whole body aligned to the sound of passion in
the voices: the delicious pain of love, the beauty, the intensity. To be
able to sing like that, he thought, would be like being able to fly. And
now that he was a lover himself, he understood: that was what it was
all about—desire and suffering, betrayal and madness, reconciliation,
the joy of being united in love.

Long ago opera had taken the place of a friend. Now that he had
someone of his own, he hadn't lost his affection for it, but its use had
changed. It supplemented his life, where before it had been a substitute. Jean had become his life. And he was living for the first time, as
if he'd just woken up, having slept to his music all the time when he
might have taken part in the world.

Eventually, after several months, Jean got pregnant. She didn't tell anyone. Even though her period had never come late before, she hoped and expected and prayed that it was late just this once, and it would come at any moment. When it was three weeks late she still hoped, doggedly and miserably. She threw up twice—once after she'd been drinking, so that didn't count. Her breasts began to hurt. But she told herself that if something had gone wrong with her period, she'd probably feel strange symptoms anyway.

Eleven days after she missed the second period, she told William she thought she might be pregnant. She might be; in fact, she was sure now: she was. She'd have to have an abortion straight away. How could she get one—what could they do?

William was so amazed that for a while he could only say, "It's all right." Then he told her he blamed himself for not trying to be more careful. He wasn't the one who'd get stuck, so he hadn't worried. He should have thought about her. Now that it had happened, he said, he wanted her to have the baby. It was his; he was proud of that. And it was natural. To do anything against that, he figured, would be somehow wrong. He was stunned by the idea of a new life that the two of them had made together. "Because we loved each other," he said. The only reason why she didn't want to have it was that all the people in town were such hypocrites: wasn't it? She was afraid that they'd take it out on her, start talking about morality and do a lot of preaching at her. But everything was going to be all right. He wouldn't let them.

It wasn't going to be easy. He could imagine how bad things would be for her. He'd known for a long time how strongly society felt that any kind of love outside marriage, and sometimes within marriage, was bad. The physical expression was bad. In fact, the emotion itself, the idea, was suspect. Platonic love could sometimes be the worst because it bound two souls together regardless of age, sex, color, belief, or marital status. The movies you could see in town were almost as repressed as real life; people were given their just deserts if they stepped out of line by a fraction. You only saw how beautiful love could be—the way everybody their age knew it had to be—if you could get to a foreign movie, where they showed people in their underwear and sometimes even, from far away, naked; at least, the women.

It would be bad for her, but it was going to be bad for him, too. Once people knew, the small town would close against him. It had never had anything in common with people like him, anyway.

As for her, she knew that what had happened to her was the end of a girl, unless she got married. Everybody knew what became of girls who got pregnant: everyone talked about them and the girls went away forever, or they came back later and no one talked about where they'd been. They were like women who had died.

If she got married, then it would be all right. She would escape from her parents, who were wrong about everything anyhow, and she'd be with William. He won her over. She'd do anything for him. He'd tell his parents. They wouldn't be able to fight it; they'd have to let him marry her in one of those states where the age limit was lower. And if his father and mother accepted that, the rest of the town would, too.

He talked to her parents. They were impressed by him and by his family. "As far as I'm concerned," he said, "we're married." But Jean's mother thought, despite everything, it was a terrible shame—the ruin of at least two lives—for a girl to have a baby at such a young age: she'd be only just sixteen when it was born. And Jean's father got to thinking that there should be some legal safeguard for his daughter, so that in three or four years' time, or even ten, she and the child would be provided for. Young men sometimes changed their minds.

"I'll see to all that," William said. He was still only seventeen. He wouldn't be eighteen till the spring. He hadn't told his own parents anything yet. Knowing them and their views about who was or wasn't worthwhile, he'd prejudged their reactions and chosen, for the moment, not to speak out. In any case he'd wanted to be with Jean when she had to face her mother and father. The money he'd have when he was eighteen wasn't much, but it was enough to start out on. If he had to, he could handle everything all by himself, though he'd rather have his parents' help. He'd rather have them understand, too.

He was still mulling over the wording of the speech that would overwhelm his parents, when he was beaten to the punch by Jean's father.

Her father had first of all let his daughter know what he thought of her. "This is all the thanks we get," he'd said. His wife backed him up. Jean ran upstairs, crying, and slammed her door, leaving her parents to talk about what should be done.

Her father decided there ought to be a discussion between all four parents on the matter of financial arrangements. He telephoned William's father. He assumed that the man knew what was going on.

Jean's father talked to William's father for twelve minutes. He brought up the subjects of rent, food, clothes, the price of baby carriages, hospitals, and so on.

William's father didn't say much, except that he'd remember all the points raised: he'd have to go over them with his wife before he could say anything definite. He left the office immediately. He went into conference at home with his wife. Together they greeted William on his return from school.

He opened his heart to them. They closed theirs to him. They told him that he had no idea how difficult it could be for a young couple with a baby—especially hard for a girl, who would have to become a mother before learning how to be a wife.

"We know that already," William said. "What it means to be man and wife. We don't need a piece of paper."

"Without a piece of paper, and without being the right age, the child may not be legally yours," his father told him. "Or hers."

"That can't be true."

"You can prove you're not the father of a child, but it's impossible to prove that you are. You didn't know that, did you?"

"I guess so," William said. "Why does it matter?"

"She's still considered to be under the care of her parents. And now her father's trying to get money out of us. He called me up at the office, started talking about hospital bills and the price of maternity clothes and everything. He seemed to think I knew all about it."

William was sorry about that, he said; he'd been racking his brains, wondering how to tell them: he'd known from the beginning that they didn't like Jean.

His parents denied it; they had nothing against the girl. Of course not. But as things stood now . . . well, there were so many difficulties.

If they wanted to, his father told him, her parents could get really nasty. She was still a minor. If William were one year older, they could charge him with rape on the mere fact of her age, and send him to jail. Even as it was, they could put her into some kind of reform school until she was eighteen. For immorality.

"That's crazy," William said. "And disgusting."

"It's the law."

"Then the law is crazy. It ought to be changed."

"Maybe so. But it isn't changed yet."

William wanted to know what people were doing, passing laws like that: were they all religious bigots? Even bigots went to bed with each other; or did they just want to stop everybody else from doing it?

Laws, his father said, usually had some sense to them. This particular one was meant to protect people who had no defenses: to prevent men from fooling around with young girls who didn't know how to take care of themselves and who wouldn't be able to raise a child on their own.

"But this isn't like that," William said.

"Nothing is ever like the textbook case till somebody takes it to court, and then it's got to be argued like the book, because that's the only way you can figure out how to deal with it."

"It doesn't have anything to do with other people."

"Could you support a wife and child right now?"

"Yes," William said, wanting to win the argument.

His father didn't tell him he was wrong. He simply pointed out how hard it would be, and added that the kind of salary and career available to a college graduate was a lot better than what a man could hope to work up to after five years of living from hand to mouth.

William thought that over. He saw that he'd have to have his parents' help. He knew he'd be able to count on them as long as he fell in with most of their advice.

He began to believe he might have been wrong about the way he'd handled the talk with Jean's parents. If that was the line they were going to take, they weren't worth considering, but naturally Jean would want to think there was an excuse for them. He also felt ashamed of not having trusted his own parents, who both appeared so reasonable, and so worried; they weren't angry at all.

His parents worked on him, in perfect counterpoint, until he agreed that he wouldn't see Jean for two weeks. It was an unsettling time for everybody, they said. Two weeks would be enough of a breathing space to get everything straightened out. They asked him not to telephone Jean during that period; they wanted a free hand. They didn't put a ban on letters, since his mother had long ago searched his room and found the letters Jean had written to him. Nowhere in them had there been a hint of the pregnancy, but in one letter Jean had written something about the ornamental stone jar in which the two of them had started to hide their more fervent correspondence: the jar stood at a corner of the crumbling terrace wall that bounded three sides of the old Sumner house. The house had been shut up for years. Weeks before she could have known that the letters would make any difference to her life, William's mother knew the look of Jean's handwriting. She knew it nearly as well as she knew her son's.

William wrote a letter to Jean. In it he told her about the talk he'd had with his parents. Things would turn out all right—there was nothing any parent could do to keep them apart for long, but he didn't want her to imagine he'd stop thinking about her if they just didn't see each other for a few days. They were always going to be together in their thoughts. And he hoped she'd stay certain; even though they were close in spirit, he was a little afraid of her parents' influence. He was especially worried that she might be persuaded to think everything he and she had done together was bad.

He put the letter inside the terrace urn. His mother retrieved it.

She then made a surprisingly good forgery of Jean's handwriting on paper she had bought that day. Each pale pink sheet was printed at the upper left-hand corner with a picture of forget-me-nots tied up in blue ribbon. The paper had been a lucky find: she'd bought a whole box; it was the same kind Jean wrote her letters on. William would never suspect his mother of using such paper.

The forged letter asked why his parents couldn't help out with the money, because her father was getting really mad about it and, actually, she was beginning to wonder, too; after all, he wasn't the one who was going to have the baby. Anyway, her father had told her that William's father had said something about her, something kind of insulting, so she realized that William had been *discussing her with his parents*. She thought that was a pretty cheap thing to do; in fact, it was measly.

William's mother was proud of her letter. She thought she'd hit the tone, the phrasing, and the slang just right. Her pleasure was malicious, but her purpose wasn't. She believed that William had been maneuvered into fatherhood by a girl from a family of no background; and that if events were allowed to take their course, he'd hate the girl in a few years. It would be better to break up the affair now.

His father, too, was ready to protect William. He'd run across men like Jean's father before. He telephoned back and laid it on the line: he and his wife had no responsibility toward a girl who said she was pregnant by their son. Attempts to extort money out of their family— phoning him at his office, yes—could end in criminal prosecution. Naturally Jean's father was free to try to prove that some compensation was owed. But if there were to be a legal battle, money would win it in the end.

Jean's father felt a deep sense of unfairness and injury after the phone call; he felt it more and more as he continued to brood about it. Every time you tried to make excuses for people like that, he thought, they turned around and ran true to type. They had no respect for other families. They considered themselves better than other people. He couldn't quite bring himself to face the fact that it had been a disastrous move to raise the question of money, and that by doing so he had probably wrecked his daughter's hopes of marriage. He'd never really had anything against William, only against the double sin of sexual trespass and pregnancy. But he'd been intimidated. He didn't like the idea that somebody in his family could end up in a law court. They'd always been law-abiding—all of them.

He told his wife that it wasn't going to be the way they'd hoped; they couldn't expect any help from the boy's parents. They'd have to start thinking about those doctor and hospital bills, not to mention the embarrassment of having to go on living in the town afterwards. Jean's mother got scared. She had never done anything underhand or shameful; she'd worked hard and made a good home for her family. And if Jean didn't get married now, it would be her parents' lives that would be destroyed, not hers.

She had a little talk with her daughter. She told her that no matter how things went, Jean wasn't to worry: it still wasn't too late to do something about it.

Jean pretended to be reassured. She wrote a long letter to William, asking him what was going on at his house, and telling him that her mother had changed, and wanted her to get rid of the baby. She had to talk to him, she said.

She ran to the Sumner house, to the urn on the terrace. She left her note and hurried away with the letter she'd found addressed to her in an excellent facsimile of William's handwriting.

His mother saw her come and go. And she picked up the letter meant for William. If she or her husband had stopped to think, they might have said to themselves that many boys and young men will sleep with the wrong kind of girl because there's nobody else around, but that this affair wasn't like that: the two were in love. Traditionally, that was supposed to make all irregularities acceptable. Therefore, if the parents disapproved so violently, it might be because they actually wished to discourage the young from loving.

William's mother realized that she could keep up the letter game for only so long. It would be stupid to assume that one of them wouldn't catch her at her substitution; or, they might come across her while trying—in spite of their promises, and against their parents' wishes—to meet each other. Nor did she look forward to having her husband discover the exact extent of her interference. She could justify her actions if she had to: a mother has excuses not available to other people. But she'd rather not have to. All she had said in the beginning was that she was going to read the letters, in order to figure out the right way to approach William: as long as she was free to act on her own, everything would be fine. Of course, if her husband wanted to read their letters himself . . . no, he'd said; he didn't think it was necessary to read anyone's letters, but he'd leave the matter to her.

She was excited, frightened, and should have been worried about her rapid heartbeat. The thrill of participating in William's drama, of saving her son from making a mess of his life, kept her at fever pitch. She was happy. She'd never had a real romance herself: the secret, stealthy, illicit going back and back again to temptation. She was having her romance now, fired by the heroic part she was playing—a woman rescuing her innocent son from ruin. She didn't blame the girl especially; it was just that a girl like Jean wasn't good enough. Girls like that wanted to get married. It didn't usually matter who was picked out to marry them. Jean would have to release her hold on William and find someone else.

Jean took her letter home and read it. She cried over it. Everything was going wrong: he was changing. If she could see him and try to talk to him, she wouldn't know what to say. His letter almost sounded as if he didn't love her anymore. But that couldn't be true.

Her mother made an excuse to the school, to keep Jean at home for a while. She thought her daughter needed time to think. Besides, Jean was looking so unhappy that her classmates might start to ask her questions; or, she might just decide, out of a need to feel comforted, to talk to someone herself. Then, later, if she had to be sent away, everyone would know why. That wouldn't do. And William was there at school, too. Although he wouldn't be able to see Jean without cutting classes, he was there. He might wait around for her in the morning, or later in the afternoon.

At the same time, William's mother asked her husband to arrange for their son to take a break from school. She wanted to make sure that William and Jean didn't get a chance to plan anything on their own. She made the first suggestion herself: that William might like a change of scene for a short while, to get things clear in his mind; how about a trip somewhere nice for a couple of weeks? Nassau, perhaps; with his uncle Bertram. William said no. He couldn't leave now. As soon as the time limit was up, he'd get together with Jean. He already wished he hadn't given his word.

He couldn't bear the thought that Jean had lost faith in him. He broke his promise to his parents and went over to her house at night. He stood under her window, where the light was out. He threw small stones up at the panes. If he'd had a long, black cloak, he'd have felt safely disguised: covered by darkness, the lover's friend. On the other hand, it would have made throwing the stones even more difficult. It was impossible to hit anything in the dark. He might break the glass if he wasn't careful. He began to get mad enough to risk it. Her light went on. Then other lights came on, too, one near her window and another downstairs; her parents had heard. He retreated. Maybe she hadn't even realized he'd been there.

He looked for her at school. He asked one of the girls in her class: where was she? "She's sick," the girl told him. But it wasn't anything serious, she said. Just a bad cold.

He stopped playing his records so often. He couldn't concentrate on them. The most beautiful parts upset him: and everything in between made him impatient. He wrote a letter to Jean, though he knew she wouldn't be able to go get it till she was better. He worried about her. She shouldn't be sick if she was carrying a child. He put his letter in the urn and took out the one that was waiting there for him.

His father had a long talk with him about money and compensation, college and law school. William was so distracted he could barely understand what was being said to him. The letter he had just read, and which he believed to be from Jean, told him in plain terms how little she thought of his conduct, said there were others who wouldn't have treated her so badly, talked about his petty-mindedness on the subject of money, sneered at his mother's fur coat, claimed she could sue him, and complained that he'd talked her into keeping the baby: now she was stuck with it while he was as free as a bird.

His mother was just in time to intercept his desperate answer. In its place she put a letter containing a key to a box at the post office. The letter said that William was afraid he might be followed or sent away, so it was safer to use the post office.

From then on, it was easy to deceive the young couple without danger. William protested when he was sent to the Caribbean, but he gave in; the fight was going out of him. He, too, had been given a key, to a post office box with a different number. His mother was therefore able to make her exchanges without fear that a letter would slip through. She could also use William's stamped and canceled envelopes sent genuinely from the West Indies; a single numeral altered the box number. And she brought the affair to an end quickly. She sent Jean a letter that described William going to a party given by friends of his parents. These friends had a daughter he'd met years ago when they were children. He couldn't believe now, the letter said, how much they had in common. Although he'd always be fond of Jean, he thought they'd better both admit everything between them had been a big mistake. He felt pretty upset, but he had to be honest and say he wanted to do lots of things in life—starting with college and law school—that wouldn't be possible with a wife and child. He'd come to believe, from hearing some interesting theories on the subject recently, that it was better in every way not to start having children till you were about twenty-eight. He did realize, naturally, that in a certain sense he was to blame. But she couldn't deny that she'd said yes in the first place, and nice girls didn't—he knew that now: they just had strong principles about the right way to behave in life. You had to have those high standards in order to become a mature human being. Of course he still liked her, but he thought she'd better take her parents' advice, except not about trying to get money out of his father, because that could land them in a lot of trouble, she'd better believe that.

The letter ended, *So I guess this is good-bye.*

Jean wrote back. She pleaded with him. She thought that he couldn't have meant to send her a letter like that. She asked him to read it over, and to think about what he felt, and to try to remember the way he'd known her. She enclosed his letter. She said she loved him; she'd wait for an answer.

He didn't answer. He hadn't seen her letter. She wrote again, almost immediately, telling him that her parents were taking her out of school for the rest of the year and sending her to live with her maiden aunt in the next state. She was going to have the baby there. She gave him the address and begged him to help her: if he didn't help, they could take the baby away from her as soon as it was born. That was what they wanted—for the baby to be adopted by somebody, so then nobody would know she'd had an illegitimate child.

William still knew nothing. His mother had written him a master-piece of a letter, filled with accusations, silliness, and platitudes. It also compared parents, saying that her father had worked all his life, which was more than you could say for his father, who spent all his time swindling people and called it big business: she didn't know why he was so stingy, either: William was going to be just the same when he grew up, which would probably be never. And she was taking her parents' advice, by the way, and having an operation because she didn't want to have anything more to do with him: she was hoping to get a steady job some day and meet a real man: and she was staying away from home for good, so he didn't need to write any more dumb letters to her.

A key was enclosed. His mother had had duplicates made. She hadn't worked out the details of her scheme at the beginning, but every-thing had seemed to go very well. She stopped writing any letters her-self. She merely collected and read theirs. At any moment she expected to find that William had written to Jean's parents—that would have spoiled everything: but he'd lost his trust in them. He stopped sending letters. He'd come to the conclusion, suddenly, that it was over between him and Jean. He hadn't done anything, or been able to do anything, to make a difference. She had changed; she wasn't sorry about what had happened. She hadn't loved him, after all.

His uncle Bertram said over the phone that William was desolate: he swam, and he went out in the boat with the rest of the gang, but he was so unhappy it was pitiful to see. And he'd gotten drunk one night and passed out cold. "He's getting over it," his father said.

When William returned to town and to school, Jean had gone. He finished his school year. His mother continued to collect the letters Jean was sending to the post office. At last a letter arrived that was much shorter than the others: it said simply that she loved him but she couldn't go on—she knew they were going to take the baby away, and she was tired of everything anyway. She'd decided to kill herself.

Her mother didn't believe it. Girls tried that kind of threat all the time. She put the letter with the rest of them. She kept a regular check on the mailbox. Week after week there was nothing. Nothing for months. If Jean had killed herself, if she'd died—what could anyone do? It would be too late to go back. Long ago it was too late. But there was no question of suicide; that couldn't be. Obviously the girl had just given up, finally. There was no reason to wait for more letters. The keys could be turned in at the post office.

William did well at school. He drank at parties, but he stayed away from drugs like Benzedrine and Dexedrine, which had begun to make an impression on the college campuses of nearby states. He started to go around with a girl from his own graduating class, and then went out with her friend. He slept with both of them. He had fun. He didn't intend to get serious again. He began to feel better and to think of Jean with a sense of disappointment and revulsion. She had let him down. It seemed to him that all women would act the same way in the end. They didn't want love. Their sights were fixed on other things: safety, pride, interior decorating. He saw Jean's mother in town one day. They both turned away at the same time, instantly, as soon as they recognized each other.

He went away to college, where he also did well. And to law school. He came back briefly for his father's funeral and then, after he'd started work with a law firm, to visit his mother. She'd had a heart attack. She was only fifty-seven. William was horrified by the injustice of her illness. Because his father had been so much older, that death had seemed to come at a reasonable age. She was too young. He knew she still had hopes that he'd marry one of the girls she'd introduced him to. He hadn't come home so often as she'd have liked, either. He had been thoughtless. He'd neglected her.

She had a series of slight attacks and then the massive failure that carried her off. William phoned every relative he could think of. He asked them all to come to the funeral: stay at the house, be with him. He had nobody now. When the funeral was over, he sat downstairs with Uncle Bertram and his cousins from Kentucky. He told them he felt like the last of the dodos; for the first time in his life he thought it might be nice to have some brothers and sisters. "Even though all of you turned up trumps," he said. He thanked them for coming. They spent a long and raucous night reminiscing, but they were gone the next day.

Later there were the clothes to give away, the accounts to put in order, the question of what to do with the house when he was away—whether to sell it, or rent it, or leave it standing empty. There was a lot of junk to sort through. And his mother hadn't thrown out any of his father's clothes; she'd just left everything of his the way it had been.

William took a bottle of whiskey upstairs with him. He plugged in his father's portable phonograph and turned it on in the empty house. He put the volume way up. He played Verdi. He started with his father's study; moved to the attic, and then to his mother's room. He was glad he was alone. He could cry without restraint.

He stuffed his parents' clothes into suitcases, laundry bags, and cardboard boxes. He threw combs and brushes and shoes after them. He opened drawers containing half-used lipsticks and unopened per-fume bottles. He discovered all his old school reports back to when he was six years old. And he found the box that held the pink, flow-ered notepaper, the sheets covered with repeated phrases scribbled as practice for the final draft. He saw the originals in his mother's handwriting, the bundle of letters he'd written himself, and the ones from Jean: all of them. He went out of his mind.

He smashed the empty whiskey bottle, the mirrors, the windows, the phonograph. His hands were cut and bleeding. He threw the unbreakable records out of the windows and snapped the others over his knee: all his precious collection of 78s. He picked up chairs and banged them down on the tables, threw vases against the walls. He screamed unceasingly, like a monkey in the forest. He slashed all the paintings in the house, even the ones he had known from his childhood and had loved most—the portrait of his grandparents as children, the view of the summerhouse from the bay. He tore up all the photographs of himself and his parents, set fire to the Anatolian rug, and walked out of the room while it was still smoldering. He took his father's bird guns from their cases, loaded them up, and began to shoot into the walls, sideboards, ceilings, stairs. After a while people out in the street called the police, who came and broke down the back door. They got a doctor to give William an injection. He spent a couple of days asleep.

When he woke up, he didn't realize where he was. A private nurse had been left with him. She fed him some soup and said, "You feeling better now?" She made it plain that she expected him to answer yes.

"It was the shock," he said.

"That's right. You take it easy," she told him.

He took it easy. He began to think. He thought for the first time in years about Jean; about how he and she had been tricked, treated with contempt; and how his parents' hatred—especially his mother's—had not been satisfied by merely frustrating his hopes and plans: they had had to destroy his chance of any kind of love for the rest of his life. Jean's chance, too. What had happened to Jean?

As soon as he was on his feet, he went to her parents' house. They were there, but they wouldn't let him in. To begin with, they wouldn't even answer the door. His shouts and sobs convinced them that it would be better to talk him into being quiet than to have the neighbors hearing that old story dragged up again.

Her father opened the door a crack. The safety chain—a recent installment—prevented entry. "We don't want you here," he said. "Go away."

William started to explain—fast, gasping, and doing his best not to yell—that his mother had written forgeries to Jean and to him, too: she'd lied to both of them and now he had to find Jean, to ask her to forgive him and to make it up to her.

Her father said, "We don't know where she is. That's the truth. And it's on account of you. She was staying with her aunt and she was five, almost six months to—you know. She couldn't stand the shame. She took some kind of poison."

William stopped breathing for a moment.

"She nearly died," her father said.

"But she didn't?"

"They had three doctors working on her for twenty-four hours. They couldn't save the baby: nobody in the family wasted any tears over that. They only just pulled her through. Soon as she was getting better, she ran off. Her aunt says she told Jeannie she'd better behave herself from now on, seeing as how what she did is a crime you can get put in jail for; and she would be, if anybody wanted to arrest her for it. It would be murder. I guess she took it the wrong way, got scared the police were going to come after her. That woman never treated her too kindly, from what I can make out."

"Where is she?" William asked.

"Like I told you, we don't know. We haven't heard from her since that day. We haven't heard anything about her at all. All we know is, her aunt said her mind was a little unhinged from the time she took that poison. I reckon you'd better forget about her. That's what we had to do. It's like she was dead."

William was about to ask some more questions when Jean's mother called out from the hallway, "What are you telling him? Don't you say anything to him." She sounded drunk. She raised her voice and screeched, "You get away from us. Haven't you caused enough trouble? Go on, go away!" William turned and ran down the street.

He believed what her father had told him. He went back to his parents' house. All night long he howled and wept. He cursed his mother, he called on Jean, talking to her, explaining. He beat his head against the walls. He slept.

When he woke, his madness had developed into a quiet conviction. He was no longer violent; the thought just kept repeating itself in his mind: that Jean was somewhere waiting for him, and that he had to find her. He'd find her if he had to search the world over. He had plenty of money: he could spend his life on it.

He got into his car and drove to the capital, where he hired a firm of private detectives. There were several clues, he told them: the hospital she'd been admitted to would have her name and address in its files. It would be in the same state where the aunt lived. He could let them have the aunt's address, but he didn't want them to go near her. They should concentrate on the medical register; there might even be a record of fingerprints.

He gave the agency approximate dates. Nothing could be learned from her parents, he said. It would be better not to disturb them: they might decide to get in touch with the aunt or somebody, and everyone would clam up. And maybe if the detectives got close to Jean or anyone who knew where she was, they ought to say they were looking for her because of a case that concerned distant relatives. They could pretend it was something to do with a legacy.

He couldn't understand why her mother and father hadn't tried to find her. Even though they wouldn't have had the money for detectives, they could have tried the police. It seemed to him that if you looked at the whole story, right through to where it stood at the moment, her parents hadn't behaved any better than his—maybe even worse, because Jean was their own child, whereas to his mother she'd been an outsider.

His detectives also had the clue of Jean's illness—her reported illness, anyway, which meant that she could have been in hospitals afterwards. Her father had specifically cited mental instability, so the investigation could start there, with a check on all the public asylums and private clinics in the general area. She might have changed her name; the detectives should concentrate on anyone who was the right age. He had photographs but he knew, as the agency men undoubtedly did, too, that people sometimes changed radically in a short space of time, especially if they'd been sick. The expression of the face, the look in the eyes, could become like those of another person. A gain or loss in weight could also make someone unrecognizable. Thirty-five pounds either way was a better disguise than a wig and glasses.

William said, "I guess maybe the thing for you to do is to go through all those places, get the possible names and then, if you think you're on the right track, I should go see for myself."

One of the partners in the firm, a Mr. McAndrew, presented William with a businesslike sheet of facts and figures, plus an estimate of costs. "Those are the short-term calculations," he explained. "This could take a long time. But if it does, our charges would drop significantly. We believe in keeping our customers happy."

William said that all sounded fine. He hoped they'd phone soon because he was eager for news. He got up from his chair jerkily and lurched toward the door. Ever since finding the letters, his movements had become slightly uncoordinated. And he'd fallen into the habit of looking off into space, as if searching or remembering. Mr. McAndrew might have considered William a fit subject for the clinics himself, if the princely retainer he'd pushed across the desktop hadn't proclaimed his sanity.

Weeks went by. William kept himself busy with the house. He couldn't decide whether or not to sell it. He took a leave of absence from the office. His hands healed. He hired painters to clean up the house, inside and out. And he got other workmen in to repair the damage he'd done.

Mr. McAndrew found four patients in public wards whom he described as "possible suspects." Two of them were in the same hospital. If William wanted to go look for himself, one of their operatives could take him along. William said yes, he'd like that.

The detective called early. He was driving a company car. He was young, about thirty—only a couple of years older than William. He looked tough enough to deal with the rougher side of detective work, if he had to. He introduced himself as Harvey Corelli.

"Like the tenor?" William asked. "Franco Corelli?"

"Don't know him. Call me Harvey, OK?"

"Sure. I'm Bill."

"Yeah, but you're the client. You're supposed to be Mister."

"If I call you Harvey, you call me Bill," William said. People had started to call him Bill as soon as he got to college.

"Right," Harvey said. "That suits me fine." He'd noticed the sudden far-off look his boss had mentioned. He got behind the wheel.

On that first trip they spent a week going from one hospital to another. Harvey handled the receptionists and doctors; William took a quick look at the patient and shook his head. Sometimes it was enough just to have her pointed out in the distance.

Two weeks later they started out on a second trip. They visited three institutions, all no good. While they were still traveling, McAndrew came up with some more names. Harvey passed on the information after he'd made his routine call to check in. "You want to leave them till another time?" he asked.

William said no—he'd rather keep going, and follow up as many leads as possible. They could stay in motels and go down the whole list in a few days, unless Harvey had another case he was working on.

"Only this one at the moment," Harvey said. One, to his mind, was usually one too many. He had always found it less easy to sympathize with his clients than with the people who had run out on them, cheated them, or otherwise let them have what they deserved. William was no exception to that rule, but he seemed like such an idiot that he actually had possibilities. Harvey knew the area. He could speed up the chase or slow it down. He figured that he could spin it out for a long time; he could be collecting a salary practically forever, if he played his hand right. He didn't like taking orders from McAndrew. He'd been bawled out in front of other people once: he hadn't appreciated that. He wasn't going to forget it. William, he thought, could turn out to be a pretty good meal ticket; he wasn't up to much in the way of fun, but Harvey knew the ropes: he'd get William interested somehow. It might be a good idea for all concerned to give old William something to think about besides his quest for the holy bride. There were a lot of moneybags in the family vault; Harvey could think of several uses for them.

William was lonely, so it wasn't hard, despite his mania, or obsession, or—as he preferred to think of it—love. One evening Harvey suggested that they call up a couple of girls: he knew one or two in the neighborhood. William said no, he didn't feel like it.

"Do you carry on like this all the time?" Harvey asked.

"Carry on?"

"*No thanks, I don't feel like it?*"

"Well, I don't."

"Never?"

"I've got other things on my mind."

"Mind isn't what I'm talking about, Bill. Come on." He called up a woman he knew. He poured William a few drinks. When the woman arrived, she dropped her coat on the bed and said, "Hey Harve, just like old times." She then whipped off her dress and underclothes. William jumped to his feet. He intended to go to his own room, but he was too drunk. He fell over the corner of the bed. Harvey picked him up and slung him on top of the bedspread. The woman threw her arm over him. His buttons were being undone, his belt was being unbuckled. He heard Harvey going out of the room.

In the morning the woman was gone. Harvey knocked on the door. He dragged William into the bathroom and gave him two Alka-Seltzers. He said, "Now you've got the hang of it, you won't have to get so plastered. Next time, we'll have a party."

"I feel god-awful," William muttered. He had such a headache that he had to wear a pair of sunglasses all day, except for the moments when he looked at the hospital patients who might have been Jean, but weren't.

They kept traveling for another week. William talked to Harvey about his story. He explained why it was so important to find Jean.

Harvey didn't seem to think the story was anything special. He said it was a tough break, but it happened all the time. "You got to move on in life," he told William. "You got to move forward."

William was sorry he'd said anything. That was another thing loneliness did to people—they'd spill out all the most secret, private details of their lives to complete strangers: they'd get drunk and try to obliterate themselves for a time, to get rid of the past and of themselves, too, by transforming everything into talk. You could always change events by describing the truth another way, remembering it differently. It was a method of controlling your life, of understanding it.

Harvey, in his turn, talked. He had dozens of schemes for becoming famous, making money, cornering the market on something nobody else had thought of. He had ideas about travel, international finance, import-export. He wanted to buy a boat some day and trade between Florida and the islands, like everybody else: that was where the big money was.

William nodded and said, "Yes, I see," and, "That's interesting." He was looking into the distance again. Harvey phoned two girls. He wanted an evening where he'd trade girls with William; after they'd tried out their own, they'd swap. William said all right: he didn't mind.

"Picking up some tips, kid?" Harvey asked.

"I hope that's all I'm picking up," William told him.

Harvey began to wonder how far he could push William. He'd gotten him in with the girls; the next step could be a couple of other, more expensive habits. He didn't want to take things too fast. William looked nearly ready to crack. Harvey thought hard about how to get him lined up just right.

Before he could do anything, they came to a sanatorium called Green Mansions. It wasn't green and it didn't look like a mansion: a three-story brick and concrete building that lacked the architectural charm of some of the older asylums. It was privately run.

There were three candidates for inspection—young women of the right age. Harvey saw at a glance that none of the three would fit the photographs. The women were seated around a table at the far end of a large hall that—on the evidence of the drawings, announcements, and other pieces of paper tacked to the walls—was the patients' recreation room. It was the room where they'd taught gymnastic exercises and would take part in dances. Scuffed linoleum covered the floor. There was a piano in one of the corners. The lid was down over the keyboard. In a place like that, it would have to be locked, too.

Right at the back, a line of folding chairs ran around three sides of the room. Patients and possibly nurses sat together in groups. There were no white uniforms. Many people were sitting quietly on their own, or standing. One man who tried to sit on the floor was immediately pulled to his feet by two other men: he didn't appear to be pleading for attention—it was as if he'd temporarily forgotten that people were supposed to sit on chairs instead.

A doctor led the way across the room. William followed, keeping pace with Harvey. When they were still several yards away from the three women, William said, "No," in a low voice. "I don't think so."

"Well, why don't we sit down?" the doctor suggested. "I can tell you something about the work we do here."

Harvey made a face at William. He saw the propaganda coming: *Our worthy cause, insufficient funds, these unfortunate people.* William ignored him. He told the doctor he'd be interested to hear what he had to say. Even if Jean wasn't at Green Mansions, she might be in a similar institution; he wanted to know about anything that could have a bearing on her life.

They sat. Harvey longed for a cigarette. Signs on the walls told him he couldn't have one. More than any of the hospitals and rest homes they'd seen, Green Mansions reminded him of a school he'd been sent to once. He'd stayed there for a year, and he'd hated every minute. It was one of those schools where they were supposed to straighten you out.

The doctor talked about state funds, federal grants, and private subsidies. William nodded and looked out into the center of the floor. It was surprising how many people were just standing there, not talking to anyone—just standing alone, looking like machines that had been switched off: nothing registered on their faces. "Do you use drugs?" he asked.

"In the case of a violent patient it's sometimes advisable," the doctor answered.

"But not regular doses as a matter of policy?"

"No, of course not."

Harvey turned his head to look at the doctor. Naturally they'd give drugs as a routine. It would make all the supervisory work easier. He was pretty certain that all those places did. If you weren't loony when you went in, they'd soon mess you up enough to pass for crazy.

William wasn't looking at the doctor. He was staring at one of the patients standing alone in the middle of the floor, a girl with straight, orange-blond hair and a pale face that had a sweet, absentminded look. "Jean," he whispered suddenly. He grabbed Harvey's arm. "There," he said. "It's her."

"It doesn't look like her," Harvey said.

"It's Jean."

"Doctor, who's the thin girl with the long hair?" Harvey asked.

"That's Coralee. She's been here eighteen months now. She'd be about five years younger than the girl you're looking for."

"That's my girl," William said.

"Her parents—"

Harvey said, "She doesn't look like the photographs, Bill."

"Well, she's changed. It's been years since those pictures were taken. As for her name being different, I'd expected that."

"Oh?" the doctor said.

Harvey put his hand on William's shoulder and told him they'd better talk things over. William agreed. He'd found Jean. Nothing else mattered.

He'd known that when, at last, they found each other, the healing power of love ought to cure her, although in an opera the heroine usually died at the moment of reuniting, having undergone too much. This was real life. Jean might never recover her reason, but they could live together as man and wife and be happy. He accepted the fact that she'd been committed under a different name and by people who claimed to be her relatives: naturally, if she were afraid of being sent to jail, she'd have made up a new name for herself. She might even have found a new home for a while. He was willing to marry her under any name at all.

While Harvey wrote down notes about the circumstances of her admission, William put questions about getting her out. He wanted to know what objections there might be from the authorities as well as from her family. He was hoping that both could be bought off: the clinic with money and proof of good intentions, the family with belief in his love.

Her parents—the doctor said—seeing that she seldom recognized them, had quickly found it too painful to continue their visits. They got into financial difficulties, stopped paying for her upkeep, and moved away. Coralee was due to go into a state asylum at the end of the month.

"I know this story may sound unbelievable," William said, "but to me everything makes sense now that we're together again. I'd be glad to pay whatever Coralee owes the clinic." He spoke for a long time. He was persuasive, partly because the doctor and his staff wanted to be persuaded, but also because his need inspired him. As he dug deeper into his fantasy, until he finally merged with it, his outer actions began to appear more normal and relaxed.

"I knew her before," he said, "and lost her. But I've been looking for her. And now I've found her, I want to take care of her."

The doctor was favorably impressed by William's story, his future plans, his wealth, and his ability to treat a madwoman with kindness for the rest of his life. He didn't consider the possibility that William himself was crazed. He promised to do what he could; and to meet again the next day. He introduced William to Coralee before escorting him and Harvey out of the sanatorium.

William took her hand in his. Her eyes moved back to the world where she was standing and where he stood, his hand touching hers.

Her smile reflected the one he showed her. He told her his name, and said that he was going to see her the next day: she might not remember, but he had known her a long time ago. He'd loved her. He'd been looking for her, to rescue her, and he wanted to make her happy.

He talked to her slowly and clearly. For the first time in days she spoke. Her voice was feeble from lack of use. Later it would turn out that part of her disability was caused by deafness, for which she'd never been tested.

"Oh," she said. "I don't remember."

"That's all right," he told her. "We'll get to know each other again from the beginning. We'll have a nice time."

She smiled again. He let go of her hand. She looked after him as he walked to the door. He turned and waved. She came forward.

She walked up to him and put her hands on his jacket. "What did you say your name was?" she asked.

"William," he told her again. "Will."

The doctor was astounded. She'd never acted that way before.

She said, "You come back soon, Will."

"Tomorrow," he promised.

As soon as they were in the car again Harvey said, "Listen, Bill, it isn't the same one."

"This is the happiest day of my life, Harvey. There's only going to be one happier one, and that's when Jean and I get married."

"She doesn't look anything like the pictures."

William smiled. He'd stopped staring strangely or seeming to go off into another dimension. Still smiling, he said, "Her sufferings have changed her."

"I just—you ought to think it over. You could be making a big mistake."

"The mistake I made was to let you talk me into going with whores."

"You liked it fine at the time."

"I was so lonely, I couldn't stand it. Now I've found her, I'm never going to be lonely again."

"Are you sure she's the same one?"

"I'm positive. She couldn't be anyone else."

"But she is somebody else. Even if she wasn't goofy, she just isn't the right girl. Different age, different name—she's got a whole different face, man."

"Unhappiness can practically destroy people. You don't know."

"It can also prevent them from seeing what's right in front of them. I can't let you do it. Just think—maybe the real girl is still somewhere waiting for you. She'd have to wait forever, if you tie yourself up with this one."

"I know you're worried," William told him. "I don't believe you're just thinking about the money and the case coming to an end."

"What's that?"

"No. I know what worries you. It's love. It makes you uncomfortable. It isn't what you're used to. You see it, and you get scared."

"Don't give me that horseshit."

"Harvey, one day it's going to happen to you. Listen—one day you're going to find the right one: the only one for you. And then you'll be happy. Like me."

"Christ," Harvey muttered. He didn't trust himself to say anything more without losing his temper. He couldn't believe that William had ducked out from under him so neatly, taken the first opportunity he saw, to escape: in the company of some jerk girl with a dopey smile, who wasn't even the one he'd been looking for.

William got on the telephone at the motel. He arranged through his lawyers to have people waiting for him at the house. He said that calls would be coming in soon, asking questions about him, but that everything would be all right.

And it was all right. Good credentials, his family's name, the record of their holdings, their history in the town they'd lived for four generations, guaranteed William's fitness to remove a patient from Green Mansions. His money ensured speed.

The girl didn't mind. She'd taken a liking to William. When he spoke, she leaned into his face. He held her lightly by the hand and—

once they were away from the clinic—by the arm. The drive home was made in almost total silence. At the house William helped her out of the car. He said, "This is where I live, Coralee. I hope you'll be happy here."

She looked pleased. She seemed to be taking in what was happening. "Big house," she said. William handed her over to the maid, housekeeper, and cook he'd hired. That evening he asked her if she'd marry him. She said yes. In the morning he made plans for the wedding. He also asked a doctor to come on a house call to have a look at Coralee.

He phoned the detective agency and he went there, arriving just as Harvey was coming off work for his lunch hour. Harvey had registered a formal, written protest against the ending of the case. If anything were to go wrong with William's choice, Harvey wasn't going to be held responsible. Mr. McAndrew had taken the matter calmly; he'd been content with a quick result, a large fee, and a satisfied client who admitted to overriding the objections of the agency.

"You're really going through with it?" Harvey asked.

William beamed. "She's accepted me," he said. "She likes it here."

"I bet she does. It's better than that place she was in."

"I'm giving you a bonus. That's what I'd do anyway. But I also just wanted to say I appreciate the hard work you put in on the case, even when you didn't believe we were going to get anywhere. Well, you know what it's meant to me. It's saved my life. I want to thank you." He handed over two checks, one for the firm and one made out to Harvey by name. They shook hands. William walked to the door, went down the steps, and got back into his car.

Harvey looked at the amount on his check. He started to think about William and his search, the girl he'd discovered and the life they'd have together. They were both crazy, so what did it matter? And why should he be thinking about them? They might make out fine. There was no reason to feel that what had happened was such a terrible thing. And the check was for a lot, so what the hell?

Plans for the wedding went forward. Coralee had doctors' appointments to go to. William was told that she could live a normal life, but her mind would probably never develop. Everything had been left for too long. She didn't appear to have any mental illnesses—she was, as far as they could tell, just stupid, or—as they phrased it in that part of the world—slow. Of course she'd been sick, but that would leave her as she became accustomed to her new home. Some of her debility had undoubtedly been induced by her surroundings: first her family, then the institutions they'd put her in. With kindness and patience there would be some improvement, there always was. She might not become completely well, only enough recovered to believe everything William told her: to adopt his madness in place of her own.

She liked William. She was acquiescent, dreamy, vague. She was like someone asleep. He didn't mind. He liked her quietness. There was nothing to disturb his idea that deep down, under the different face and body, she was Jean.

He told her many times, simply and clearly, how they'd loved each other and been parted. Now that they were together again, their lives were going to be full of joy. He handed her the packet of letters his mother had kept tied with a ribbon. She held the letters to her face and smiled gently. Then she dropped them on the floor. He took her action to mean that as far as she was concerned, the past was over: they would get married and be happy.

The wedding was announced. Coralee was fitted for a wedding dress. The dressmaker called at the house to measure and alter. Coralee delighted in the fitting sessions; she played with the veil, she danced around, holding the partly competed skirt, she tried to sniff the artificial flowers. The dress was made with plenty of tucks that could be let out easily for extra width; Coralee had gained sixteen pounds since leaving Green Mansions and was still putting on weight. Apparently the inmates had been kept on a meager diet.

He didn't try to reunite her with her parents, nor with the people who had had her committed under her new name. He didn't think they deserved a reconciliation of any kind—in fact, he didn't even send them an invitation.

The wedding was to be a small affair. Hardly anyone from his old days in the town went on the list of guests. He could have asked men and women he'd been to school with, but he hadn't kept up with them. He still said hello to people on the street when he ran into them— that was all: he'd made no effort to pick up old friendships again, and when pursued, he declined invitations. He didn't need anyone except Coralee.

He invited his lawyers, the local doctor, the dressmaker and her family, the women he'd hired to work in the house. He didn't bother to notify any of his aunts, uncles, or cousins; he thought he'd write to them afterwards. As soon as Coralee got used to married life, they might take some trips, meet people; there would be time for everything. And then he'd get back to his job with the law firm. As an afterthought he picked up the phone and issued a formal invitation to Harvey.

Harvey said he'd really like to attend, but he just couldn't: he had too much work to do. It was nice of William to ask him, he said. His voice sounded right, but the truth was that after he'd banked his check, Harvey had begun to detest William and his love and the misery of it. He hated fools. He thought of them as people who had the sanction of the law to cause more damage than criminals. He didn't consider them funny or lovable.

William wouldn't have minded if nobody turned up but the preacher and a witness. He'd have had the whole business done in a registry of-fice if he hadn't believed it would be more fun for Coralee, and more like a party, to have a church ceremony. When he saw the way she took to the white dress, with its train and veil and little crown of flowers, he knew he'd been right. She glowed with pleasure.

The dressmaker's two small nieces had been chosen to hold up the train. During the rehearsal Coralee kept turning around to peek at the children and then all three would laugh wildly. The cook's family arrived and sat proudly near the front, as William had told them to. Other people from around town were scattered among the pews. A bass and soprano sang to piano accompaniment. The pianist was a relic from William's schooldays; she was blind now and had almost cried with gratitude when William telephoned her. On the day of the wedding she did a good job; the singers, too, suddenly came into their own, delivering without affectation the simple old hymns about belief in the Savior, love of the Lord. *I believe,* they sang. *I believe.* William could feel that beside him Coralee had realized all at once where she was. He held his arm around her lightly, protectively. The singers' last words rang in the air, stopped, and echoed, and left. The minister said afterwards that it was one of the most moving betrothals he could remember: sometimes it was like that—the spirit would seem to be fully present. The importance or grandeur of the family made no difference, nor the size of the congregation. Sometimes it was especially touching to have just a few witnesses there, when those few had love in their hearts.

To the people in the first three pews the church didn't seem empty; they sensed only good feeling and friendliness. There were even a few strangers who had wandered in and—seeing that there was a marriage ceremony in progress—had sat down to watch. The minister felt that their presence conferred additional blessings upon the happy pair: it was as if the extra observers stood for the rest of the world, who didn't know the couple being joined together, but wished them well.

Among the uninvited audience, almost on the aisle at about the midway point, was Jean. She'd seen the announcement in the papers.

She had changed: the shape of her body, the way she sat, her hair, the expression on her face where the action of the poison she'd taken had caused scarring. The damage to the skin was mild, but it was there; it made a slight difference to the overall facial look. If her parents had been at the wedding they would have known her. And Harvey would have recognized her from the many photographs he'd seen of her; he'd been trained to spot resemblances, even if a face had aged or been deliberately disguised.

She wasn't disguised, nor was she disfigured, although she looked old and clumsy. The doctors had told her that she was always going to have trouble with her health, and so maybe it was just as well that she didn't have a husband or children.

When she saw William with his bride, she knew it wasn't her health that was to blame for everything going wrong in her life—it was being without him. It was the fact that he hadn't wanted her.

She watched the whole ritual: the ring being put on, the kiss. She heard the promises: *till death*. And William turned around, his strange, vacant companion on his arm. He shook hands with people in the first rows; he pulled the bride along with him down the aisle, coming nearer. He bowed to a couple of women in front and to the left of Jean, then he looked at her: right into her eyes.

He moved forward, still looking at her face. He came closer, near enough to speak to her. Her lips parted, as if to shape his name: she almost said it out loud.

He smiled, his eyes going to the doorway beyond her. He passed on by. He didn't recognize her.

THE ARCHAEOLOGIST'S DAUGHTER

The Norbert family had lived in Switzerland for generations. Although they had originally come from farther north, by the 1830s, when Professor Norbert was born, his relatives had forgotten most of the habits and languages of their former homelands. He didn't try to find out about his ancestors; his interest lay in the distant past, among the great progenitors of humankind: their cities, statues, buildings, paintings, and religions. He passed on his enthusiasm to his young daughter, Beatrice; she came to share his passion for lost civilizations because, from the very beginning of her life, the times when he was explaining the past to her were those when she was most certain of his paternal affection, pride, and attention. She did not share his merry and inquisitive temperament. She was a quiet girl, serious even when she was happy, but often melancholy.

The house of Beatrice Norbert's childhood seemed to her to be set in a landscape that was reminiscent of the south—that is, the south of Europe. Later she would become acquainted with the sweltering countries of the equator, the deserts and plains, where people wrapped up their faces and bodies against the heat as if protecting themselves from a winter storm. Her parents took her along on their travels only once, when she was four years old; the journey so broke her sense of time that she forgot all of it but a few moments that she could call back like pictures out of a dream. What she remembered and thought of as her true life was home, in Switzerland.

The summers were hot and hazy, the parklands lush with flowering plants. Their house had a large garden that led down to a lake. And she remembered her mother as a lovely creature who was always wearing white dresses and standing under a blue sky. They had gone on picnics and boating parties together.

Her mother's name was Celeste; she had died young. Beatrice's memories for a few years on either side of the funeral were disrupted: she recalled staying in places where her mother, talking, had once walked with her, but to which her mother would never return. She remembered looking up for long periods at the sky and being confused between the words Celeste and celestial. Someone had foolishly told her that the dead went to heaven and became stars: that was why there were so many stars—innumerably, inconceivably many.

She was still a child when they moved away from the lake so that her father could be near town. He taught and lectured at the university. He wrote his books. And for a while he took her on his travels. They went to Turkey and Syria, to Petra; to Cairo, where Beatrice spent three years in a French school for French- and English-speaking children. Most of the other girls were the daughters of diplomats, lawyers, or bankers and they talked about the fashions and gossip of Paris, the theater and opera and the magnificent evenings—dinner and dancing in the ballrooms of palaces—for which they were destined: at which they would meet the men who were to become their husbands. She became enraptured by all things Parisian. She was sure that Paris had to be the center of the world. She listened avidly to the stories told by girls who had been there during the holidays. What was everyone wearing, she wanted to know; what had they had to eat? And the weather? Even the smallest scraps of information were enthralling.

It never occurred to her that there might be girls in Paris who would think Cairo exciting and exotic, and who would long to go there. For her—at that age—wherever she was, was normal. What most people considered ordinary had always seemed strange and marvelous to her, and unknown: the life of children who had both a mother and a father, and who stayed in one place until grown up. That was normal, but she couldn't imagine it.

She did well in school. Her father was proud of her. He'd made arrangements that she should study subjects not ordinarily taught by the school. Special tutors arrived to give her lessons in languages, architectural design, the natural sciences. Fortunately there was one other girl, Claudia Schuyler, who shared these extra classes with her. If Beatrice had been the only odd one, she might have been singled out by the other girls as hopelessly different and therefore perhaps an object of dislike. Claudia soon became her best friend, although she was a year younger than Beatrice. They studied together every afternoon, listening to the instruction of four different men—two quite young—who had been chosen to teach them. Mlle. Dubourg, their chaperone, sat on guard at the back of the otherwise empty classroom. The high windows looked out onto the tops of palm trees.

Claudia's mother was half English, half Italian; her father, American. She had a younger sister at the school, one younger brother at home, an older one at a boys' school a few streets away, and another older brother who was just starting work in a bank. She invited Beatrice home for weekends and holidays.

Beatrice had dreamt for several years about the family that would one day be hers—when, of course, she found the right husband. But the desire for a husband had been prompted by her wish to have sisters, brothers, and a mother. She didn't feel the need for a different father, despite the fact that her own father was so often away; he wrote regularly to her, and besides, was so loving and so willing to share his life with her when he did see her, that she was never without the sense that his presence was with her, nor that she was always in his mind and heart.

One day when Beatrice was staying with Claudia, Mrs. Schuyler said, "You know, I think I once met your father, many years ago. In Rome."

Beatrice was too old to think it natural that somebody else should know everyone she knew. She had also passed the stage where it seemed an amazing coincidence that anyone should have thought the same thought or visited the same city, or loved the same person as someone else. But it did strike her as unusual that she and Claudia should be daughters of two people who had met years ago in another country; it seemed a good omen. She asked, "Did you also meet my mother?"

Mrs. Schuyler paused and then said no: she hadn't had that pleasure.

Beatrice was to remember the small hesitation when a week later she was in a shop with Mlle. Dubourg to buy copybooks for the German class. A young man behind the counter was helping the chaperone to decide between different qualities of writing paper. The old woman who ran the shop was already occupied with a girl about five years older than Beatrice; the girl also had an older person with her—a man who was evidently her servant; he was Egyptian, whereas the girl herself had the look neither of an Egyptian, nor a European. Her eyes were light, her hair and skin—in striking contrast—palely brown. She resembled women Beatrice had seen in the south of France—light-complexioned dancers and singers from the West Indies and South America. As the girl turned to go, she looked briefly at Beatrice. The look said that Beatrice wasn't worth considering. She went through the doorway, followed by her servant, who carried all the packages.

The old woman shut the door behind them. She said to Beatrice in French, "That was your sister."

"I don't have a sister," Beatrice told her.

"Maybe you don't," the old woman muttered, "maybe you do." She started to walk away behind the counter.

Beatrice went after her. "I've never seen that girl before in my life," she said. "Who is she?"

The woman pretended that she didn't understand French. When Beatrice changed to Arabic, she turned quickly and went through the curtains at the back of the shop, where the living quarters were.

"Is something wrong, Beatrice?" Mlle. Dubourg asked.

"Did you see that girl? The one who was in here just a minute ago?"

"I didn't notice. Why? Have you lost something?"

Beatrice repeated what the old woman had told her. "And she went behind there. She doesn't even know me. What did she mean?"

Mlle. Dubourg called the young man over to them. But no amount of discussion could persuade him to make his grandmother come out again; she was ill, he said: forgetful, her thoughts not always completely collected. She often said things that made no sense. She was old.

The incident troubled Beatrice for days. If she'd been staring pointedly at the other girl, the old woman's remark might conceivably have been a rebuke—a way of saying that one girl was no better than another: all were alike. Such an explanation seemed far-fetched. And anyway, she hadn't been staring. She wanted to talk to someone about it, but she felt that Claudia wasn't the right person to go to. She needed someone who was grown up and who had lived in the city long enough to know who everyone was. Was it possible that her father had been in love with another woman before he'd married her mother? Perhaps if she'd had a sister, or even a brother, the idea wouldn't have made such an impression on her. As it was, her sleep became so disturbed that at last she was summoned to the office of Mme. Bonnier, the principal of the school.

She stood by the desk. Madame sat on the other side; she was impeccably dressed, as usual, and looked as if she found life highly enjoyable. She told Beatrice to sit down, asked her the cause of her distress and said that it simply wouldn't do to drift around the schoolrooms, looking like a ghost and falling asleep over her lessons.

Beatrice told her. She described the girl from the shop and said, "Do you know who she is?"

Mme. Bonnier dismissed the story. The old woman, she said, wasn't right in the head; you wouldn't believe the things people muttered to themselves when they relaxed their concentration—even young, sane people.

"But who is she?"

The identity of the girl couldn't possibly be of importance, Madame said, because the old woman didn't know what she was talking about.

Mme. Bonnier was embarrassed. Years later, Beatrice was to understand the nature and extent of the embarrassment: once she'd realized that her father had been quite a ladies' man and that he'd known Mme.

Bonnier, as well as many other women. Beatrice might have had sisters and brothers over half the globe.

But at the time, her attention was trained on one person: the girl in the shop. And her worries were mainly theological. If the girl were a sister, she reasoned, that would mean that her father had been married twice. It followed that the other wife had to be still alive, otherwise the daughter would have stayed with him.

"And if that's true," Beatrice said, "then in the eyes of the Church, his second marriage, to my mother—you see what I mean? I might be the child of sin. One of us has to be."

"Nonsense, Beatrice."

"Well, is that girl's mother still living?"

"Yes."

"Then she's the real daughter. And that makes me—"

"Your father," Mme. Bonnier said, "was never married to this girl's mother. Nor, as far as I know, to anyone but your mother. Does that make you feel better?"

"Of course," Beatrice said. "It's a great relief."

"Good. I'm glad to hear it. Now you can get some sleep."

"But is it true? Is she my sister?"

"I've just told you."

"No, Madame. You've just told me that they weren't married."

"I see. In that case, I must say that to the best of my knowledge, no: she isn't. But her mother is one of those women who's always lived a very free life. So, people gossip about her."

"And my father?"

"I've never heard anyone say a malicious thing about your father. He's always talked of with kindness. This is more the sort of tittle-tattle you'd expect to hear directed against a woman."

"It was directed against me. She wanted to hurt me."

"You know the kinds of people who gossip," Mme. Bonnier said. "And you say she was old. Perhaps she didn't see well. There seemed to her to be two girls in her shop, both of them to her mind looking foreign. Do you understand? There's no great mystery about it."

Beatrice had once heard her father say that when it was a matter of something serious, it was always a good idea to get a second opinion. She went to Claudia's mother.

Mrs. Schuyler knew the girl as soon as Beatrice described her. "Ernestine," she said. "It's a peculiar family. They came here from Brazil. They were running away from something." She appeared to think that the question had now been answered. She reached for another almond cake. The family was at the dining table for tea; one of the younger boys had broken a leg off the tea table: he'd been jumping on the top, but the parents weren't supposed to find out about that. Beatrice felt honored to be treated so completely as part of the family that she was expected to keep from one member of it the secrets of another.

"What were they running away from?" she asked.

"Oh, I don't know."

"Something political," her husband said, getting up from the table. "In that part of the world." He put down his napkin and took his teacup with him into his study.

Mrs. Schuyler said that every country had its politics. However, in the case of the Cristo-Marquez family it was probably something simpler: debts, or a partnership that had fallen to pieces. "There are lots of reasons why people leave a country. If the whole family has to get out, it's liable to be business, I suppose."

"Or politics," Claudia repeated.

"Yes, but they aren't that kind. The mother's a stay-at-home, the father's reserved and silent. They hardly talk to anyone. You see them out shopping with their servants and they never open their mouths. I don't think anyone in town has ever been inside their house."

"Is it a very small house?" Beatrice asked. People who shared a small house with a staff of servants might not have room to ask anyone in.

"Enormous. Like a palace. One can't imagine what they find to do with themselves. Unless you believe the gossip, of course."

"What does the gossip say?"

"We'd better not talk about that. One never learns much from gossip."

"Could you tell me where the house is?" Beatrice said.

"Why?" Mrs. Schuyler asked. "Why do you want to know that?"

Beatrice couldn't think of any reason. Sometimes people didn't have reasons; or sometimes they didn't know exactly what their reasons were. She said, "Just to know. A big house, like a palace—is it near the legation? The one with the two white pillars and the tiled roof?"

"No, that belongs to the medical institute. The Cristo-Marquez house is on the other side of town. About three streets away from the building they call the summer palace. It stands in part of the park there. It has a garden."

"Are you sure?" Beatrice asked.

"Of course, I'm sure. What a question, Beatrice."

"It's just that if it's the same place, I remember driving past there one evening and all the lights were on—all of them. And it really is huge. I've always thought it was a hotel."

"Exactly. That's the way they live. All the lights on, and the singing going on all night. That's why people talk."

—※—

She was moved to a school in Constantinople, then to Athens and to Rome. In Rome she looked up Mrs. Schuyler's sister, a Signora Arnoldi, whose address she'd been given.

The Arnoldis had three daughters, two of whom were already married. The third, Vittoria, was exactly the same age as Claudia: in fact—a fact considered magically propitious to everyone in the family—they had been born on the same day. She too, like Claudia, became a close friend. And though Beatrice was always being shunted on to other cities and countries, she never lost touch with Claudia herself. She thought of the Schuylers as her second family, although in some respects they were her only family. Other people had aunts and uncles, in-laws: she had only her father. There were no relatives left on her mother's side of the family, either; it was as if her parents had each been the last surviving member of a tribe, or a country, or a race.

Over the next few years the Schuylers, too, were on the move: to

England, and afterwards to America, while Beatrice traveled with her father's expeditions. In his opinion she'd had enough of school; she was ready to do serious work.

They went to Afghanistan, Turkey, Mesopotamia. She kept the accounts, wrote up the day's findings, and listened to her father's theories and stories.

When she was eighteen, she and her father joined a large expedition. At the base camp there were two wives and a woman described as a niece. There were difficulties with language, clashes over customs and habits and, above all, fights about who had the authority to do what. The general atmosphere of quarrel and intrigue was further complicated for Beatrice when she fell in love with a Canadian student named Paul, who had come out with the American team. He asked her to marry him. She was still pretending to think over her answer when one of the wives spoke to her father about him.

"I don't know what business it is of theirs," Beatrice said.

"I think they probably have your interest at heart. You're so young."

"They want to stop me having any romance in my life, just because they never had any."

"I don't think it's that. Anyone can have romance, if he wants it. They may feel it's their duty because you have no mother. For a woman, there's always the question of—"

"Morality? That's what they kept talking about in school. They nearly turned me into a religious fanatic."

"Of pregnancy," her father said. "Of course, he's in the same field— you'd be able to help him with his studies for a while. When you had children, perhaps you'd leave them at home with someone. I was able to take you along with me because you were an only child, but it wasn't easy. If there'd been anyone to look after you, it would have been safer to leave you behind. And," he added, "you're a better archaeologist than he is. He's superficial. He doesn't know what to look for. He has no flair for the job."

Beatrice's need for a romantic alliance with a man of her own age was so strong that if her father had been talking about a young man's character, she wouldn't have taken his word, but the indictment of his professional abilities made her question Paul's integrity. Her father had a reputation. Paul was a newcomer. Her father was undoubtedly right. As for the rest, she recalled that among the stories circulating through the camp there was one about a girl back in Canada. And she knew for certain that Paul was writing to three women addressed as Miss: she'd seen the envelopes. She told him the next day, "I've thought about what you asked me and I think we should get to know each other better."

"But you love me, don't you?" he asked.

"Of course," she said.

"Well, that's the main thing, isn't it?"

"I think we'd have a good start because I've been trained for the same job. I could help you, even if we had a large family. But . . ." She thought she really ought to admit that despite her love, she didn't trust him. She trusted her father and Claudia and everyone in Claudia's family: if she were in trouble or ill or needed advice, she knew that they would help her, no matter what they had to sacrifice. But how long would Paul be patient or understanding? She had no idea; nor was she sure how long she'd be able to put him first if he didn't seem to be taking her wishes into consideration.

"I just think" she repeated, "that we should get to know each other better."

"How long will that take?"

"Two years," she said.

"This is a joke, isn't it?"

"I think we ought to be sure."

"Because if it isn't, it's an insult. If you don't want to, Beatrice, just say so."

"I don't even know you," she burst out.

"That doesn't matter."

"Don't be stupid," she snapped. "Of course it matters. We'd be living with each other for the rest of our lives." They'd be one. The thought suddenly terrified her. She didn't know if she wanted to be one with anyone at all, ever.

"But that's all just going to happen as we go along. The important part is what we knew from the beginning."

"I don't know."

"Yes. That instant attraction."

"I feel that way about lots of people," she said.

"Oh?" He looked so scandalized that she didn't know how to explain: to say that the kind of emotion she meant was something that would come over her suddenly or, just as quickly, would go away; and it didn't seem to have much to do with who the man was, or whether he was likeable, or what the wives would have called "possible." Sometimes just seeing the way a man turned his shoulders as he lifted a load of stones or swung a pickax was enough to make her feel interest and excitement.

"I think it's better to find out what we're like," she said.

"Is there any point? If you don't love me?"

"I love you, but why can't we wait?"

"That means no," he said. He walked off.

She was so discouraged that she almost ran after him. A long time afterwards she realized that his abrupt departure was calculated. By then, she had also understood that he'd been right: whatever she'd said, she had meant no. But at the same time, she didn't want to let go of him and of the idea of being wanted. She tried all through the evening meal to catch his eye. She stared at him across the table. He wouldn't lift his head. As soon as the company broke up, he rushed away.

She had almost made up her mind to go charging after him, when one of the wives called her back and, talking about inconsequential matters, took her arm and led her away from the others. "When I was your age," the woman said, "I never imagined that I'd be part of a scholarly expedition. It's really most absorbing, despite the inconvenience. And the many discomforts. Yes—I know this one's a model of its kind, but you're used to it, my dear. You've had invaluable training, simply by being near your father. This life was new to me when I married. But now I see the familiar faces every year. And the young ones come and go. It's a shame that Paul won't be with us next year."

"He hasn't resigned, has he?"

"Not at all. But his scholarship grant runs out at the end of the season. So, unless he can find some way of financing himself privately, I suppose he'll have to go back to Canada."

"I see," Beatrice said mildly. She hated the woman for telling her. Undoubtedly the action was meant kindly, although she didn't think so at the time. Later she would also wonder—after it was too late to ask him—whether her father had had a hand in the disillusionment: whether he'd asked the woman to speak to her. He might have felt that it was the sort of thing a real mother would do. Girls whose mothers were living, Beatrice knew, had to put up with that kind of interference all the time, and with the fear induced by constant protectiveness and warnings; whereas she had never had anything but the beauty of the dream she'd invented around the absence of her mother.

She kept quiet and waited. Paul tried to make up. He accused her of insincerity. She said to him, "That's not true," but she could tell that it was too late to go back to what she had felt before. She knew that he'd never loved her. She could hear it in his voice. She said that they'd better part and there was no reason why they shouldn't do it in a friendly way. Once more he left her abruptly and indignantly, this time calling her an obscene name: a word she didn't know the precise meaning of, although she could guess the general sense of it. That, too, was in his voice.

For the next few weeks she could feel that everyone was talking about her. The wives, unexpectedly, made an effort to keep her company. And her father was as easy to talk to as ever, as fun-loving and full of good conversation. She asked him, "Have you ever thought of marrying again?" The question had come to her in a rush, as if it were in itself an attempt to get close to him. She'd never considered the idea before.

"I thought of it quite a lot when you were still small," he said. "Not that I had anyone in mind, but—it seemed to me that you needed a mother. You sometimes looked completely lost. It upset me a great deal. But then I talked it over with one or two friends. And they told me that things would be so much worse if you didn't take to a new mother."

"I couldn't imagine it," she said. "I'm glad that you didn't. I only wondered for your sake. I wouldn't mind now, you know. I wouldn't have minded even when I was at school. It was just those six or seven years before."

"It's impossible to repeat something like that," he told her. "I wouldn't want to try. Some people find happiness more than once. More than twice. We're all different. You'll find out what agrees with you. Just try to ask yourself if you're sure of what you want."

"What kinds of people gossip, Papa?"

"Politicians, journalists, old women, old men. Girls. Boys. Everyone I can think of. Even your father, on occasion. Why? Are people gossiping about me again?"

"About me, I think. I can feel it in the air. And the way they all pretend not to be looking at me too closely."

"Let them. Don't allow it to worry you."

"If people tell me things about someone, and I don't know whether they're true or not—"

"You can ask the person. Or you can just think it over. Try to sort out the probable, the possible, and the unlikely. It's part of the trade."

"I might end up believing something bad of someone when it wasn't actually true."

"You might. What would that show?"

"That I drew the wrong conclusion on lack of evidence."

"Perhaps because other evidence predisposed you to think badly of the person."

"What other evidence?"

"You tell me," he said. "You started this discussion."

"I never really trusted him," she said. "I wanted him all the same. But not for too long. Not forever."

He gave her a complicated assignment that entailed meticulous collations of original notes and translations. The work was harder than anything she had done before. The time passed quickly for her.

The next season saw a new set of students; and the next. She became invaluable to her father and—when he was away—to many of his colleagues, who used to consult her as if she were his partner and equal.

She presided over the house in Switzerland like a curator in a museum. She loved being there, even on her own, surrounded by her father's discoveries. She was always occupied with some work of hers or of his; she began to publish under her own name. And she traveled, sometimes with an expedition and sometimes merely to see friends. She made regular visits to the Arnoldis, in Rome; and to Paris, where the Schuylers went for Easter. She'd stay with Vittoria Arnoldi for a few weeks and then both of them would take the train to Paris, to join the Schuylers—"my American cousins," as Vittoria called them. Beatrice began to remember Paul with less anger and blame. Ten years after the event, the hurt had gone. She thought of her old self as someone, like him, who shouldn't have been taken seriously, and who was too inexperienced to behave well.

She was happier than she had been when she was younger. She saw that she had a place in life and she liked it.

Her father had just come to the end of a stay in Palmyra and was back in Baghdad for a while, when he fell ill. The first indication Beatrice had of the fact was an official letter of condolence.

She was certain that whoever wrote the letter must have made a mistake; people got things mixed up all the time, even names. She wrote back, and then decided that that wasn't enough—she had to get out there and speak to the officials herself. Everyone tried to talk her out of it. They said that she wouldn't be able to help.

She made the journey anyway. How could she have stayed at home, when her father might be anywhere at all, and she wouldn't know about it? He could have written to her about plans to go on an expedition: it wasn't unknown for letters to be lost or delayed for months. He could be in danger, while some petty bureaucrat was entering his name in the wrong set of records. She remembered her father himself telling her that an acquaintance of his had had to travel all over the world as Mr. Brown Gray simply because a clerk somewhere hadn't known how to copy out the information in his papers, according to which his hair was brown and his eyes gray.

As she moved from country to country, her father's friends came to greet her; like cities on a map, they were dotted across the great distances she had to go. And when she neared the end of her journey, two of them, an uncle and nephew named Hoffmann, took on the local and foreign officials while she stood or sat silent nearby. Sometimes she felt compelled to interrupt, especially as people seemed to keep changing their stories. Her father, she was told, might not have been exactly ill; he might actually have been poisoned—that is, murdered. There was a woman in the case: more than one woman. And that always made for danger.

"This is ridiculous," she whispered to the Hoffmann uncle. "My father was used to having all sorts of friendships and so on. He never left anyone feeling resentful or unhappy."

"Perhaps a man who was a rival?"

"Much more likely to have been a poor cook," she said. Then, feeling just like Mrs. Schuyler, she asked for information about the servants.

His household had loved and admired him. According to them, he'd had a fever. One of them—a superstitious man—suspected that the professor had caught the disease from something he'd found when he was digging up a grave: everyone knew that it was forbidden to disturb the dead.

She asked where her father had been buried. They were shown to a small cemetery for Christian Europeans. The Hoffmanns stood on either side of her, in case the emotion or the climate should prove too much for her. She found it impossible to believe that her father was there, in that space of earth. Could they have buried someone else by mistake? She wanted to ask to see him—just to be sure. But that would be impractical as well as shocking. Everyone agreed that the thing had happened and that he was there. Friends of friends had been at the funeral. She simply found it against the nature of the world as she knew it that he should suddenly not be there for her to talk to or write to.

On the return journey she began to believe in his death. Everyone she had met going out tried to comfort her on the way back. So many people had loved him. It made her feel closer to him to hear them talk, and yet it also persuaded her to accept the fact that he was dead.

When she got to Switzerland there were two letters waiting for her, from him. They were just like his usual letters, with no hint of bad feeling among his acquaintance or in the household.

She began to go through his papers, which were neatly arranged, as always. She kept herself busy. There were the clothes to be given away, the boxes of papers to be gone through: letters from his colleagues, his friends, and from her. All the letters from her childhood were there—every note she'd sent him from her schools in Egypt, France, and Italy.

She used to wake in the night, choking with tears, bawling. Some-times it was as if she were in the middle of a storm. The first time it happened, her cook, Maria, ran up the stairs to pound on her door. Beatrice shouted for her to go away; the next day she said that she was grateful for the kind thought but that since nothing could help, it was better to ignore these outbursts. She didn't try to stop.

For months she carried on mental talks with him. At times they became so real to her, she sometimes imagined that she could hear his voice. Perhaps if her mother hadn't died early, there would have been another strong influence in her life. As it was, although she had loved her mother dearly and with a particular kind of love that no other person she'd met could evoke from her, her father had always been at the center of her life. He had shaped her interests, passed on his knowledge and talents to her, yet he'd given her the freedom to leave, if she wanted to. Despite the fact that she had remained an un-married daughter, she led a more liberal life on her own than any married woman she knew, whether happy or not. Her father wouldn't have minded if she'd wanted to travel to a different country, visit friends for long periods, spend her time in some new pursuit, or get married and move away. They'd known each other well enough for him not to have had to explain that, as before, he'd speak out against any admirer of hers whom he considered unsuitable; and for her not to have to say that she sometimes felt guilty about her comfortable life, knowing how much he'd have loved to have grandchildren.

She missed him all the time. For years—long after his death—as soon as she thought of him, his presence was with her. She understood how it was that many people became religious after a bereavement: it was because they were impelled by an urge to reach the other person again. In her case, she grew less religious. The act of prayer had become a process of having conversations with herself and her memory of her father. She didn't feel that she was developing eccentric habits—other people told her how they caught themselves thinking of what her father would say to such-and-such, and how dear he still was to them, how clearly recalled. She loved to hear people talk about him, especially if they were old friends who had known him before she was born, or even before he was married.

Sometimes she would remember, with a dreamlike vividness and immediacy, a phrase he used to favor, the way he'd looked at certain times, the sound of his chair scraping back over the floorboards as he stood up from his desk. It was as if in her mind she were once more writing him letters. The ancient Egyptians, he'd told her, used to write letters to the dead. They'd put up a statue of the departed person and inscribe the letter on the front. Usually the survivors wanted the dead to intercede; to help them in some way. Occasionally the letter was an accusation, saying: "Why are you causing me such bad luck, when I was always good to you?" Unhappiness, they believed, always had a cause. And usually the cause was witchcraft by other people, dead or alive. Beatrice's father had shown her one of the letter-statues when she was still a child. She had immediately realized that the writing was really for the living, not the dead, who couldn't answer. If the dead had been able to do anything, her mother would have spoken to her from wherever she had gone to.

One day while she was in Rome on a visit to the Arnoldi family, she looked up Dr. Santini. His son had been one of her father's old school friends. At the time of her father's death, the son had written to her; a year afterwards, when the son was killed in an excavation, she had had to write to the old man. She wouldn't have gone to see him, except that his name came up and Signora Arnoldi said, " I hear he's dying."

She sent a letter first, and was invited. The professor lived in a part of town she hadn't seen for many years. The house was large, underlit, and cold. It had abundant tile decoration, some marble, dark wood paneling, and many tarnished silver wall sconces adorned with ugly human figures. Three maids stood in the hallway to greet her. They were dressed in baggy skirts and shawls. For all she knew, they might have been relatives. The one who struggled up the staircase in front of her screamed down to another one near the kitchen entrance to get the tea ready.

The old man was delighted to see her. He said that he remembered her father as a young boy: when he'd come to visit his son, Giorgio, at their cousin's house on the island. The two boys had been up to all sorts of tricks. They were always inventing games and stories; her father, even then, was fascinated by the past. But he was also a boy who liked to play outdoors—not at all the bookworm type. Dr. Santini could remember him and Giorgio catching the big, hard-shelled beetles they used to have on the estate: you could pick up any beetle easily while it fed on grapes or flowers—tie a thread around the middle of its body, and walk around with it that way. The beetle would fly at the end of the thread and make a loud, whirring sound like a bumblebee. What the children liked best about the game was the noise the beetles made, but the creatures were also wonderful to look at—black on the underside and on top a bright, emerald green that changed in the sun to gold. He could remember seeing her father and Giorgio—his son, Giorgio—walking down the path side by side, and their beetles flying above on strings. Everyone had loved her father. It was a pleasure when he came to stay.

"And his mother," the old man continued, "your grandmother; sometimes we'd see her. She was the most beautiful woman I've ever met. Did you know that?"

Beatrice said no, she hadn't known.

One of the maids brought tea and propped the doctor higher in his bed. He went on to talk about his own childhood and also asked about her life. She told him that at the moment she had to decide what to do with her father's collection. Some of it would go to museums. "And I ought to sell the rest, I suppose. All those things should be in a place where they can be seen. Where people can learn from them."

"And you must get married," he said. "Don't smile. I can still see well enough to tell what expressions people have."

"If that's meant to happen—" she began.

"You shouldn't wait. I waited for too many things. Sometimes there isn't another chance."

"But sometimes it doesn't matter. I'd rather be the way I am than the way I might have become if I'd married the first man who asked me."

The doctor shook his head. He said that he'd probably been spoiled: he'd always had a large family around him and of course, he knew, it was the women who had to do the work in the house. But if you outlived all your family, it made you wonder what sense there was in anything. He blamed the French, for not providing adequate supports for the higher trenches on the site, so that when it rained the mudslide came down all in a flash and buried his son. It was a matter of seconds; nothing could be done for him. "This tea tastes bitter," he said.

Everything tasted bitter when you were sick. Her father might have voiced the same sort of complaint, and that could have given rise to the rumors about poison.

She stood up, brought the sugar to him, and offered to spoon some crystals into his cup. He asked her to take the cup away, which she did.

And soon after that—seeing that he was tired and wanted to think about his son—she left.

She went to his funeral. She would have gone anyway out of respect, but the fact that she hadn't been able to attend any last ceremony for her father made her want to be there for her own sake, too. Vittoria Arnoldi accompanied her. They, and the maids, were the only women. All the other mourners were old men. Vittoria said she thought that they were probably part of the archaeological faculty of the university; unless, she added casually, they were something it had dug up. Beatrice slapped a handkerchief to her face and exploded into giggles. For several minutes she fought against hysteria. She hadn't known anything like it since her school days. Fortunately the handkerchief was large enough so that everyone would assume her to be weeping. Vittoria, having caused the trouble, remained unaffected, and unrepentant afterwards.

The lawyers sent Beatrice a letter to say that the doctor had left her a picture, which she could come to collect. She imagined that it would be something to do with her father or perhaps with the house where he and Giorgio had spent their school holidays. But a note on the package she was handed said: *This is your grandmother. She was more beautiful than her picture.* The portrait was in pen and ink, the face lovely, and the attitude so natural and modern that if it hadn't been for the arrangement of the hair and the set of the rakish little hat—both in the style of another age—it might have been of someone who was still alive. There was no resemblance to her father, nor to anyone else, as far as Beatrice could see. She was so pleased with the picture that for a long while she didn't ask herself how the doctor should have come to have it in his possession. It was possible, of course, that her father had given it to him. And while she was still wondering about that, she thought again how strange it was that, enigmatic as these lives were to her, they were all on one side of the family. She still knew nothing about her mother's people, not even where they had originally come from. The parent about whom she kept finding out unusual facts was the one she already knew. Her mother, never known, could not be mysterious. Her mother had become a being she recognized emblematically: an unalterable, undifferentiated presence, stationed in another place, reaching her from another time; always the same. Her father had become the mysterious one: more could be known about him; more of his life revealed by other people.

Signora Arnoldi admired the grandmother's portrait so extravagantly that she asked for permission to have it copied. And when the work was done and she held it in her hands, she said jokingly, "Who would ever have thought it of old Santini?"

"Thought what?" Beatrice asked.

"That he'd nurse a hopeless longing for years. He always seemed such a dry old fellow."

Beatrice wanted to say that there was no proof of any longing, hopeless or otherwise, on anyone's part and that this was just gossip again; but since Signora Arnoldi had hit on the same suspicion she'd had herself, she let it go.

That summer in Switzerland she hired a young student named Ernst to help her with the recataloguing of her father's library. She also made preparations to sell most of the Greek and Roman sculpture and the larger objects from ancient Egypt. Some of them were very large indeed. Even statues smaller than life-size required the kind of lifting gear normally found only among the loading equipment in a harbor town.

She took photographs of everything and was so satisfied by the results that she went on to take pictures of Ernst, his fiancée, Marta, and Marta's parents, who came to visit her one day and were frightened by the statues and helmets, and the vases and jars emblazoned with animal heads. They had never been in a museum before. They thought that everything was slightly sinister. They went down the hallways behind their daughter and said, "My, how interesting. Think of that." They held hands and looked as if they were prepared to protect each other if anything strange were to happen.

Beatrice chattered on in an attempt to put them at their ease. She told them about the gods and goddesses represented in the works of art. She described aspects of religion that the couple wouldn't find too shocking. "I didn't realize how much there was," she ended. "I'd never thought about all those boxes out in the old barn. And the things stored at the institute. At least a third of the collection was given to him by his teacher, long ago. I don't suppose there's anyone nowadays who has anything like this—certainly not like the big statues. They really shouldn't be in private hands."

Marta's parents shook their heads. They agreed: Get rid of things as soon as possible.

The auction was held eight months later. It went well. Several American museums joined the bidding, which knocked the prices up considerably. Beatrice sold to the United States, Great Britain, Germany, Austro-Hungary, France, Russia, and several countries in South America. Private collectors accounted for over 50 percent of the sales, despite the size of some of the statues. There had been a great demand in recent years for garden statuary of any kind and in any condition. It pained Beatrice to think of the Greek Apollo outdoors in a German winter; the Roman cupid with his pet deer had gone to St. Petersburg and the two Etruscan sarcophagi to Vienna. She was glad to hear, however, that most of the Egyptian treasures in the sale had gone back to Cairo, to a bidder named Hassan. She assumed at first that that meant purchase by an institution, but a man on the auction-house staff told her that the largest of the Egyptian lots were all going to a private family. "Oh," she said, "to a private museum, like my father's."

"Well, possibly," the man said. "I'd understood it to be a private collector."

She thought that that couldn't be: she knew what the prices were. For a single family to buy such things might have been possible in North or South America, or in Russia, but the sort of millionaire who might have a weakness for Egyptian statuary didn't live in Cairo. A rich Egyptian collector would be looking for French and Italian paintings, German machinery, South African diamonds; or, at least, small *objets d'art* and *objets de vertu*. The father of one of her school friends in Cairo had had a vast collection of enamel boxes; he'd once said to her that the ancient art of the Pharaohs gave him the shivers—modern life was much more to his taste. He'd also had a passion for sweet liqueurs, Irish racehorses, the operettas of Jacques Offenbach, and English tweed jackets. She remembered him as a very agreeable man.

She thought suddenly that there had been many pleasant people in her life with whom she'd fallen out of correspondence. It was possible that they'd moved, or—like her—suffered bereavement. Most of the girls would be married by now, and would have children. Claudia already had three and her American husband, Charlie, was putting on fat and beginning to look important.

As long as the collection had been unbroken, she'd had so much to do that her life was full. Now that most of the pieces were disposed of, she felt that she'd lost her occupation. She sat down at the desk that had been her father's. She wrote to Claudia. As her pen shaped words on the paper, she remembered their school days. She felt a longing for the friendship of her childhood and for the family that had seemed to be hers: among whom she was at home, never just a guest.

Claudia wrote back; she was coming to Paris and going on to Florence: Beatrice must stay with her.

They met. On the morning after Beatrice's arrival, Claudia told her, "You should come to New York. You need something entirely new."

Beatrice said, automatically, that that was certainly something to consider. Later in the day she did think about the possibility, and asked herself: Why not? Some of the treasures from her father's collection had gone as gifts to museums and some—but only a few—he'd held in trust for archaeological foundations that were looking for places to house them. Most had been his. They had brought her a huge sum. She hadn't yet begun to contemplate what she was going to do with it. She could go anywhere in the world.

"I just might," she said the next day.

"Good. Come to town for the spring and spend the summer with us at the seashore. And during the winter—we're going back for a visit to Egypt. You've got to come. You can help to cheer up Jack. Did I tell you about Evie?"

"Yes," Beatrice said. "Such a simple thing. And so quickly. It's terrible to think about." Claudia's sister-in-law, Eve, had developed a cold sore on her lip. She'd tried to cover it with powder and some sort of liquid makeup and then it had become infected, either as a result of what she'd put on it or simply because it wouldn't heal. At any rate, the infection had turned septic and it had killed her. She and Jack had two small children. "He's still knocked sideways," Claudia said.

Jack met them in Florence and did the museums and galleries with them. Beatrice felt that, after so many years, it was still as though they were her family. She found that she seemed to know Jack just as well as she'd always known Claudia. When Claudia said that she wanted to stay in the hotel one rainy morning, Beatrice and Jack went out together. After that, they'd often go out with each other. He began to court her. It happened so easily, and her response was so wholehearted, that it was as if she'd burst into flame. She knew that he'd loved his wife and undoubtedly still did, and that he was lonely and needed a mother for his children. She also knew that he genuinely wanted her and had always been her friend. She didn't mean to wait an instant: she was afraid of losing her happiness before it had begun. But it wouldn't look right to be in such a hurry, and before his year of mourning was over. "After Egypt," he told her.

Claudia said, "It was my doing, of course. You two didn't stand a chance."

Beatrice smirked and blushed. She was blushing all day long. She considered it ridiculous for a woman in her early thirties to be overcome by such feelings of maidenliness, but she was also happy. She made plans. She prepared to sell the house in Switzerland.

She arrived in Egypt two days before the others and had time to settle her luggage and unpack her clothes. As soon as the Schuylers joined her, they began a series of parties at the hotel, at friends' houses, at restaurants. All the family was there, including some of the Arnoldis, with in-laws and children. In the daytime they enjoyed the sunshine, at night they ate and drank and danced. Jack presented Beatrice with her engagement ring—an emerald centered between two smaller diamonds.

The next morning an invitation arrived for Beatrice; it was delivered to the hotel by hand. She'd never heard of the people. While she was puzzling over the question of why strangers should ask her to their house, she picked up the envelope again and saw that there was a second piece of paper inside. She pulled it out and read the explanation: the stranger, a Mme. Cristo-Marquez, thought that Beatrice might want to see her father's collection in its new surroundings.

"How nice," she said. "It's the people who bought Papa's statues." She read out the name.

"Not them?" Mrs. Schuyler exclaimed from her end of the breakfast table.

"Don't you remember?" Claudia said. "You once told me about meeting the daughter in a shop. There was something unusual about it—I can't remember. She said something to you."

"No," Beatrice said. "I don't remember."

"Of course you do. In that shop that sold the rugs and the paper. Where I bought my silver bangle. She was going out and she said something that upset you so much that—"

"Oh," Beatrice said, remembering all at once. The family must belong to the strange-looking girl she'd seen shopping with a servant nearly twenty years before. "Now I know. What an odd coincidence."

"One couldn't possibly go there," Mrs. Schuyler said. "No one could. It's out of bounds. And certainly not at night."

"Mother, dear," Claudia said, "what difference could that make?"

"It makes a difference in that house. The whole of Cairo knows what they get up to at night. I won't tell you what they used to say about that family."

"Why not?" one of the children said, and was immediately shushed. Beatrice, too, would have liked an answer, but the interruption had brought the topic to a close.

She accepted the invitation. When the fact came out during a comparison of dinner dates, Mrs. Schuyler expressed such concern that Beatrice began to feel unsure about her decision.

"You mean to say, you accepted?"

"Yes, of course. I thought it would be so lovely to see the collection again. It was thoughtful of them to ask me."

"They aren't thoughtful people. You can't go, Beatrice."

"But I've accepted."

"You'll have to cancel."

"No, I don't do that kind of thing."

"My dear, this is serious. I should have made it clearer. These people are much more than simply undesirable. They are extremely unsavory. They indulge in practices that—that—I don't quite know what to call it. A great deal more than the ordinary sort of orgy. And the servants join in."

"I've accepted," Beatrice said.

"You can become ill at the last moment."

"As soon as I'm well, they'll ask me again."

"And you'll still be unable to go, until finally they stop asking."

"I couldn't do that."

"Beatrice, it's not a house to go to at all, but if you can't get out of it, at least it's not a house to go to alone. I expect Jack will have to go with you."

"He isn't invited."

"If they try to turn him away, you leave with him."

"But it's for dinner. And I can't bring an extra guest anyway, if I don't even know the people."

"You can and you'll have to," Mrs. Schuyler said.

Beatrice recalled her school days, the incident in the shop and the effect it had had on her. Of course, it had been the old woman, not the girl, who had spoken to her. Even so, she began to sense again the mixture of curiosity and panic the event had aroused in her. The prospect of visiting her father's collection no longer appealed to her. She thought about entering the Cristo-Marquez house. She tried to imagine what it would look like inside, and what the people would be like, but she couldn't. All she could think of was that everything there would be dark. She said, "Well, I can't say I'm very anxious to go now. I'd be glad if Jack could come along."

Jack took the affair as a joke. "That old place," he told her. "We used to believe it was haunted. Mother's always distrusted the family. It probably goes back to sometime in the past when they managed to outbid her at an auction. Something like that."

"Didn't someone mention singing? That they sang at night?"

"Yes. Chanting. Wailing. Religious, I guess."

"At night?"

"Yes. I used to hear it myself."

"What was it like?"

"Rather like . . . like what I said: the kind of chanting you'd hear at a religious ceremony."

"Just the thing to brighten up a dinner table."

"Should I go armed?"

"That's another thing—don't start me laughing. I'm beginning to feel nervous about it. I'm quite capable of bursting into laughter the moment we get in the door. So don't make jokes."

He promised, and then told her several terrible old jokes that doubled her up with giggles.

They held hands on the drive to the house. A friend of hers in Switzerland—not a very close friend—had once accused her of being interested in the past because she was afraid of the future. The comment had hurt her deeply; she'd feared that it might be true. Now she knew that it hadn't been true at all. It had simply been a spiteful remark. She loved the past because she was able to imagine it. She could see it clearly. And now, all at once, she saw her own life, too, as it was and as it could become.

The driver deposited them outside the railings of the garden fence. He left as soon as he was paid. There was a small, inadequate streetlight above the gates. Jack looked for a bell. There was nothing. Through the open ironwork they could see the path, the trees, the gigantic, partly lighted house beyond. He pushed the gate, which opened in the middle and gave a loud, wrenching squeal. "Come on," he said.

She stumbled along beside him over uneven stones. They went up a flight of steps and stopped at the front door of the house. Again he hunted in the dimness for a bell, and at last found the button. They waited a long time. Just as she was feeing relieved at the delay and thinking that they could leave, the door was thrown open and it was too late.

"Mlle. Norbert and Mr. Schuyler," Jack said.

The servant who had opened the door stood back to let them in. As they passed him, Beatrice thought there seemed to be something wrong with his back or shoulders. He held himself stiffly.

The corridors weren't so dark as she'd imagined. On the other hand, they were extremely narrow, without room for decoration or hangings other than the light brackets, and the ceilings were so high that it was like being in some vast, underground cave.

They had to walk in single file, the servant leading, over an old rag carpet; in several places it wasn't securely attached. Twice Jack had to catch Beatrice as she skidded to the side. The floor underneath was stone. And the house was quiet enough so that as they shuffled forward, the only sound other than that of their moving feet was the wheezing of the man in front.

They came out into a space that in another house would have been the hallway by the main door: well-lighted, with plenty of room to stand. There were chairs against the wall and carpets on the wooden floor. A large Venetian mirror hung from a ceiling rail. Beatrice wondered how old the place was. The curiously labyrinthine entranceways might have had something to do with an ancient system of defense.

A butler took their coats and showed them down two steps and through a door, into a reception room filled with people talking and raising glasses to their lips. An Egyptian in his midforties came up to them; he introduced himself as Hassan, the son of the house. "My mother is resting," he told them. "But you must meet my sister and my uncle, Constantine."

Uncle Constantine was a desiccated old gentleman who immediately attached himself to Beatrice and began to tell her about his young days in Paris. She enjoyed his stories, despite the fact that occasionally he'd repeat phrases or ask all at once, "Where was I?" or, "What was I saying?" The daughter, Ernestine, was also presented. Beatrice didn't recognize her until a few minutes after they had been introduced; she now wore her hair pulled back into a knot. Her face was thin, the skin dried out, and the light eyes—which had made such a startling effect in her youth—had lost their clear, open look; they seemed sunken into her face and their color no longer appeared remarkable. Her hair was lighter than before. Beatrice suspected that she'd been putting henna on it. That was surprising, but merely a detail. What troubled Beatrice was the greater change that had taken place: from the striking-looking girl to this unsmiling, charmless woman.

Two waiters circulated through the room with trays of wine. Jack engaged Ernestine in conversation. Like all the Schuylers, he could talk to anyone, and on any subject. He could talk to anyone, and on any subject. Beatrice said to Hassan that she hadn't realized there was to be such a large gathering.

"Every week," he told her. "They come for the ceremony."

"Oh?"

"Recitations from the classical texts. My mother started the custom years ago. This is just the usual crowd." As he finished his drink, one of the waiters whispered to him. "I'll be back in a moment," he said to Beatrice.

She could see Jack edging toward her. He waited until Ernestine and Uncle Constantine were drawn into larger groups and then eased himself away from them.

"I recognize the son," he told her. "We used to see him at the bank. He's got a reputation for business transactions that go a bit wrong for other people. He always seems to come out of them all right. Quick on his feet. Makes a lot of money and loses a lot, too."

"Hush," she said. "He's coming back."

Hassan bowed to Beatrice. "My mother would be very happy to show you the sanctuary now. Will you come this way, please?"

Beatrice and Jack moved forward together. Hassan said that it wasn't necessary for the gentleman to come: he could stay and amuse himself with the other guests, if he so wished.

"I'm looking forward to seeing the statues," Jack said. "Immensely."

Hassan hardly paused. He said that his mother would be delighted. He led them up a staircase, down a long corridor, and up another flight of stairs. Beatrice had to stop for a moment to catch her breath. At the end of the hallway two men who looked like bodyguards stood to attention in front of studded double doors.

"Are you not well?" Hassan asked.

"Very well, thank you. Too much dancing and champagne this week, I'm afraid. I'll be all right now."

They moved to the doors, which now seemed to Beatrice like the entrance to a tomb. The guards swung the doors open to reveal a long, high, wide room like the main showroom of a museum. She recognized the sitting hawk and baboon, the two rams, and in the far distance the torso of Tuthmosis the Third. She did not recognize the woman who glided toward them, but felt that she ought to have.

"Mother," Hassan said, "this is Mlle. Norbert. Mademoiselle, allow me to present my mother: Mme. Cristo-Marquez."

Beatrice stepped forward, smiled, and took the woman's hand. She tried not to stare at the long, square-cut, dead-black hair that must have been a wig, or at the extraordinary, flamboyant makeup on the face in front of her. Mme. Cristo-Marquez was painted to resemble an ancient Egyptian queen or goddess: the eyes were heavily outlined with black, the lids azure-shaded. The eyes themselves never stopped moving. She greeted Beatrice and Jack, looking at them and away again— at a stone jar, at a blue bead necklace, at Hassan, and at Ernestine and Uncle Constantine, who had followed them in. It took Beatrice a few moments before she realized that the woman was insane.

Mme. Cristo-Marquez described an outward arc with one hand. "He would have wanted me to have them," she said.

"It's wonderful to see them again," Beatrice told her. "But shouldn't they be on the ground floor? The weight—"

"The weight of the past," Mme. Cristo-Marquez said portentously, "is always with us." "They might actually go through the floor. We had a bad accident at home with a granite cat—quite a small statue, but it weighed—"

"It weighs on my mind," Mme. Cristo-Marquez said. She laughed. Beatrice heard Jack draw in his breath. "Do you see my daughter there? My daughter, Ernestine. She looks like an Arab, doesn't she? And sometimes she looks almost like a Nubian. Do you know why? It's because of our association with the past. With history." She prowled toward a lidded sarcophagus in the center of the room and turned back without warning. "It's caused by thought," she declared.

Beatrice took Jack's arm. She prepared to make an excuse to leave.

"She's your father's daughter," Mme. Cristo-Marquez proclaimed. Ernestine showed no response, nor did her brother, nor the uncle. Beatrice began to feel angry as well as uneasy.

"He loved me," Mme. Cristo-Marquez murmured. She closed her eyes for a moment, displaying the blue color to the full.

"He loved everyone," Beatrice said. It wasn't quite true. He'd had no time for women who were silly without being beautiful or charming enough to make up for it. He'd never had much patience with posturing and melodrama: he liked people who had some sense.

Mme. Cristo-Marquez swept toward the sarcophagus and draped herself against one of its corners. "I was the only love of his life," she said.

Beatrice wanted to say: *How long did you last?* She felt herself being overtaken by the indignation of the legitimate. She tried to stop herself from saying anything that would hurt the woman. Mme. Cristo-Marquez was repulsive, outrageous, and offensive, but she was also ludicrous, pitiable, ill. And the rest of her family knew it. Her painted face, her stories about her daughter's parentage, her collection of objects, were all for nothing. *The things people will do out of despair*, Beatrice thought. *And then afterwards they sit there with a handful of trash, and tell themselves that they're happy.*

"And in the end, he came to me. He came back to Cairo, to seek his final resting place. He died of love."

A sense of her father's personality came to Beatrice so strongly that it was almost as if he were near her in the way people describe the presence of ghosts. *How he would have detested the impertinence of this woman*, she thought. *How he would have disapproved of all these theatrical trappings. He liked reason, science, logic.* It was impossible that these people could have known him. "He died," she said, "of food poisoning."

"There are poisons and poisons, you know. Some can work at a distance, and some over a period of time. Love is a poison."

"Love is a pleasure," Jack said. "Always." Beatrice squeezed his hand.

"Not always," Mme. Cristo-Marquez shrieked. "But he knows better now. Now he's come home to me."

"He's buried near Baghdad," Beatrice stated coldly.

Mme. Cristo-Marquez made a snarling noise. She slapped the side of the sarcophagus. "Here," she said. The other members of her family still hadn't moved. "Shall I show you?" she shouted.

Although Beatrice was incensed, the fact that she hadn't seen her father die—that she hadn't even been able to look at the body—suddenly made her fear that there might be something inside the sarcophagus. It was even possible that a crazed woman with enough money could bribe people to dig up a corpse and transport it from one country to another. She said, "Jack, would you take me back to the hotel, please?"

"Certainly. Will you excuse us? It's been a delightful evening, but a long day. I'm afraid we must be going." He drew her away, heading toward the doors. Beatrice said, "Good night," as they turned.

Hassan made a move to follow them. His mother screamed that they were to stay, but he didn't try to stop them. He told Ernestine, "Stay with her," and ran ahead of Jack. "Let me show you the way," he said.

They went down the staircases in silence, across the carpeted lobbies, down the narrow hallways. In the foyer where the mirror hung, a butler presented Jack with his cape and Beatrice with the velvet cloak she'd bought in Florence. Hassan proceeded to the last, dim corridor and the door to the garden. Jack put his hand on the latch and opened the door before the arthritic servant could move. The cool air came in to them.

Beatrice stepped out so that she was halfway through the door, and turned. She asked Hassan, "What's in the sarcophagus?"

He shrugged. "My father or your father—perhaps more than one person. Why should it make a difference to you?"

"Do you mean that she'd really go so far as to dig someone up in order to put him in there?"

"And why not? It's what archaeologists do all the time. That's their job: digging up the dead."

"Their job is to add to the sum of human knowledge," Beatrice said.

Hassan started to shut the door in her face. He'd forgotten that Jack was still inside. Jack threw him against the wall and pushed his way out of the door. He caught Beatrice by the hand.

They ran down the path to the gate. As soon as they were out on the street, they turned around to look back.

"Those horrible people," she said. "Your mother was right. My God, what a nightmare."

"Not a nightmare. A farce. Listen," he said, freeing his hand and using both arms to imitate the dramatic movements of Mme. Cristo-Marquez, "there are poisons and poisons."

Beatrice laughed. From the house, faintly, came a doleful wailing.

"I suppose that's from *The Book of the Dead?*" he said. "They'll get a surprise when all that masonry comes thundering down on them one of these days. That'll really give them something to moan about."

He led her to broader streets, more densely populated, bursting with crowds and brightly lit. Every once in a while he made her laugh by leaning to the side and whispering into her ear, "Love is a poison."

SOMEWHERE ELSE

Beth was still working on the crossword puzzle when Alan finished his section of the paper. He reached for the pile of letters that looked like bills and throwaways. There was a time when the mailman delivered letters from living people, not just from organizations and offices. Of course nowadays practically everyone picked up the phone instead of a pen. Beth, and Alan, too, preferred the telephone. Unless they had to send a contract somewhere, nearly all their business was done over the phone and by fax. They had answering machines at the office and in the house. The telephone dominated their lives. It was a blessing; and it was a nuisance.

He lifted the heap of catalogues and magazines and dumped them at the right of her coffee cup. "Clothes, handbags, shoes," he said. "Save the environment. One for jigsaws, one for music boxes, one that sells replicas of prehistoric animals. Two book clubs you can join."

"I don't have time to read anything."

"Except the catalogues, and that's a real waste of time." He shuffled through some more bills. She went back to her puzzle.

"Hey," he said. "I think I've won a prize."

"What for?"

"Being good, of course."

"Oh, ha ha."

He held the paper up to her, but she didn't bother to look. She was trying to think of a six-letter word meaning stop. "Listen to this," he told her. "Two thousand dollars if I apply within forty-eight hours of receiving the enclosed. It's got a date and a time-stamp on it. We've got a day more than they say."

"Desist," she said. "Those urgent things are never important. Alan Q. Beasley, you could win a million dollars: remember?"

"This looks OK. No pictures of Colonel Kentucky. No free stamps."

"Another bonanza from the black-diamond mine," she said.

The black-diamond episode had been about three years before; they'd been carrying on a smoldering quarrel for a couple of months. She'd begun to think they weren't going to pull out of it—that this time their marriage would end: and she wouldn't have cared a bit if it had. One morning, another of those prize envelopes arrived for Alan. He'd actually sent for it. How dumb could you be, she said. He told her huffily that he'd written back to them just to see if they were crooked. "And," he announced, "I've won a black diamond." He opened the envelope and took out a little transparent plastic pocket, in one corner of which rested a tiny brown ball of something that might possibly have been a piece of low-grade coal. He held it up. They stared at it. Then, both of them burst into laughter. They laughed so hard that they had to hold their heads in their hands. "A putative diamond," he shouted. "An alleged diamond," she gasped. They stopped for breath and started each other off again. They laughed, uncontrollably, until they ached. And somehow the quarrel had ended.

"Two thousand bucks," he said, "if I apply within the time limit."

"What's the hitch?"

"You'll never guess. It's got to be used on travel."

"That's a joke."

They ran a travel agency. They'd been in the business for six years. It took all of their energy and thought. It was the reason why they didn't have any children: they kept figuring that next year they'd find time to plan their own lives. But they couldn't even squeeze in the hours to work on future holiday schemes. They only just managed to keep up. Their range of vacation trips was still the same as when they'd started. If your standards were high, you had to spend money. Alan saw it as his joke to make the past—from which we ought to be able to learn—usable and habitable in modern terms. There was no point in going to a quaint English village or a picturesque Greek temple if you were going to have to sleep in a place with no running water. That would be ridiculous. Even Beth, who tended to get worked up over authentic atmosphere, agreed with him about that.

"We do need to do some research," he said. "Find a couple of new places."

"We can't spare the time. We'd need lots of . . . we'd need weeks. Can you see Rosa in charge for that long?"

"The Stones might help out for a while."

"And you know what they'd expect in return. They want our list. If they got their hands on that, we could say good-bye to the business. I don't just mean what they got out of Mr. Pettifer."

"I'm going to put in for it anyway. It can't hurt."

"That's right. We might win a fun-filled holiday in Butte, Montana."

"With two thousand extra, you could come, too."

"Too?"

"Two thousand. That's what it says. What we should really do is go over our itinerary. I wish people would let us know how things went."

"It's like everything else, she said. "Who's going to spend the time on it? People don't like writing letters. Except cranks."

"If they send the money, would you come along?"

"We can't both leave the office at the same time."

"For a week, we could. Just."

"What could we do in a week?"

"We could go over the part of the British tour we never got to. Wouldn't you like that?"

"Well, sure. I guess."

"Fine," he said. "That's settled."

Beth still wasn't certain, but since she thought nothing was ever going to come of the idea, she didn't say anything.

It was her day to have lunch with Faye. Faye worked in the magazine office a few doors away. Ella, Beth's other lunchtime crony, was at the opposite end of the shopping mall. Beth had once tried to introduce them to each other; everything had seemed to go well, but the next time she suggested a meeting, Ella and Faye complained so much about the distance, the dates, the pressure of work, that she knew it hadn't been a success. So, she saw them separately, which took twice as much time. That was another thing, she realized: she'd been trying to get her two friends together in order to save herself an hour or two.

For three years, until the crisis in Ella's life, Beth used to see her for a coffee break in the afternoons. Ella now needed that time for what she called "contemplation" and what Alan described as "goofing off." Ella's life had been irreversibly altered on the day she'd lost her Filofax. She'd had a breakdown. Her doctor had referred her to a psychiatrist and a time-management consultant, but neither one had been able to help her. Someone—an aunt, or some other relative—had advised her to pray. Ella did better than that; she went on a pilgrimage. She got on a plane to Venice, took the train to Padua, and joined the crowd of people waiting to beg St. Anthony to find things, or people, they had lost. She moved with the others to the left of the silver altar, filed past the stone carvings that illustrated the miracles worked by the saint in his lifetime, and at last reached out, put her hand on the casket, and asked him to get her Filofax back.

When Beth told the story, Alan said, "I can see it coming: she got home and there it was, right where she'd left it."

"No, she really had lost it. But when she got home, there was a package waiting for her. Somebody'd found it and mailed it back."

"St. Anthony, no doubt," he said. He thought Ella was crazed and affected. To Beth, the story seemed a little zany but it made perfect sense. If there were such things as saints, no task could be too enormous for them, no request so silly that it was unimportant: they could do anything.

He said, "Why would a saint bother about something so trivial?"

"Why not? For a saint, a big favor would be easy. So, a little one wouldn't be any trouble at all. I think you could also count on his tolerance of human folly and petty-mindedness. It wouldn't be any skin off his back to grant something really idiotic. If you accept the basic principle—"

"Well, if you accept that, you're beyond hope to begin with."

"Maybe," she said, meaning that she didn't agree. It wasn't surprising to her that ever since Ella had had her Filofax restored to her, she'd been preoccupied by questions of religion; she hadn't gone so far as to take instruction, but she'd begun to spend a lot of time reading, meditating, and trying to pray, which—she told Beth—wasn't so easy as you might think. It took discipline. It was hard work. The afternoon break was no good anymore. Ella became another lunchtime friend, like Faye.

On three days of the week, Beth would usually stay in the office through the lunch break. Rosa, their secretary, would run around the corner to buy her a sandwich from the delicatessen. Occasionally Beth would say to Rosa that this was going to be a diet day. She never made it past two-thirty. Rosa didn't mind the extra trip; she was on good terms with one of the boys behind the counter.

Their office was in an arcade, one of four that radiated from a central area where trees in tubs surrounded a large fountain. Between the trees there were benches. It was a pleasant spot for people to sit in after they'd done some shopping and were wondering where to go next. It was also a meeting place. The planners of the mall had originally called the center a piazza; when most shoppers were making an effort to get the name right, they'd come up with the word "pizza," although normally everybody just said, "By the fountain."

You were doing all right to have an office in one of the arcades near the fountain. The only trouble with the location was that a customer who tried to find you for the first time could get mixed up between the four arcades, which looked alike: they had been given the names of the four main points of the compass, but who knew one direction from another? Left and right were fairly easy for most people to remember, but you couldn't expect everyone to race outside in order to check where the sun was; and anyway, that depended on something else, too. A mapmaker or a navigator would know about directions. Ordinary shoppers didn't. They got lost. That was how Beth had met Ella, who had ended up at the office after her first morning in the mall. "Where am I?" she'd said, like someone coming out of a faint.

The great advantages of the mall were for those who worked there. Almost all the people Beth thought of as her friends were her neighbors at work. In fact, it seemed to her that the mall was really the neighborhood where she lived. The house that she and Alan owned was just for sleeping in and for giving parties.

She wouldn't mind getting away from the house for a while. She wouldn't mind leaving everything for a week.

As she picked up her tuna-fish sandwich, she asked Faye, "Have you and Hutch had one of those prize envelopes offering you two thousand dollars to travel with?"

"No. Wish we had. What is it—something to do with a rival firm?"

"I don't think so." She bit in and munched, thinking that she'd have to ask Alan about that: it hadn't occurred to her. "As far as I know, it's just another one of those win-a-million things."

"But if you got the money, you'd go, wouldn't you?"

"You bet. I wasn't so sure this morning at breakfast, but I am now. We both need a break. And I need some time to think about things. We just keep going and going."

"You love it."

"In a way."

"In every way. You thrive on it."

"But it's taken over. I'm beginning to suspect that it's done something bad to me. I think maybe Alan would like to get out, too. At least—well. I don't know. We don't have time to talk about anything at all anymore."

"That sounds like a good time to take a vacation. You two should read some of your little leaflets."

"Aren't they brilliant?"

"You'll have a great time."

"We haven't won it yet."

"Don't wait to win anything. Just go."

"That's the trouble with you, Faye. You encourage my weaknesses. Act now, think later."

"It's a good idea, isn't it? You could afford a week off."

"Afford, sure. It isn't a question of the money. Not really. It's the time, as usual. The thing is—I have a feeling that if I went, I might not come back I've been feeling that way for a long while."

"Something wrong at work?"

"Nothing's ever wrong at work. That's the point. The work is always just great. It's a substitute for everything else. I'm beginning to think it's my excuse for not living my life."

"Oh wow, Elizabeth. Let me write that one down."

"You know what I mean. It's everything; not just that we don't have kids. Well, that's the main thing. I realized a few months ago, last year: I kind of feel like I've left it too late."

"What are you talking about? You're still in your twenties, aren't you?"

"Well, not quite." She wasn't prepared to say anything more exact, unless Faye spoke first. From the beginning of their acquaintance it had been obvious that Faye didn't want any questions asked about her age; or, for that matter, about her first husband, her daughter's experience at the boarding school they'd sent her to, or about anything at all connected with Trenton, New Jersey. "You know what I mean," Beth told her. "I've sort of run out of steam. I've put it all into the agency. Now I couldn't start a family unless I gave up work. But that's the one thing that keeps me going. It's fun."

"It's fun, but it's killing you. I see."

"I guess I'm what they call a workaholic. Alan's the same."

"Does he want to go on this trip?"

"He was the one who suggested it. He's sending in the form."

"Good."

"You could be right, you know. Maybe some other travel company's doing a promotion. I'd better ask around."

They said good-bye at the fountain. Beth turned off into her arcade. The clock in the jeweler's window caught her eye. She began to hurry.

As she opened the agency door, Alan came out, saying, "Where were you? I've got to get over to Meyerson's." He ran off, not looking back.

She sat down at her desk and reached for the telephone. She didn't stop working until four o'clock, when she asked Rosa to go across the arcade for some coffee. She stretched in her chair and yawned. It had been a good afternoon.

The pleasure she took in describing places was founded on her need to communicate enthusiasm. You couldn't call her exaggeration false-hood: it was a slight emphasis in the process of persuading and convincing someone about the fictions she already believed in. It wouldn't be right to say that her work required her to engage in deliberate acts of dishonesty. She simply tried to get prospective clients into the right mood: to create an atmosphere. If people took off on their holidays with a few skillfully devised impressions in mind, they were pretty well certain to find them justified. That wasn't doing anything wrong. It was smart salesmanship backing up a worthwhile product—that was what Alan said.

She picked up the receiver and punched the buttons for the Stones' number. The Stones were their friends but it was a business friendship, not personal. A personal friendship might be like marriage, whereas this particular business friendship was like having a lover who lied and cheated and was unfaithful with friends and enemies, yet who managed to remain so attractive and charming in other ways, so desirable, that one didn't want to break off the affair. They liked the Stones and they didn't trust them an inch. Several times Pete and Marcie Stone had tried to poach customers away from them. They were, Beth believed, the kind of people her grandmother had once described to her: they'd come to dinner and try to hire your cook out from under you. Once or twice Alan had done things back to them, just to show that he and Beth weren't pushovers. There was no point in ending the friendship, as long as the others kept within bounds; Marcie and Pete had shown that they could be useful people to know. On the other hand, one more outrageous stunt like the one with Mr. Pettifer, and Alan and Beth would cut them adrift.

She got Marcie at the other end of the line. They talked about the new airline prices, and Beth asked about the two-thousand-dollar offer.

Marcie said, "It's news to me. But I'll ask around."

"I was thinking: it might be nice to get away for a week anyhow. We could check out the places they never bother to tell us about."

"Hey, I got news about that. I had a customer drop in. Two of them—husband and wife."

"I don't believe it."

"Honest to God. Five years in the travel business and these are the first people that ever came back to tell us what the trip was like. When you see them again, they never stop to talk—they just ask how much it's going to cost to go somewhere else. Nobody's ever got a spare minute. God, they were so nice. I nearly cried. They said they just wanted to thank us, because they'd had such a good time."

"I hope you asked them a lot of questions."

"I certainly did. And there were a few changes I thought I'd pass on to you: opening times at a couple of country houses, restaurant hours—that kind of thing. It was the south of England, including London, and over to Paris and Rome."

"We'd love any information," Beth said. She thought Marcie must be feeling guilty about wangling Mr. Pettifer's little list away from him.

"OK. I'll send you a copy of what we've got. And if you're taking a trip, let us know what you find out, hm?"

"Sure," Beth promised. "Unless we have such a good time that we just never come back."

After she'd hung up, she thought *I've said something like that before today, at lunch. When I was talking to Faye.*

Rosa brought some hazelnut cookies with the coffee. The delicatessen was giving them away as a special, introductory offer. She had a big bag of them, and she was chewing on one as she came in. Beth said, "Don't let them near me." Rosa tried to break her down, but she wouldn't be tempted. She concentrated on work until closing time.

꽃

She sat in the rush-hour traffic with Alan and blanked out a little, while he complained about Meyerson's. They were always having trouble with the brochure, but they never did anything about it. There weren't any other printers around who could do a good job. It was specialized work. Their only consolation was that half of the other agencies in the vicinity used Meyerson's, so they were all in the same boat.

When he'd talked everything out of his system and then done the paraphrase, Beth told him about her afternoon phone call.

He'd been thinking all day about a trip, he said. "I think we should go anyway. Cassie could take over for a while. She's always said she'd be happy to."

"But it might not be a good time for her."

"I don't want Pete and Marcie in there, not for a hundred peace offerings."

"Why don't we just close for a week? We could send out a leaflet to everybody."

Alan thought the idea was impossible. Cassie was related to his brother-in-law and was trustworthy. She and Rosa could keep things running: he thought so until they got through the traffic, reached home, and sat down to cocktails. He thought so until well into the first bourbon; but by the end of his second drink, he'd changed his mind. "We'll wait a week," he suggested, "to find out if we've won the prize."

"Nobody wins those prizes."

"We'll see."

He made the airline reservations for two on the transatlantic flight; it left in the evening and arrived in England early in the morning, London time, which would still be night for them. He bought himself a new suitcase. She tapped out a letter on the computer, printed out stacks of copies, and gave them to Rosa. Then she had a quick word with the people next door, before running into town to buy a new raincoat. While she was hanging the coat up in the front-hall closet, she saw Alan's suitcase and decided that it was just the kind of thing she needed. The next morning she went out and bought one, to find on her return that he—having admired her new raincoat on its hanger— had gone shopping again and had found a coat just like it for himself.

"We ought to have done everything together," she told him. "We'd have saved a lot of time."

He said, "I'm looking forward to this. We should have taken a trip a long time ago. I think I was in a rut."

"And I was in something worse. I didn't realize until a few days back. I'd lost hope."

"About what?"

"I'll tell you when we're away from everything."

"Let me take you away from all this," he said, throwing an arm around her.

The day before they were set to fly out, a check came through from the prize people. There were no stipulations, no strings attached.

"See?" he said. "I was right."

The check was issued by an organization called *United Holdings and Travel Co.* They'd never heard of it. Beth picked up the brochure that came with the letter of congratulation. She flipped through the pages, saying, "I'd like to know who their printers are. Look at the quality of the pictures. Isn't that incredible—color reproduction like that? This is as good as one of those art magazines." She reached the section where, at last, they found the catch. She read out the passage: *Prizewinners who apply for the Finborg weekend will automatically receive a further one thousand dollars.*

"It's in the letter, too," Alan said. "You agree to go there, all the expenses are paid, they give you the round-trip ticket from whatever city you name, and you've got a luxury weekend in this top-notch castle full of swimming pools and gourmet cooking. It's a promotional gimmick. I guess they've just converted it."

"Our clients aren't in that league. I suppose we wouldn't have to tell anyone that. Just turn up and have a ball."

"We aren't going to have the time, unless I change the plane tickets. We have to tell these United people right now."

"For an extra thousand?" she said. "And it might be interesting. If all the other people they wrote to are travel agents, we could learn a lot."

"That's a point," he said. "OK."

***

They stayed up all night, writing memos and leaving messages, taking things out of their suitcases and putting them back again. When, the next evening, they were finally on the plane, they both felt slugged. He wanted to order some drinks, to relax.

"You can't be serious," she told him. "That dehydrates you. It'll make you feel terrible. And they say jet lag hits you a lot worse if you drink. That's what I read in that body book."

"Well, my body book says a little drink never hurt anyone." He ordered a double for himself. She stuck to water. They came out nearly equal because she'd been tired to begin with, and she always fretted more than he did.

They landed in the morning, had an hour's sleep, made themselves get up and go sightseeing, and ate their evening meal early. Already they were glad they had come. Beth kept saying, "Isn't it wonderful? Isn't everything beautiful?" He said yes; he was more interested in seeing what was happening to her than in looking at the sights. He'd been worried about her for a long time. Her friend, Faye, was all right but the other one, Ella, was certifiable: she had a bad influence on Beth. Ella had turned into some sort of religious or ESP fanatic. She'd tried to make Beth believe totally crazy things, such as that it was possible to go through walls by concentrating on an imaginary black dot in front of your eyes. She'd told Beth to meditate and to sing certain notes and melodic phrases and to go on diets. Luckily Beth couldn't prevent herself from nibbling potato chips, wasn't able to carry a tune for long, and fell asleep as soon as she relaxed; she hadn't needed all that. One look at her now would have convinced anyone: what she'd needed was a break. She'd even become flirtatious.

"It's like our honeymoon," she said.

"Without the mosquitoes," he reminded her.

"But, darling, that was the best part." She made a face at him. The phrase was from a family joke—something to do with the part of a lobster you weren't supposed to eat because it could kill you.

"The second-best," he said, leaning over from the other side of the table to catch hold of her hand.

They spent the weekend in London, then they visited the two Devon hotels on their list, looked in at the Stratford guesthouse, and did the Stonehenge trip. On the fifth day they felt tired, but that was simply the reaction they called "traveler's dip": everyone had at least one day of it. After that, you straightened out.

The temperature dropped as they boarded the plane. Beth wondered if she should have brought an extra sweater with her, she'd had her shopping-spree clothes sent back home.

"Cold," Alan said, lifting his head. "Scandinavia, here we come." He settled down to read, while Beth shut her eyes and tried to doze. She didn't like flying. What she used to tell her clients was that it was exactly like a bus ride, only safer; but naturally, that wasn't quite true: even if you could adjust the air-conditioning nozzles so that they didn't shoot jets of air straight on your head, the pressure made a difference. It did something to the fluid in all the sinus passages. It gave you a headache. That was funny, she thought: the travel agent who didn't like to travel.

She went right under for a few minutes. Alan had to touch her shoulder to wake her up. They were beginning the descent.

She got her handbag from under the seat in front of her, redid her lipstick, and combed her hair. She pulled her seat belt tighter. At the same instant the plane braked suddenly, unnaturally; everyone was tossed forward. A steward's voice, omitting the usual, "Ladies and gentleman," spoke loudly over the address system, saying, "Fasten your safety belts, please. We're experiencing some turbulence." Although there was no indication of what it could be, everyone knew: something had gone seriously wrong. This wasn't a small or incidental disturbance.

There were murmurs of distress among the passengers. Several people had been thrown against the seats and hurt their heads or broken the glasses they were wearing. And they were frightened.

The engines of the plane began to roar. Beth wanted to reach for Alan's hand, but she knew he wouldn't like it. She was relieved and pleased when, without saying anything, he placed his hand lightly over hers.

The noise stopped, but they seemed to be falling fast. All at once they were plunging, rushing. A man's voice, abruptly, announced, "Attention, all passengers. Prepare for an emergency landing." The rest of the message was cut off as the plane screamed. Many of the passengers, too, were shrieking, crying, moaning. Beth and Alan looked at each other. His hand gripped hers. Her lips moved. She said, into the uproar, that she loved him. He said something back, which she couldn't lip-read; it might have been *Thanks for everything, Happy landings*, or *We should have drunk our duty-free bottle*. The plane crashed.

She was still trying to undo her belt while he was up from his seat and out into the aisle, pushing a space clear for both of them. The air was bitter with smoke. Everyone was yelling and fighting. Fire fanned toward them from the rear of the aircraft. She kicked herself free of the seat in front of her. She scrambled to her feet. Alan had gone. The thrashing crowd had carried him away from her. She could just see him, a long way off. He turned back. He was shouting. She tried to get into the aisle, but it was no use. She held her arms out to him. There was an explosion. High flames shot up from the seats near the front exits. Across a wave of fire she saw him, looking back at her. A fierce heat blasted the left side of her face, her shoulder, and hand. She jumped back. She couldn't protect herself: the flames were everywhere. She knew it was too late.

She woke up. Alan was standing in the aisle. He was getting the coats down from the overhead locker. They had landed. The other passengers were collecting their belongings.

"OK?" he said. She nodded, unbuckling her seat belt. She was too shaken to speak. She never wanted to talk about the dream. She didn't even want to go over it in her mind. It had made her feel sick in a way that was worse than anything she could remember, even the nightmares of childhood. She kept herself busy with her flight bag and shoulder bag until everyone began to move down the aisle. Alan said, "All we have to do now is find that other plane."

They put their carry-on luggage on a trolley they found in the airport building. Beth stayed with it while Alan went to investigate. Now that she felt calmer, she would have liked to tell him something about the dream—only a hint, to get rid of it herself by sharing it; but she had the feeling that to mention it at all would bring bad luck. It might turn something into a reality that, so far, was only thought.

It would be nice, she thought, to have a long, cool drink; better yet, to wade into a pool of refreshing water. She imagined doing it— stepping in slowly. She could picture the water, pure and effervescent as a drink of bottled mineral water. She thought of the fountain back at the mall, in the center of the meeting place by the arcades, near their office, at home.

Alan was at her side again. He said, "I've found it. We'll have to walk a long way, but there's plenty of time."

"Good. I'd love a nice, big drink of springwater."

"Oh, Beth. Can't it wait?"

"I guess so. I thought we had so much time."

He started to push the trolley forward. "We've got time to catch the plane," he said. "No customs. They'll look at our passports and cards at the gate."

She followed him. She wondered if her thirst had been brought on by dreaming of fire; or, it might have been done the other way around—that her mind had produced a fire dream to account for a thirst she'd already felt in her sleep.

They reached a smooth passageway, slightly ramped. Alan raced along it with the trolley. She trotted to keep up. "I had a terrible dream," she said.

"So did I."

"About the plane."

"Uh-huh. Don't tell me."

She didn't think he'd had any dream. He simply hoped to stop her talking. There were times when he didn't enjoy keeping up a conversation: when she'd be rattling away on some topic and all at once would notice that he was taking part reluctantly. In the early days of their marriage she'd been hurt by that kind of thing. Now it didn't bother her. People were different not just in temperament but in their sense of pace. There was no reason why they should be in perfect symmetry every moment of the day and night; it was probably just those incongruities that kept them attached to each other for so long.

They had to wait for two officials to look at their airline tickets and passports, then they were motioned toward another hallway; it led to a waiting room where their bags were taken from them, to be loaded onto the plane.

They studied the other people in the room—four couples, one man on his own, and a single woman. The couples seemed to be much like themselves; one of the women was pretty, one had red hair, one was fat. The redhead's husband had a mustache, slicked-back hair, and a sharp-featured face. He looked like a bandleader from the thirties. Another husband, standing up, was tall and beefy and was dressed in a frontiersman's outfit: fringed deerskin jacket, Stetson, and Western boots. "Myron," his wife called to him. Myron returned to his seat. He put his hands on his knees. His wife—definitely a city type—had on a dark business suit and black patent-leather shoes with very high heels. She handed him a map, which he accepted without interest.

"Look at that woman's shoes," Beth said to Alan. "I thought we were all supposed to be travel agents. One of the first things I tell a female client is not to wear exaggerated heels on a plane. She must be incredibly uncomfortable."

"Maybe they came here by car. It's a short flight, anyway."

"Well, just the same."

The single man—tidy, bespectacled, and wearing tweeds—resembled a math teacher at the school Alan had gone to the year before high school. The man reminded him all at once of the whole year: of the street corner where he'd waited for the bus; and the drive out to the school through the suburbs and into what looked almost like real country. There were several nice houses they passed; a park, and streets with big trees on either side. There was one particular part of the ride he'd never forget—a stretch of road lined by tall maple trees that arched over and formed a tunnel: in the fall it was like driving through a land of jewelry, the leaves scarlet and gold. Every morning for about two weeks he was made happy by the sight of that gorgeous avenue. He would have liked to see it going in the other direction, too, but in the afternoon the bus driver took a different route. He'd thought then: some places made an impression on you that you never recovered from. They were special. Some of them used to be hard to reach, yet now that air travel was so easy, it was possible to get to countries and landscapes that—only as far back as the last century—couldn't have been visited by anyone but explorers and pilgrims. That was one way in which the world had improved; the convenience of modern travel was wonderful.

At that age, when he was young, he'd wanted to go everywhere, anywhere: after Europe, to Asia, the South Seas, Africa, and South America. He'd wanted to get to the Arctic. He'd yearned for places where no one else had ever been. And later, he'd hoped to open up the world to other people; to allow them to be in marvelous places and see fascinating things. He'd never quite outgrown his adolescent longing, never completely achieved his dream, which was to find himself suddenly, and as if magically, somewhere else. And, as it had turned out, the one place that was the most beautiful for him had been at home: on that ride through the maple trees. They had remained his vision of beauty on earth, of the best from all the world outside the school bus. He hadn't realized it before. He'd forgotten, for years.

"That woman looks like your aunt Nora," Beth said.

He looked. The woman was the one he'd decided was unattached. When he'd first noticed her, she'd had her head down and was reading a booklet. Now that she was talking with the tweedy man, he could see what Beth meant, although he didn't agree. "Sort of," he told her, "but not much."

Two airline officials, a man and a woman, came through the entrance. Their uniforms were immaculate, their smiles toothy. They looked a little like manikins from a store window—perfectly regular and bland. The woman stood at the microphone and made an announcement: they could board the plane. Everything was ready. The passengers stood. Beth and Alan joined the group.

They had to duck to get into the small plane, and to crouch as they moved to their seats. The aircraft had fourteen seats, seven on each side.

It was a bumpy ride. The engines made so much noise that conversation was out of the question. Beth tried to sleep. She closed her eyes, but couldn't drift off. She felt as if they'd been traveling for years. It was impossible to imagine going back home. London had vanished from her mind, together with America. The house, work, the office in the mall, were like memories from as long ago as early childhood.

Alan looked across the aisle at her. They were near enough to hold hands without stretching, if they wanted to. He would have liked to reach out to her, but he saw that she was trying to sleep. He had no wish for sleep. He'd had his fill of nightmares. The one he'd had on the plane from London was enough to last him a lifetime; he'd dreamt that they'd crash-landed in flames, that he'd jumped out of his seat to get a place for both of them in the aisle; and as soon as he'd turned around to help pull Beth clear, the other passengers had swept him away. The dream ended as she was holding her hands out after him, the fire roaring toward her, and he was being carried ever farther away.

It was only a cliché, of course—one of the basic dreams; one of the earliest myths: Lot's wife, Orpheus and Eurydice. You turned around and she was gone, or dying, or transformed. Or, maybe, just divorced. It was possible that that was his real fear. Years before, for a long time, he'd wanted to leave her. He'd waited for the right moment to talk about it. But time passed, the moment never came and suddenly everything was all right again. Now he was afraid that perhaps what had happened to him could happen to her. One day she might feel that she'd just had enough, and she'd want to get out.

Their landing this time was easy. All the passengers had to stoop, almost to crawl, out of the cramped cabin. It was like emerging from a cocoon or coming up from a tunnel.

The plane sat in the middle of an enormous clearing surrounded by pinewoods. A road ran across one end. Near the road stood a shed with a corrugated metal roof. Boxes were stacked against two of the walls and piled up next to a neighboring shack. A mound of fuel drums had been set some distance away from the buildings and also from the trees. There were no other planes in sight.

Their transportation was waiting. As Alan and Beth stepped down from the narrow ladder, people were already pointing at two old-fashioned horse-drawn carriages that were heading toward them from the shelter of the woods.

"Not bad," Beth said. "Right on time."

"They probably pulled up back in the trees there," he told her. "Otherwise the horses might have been spooked by the plane." He knew nothing about horses. He was guessing. In the early days of their marriage she'd been in the habit of asking him all kinds of questions, as though he were an authority on everything; and he'd taken to acting like one: if he thought or suspected a thing, he'd say it was true, certain. It gave him confidence in his abilities. His speculation became fact. The odd thing was that so often he turned out to be right. Sometimes he even felt that he had insights of a kind that could be called psychic; he'd know things almost before they happened—not that he really believed in such powers, but belief was part of the phenomenon: her faith in him had made him capable. It might also be true that his unwillingness to concede an equal capacity in her had kept her in a state where she didn't feel that her life was important, or that she had anything special to contribute. He'd taught her to assert herself when she was at the office. Outside business hours, she was unchanged. What she needed, he thought, was just one or two friends who weren't crazy. A woman should have a few women friends, so that they could all get together every week and complain about their husbands and families, not bring everything home to the dinner table.

The robotlike steward and stewardess unloaded suitcases. The carriages stood one beside the other, facing the same way; every so often one of the horses on the inside would swing its head over and try to nip the nearby horse of the other pair.

They joined the rest of their group, who were already getting into the high seats. Alan chose the carriage that had their bags on it. He climbed up and held out a hand to pull Beth after him. They were sitting next to the redhead, Gina, and her bandleader husband, who was called Sonny. Like Beth, Gina worked in her husband's business. "We met," she told Beth, "when we were both operating one-man outfits."

"She kept cutting my sales down to nothing," Sonny said. "I got to thinking: Who is this broad? I figured I'd better go straighten her out, make some kind of a deal with her. So, one day I drop in at the address, I open the door, and—wham, it's just like the songs: there she is sitting there, and Love came and tapped me on the shoulder. That's how we amalgamated."

Gina said, "We sure did. We amalgamated in under twenty-four hours."

The single woman, who had taken her seat in front of them, turned around and smiled. She introduced herself. Her name was Myrtle. She'd been talking to the tweedy man, Horace, who was worried about whether the coachman had packed his bag upright and not sideways. "I've got a lot of bottles in it," he explained.

"Don't they have any liquor over here?" Gina asked.

"Oh, it's just aftershave and that kind of thing. But I don't want it to spill all over everything."

They started off. The fat woman, behind Alan, spoke with approval of the wide, comfortable seats. "They should build things like this nowadays," she said.

"Nancy," her husband told her, "that's asking too much."

"Trains, buses, the subway—everything nowadays is plastic. And skimpy."

"It's the times we live in," he said.

Beth and Alan turned their heads and said hello. They exchanged names. Nancy's husband was called Ed.

The coach entered the pinewoods. All at once the world was darker, quieter. It was like going from daylight into night. Beth looked at her watch. What it said meant nothing to her. There were time differences between countries; that could mix you up to begin with. On top of that, you got tired. She asked, "Does anybody know what time it is?"

Gina said, "I always lose my sense of time when I'm on vacation."

"You find another way of measuring it, that's all," Alan said.

Nancy and Ed told a story about ordering breakfast in Mexico, but because they hadn't specified whether it was to be at a.m. or p.m., the waiter brought it up at eight-thirty in the evening, while they were still drinking their cocktails on the balcony. "That was a different sense of time, all right," Ed said.

Beth began to feel strange. She waited until it wouldn't seem that she was spoiling Ed's story, then she asked again if anyone knew what time it was. No one did. "Relax," Alan said to her.

The carriage rolled on. The landscape around them seemed without sound. They were the only noise passing through, their chatter foreign to the place, the steady rhythm of the horses' hooves like the muffled pounding of a machine.

Beth said, "Maybe this is that famous Scandinavian long night you read about."

"But this is the wrong time of year for it," Myrtle said over her shoulder. "That's in the winters."

"It feels like winter."

"I didn't get any information at all on this part of the trip. It's all very mysterious. You know what would be fun? If it's one of those mystery games—know what I mean? They give you characters to play, and then there's a murder and you have to solve it. I had a couple of clients who wanted to go on one, but the price was too steep for them."

Horace said, "I heard about one of them they held in Venice. Somebody fell into the canal."

"We're all tour operators, aren't we?" Alan asked.

From the backseat Ed spoke up. He said, "What do you mean, Scandinavia? We were booked for Yugoslavia."

"Austria," Horace said. "But it could be a lot of places. It sure looks foreign. That's about all you can say."

"Well, where are we?"

"Ask the coachman," Nancy suggested.

The coachman, sitting high up and beyond the barrier of his seat, was too far removed from them to be reached. They called out to him, but he didn't turn around.

They made conversation, stopped, started up again, and waited. At last the carriage came to a halt.

They all got down, although they could see that they hadn't arrived yet. They were at some kind of way station. There was a small hut and a dim light in it. The passengers from the other carriage joined them.

They tried to get some information out of the two drivers, who didn't speak a language any of them could understand. By signs everyone was told that they were all to keep going.

They got back into their seats and started off again. This time, they felt, they were on the last lap; they'd be welcomed with light and warmth, a drink of something: their host would give them explanations, facts, plans.

They became talkative. As Alan and Beth's carriage moved through the forest, they called out stories to each other, leaning over the seats and saying, "But this is the best part," and "You aren't going to believe what he said then." They talked about funny things that had happened in their businesses, swapped anecdotes about cities they'd been in, asked each other to describe the worst and best clients they'd ever had. And they all agreed that the brochure was a problem every year.

The coachmen pulled up again at a spot so like the first one that for a moment the passengers were bewildered. "Isn't this the same place?" Myrtle asked. "Do you think that man knows the way?"

"It isn't the same," Sonny told her. "I remember there was a log out of line up near the top there." He raised his arm. "It does look a lot like it, though."

Nancy said, "At the rate we've been traveling, they could have fixed the roof while we were gone."

Myron, the man in the frontier costume, came over to where they were parked. He suggested that since it was turning out to be such a long drive, they might switch around: that way, they could all be acquainted by the time they got to their destination.

Alan was happy where he was. Somebody in the other carriage, he thought, must be a bore; but there was no polite way out of the invitation. "Sure," he said. Behind him, at the same time, Ed said uncertainly, "Well, I guess so."

On the third lap of the trip there was plenty of time to get to know Myron and his wife, Cora Bee. And after that, on the fourth stage, Sue and Greg, from Omaha. By the fifth and sixth times around, they all knew each other very well.

They traded family histories, got to know about the children, ex-partners, and in-laws. They sang songs, played word games, wondered about the existence of God; and they asked themselves whether a unifying set of physical laws in the universe might do just as well as a divine being if you didn't want to take such things personally. They tried to remember lines from poems.

Alan began to lose heart. That was another trouble with traveling: everything was out of your hands. Someone else was behind the information counter and on the telephone and at the controls of the plane. You had to wait, patiently, as if you'd given up being human and had become just a package to be transported. If you were used to doing your own organizing, it was difficult to put up with that. He always felt more confident when he was the one in charge.

They ran out of things to say. Beth began to feel strange again. She whispered to Alan, "I'm getting a funny feeling about this. It's weird."

"Just relax, like I told you," he said, "and enjoy the scenery."

She thought: *What scenery?* There was nothing but pine boughs, the darkness, and silence, except for the creaking of the wheels and the sound of the horses' hooves on the dirt track. There were patches of leaves on the ground, then sandy soil and pine needles, but no other variation in the landscape. She tried to think about getting to their destination; her mind went blank. But they had to stop. They had to get somewhere, otherwise nothing made sense. She made a great effort to hold within her mind some picture of the place they were meant to find. If she concentrated hard enough, they might get there.

They stopped again and changed around and started off once more. Alan looked up at the dark shapes of the trees that passed, in unceasing progression, above and around him. Everyone nowadays worried about conservation and the environment, yet it seemed that the forest they were in was limitlessly huge, its growth encompassing time as well as space—as if they were seeing all the trees that had ever been alive since the beginning of the world. It was—like the journey itself—unending. He changed his mind. He gave up.

The two carriages continued to roll forward. The hoofbeats sounded on the track. The wheels kept turning. Eventually the others began to feel that something was wrong.

"We've never going to get there," Nancy stated. "This is it." Ed told her not to be silly: of course they were going to get there, in the end; it was just taking a long time And if she started to complain, it was going to seem even longer.

"I think she's right," Alan said. There was no other outcome he could imagine. They were going to keep traveling, forever. "You'd be kidding yourself to think anything else."

"Don't say that," Beth told him. "We'll get there pretty soon now. We've got to." She was too frightened to allow for doubt. There could no longer be any question. She'd come to believe, like her friend, Ella, that all events were a matter of faith. And anyway, she'd decided that this holiday was going to make up for everything else. She'd been looking forward to it too long to let herself be disappointed.

She kept on believing. She never lost hope that if they continued to move ahead, somehow—all at once—they would reach the light. It would come upon them like a revelation of truth, a burst of sunlight. It would be amazing, overwhelming, and out of this world—like the coming of spring, or like the sudden appearance of fire in the dream she and Alan had had, a long time ago, when they thought that they were dying in a plane crash.

CORRESPONDENT

Joan met Max when she was working at the library. She hadn't seen him come in because she was reading a book under the counter, but she heard him and, as he approached the desk, she prepared to release her attention from the page.

Every day she read books and magazines, only occasionally looking at a newspaper and then often preferring the less respectable ones that had the scandals and amazing stories and the little snippets of weird fact. At the end of the previous week she'd read that—according to the latest research—four out of five women succeeded in business, whereas three out of five men failed. She'd been wondering about the statistics for most of the morning. Were those numbers just for a few countries? Did they include only particular trades or types of job? One of the other girls at the library had suggested that probably what was meant by business was small businesses started up by a single person who had taken out a loan from a bank: that might make sense because the women would have to have serious intentions; and the men might just want to raise money to spend on something else.

The best stories, and the one subject that held everyone's attention, found full scope only in the three or four tabloids regularly read by everyone on the staff. Crime was the favorite issue; from the information desk to the archives, crime reports had become an addiction with all the librarians. Whether their need to read about it sprang from fear of becoming victims of violence or from a suppressed wish to lead a more active, passionate—or even lawless—life, they were so eager to get at the latest installment of murder investigations that often one of them would have to hold the paper and read it out loud to the others.

In recent years there had also been many national and international crises and catastrophes, but wartime made the act of killing so lacking in personal detail as to be almost anonymous. That thirty people had died in a mortar attack was horrible but not interesting; that someone had killed someone else was shocking and at the same time fascinating. Everyone at some point had the wish to murder; most possessed the ability to suppress it. Both the hideousness and the allure were immediately understandable. Murder was a civilian crime and for amateurs. Military matters lacked the personal touch. They were for the professional.

Max's specialty was war. He'd begun on court cases, accidents, political interviews, and natural disasters: fire, flood, avalanche, earthquake. Only gradually had he been drawn toward what was to become his chosen field. He'd started with a good ear for languages—that had turned out to be one of his greatest assets: it had allowed him to communicate with all sides in a conflict and then to translate the general sense without being too literal. Experience taught him which people to approach and how to frame questions. And thanks to an ability to speak calmly and clearly while observing turbulent events, his eyewitness accounts sounded real. Most newspaper readers or radio listeners, like Joan, thought that his reports from the front were completely true. What he told them was better than one man's opinion: it was information. After a while it could be considered history—a personal account, but one that didn't twist the facts.

He was at the top now, at the peak of his profession.

Joan, on the other hand, hadn't really started to do anything. She'd just been reading about it.

With her eyes still on the page, she sensed him coming nearer. She picked up her Degas postcard to mark her place in the book. Just at that moment he asked her to find a title for him.

She recognized his voice and she looked up with an expression of delight on her face, but she couldn't place the man in front of her.

As for him, he was so taken with the change in her as her concentration passed from her book to him, that he, too, felt an agreeable sense of recognition, almost like a sudden appreciation of beauty.

She wasn't beautiful, but she was pretty enough to give that impression every once in a while.

He also saw that she liked him and that she was somebody he could talk to.

He spent most of his time talking to people. In war zones and conference centers he talked and listened. And afterwards he'd unwind, also by talking and listening and, sometimes in addition, by making love.

"I know your voice," she said.

"Do you ever watch the news?"

"Never. I listen. I watched so much TV when I was fifteen that I'll never have to have a set of my own, even if I live to be a hundred. But I do lean on friends every once in a while. Are you on television?"

"Sometimes," he said, as if it didn't matter.

"By the tie I was sixteen, I'd seen every B-feature ever made. It saved my life. Now I go out. Or I do something while I'm listening to the radio. Is this research for a show?"

"Background information. Just to check if my possibly unreliable facts line up with the possibly unreliable history books."

"My grandfather used to say that history was the great subject. History and law."

"I think I'd agree with that."

"I guess most men would."

"Wouldn't you?"

"Maybe."

"Why? What do you think the most important subject is?"

"Oh, religion. Not that I've got one, but I've always wished that I'd been brought up in a faith."

"Why?"

"Well, otherwise everything's just bits and pieces. Nothing to live by."

"That's a lot better than war. Religious certainties and intolerance can lead to some pretty nasty activity."

At the mention of war she recognized him: Max Dangerfield, the famous foreign correspondent.

"Oh, my God," she said, "that's who you are. Of course. That recording where you could hear the bombs going off. And then the earthquake. And when you were shot and you kept right on broadcasting. I must be the only person in the world who doesn't know you by sight. How rude of me. I'm really sorry."

He told her that it was refreshing to meet someone who still listened to the radio. And to find anyone who could remember his work in such precise detail was flattering in the extreme. The trouble with television was that after a certain point audiences tended to think of you as if you were the lead actor in their favorite soap opera or the star who advertised the breakfast cereal. You became part of a pantheon; your appearance on the screen was congenial and reassuring, but nobody really listened to what you were saying."

"Oh, they listen to you," she said.

He asked her if she'd still be at the desk in another forty minutes or so. He wondered whether she'd come out for a cup of coffee with him.

She told him that she'd have loved to, but she didn't get off work for another two hours.

He repeated the title of his book. There was plenty of reading he could do, he said. Two hours would go by in a flash.

If everything hadn't happened so fast—if there had been a day between his invitation and the evening out—she'd have been too nervous to open her mouth. But while they were talking she'd felt so easy with him that when he reappeared at the desk with the book in his hand, she was elated. She was ready to enjoy herself.

⁓

They took a stroll until the buses and subway trains thinned out the rush-hour crowds.

As they walked, their conversation jumped from one topic to another until something he said reminded her of a newspaper report that morning, about a player of loud music and an old couple he'd had killed because they'd asked him to turn the volume down. NOISE THUG KILLER SHOCK VERDICT, the headlines had read. The aggressor himself had received a fairly light sentence: a matter of months. The two boys he'd hired, who had ignited a gasoline trail into the couple's apartment, had each been given a few years. "That's what I can't figure out," Joan said. "Not just that the incredibly painful, terrifying death of two innocent people is only worth a couple of years, but the fact that the really guilty one was the man who hired them and yet he's gotten away with a shorter jail sentence. None of it would have happened if it hadn't been for him."

"He didn't do the killing."

"But he started everything. That's the strange thing about the law—it's so unfair."

"It's merely inexact, like us. It has to cover all kinds of situations and combinations."

"Subjecting people to that kind of noise—that unrelenting beat—it's a recognized torture technique, a form of assault, a kind of oppression. People who inflict it on someone else think they can do what they like and at the same time diminish everyone else's capacity. It's an abuse of the powers that freedom should give you. In a free world you ought to be able to have everything you want without making life intolerable for the rest of society."

She laughed a little and felt embarrassed at having talked so much. "A completely uninformed view," she added. It was then that she realized what had made him ask her out. It might have been loneliness, but it wasn't. It was desire. She could have said just about anything and he'd be interested. She wanted to say that without equality there were no relationships; there was only the oppressor and the slave, the host and the parasite. Later on she was glad that she'd shut up for a while. It was his turn to speak. And it wasn't long before she'd changed her mind about equality, anyway. Once you were living with somebody, you had to reorder your ideas.

"The younger generation has always been loud," he told her. "Loud, selfish, and careless. I think the only difference nowadays is that the technology is capable of boosting sound so high without distortion that most Western kids are partly deaf. So then, of course, they have to turn the volume up higher and even more of their hearing goes. I think I'm beginning to suffer some hearing loss myself, from gunfire and other explosions. But you're right. Noise is going to become an increasingly unattractive aspect of modern life unless there's some way of keeping it under control. In most countries it seems to fall into the category of environmental pollution rather than simple assault."

"If you're the one whose walls are pounding with it—like my friend, Katie—that's juggling with words. Not even earplugs work against that. She's had to move out twice. The law can't help you against neighbors like that."

"Of course it can. The law is for people who can't come to an agreement with each other. They need a third party to make a decision that's going to be binding on them both."

Before she could stop herself, she said, "And wars are for people who don't want to get along together, no matter what the law says."

"Is that really what you think?"

"No. It's what I feel. When it's too late, you destroy everything and start again."

"That's a counsel of desperation. I'd rather have as little as possible destroyed. The big difficulty is getting people to the bargaining table."

"That's right. After a while, they don't want to talk. They want to rip it all up and walk away."

"But once you can get them to sit down around a table, you can make them see that there's no need to do that. It's always better to remain friends, even if it's only on paper and you never actually like them."

"Isn't it harder to make them listen when they're in the same room with each other?"

"On the contrary. You throw a bone to one side and then you slip a tidbit to the others. And if you time it right, pretty soon they're accepting things they don't want, so that they can have what they do want. They'll even give up an advantage in the hope of gaining a different one. No. The difficulty is getting them there in the first place."

He had a wife—a fact he mentioned that first evening, letting Joan know that the marriage wasn't working out and that it no longer meant much to him. They didn't talk about it.

They talked about trivial things or about their past—each bringing out favorite stories and memories: the ones that had become introductory gifts for people they knew they were going to like and wanted to hold onto. She told him about her great aunt and the handkerchiefs; he gave her the ghost story about the apple tree in his grandmother's backyard. Then there was a pause before he decided to take things further or she let him know that he was the love of her life so it didn't matter to her whether he was married or not. Anyway, she wondered, if he could understand all the intricacies of hostility and negotiation, and could explain them to other people, why wasn't his marriage all right? Obviously, something was wrong with the wife.

In the interim they traded opinions and once or twice during the last kicks of the Noise Thug case—when the parents and other relatives of the two teenagers came forward to sell their reminiscences to the papers—went back to the subject of the old couple who were killed for complaining.

"Isn't that what wars are about, too?" she asked him. "The abuse of authority and wanting to do whatever you like at the expense of everybody else? Encroaching on other people's freedom and privacy?"

"Oh, neighbors' quarrels," he said.

"What about a disputed boundary line between neighbors—wouldn't that be the same as a country and its borders?"

"No. Besides, some wars are fabricated to keep certain people in power or to maintain sovereignty."

"Some neighbors' arguments, too. They go on and on because one of them has to have the upper hand. It's always somebody who can't stand to be equal because he won't trust the other person not to try to take more power. An aggressive personality."

"It's a question of being able to get along together. That doesn't always mean equality. It might be symbiosis: a small country and a larger one agreeing to share by trading with each other and remaining separate."

He was right: it was impossible to draw analogies. His wife, for instance, decided not to fight. She gave in. And yet she'd loved him, hadn't she?

He wasn't just famous—he was the youngest of the seasoned campaigners and he had the reputation, even among his colleagues, of being the best. Less respected correspondents went out to the battle zones in ex-army camouflage jackets and special heavy-duty boots lined in the latest scientifically perfected materials. He and three others—a Dutchman, an Englishman, and a Spaniard—faced the mortar bombs in an eccentric collection of good-luck clothes, which among the four of them included a tartan hat, a pair of patent-leather pumps that looked like dancing shoes, a cream-colored suit, and a purple Hawaiian shirt printed with orange pineapples and worn over a Los Angeles Rams sweatshirt (or a white T-shirt, depending on the weather). His own outfit incorporated several eye-catching items that might have been designed specifically to draw attention, and therefore, gunfire. But he wouldn't have dreamt of leaving any of them behind. And as he and the other three went about their business of observing and interviewing the villains and victims of war—or those affected by flood, explosion, earthquake, and other disasters—they left younger men shaking their heads and refusing to cross the airfield guarded by snipers, or the clump of burning vegetation next to a lava flow, or the slippery stone pathway across the flood.

Generals listened to his broadcasts. They approved. Here was someone who got it right, they'd think; at other times they'd be enraged by what he was saying. They'd want to meet him so that they could correct some detail in his reports or change the overall impression he'd given. They knew that he didn't care about anything except the truth and that, if he believed them, he'd pass on their version to the world. He was willing to listen to any side. But he also spoke out. He reported his thoughts and that was what his audiences loved. Over the years they had come to think that they knew him. And they felt that he was a friend. He had the right reactions. He was sympathetic in the manner of an artist, not merely an observer; he made people believe that his point of view was correct because it was the only reasonable one.

Joan didn't understand how he could have survived everything he'd seen—as well as the guilt of being a bystander to others' suffering—and how he could continue to go back again to the horrors without having some sort of religion to sustain him. And yet he didn't. Neither did most of his fellow reporters, although that didn't surprise her—so many of the ones he introduced her to were obsessed by competitiveness and self-aggrandizement.

He'd been brought up to put his trust in a mild form of Christian ethics mixed with the principles of Humanism: a system of belief that didn't take seriously the forces of evil in the world. Being present at the battlefront had done nothing to strengthen those ideals, nor had it undermined them. The ethical basis of his upbringing held firm. But he lost faith in the idea of God as soon as he saw how many massacres were instigated or avoided by purely human endeavor. They were caused by man and could be changed by man.

The less he believed in God, the more he valued the importance of what he wore into the danger zones, how he wore it, what he carried with him, and the order in which his possessions were packed or unpacked. A few of his finicky notions had begun as practical time-saving devices and as the result of losing a shoe, twisting an ankle, or getting a sleeve caught. But the rest had to do with a kind of therapy. While he was concentrating on getting all the details in place, he didn't have time for nerves.

He told her often enough that he'd been scared out of his wits on assignments, but he always said that kind of thing jokingly, as if consciously exaggerating. She understood that he wouldn't want to talk about feeling afraid. Fear was something he lived with all the time, even when not on duty; it was part of everybody's psychological defense system and in his case it would have to be working overtime. He didn't mention his good-luck charms either, except laughingly, in a way that was slightly coy. Yet whatever they gave him was a necessity. They seemed vital to his sense of hope.

He had more lucky charms than a tennis player or a teenage girl. And he took them all with him whenever he set out for danger.

The collection had started a long time ago. Some had been his as a child, others were small trinkets he'd picked up on his travels, usually one per trip. But the majority had been sent to him by fans. Only three had lasted from the very beginning: a silver teddy bear, a blue enameled St. Christopher medal, and a gold-colored souvenir keg from the neck of a whiskey bottle. The keg was the largest—about the size of a fingernail—but practically weightless.

Over the years there had been many additions and subtractions as new items were proved to bring either good or bad luck. There was the safety pin, the dime, the brown bead that looked like a vitamin pill, the flat metal ring that might have been the backing for a button; a theater ticket, now no more than an illegible scrap of cardboard; a red metal paperclip. The paperclip had arrived at Christmas and he'd used it to attach an official letter to his passport. It had been responsible for gaining him entry to forbidden territory. It had brought him a lot of luck, so it had been kept.

He traveled light. A waterproof shoulder bag held the essentials, including the tape recorder, extra notebook, pencil and pen, and the Swiss jackknife with its nail file, corkscrew, and fish-scaler. There was room for a shirt, two pairs of underpants and socks, a T-shirt, sweater, a raincoat that folded into a pack hardly bigger than a slice of bread; and a pair of sandals in case he lost his shoes or had them stolen.

The duffel bag contained more shirts, boots, an old wool shawl that could be used as a blanket, a second suit, a portable phone, and a laptop computer, which he'd never used. He hardly ever took anything out of the main bag, other than an extra shirt.

Gradually he had varied his routine of preparing for the front line. At the time when they first became lovers, he allowed Joan to do most of his packing. But after a few years she was hardly permitted to go near the shoulder bag and certainly not to approach the sacred talismans in the security belt, all of which had to be packed in the right order. He might give her a list of what he wanted, but he always took care of the most important things himself. And if he allowed her to slip something in at the last minute, that was an exception.

"What's this?" she asked one day, coming into the bedroom while he was packing. "Your magic underpants?" She reached over and held up the garment for inspection. He snatched it from her, saying, "That's exactly what they are."

"Max, they're full of holes. How did you get them past me? I haven't been washing anything like this—I would have noticed."

"It's all right. I wash all these myself."

"At least let me sew up the tears."

"No sewing, no replacement. They're fine."

"We could sell them to a museum and say those were bullet holes."

"Don't joke about it."

She opened her hand above the array of trinkets, being careful not to touch them, which he wouldn't have liked. They were laid out on the bedspread in a sequence that—apparently—corresponded to the order of acquisition.

"A man of many charms," she said. She put her arms around him. And he didn't push her away, but his mind was on other things. He continued to pack while she rubbed her face against his shirt.

She didn't understand how a man of his intelligence could really believe that primitive rituals could save his life. That was faith as misplaced as the extravagant notions held by high-school girls and boys who were anxious to ward off pregnancy.

"If you tell the truth and do what's right," he'd once told her, " you automatically fall into harmony with the world: your pace is one step ahead of the bomb and one behind the mien going off."

"Because you deserve to escape?" she'd asked. "Because your good intentions actually mean something?"

He'd shrugged, saying that he couldn't explain it any other way and that if there was a chance in hell of his being right, he certainly wasn't going to start changing his habits: in fact, it made him slightly uneasy to refer to the matter at all.

He knew as well as she did: there was no physical armor that could protect you against modern weaponry. And as for psychological defenses, they worked only on and against the mind. They got you out there and they got you through it. They were important. But they couldn't save you.

She'd thought up many theories to account for the discrepancies in his behavior. One had something to do with surrogate emotion and the suppression of anger. But none of them lasted; in the end she knew him too well to be able to explain him and she stopped trying to question what he was or how he thought. Often she didn't understand her own motives, either.

The only time he made a comment about suffering a possible reaction from his work was once when he said to her, "The ones who survive are all crackpots." He seemed to think that he was just stating a fact and that there was no sense in trying to change it. Presumably the other war correspondents—who weren't in some way damaged— didn't survive. He said nothing about the ones who stayed alive and continued to broadcast despite the fact that they were so stupid, lazy, and dishonest that they regularly used large chunks of other people's material, sometimes simply by asking a girlfriend to translate published or broadcast passages for them. He was too engrossed by the iniquities of politics to become exercised about lesser questions: every discipline had its cheats.

In his profession the cynical were looking for money and fame; the morally committed took their trips into the death zone because they would have liked to be priests and saviors—to make people better, to force them to look at themselves; and to lead them toward an understanding of the brutality and irrationality of certain actions. Max was one of the moral ones: there was no doubt about that. As Joan began to know him better, she sometimes thought of him as a valiant knight, like a figure from a storybook—a man who was driven into danger by his sense of chivalry: to rescue the truth.

She loved to listen to him talk about his work. Even when the facts were unpleasant, in the recounting he could transform them into something close to art. He told her stories of poverty, disease, political and military mismanagement, torture, and imprisonment. The long stream of reported injustice would have been too much for her to bear if it hadn't been for the fact that among the victims and dispossessed there turned out to be as many liars, chiselers, frauds, and killers as among their oppressors. That added a touch of monstrous comedy to the tales. At times she thought of his job as a combination of police work, priesthood, and stage management. And he seemed to know everyone.

His acquaintance included soldiers of every rank, ambulance drivers, librarians, poets, assassins, Red Cross workers, photographers, health inspectors, forgers, explorers, helicopter pilots: anyone who wanted to talk. And women; women from all over, of differing ages and shapes and various degrees of beauty, suffering, health, deviousness, intelligence, and despair.

What he got up to out there with other women didn't matter to her. Out there would stay where it was. She was sure that any amorous adventure he might engage in while on an assignment would be a thing he'd consider, from the very outset, temporary. She didn't really believe that he'd ever be tempted because he was so fascinated, appalled, and excited by his work that nothing could distract him. While his concentration was fixed on it, warfare itself became a substitute for the erotic.

The first marriage hadn't been in such bad shape as he'd hinted. Not that his version was dishonest: as anyone sensible or practical would do, he tried out the new relationship before deciding to leave the old one. And Joan, knowing that he was married, had still been eager to hand over her life to him. She'd wanted to throw herself into her fate, making the attachment more intensely romantic by believing that right from the start it was too late to turn back. But as soon as she really fell in love with him, she stopped having fun being the other woman. She wanted to be the main woman—the real one. She was ready to fight for him.

Then came the surprise: there wasn't any fight. The first wife stood back, agreed to a divorce: disappeared.

Joan grabbed her good fortune and held on. She and Max married. They settled down; they had children. They continued to love and, for a while, to be happy.

For the first three years of their marriage she was able to concentrate on him to the exclusion of everything else. And after the children were born, she usually managed—in the early days—to get them tucked in for the night so that she and he could be alone. But with time, that changed. When the family was suddenly all together again, the children needed reassurance that she still loved them; they'd call down from their rooms that they couldn't sleep; they'd ask for glasses of water and—simplest of all—they'd cry. Even the baby would become additionally demanding when Max was at home. And then Joan would worry that because of her need to be with him, she was neglecting her children.

Sometimes it seemed to her that he'd passed his fears on to her: that she'd been delegated to keep them safe until he got back—that he left all the dangerous emotions with her and took with him only his talismans, his special clothes, his lucky boots—like a child going off to war with a peashooter and a rabbit's foot.

She worried about his comfort, feared for his safety and his sanity. Within moments of his departure she longed for him to come back. And the more she feared, the more surely she believed that, while he was gone, he was protected by the way she felt about him.

On the two occasions when he'd been wounded, she'd known about it before being told. The first time, she was in the kitchen and about to reach up for a coffee cup; the second time, she was with a friend at a play. That initial warning instant, at home in the kitchen, hadn't told her what her alarm might indicate, other than that something was wrong. When the same thing happened again, she knew that it had to do with Max. She was convinced that when he was closest to death, her love was what shielded him.

She was glad that his first wife hadn't wanted children. That had been one of his greatest disappointments in the marriage: his wife had refused to have children until he changed to a less dangerous branch of his work.

Joan had imagined that children would bind her and Max more closely to each other, but soon it began to seem that always—at just those moments when it was important that he and she should be together—the kids did what they could to come between them; they wanted him all to themselves and at the same time they resented him for interrupting their hold on her. Max would load on the entertainment for a solid two hours and then pick up the phone for a babysitter.

They'd go out to restaurants. They'd walk arm in arm. Once they checked into a hotel for a couple of days, leaving the kids with relatives who boasted afterwards about how well-behaved the children were: good as gold—no trouble at all.

While he was away she read the children bedtime stories. All they ever wanted to hear about was kings and queens, fairy-tale princesses, castles and dragons: the past as it never was, the era of Romance. She loved their insistence on the stereotypes and clichés of good fortune. She saw it as an innocence to be fostered. When they grew up, they'd be bored by the trials of true love and the daring of knights on horse-back. They might even want pictures of car crashes and machine-gun massacres, blood and wreckage. They'd be able to appreciate their father's work and to know why he'd had to be away from them so often. But until they were older, his absences were going to disarrange what should have been the regular pattern of their lives.

When he came home, he wanted to tell her about what he'd seen and what he thought about it—everything he'd been through. She understood that and it saddened her that the constant interruption of children's complaints and questions, the ringing of the telephone with urgent messages about mothers' meetings and carpool dates and so on, interfered with her desire to know his news, his mood, and his heart; with her capacity for listening and his to tell; and eventually, with their ability to keep in step with each other.

She didn't mind the professional bond that drew him to seek the company of fellow newsmen and television cronies as soon as he arrived home. What began to make her anxious was the knowledge that two or three of his favorite lunching companions were pretty young women in the business. As soon as she was certain that he'd slept with one—and then another—of them, she felt a spectral presence beside her of the first wife: the one to whom she'd so casually done a greater wrong than at the time she could have imagined being done to her. How could the same thing ever happen to her? She was the one who loved. And if you loved, you were in the right.

He had a friend named Bruno. Ever since she was introduced to him, Bruno had flirted with her in a way that was more than just single-minded: he was hoping to start something up with her that would be serious enough to threaten her marriage—to get her away from Max and to marry her himself; or not to. Maybe what he had in mind was to seduce her, expose her to Max, and drop her without warning while her husband walked out on her with any one of the many women who were in love with him.

She'd seen from the beginning that what Bruno wanted was to outdo Max and because he didn't have the drive, the brilliance of expression, or the quality of mind to equal Max professionally, he'd always be willing to take a stab at his personal life instead. The flirtation had nothing to do with her, although often—especially when a party ended up with Max being surrounded by good-looking, younger women for whom he was putting on a show—she was glad of the distraction. Her party talks with Bruno could sometimes make her feel desirable and, because she was always saying no in the nicest way, respected. This game of lies had been carried on between them for years. Since both of them were getting something out of it, she'd developed a kind of fondness for Bruno in spite of what she thought of his motives and what she suspected was his real opinion of her.

At Max's most recent homecoming party, she and Bruno spent the end of the evening sitting side by side on a staircase and looking down into a room filled with a loudly animated crowd of guests. Bruno said, "I can't stand it any longer, Joan. There's never been anybody but you. Why do you think it broke up between me and Pam? I keep thinking about you. I dream about you."

She turned to him sweetly, as if not wanting to hurt him. Beyond his face puffed with drink, his hangdog eyes beginning to water, his whisper trembling with urgency, she saw a flash of malice that would have made her nervous if she'd been on her own. There was nothing this man wouldn't do, she thought, to pay Max back for being better. What Bruno needed was victory. All the wars Max had observed were caused by quarrelsome, greedy, envious, and petty men like this one: he thought that taking her away could damage Max. And if it destroyed her, he wouldn't care. He despised her anyway.

For the first time she understood how intelligent she'd been to remain gentle, to play dumb, to pretend that she felt sympathy and believed him to be an honorable man who was struggling with his passions. She said lightly, "You're supposed to be my husband's friend."

As soon as he realized that she was definitely saying no for the evening, he pulled back, pretending to be drunker than he was. He had the look all of a sudden of a man who was about to say something really wounding because it would give him such pleasure to get it out. She added quickly, "It isn't that I mind being asked, because I've always liked you, so I'm flattered. But I don't want to start doing what everybody else does—and against a husband I love."

"He does it, too. With Alice. You know—that girl on my team. There she is, over there."

She looked. She saw Alice: face-to-face with Max, a packed mass of noisy people around them. The fact that they were nearly close enough to be dancing could have been excused by the crush of other guests, but not that—as he was about to raise his glass to his lips and the girl began the same gesture with her own glass—Max brushed his hand against hers, the knuckle of his little finger rubbing back and forth against the edge of her hand.

It happened so quickly that the next moment all anyone could have seen was two people sipping their drinks and talking.

The speed and minuteness of the movement helped to make it seem the kind of intimate contact two illicit lovers might feel they could get away with: allowing themselves the indulgence of touch while the rest of the world looked on.

Nothing Bruno had to say could have made her so unhappy as seeing—from all the way across the room—that tiny joining of finger and hand. It was a love gesture. What caused Joan such pain was not that it was something Max had done before, with her—part of their private code: on the contrary, it was new. He'd thought it up for the other woman at that moment, or perhaps he'd invented it at some earlier party and now it was incorporated into their special language. Maybe it had even been started by the hateful Alice. And now the two of them were using it between themselves like a wink.

She'd have liked to storm down there, push the girl aside, and tell her, "Get your own husband."

"See what I mean?" Bruno asked.

He couldn't be referring to what she'd seen. She said, "Even if he did, I still don't see why I should start to act that way, too, just to make other people feel better about being unfaithful." She smiled, and said, "You were only offering to pinch-hit anyway, weren't you?"

He started to protest. She stood up. He promised to change the subject. He spent the rest of the evening telling her entertaining anecdotes about his colleagues. She concentrated on remembering what he was saying while her mind was on Alice and Max.

She was still good-looking and nowhere near middle-aged. And it wasn't as if anything had ever gone wrong with her marriage. Everything was fine.

Bruno shouted something at her. She mouthed that the music was too loud and she couldn't hear. She didn't even want to know what he'd said. She was thinking that there hadn't been anything wrong with Max's first marriage either, except perhaps that his wife hadn't been willing to make a full commitment until she'd been sure. If you risked everything, you could lose everything.

She looked back into the crowd and wasn't able to find Max and the girl. While Bruno had held her attention, they'd moved. It took only a second for her to locate them off in a corner. Love was so quick to discover. And jealousy. And fear: all those things. She couldn't lose him. There wasn't anything else, only him. As she began to panic, the dislike of Bruno and the girl seeped over other parts of her life and memory until, at last, it touched Max himself. She blamed him. He was treating her badly.

For the next few days Max talked to her as he used to before their marriage, when he'd come back from an assignment needing to get everything out of his system by talk even more than by sex. For once the children didn't interrupt; one was staying at a friend's house and the other two were away on a school trip over the weekend. She listened. She didn't try to tell him about the failed exams, the trips to the doctor, the broken friendships and quarrels, the bicycle that ran into a brick wall, the nosebleed and so forth. His worries were on an altogether grander scale: they were international. And somebody else's.

She pretended that everything was normal. And he appeared to be the same as usual. Their life together still seemed to be all right.

Max was always complaining that the networks refused to broadcast the most upsetting parts of his war coverage or to show certain film clips or even stills from some of the footage Bruno and his friends brought back. And they wouldn't schedule broadcasts at lunch or supper, when most people switched on to look at the news.

They should, he said. People ought to be made aware of what was going on in the world, particularly if there were crimes being committed in their name.

He'd begun work thinking that you could show the truth and make people change things for the better. But he'd soon realized that it was hard enough to get anybody to do something about what was happening in the next street. You had to shove it in their faces, make them feel threatened or ashamed or sickened: shocked, appalled.

When his first marriage was at last beyond help, his wife had struck exclusively at his belief in his work. The affair with Joan hadn't been mentioned; everything was supposed to be a problem of work. She'd said that far from helping people, Max was nothing more than a pornographer: he showed everyone pictures of horror—agonies about which they could do nothing. His broadcasts were accompanied by photographs of burned cities, starving children, the beaten and limbless, the disgraced, homeless, and bereaved—and these images were set out in front of the rich, safe, happy citizens of a more fortunate part of the world so that those viewers could eat, drink, and go to parties with more enjoyment, knowing how lucky they were: lucky enough to be free from all those miseries as well as being free of responsibility, since there was certainly little they could do about someone else's war taking place thousands of miles away. She'd told him that the people seated in front of their television sets around the world were exactly like the crowds that used to attend games at the coliseum in ancient Rome. They were there for the spectacle. To imagine anything else was dishonest. It was wrong. His work was just entertainment. People could hear him, and watch what Bruno filmed, and be able to imagine from a position of comfort what it might be like to be caught, inescapably, in a different life. The effect was the same as that of a television drama, only more unpleasant and less memorable. Did he himself, she asked, do anything about these crises? No. His job was to package and present. And to become famous: the man with integrity, who gave the balanced view. The view wasn't truly balanced because the military leaders of all sides had their reasons—sometimes tactical and sometimes propagandistic—for not wanting certain information to be let out. That, too, annoyed Max. More than once he'd been told point-blank that no army intended to allow some news-hungry crap-merchant to divulge facts whose release might cost the lives of military personnel, not to mention the civilians.

What he was really famous for, the other wife had said, was going through dozens of grisly scenes and coming out alive. And the fame was what he liked. He wasn't driving an ambulance and staying out there all year, year after year, for the whole of a war. He'd drop in for a look and go home again.

Joan knew that she herself had been at the root of these accusations. What the first wife had really meant was: *You're mendacious, superficial, and a hypocrite because you're unfaithful. You're no good because you're no longer good to me. You don't love me anymore, therefore nothing you do can have any validity.* It was jealousy.

And now she was the wife. But she was still on his side. And again there was the new girl and once again she was changing places.

Now he's sleeping with her and talking with me. Maybe that will make him fall in love with me again, the way he did with her—and with me— back at the beginning: through talk. Or maybe I'm being let down gently and this is the start of solely conversational intercourse for the rest of our lives.

As she stirred a pot on the stove, the picture of Max and Alice— their hands touching—came back to her, the gesture quick, charged, alive. *Don't do that,* she thought. Once you allowed jealousy, you began to like it. You became the kind of person who saw things in that way— one of the envious, who thought that everything missing in their lives was absent because of someone else's fault.

The caress between their hands as they'd raised their glasses—had it really been so special?

She was at the stage where she was doubting that she'd actually seen anything. What she expected to believe was beginning to change what she knew to be fact.

On one of their sightseeing trips—before the children—they'd visited a great cathedral of the Renaissance. She'd been overcome by the building and by the paintings, chapels, altarpieces, and the many pilgrims and worshippers. She'd never been able to believe, but she'd always felt that something was there and that it was responsible for the good things in her life. By the time she met Max she would have described herself as a nonbeliever or—more accurately—she would have said that above the neck she was an atheist, but her heart knew better.

As she'd stepped back out into the daylight, she'd said to him, "Wouldn't it be wonderful to believe?"

He'd said, "Why? You'd just be deluding yourself."

"You'd never be afraid again, or even uncertain."

"Of course you would. That's what the whole thing is about. That's why people go to church."

"But I knew a woman, a friend of my parents—one of the nicest people I've ever met—and she told me once that she loved going to church because it just made her feel happy."

"But organized religion means you have to accept the whole kit and caboodle. What about life after death?"

"I don't know."

"Come on, Joanie."

"Well, no. I don't see how there could be."

"Exactly," he'd said. "Ridiculous."

He was what she believed in. He knew that. And, in a different way, millions of others believed in him, too. Public broadcasting had made him a kind of god.

He might have the public glamour, but she was attractive, too, and still young. She could pay him back in the traditional manner by having a fling with one of his friends. She could think of several. Not Bruno.

She looked into the mirror and combed her hair a different way. She tried on clothes she hadn't worn for a while.

No change would make a difference if his thoughts were with someone else. She'd have become an object. She'd be the thing left behind to stay at home and take care of the children and the house.

Never trust a betrayer, she said to her face in the mirror. *If he did it once, he'll do it again.* Maybe that really was true. People tended to stick to familiar patterns of behavior. In his case . . . but that was nonsense. She knew that he loved her. And the children, too. He wasn't promiscuous by temperament. This was all silly. What did it mean? It meant that whether he was in danger and under stress or whether he'd just escaped from the fighting and was feeling good, a pretty girl who made a beeline for him was going to hold his attention and possibly his affection, too, for a while. But as long as his wife pretended not to notice, he'd never think of breaking up the marriage. Although why she should have to put up with that . . . and anyway, how could anyone love that girl, Alice, who looked as blank and empty as a doll?

Anybody could love anybody, of course. No rules applied. But Joan didn't think it was love. That might develop. It had happened before and then, without any admission or even discussion, it had ceased to be noticeable, and then it was gone.

She stamped her foot at the sight of her reflection. What was wrong with her? Everything was still all right. Why was she scared now?

The one person she could have talked to, who would know about everything, was the first wife: the woman she had wronged. Joan's part in the business hadn't been nearly so bad as the wrong Max had done; still, it meant that the two women who loved him could never talk. No trust could be established following an act of such treachery. They would remain enemies.

It was just as possible that if Max walked out, then after he became bored with the insipid, fame-hunting Alice, he'd go back to his first wife, leaving everyone else high and dry.

What would she do then? She'd be taking care of the children and doing the laundry for the rest of her life; never having the love, never even having the sex.

Who was it who had once said to her that she'd rather have good sex than love? And the reason given was that love invariably fell apart on you, whereas good sex always gave you a bang. Somebody she'd been to school with. The school reunion. A career girl who liked the footloose life. She couldn't remember.

The children were in a rare period of unbroken routine. No crisis appeared near, or even possible, and Joan had the freedom to give in to her worries about herself. When Max was suddenly called out on an assignment again, she was partly taken up with other thoughts.

Bruno would be setting out a week later on the same job, to follow in Max's footsteps as far as he and his field team were able to go. Max didn't have the TV cameras, the connection with NATO forces' equipment and French army food supplies. He had personal contacts among the people who were fighting and killing. He had his eyes, his voice, the two spiral notebooks, two pens, two pencils, and the miniature tape recorder. And his charm. And all his lucky talismans: the other charms, worn into battle like the witch doctor's pouch belonging to a spear-carrying tribesman.

She had to admit that the tiny objects annoyed her. It wasn't just the fact that her husband treasured things given to him by strangers, that he insisted on keeping them by him in his darkest moments, and that not one of them was from her—he didn't, for instance, wear a wedding ring; her dislike of them had more to do with his need. If he had clung to a memento of her in that obsessed, fetishistic way, she'd have been pleased. But he had to have something else: some source of strength that excluded her. Other people's presents, and their love, retained a magic property that her gifts no longer had; they were never used up or made ordinary. For him to care so much about them was like telling her that she had no magic.

His need for them also reminded her of their youngest child, who, when he was still a baby, took delight in the bright toys she hung around his crib: his rattle, his twirling clown, his striped ball, and the hanging mobile from which depended eight little blue birds that flew in a circle. And if all those baubles weren't lined up in exactly the same order and height as usual, with the customary width of spacing between them, he'd scream with rage and then cry as if heartbroken: because nothing was right any longer.

What would happen if Max decided that she was bringing him bad luck? Would he just throw her away, like the dud talismans? Like the first wife?

He went upstairs to begin packing and then came down to make a phone call. As he reached the living room, she started up the staircase with two ironed blouses and a skirt on a hanger.

She put the clothes in the girls' room, moving a few dresses along the closet rail to make room for the skirt, which she hung next to her older daughter's "lucky" blouse. It had taken hours of persuasion and lecturing before the girl had stopped wanting to wear the blouse every day. The most difficult argument to deal with had been the one following the statement, "School is definitely a war zone."

As she passed down the hallway again, she looked through the bedroom door. There on the bedspread was Max's security belt and, visible through the unzipped opening of its pocket, his special package of charms: a narrow, flat triangle made by folding a handkerchief the way a flag is packed up, and at each crease adding a charm. The convenient shape and firm binding wouldn't allow anything inside to jiggle around or fall out. Next to the charms was a pile of handkerchiefs and the front door keys, which Max kept separately and always left at home when he was traveling. Seeing the keys gave Joan the idea. There was an extra set up on the closet shelf.

She brought down the spare keys, took one of the handkerchiefs, flattened it out and began to fold a section of the material until it formed a shape almost identical in appearance to a corner of the original. She wound the keys into the rest of the cloth, making a loose knot that could be mistaken for a natural entanglement: the result of one thing covering up another when all the clothes were being moved. The carefully constructed point could be taken for the remaining lines of ironing.

She slid the substitute into the pocket of the security belt, leaving the zipper still open so that Max could check, just by looking, that the triangle was inside And she put the one containing the charms up into the closet where the keys had been.

And now they'd see, she thought. Maybe he'd never know. And then afterwards she could say, "See how silly that is. You didn't have them this time and everything went fine."

If he did notice that the charms were gone, would he think it was an accident and that he'd grabbed up the wrong thing before rushing off to make his telephone call; or that she'd rearranged his packing in an effort to help?

He'd have to think something like that, unless he noticed within the next few minutes and thought she was playing a joke on him. He wouldn't suspect her of deliberate sabotage. Otherwise, the first thing he'd do when he came back would be to go straight to Alice's place, where he'd spend five days talking, relaxing, winding down, and of course giving that Alice plenty of what he didn't seem to think his own wife needed very much of. That was how his first marriage had broken up. She ought to know. First came being taken for granted, then the complaints started. It was always better to stop talking and start doing something that made an improvement.

If he discovered the keys, they might inspire him: he was a man who was stimulated by danger. It was possible that a happy, predictable family life was too safe for him.

Early in the afternoon he looked at his watch. He ran his hand over the outline of the security pocket under his belt. Then he checked that he was carrying or wearing every essential official document and that the two bags were on or under the front hall chair.

He gathered everything up. She opened the door. He moved out onto the step, set the big bag down, and put his arm around her.

As she kissed him good-bye, she told him, "Don't forget: you hold the keys to my heart."

"Mm," he said. "Behave yourself while I'm gone. Lay off the ice cream. Don't speak to strangers."

"Bye, darling," she answered. "Don't sleep with strangers."

"I said 'speak to.'"

"I can't tell you not to do that. It's your job."

He picked up the duffel bag again, backed down the front path, and waved. From twenty feet away she got the full force of the famous smile, with the warmth of his personality aimed straight at her. She waved and blew kisses to him, all the time thinking: *Don't get hurt, don't go near the shooting, don't come back dead, don't disappear out there, lost somewhere in a mass grave or a muddy field. Don't go till tomorrow. Let's be happy a little longer.*

That night she dreamt that he was shot, that they sent his body home in a coffin, and that she had to go to the airport to pick it up. The coffin came around on the luggage carousel and, when it reached her, all movement stopped. She heard a faint hammering from deep inside, under a large keyhole right over the place that would line up with the heart of the corpse. Max had been put into the coffin while he was still alive: he was trying to get out but the key to the lock had been shut in with him. It was one of the keys she'd wrapped up in the handkerchief that was in his security pocket. As she listened to his struggles, she realized that he was never going to get out; he was going to die and she was to blame.

In the morning she still felt shaken. After getting the children off to school, she telephoned three friends and two relatives, telling them that she might have to park the kids on them at sometime during the next few days. She started to organize a list of clothes to pack into the children's travel bags.

She was standing in the kitchen and about to put a load of laundry into the machine, when she sensed that something wasn't right. She caught no faintest smell of smoke or gas, no sinister tiny dripping or cracks or creakings that sounded out of place. And yet something was wrong. Her uneasiness increased. She turned slowly, going all the way around in a circle—not really looking, but just checking her surroundings—and stopped. The answer came to her: Max. She raced to the bedroom, opened the closet door, snatched up the handkerchief with the charms, stuffed it into a drawstring bag she used for her makeup, grabbed her jacket and keys, and ran downstairs again.

She had her hand out for the front door when she turned back to make a telephone call. In her hurry she bumped into a table. Then she pushed the phone buttons too fast and had to start over from the beginning.

She counted six rings.

A voice answered, "Yeah?"

"Bruno?"

"I don't believe it. My dreams come true. Hi."

"Bruno, this is an emergency. Are you going to be at the office for an hour or so?"

"Sure, but I could come to you."

"No, that's no good. I've got to give you something Max left behind. I'll explain when I see you. If you're going out, would you tell your secretary—"

"You stay there, I'll come right over."

"I can't," she said, and hung up.

She was bucketing through a wide, suburban street before she noticed that her foot was on the gas as hard as it could go. She slowed down and took a few deep breaths. Everything was going to be all right: panic would only make things worse.

She drove to the area where she'd lived when she was still single and, parking the car in the place she'd always used, took the subway in to the center of town.

She entered the building, running. And she was out of the elevator, pushing past the secretary, and barging into Bruno's office before she'd thought out what to do or say. As she arrived, breathless, he was getting up from the chair behind his desk. She didn't even give him the opportunity for a kiss on the cheek. She stuck out her arm and presented the pouch, saying, "Bruno, I've done a terrible thing. I still don't know how it could have happened, but Max's good luck charms were all folded up in a handkerchief and there was a set of keys right next to them, with some other handkerchiefs—and he went off with the wrong bundle. Can you get them to him?"

He wanted to take her out to lunch, to cancel meetings: to make all sorts of preliminary moves toward isolating her with him.

She shook her head and retreated.

He said, "You owe me a hell of a meal for this one."

"Yes, yes, of course," she said, rushing away.

After handing over the charms she felt better. She even felt that she'd averted any possible danger. Her relief was as great as if Max already had his possessions back. She had passed on the responsibility. Bruno hadn't meant just a candlelit dinner, of course; he thought that he really had a hold over her now. But when the time came, she'd say that this had been a favor to Max, not her. Max would be home first, anyway. She could explain everything and whatever celebration they wanted to plan as a thank you would include him.

The next day she wondered: What if Bruno didn't hand over the charms? What if he decided not to, guessing the effect it could have on Max to find himself vulnerable in a moment of uncertainty? Anything could happen.

She took a shower, packed an overnight bag, and put it in the hall. She didn't know what to do next, so she decided to pretend that everything was all right and that she ought to tackle the normal chores like the dusting and the children's rooms.

She kept doing the usual daily tasks as she waited, but she was so sure something was going to happen that when the telephone call came she was ready: the children's bags were packed and her overnight case was in the car.

She reached the hospital ahead of the reporters, twenty minutes before the helicopter carrying Max was scheduled to land on the roof.

She knew that things must be serious because the nurses kept everyone else out. When at last one of them let her see Max, he was unconscious: about to go into the operating theater. She kissed him. She squeezed his hand. She whispered into his ear that everything was going to be all right and that she loved him. "That's all, now," someone told her. She backed away.

In the corridor she spoke to the nurse who seemed to be in charge. First of all, she thanked her for taking care of her husband. That made a good impression. Then she said that she wondered if the hospital had some sort of chapel where she could say a quick prayer. That made an even better impression; it was the right thing to do at such a time and it put hospital work in perspective: there was only so much the medical profession could do for anyone and after that the outcome was up to the higher powers.

They did indeed have a chapel, the nurse told her, for use by all denominations.

"And one more thing," Joan said: her husband might be recovering for a long time, but there were colleagues of his who worked in television and you could bet anything that they'd be charging down the hallways in full cry as soon as they got wind of the story. Was there any way of keeping them out for a couple of days? One person in particular, a girl named Alice, was so persistent that you'd almost think she was intent on breaking up his marriage.

The nurse rose to the occasion. Her starched uniform seemed to expand with professional pride. She assured Joan that absolutely no one was going to get at her patient without his wife's permission.

Joan's anxiety receded. She wished that she could witness a clash between Alice—with her debutante affectations and international media jargon—and the tough, motherly nurse who knew how to deal with life, death, and people who had no business being on her ward.

The chapel was disappointingly lacking in candles. The lighting was artificial, the stained glass was fake. All over the world people were lighting candles, as she had hoped to. And they were like her. *Thank you, God, for getting me out of trouble, for letting me escape, for bringing me luck.* But eventually there would be something they wouldn't be able to avoid and there would be no point in lighting a candle for that. The material housing of everyone's world was temporary; the eyesight would go, the accuracy of the other senses, too, the strength of the muscles, the hardness of the bones. That was what God gave, as well as the people you loved. And everything else besides. And when the bad things came upon you, how could you then say: *No, thank you—why are you allowing this to happen to me?*

She stayed in the chapel for as long as she could stand being away from Max. She made her pleas for his health, she promised and apologized, and asked for forgiveness. Then she waited outside the operating theater.

She was by his side as soon as he came out of the anesthetic. She was holding his hand.

"Oh," he said, "there you are. My beautiful wife." Later he told her that she'd looked terrified and that he'd recognized on her face the same expression of calamity that for so many years he'd seen on the victims of war.

And she saw, but never told him afterwards, that he could be weakened; he could lose the energy and inquisitiveness that made him seek danger. He could be conquered, losing everything that made him what he was. Sooner than have that happen, she'd let him go to someone else. But not yet.

She told him about the lucky charms, saying that the substitution had been a mistake.

He hadn't known until they were sewing him up before putting him on the plane. But he was delighted. He said, "You know what's so wonderful? They're the keys to the front door. They mean home. Nothing else could have pulled me through this. They saved me."

Tears came to their eyes. They embraced. They rejoiced: he with the gratitude of the survivor, she was the shameless self-righteousness of the successful.

This time her prayers had worked. How long he'd be content to be safe was a question she could deal with later, the next time it came up. And how long God would remain on her side was something she'd have to stop thinking about. Loyalty from the divine was often pretty much like human fidelity—you knew about it for sure only when it changed. And by that time it was too late.

FERTILITY

When he left for the war, he left her pregnant. As soon as she realized the state she was in, she told her parents, who disowned her; they'd always preferred the rich neighbors' son next door and now she'd ruined her chances and theirs.

She went to his mother, who called her a lying whore and slammed the door in her face, saying, "My son would never have anything to do with a cheap type like you."

She got a job in the sort of place where people didn't mind who did what. She served alcohol and wiped tabletops and cleaned out greasy pots and pans. Her clothes and hair stank of fat, the skin on her hands split and bled. The waitresses who worked side by side with her told her where she could go to get rid of the pregnancy. But she was still in love with him.

When the time came for her to give birth, she couldn't work any longer. The boarding house threw her out. Her friends had no money. Only one place in town was willing to take her in: the brothel. She knew about the reputation the building had, but she was innocent enough to imagine that the real business was the bar and not the rooms upstairs, instead of the other way around. In any case, she expected to die in childbirth.

The woman who kept the place paid for her doctor. And after the birth, as soon as she was well enough, expected to be paid back: for lodging and food, too.

She refused. Every time she looked into the face of her little son and fell in love with him again, she fell in love over and over again with his father, whose presence somewhere in the world was like a promise still unbroken, although he didn't write.

She'd rather die in the gutter, she said—and take the baby with her.

"You live here," the woman told her. "You gave birth here. You know what this place is. Everybody knows. You aren't married—that makes you an unfit mother. And if I say that you're one of my girls, I can get the state to claim the child for its protection. In easier times it could be adopted, but nobody can afford an extra mouth now. That means the orphanage."

For most women at the time, it was true, an unexpected child would have been a disaster even if they were married. For most; but not for all. Not for her.

She tried to fight. Four of them came at her. One of them snatched the baby from her and ran into another room. Two others held her while the fourth began to pour liquor down her throat.

For three days she was too drunk to get out of bed. They washed her and changed her clothes, combed her hair and gave her more alcohol while the men lined up in the hallway. A year later, when she came to an arrangement with a dentist from a neighboring town, she found that several of her teeth had been cracked in that initial struggle.

Her lover's mother set about establishing legal claims to the child as soon as it was born. Since the baby was illegitimate, there was no proof either way as to who the father was, but the authorities decided that a decent home of any kind was better than life in a brothel. They took the baby. They gave him to the grandmother.

She was drunk all the time after that until the other girls let her know what had happened to some of their friends: a certain amount of drink could get you in the mood, but if you were falling down every night, you could find yourself out on the street with your ears and nose cut off.

She followed orders, obeyed requests and demands. She became a slave. Behind her mask of compliance, everything in her was dead except the thought of her child. Whenever she had any time off, she wandered near the house where her lover's mother lived with the baby.

Occasionally she'd walk by the place, looking in quickly at one of the windows, and going past without breaking stride. She was afraid that the woman would report her.

She needn't have worried. As soon as the child was old enough, it became a stranger in a way she hadn't anticipated—a way similar to that by which she had been made into what she was.

One day she saw both of them out walking in the park: the child toddling, rushing and stumbling while holding onto his grandmother's hand.

She approached the spot where they were and then stood back, as still as one of the trees, to drink in the sight of her child. In a few moments the boy seemed to notice that someone was staring at him. He stopped moving. He looked at her and smiled, making a little chirping sound of pleasure. He put his free hand into his mouth.

The grandmother turned her head. Her anger must have caused her to clench her fingers; the boy took his hand from his mouth, waved it in the air, and began to whine.

"Look," the grandmother said. "There's the bad woman." She pointed. "What do we say when we see her?"

The boy looked up for confirmation and pointed, copying exactly the direction of the gesture. "Whore," he said.

"That's right, darling. Whore."

The child laughed. "Whore-whore-whore," he chanted. He began to jump up and down with excitement. His grandmother joined him: laughing, hopping, shouting, and still holding his hand so that the two of them resembled a mismatched team of theatrical entertainers.

The tears ran down her face. She watched her child until the grandmother began to egg him on to make malicious faces, teaching him to stick out his tongue. The next step would be throwing stones.

She was younger and—despite everything she'd been through—stronger than the other woman. But her child's taunts robbed her of the ability either to attack others or to defend herself. She turned around and walked away.

She waited for her lover, not hoping for much. Victories and defeats followed each other so quickly, and the borders were altered so often that nobody could be certain who was dead or alive in the areas where fighting was going on. No one she knew of had had a letter. That was a small price to pay for their good fortune; neither the town, nor any part of their district, had yet been occupied by the enemy; nor even by front-line troops in retreat, which could also be bad, although at least only the enemy burned everything down when they left.

She prayed for his survival and, as she prayed, she dreaded the possibility of her dearest wish coming true. She shrank from the thought that he'd believe his mother; she'd had a dream in which he was the one who held the child by the hand as they both called her a whore. If the dream came true, she thought, she'd hang herself.

The war lasted almost another two years. As far as anyone could tell, they had won. Or, at least, they hadn't lost.

He came back in a gang of men he hadn't known before he'd joined up. Some of them had been from his school but not in the same class. Some had looked like children when they'd marched off in their clean, new uniforms. Now it seemed to him that they resembled professional criminals and that that was probably an accurate way of describing all of them, including himself.

There was supposed to be a parade from the railroad station and down the main street of town to the park, where there would be speeches, applause, and the presentation of flowers.

He and his friends had no desire to win approval or keep up appearances or to stand still while pictures were taken of them shaking hands with dignitaries who weren't worth the saving and ugly women who for five years had been viciously insistent that their boys get out there and fight.

They broke off from the parade as it passed the bar. A mob of them burst through the doors, shouting for something to drink. And, they wanted to know, where were the girls?

Three of the girls came downstairs from where they'd been looking out of the windows at the crowd down in the street. One joined the barman behind the counter. "Beer's on the house," someone called out. The soldiers cheered.

He tossed back half his drink and was going through the doorway into one of the smaller, less crowded downstairs rooms when he came face to face with her.

"Yes, it's me," she said. And before he could ask her what she was doing in a place like that, she told him. She described her parents' reaction to the pregnancy; and then his mother's. She explained how she'd ended up in the brothel and how his mother had legally stolen the child. "And now," she said, "she's taught him—whenever he sees me—to shout 'Whore' at me. What your mother's done to me is worse than anything the enemy ever did to my country."

"Come here," he said.

She went up close to him and stood obediently while he inspected her.

He tipped up his glass, drained it, and threw it into the corner, where it smashed into pieces. He ordered her to come with him. As he shouldered his way through the crowd and out into the open air, she followed.

The streets were empty of people and littered with flowers, confetti, and scraps of paper wrappings, advertisements, and posters. She walked behind him, wondering whether they were going to the park to search among the crowds. He began to walk faster and faster. She had to skip and break into a run every so often in order to keep up. He led her to his mother's house.

"Wait here," he said. He tried to open the door and couldn't. He stepped back and kicked out hard until the lock gave and the door flew open. He went inside.

She tiptoed up to the window, where she could see the back of his mother's dress, moving away.

His mother ran to him with open arms. He stopped her in her tracks by shouting at her, "Where's the boy you're living with?"

"Boy?" she whimpered. "Oh, I'm taking care of a little orphan child. Didn't I write to you?"

"I haven't had a letter in four years," he said. "And I haven't had time to write one. I was busy saving your neck. Where's the kid?"

"He went out to play," she told him. "Sit down and have something to drink, my darling. How I've longed for this day."

He pushed her away, ready to look through the house room by room. He didn't have to go far. At the end of the hallway stood the boy, who had heard the voices and had come to see what was going on.

"Go back to your room, honey," the grandmother said. "We have to talk."

"Soldier," the boy said happily.

The moment he looked at the child he could see that he was the father. And he recognized even more clearly that the mother was the ruined girl he'd left behind.

"She's gotten her story in first, hasn't she?" his mother spat at him. "The liar. The bitch. My God, there she is outside. Here, sweetheart, there's the bad woman again. What do we say when we see her?"

The boy ran to the window. "Whore-whore-whore," he shouted.

"I'm your dad," he said. Did you know that? Daddy, that's me."

The boy turned around.

"Your father, who's been fighting in the war. And now I'm back. Would you like to come with me? Let's go for a walk."

The boy held out his hand to be led, but the soldier picked him up and sat him on his shoulder. The grandmother screamed. "It isn't true. That slut has had bastards by every man in this town."

He ducked to pass under the door frame and walked out into the street. As soon as the boy saw his mother, he began to chant "Whore-whore-whore" again.

She fell into step beside her lover. At the end of the street he set the boy down. "Listen to me, sonny," he said in a quiet little voice. "I'm your father and this is your mother and that's a dirty word you've been taught: whore. If I catch you saying that word again, I'll wash your mouth out with soap. Do you hear me?"

The boy looked down. His fear electrified the silence between the three of them, which continued for a long time; no one knew how to break it. At last she said, "If we can ever afford to waste soap that way."

He gave a snort of laughter. She turned her head against his shoulder, her face brushing his neck. "How I love you," she whispered. He kissed her, the first time in four years. The boy, guessing from which direction harm or help might come, nudged forward and pulled on her skirt, his hands pressed to her thighs through the fabric. Like the sudden flickering of a light in darkness, warmth sprang from the center of her body, flying up to her heart and outward—igniting every part of her with a feeling of life that had nothing to do with the past and made all of it powerless against her: as if no one except her lover and her child had ever touched her.

"Fertility," her friend commented, hearing her tell the story twenty years later.

"Love," she declared.

"Don't split hairs."

"Fertility doesn't know the difference between one love and the next."

"Maybe," said the friend, who was a doctor. "And maybe not. Fertility leads to motherhood. Motherhood can take people in different ways."

"Exactly. Love is different. And anyway, he wouldn't have believed my side of it if he hadn't loved me."

"Let's just say that there's a time for everything."

"Love doesn't have set times."

"I meant," the doctor explained, "that there's a time to be a mother and a time to be a grandmother. And they aren't always the same."

"Oh, her," she said. "I didn't mean her. I understand that." She took up her work again, washing dishes in a bowl and then rinsing them under the spigot.

She refilled the bowl with water and started on the next batch. After a while she said, "I've heard so many stories about those times. And a lot of people went through much worse than anything that happened to me. I know that. You can't imagine the things I've heard. So, in one way I just think: I can forget about this or that—those things weren't important. But what I can't understand—in fact, I still can't accept it—is why my own parents would have wanted to treat me that way. Strangers, maybe: but your family should stand by you."

"You were the last thing left in their world over which they had some control. As long as you behaved according to the rules they'd laid down, they felt secure. When you stopped being the girl they'd trained you to be, they couldn't recognize you as theirs."

"Um," she murmured.

The doctor went on, "I have a colleague who says everything that happens in the world is entirely impersonal and it's brought about by large astronomical upheavals. You know, there are times when the sun shoots up fiery gases like geysers—some of them are so high that they alter the weather here on earth: crops grow better, the woods produce more lumber and—a whole generation in advance—the ratio of male to female births changes dramatically so that soldiers, who are going to be killed in a war that hasn't yet begun, will be replaced by another generation of men. Do you see what I mean? Everything that's essential happens on a huge scale and over vast periods of time. It takes centuries before you can see that a general direction has been established or that something new is being worked out. But that's what really drives us: biology. Everything else is superficial."

She stood the last of the dishes in the rack, slung the wash rag over the rail, and dumped the dirty water out of the bowl and into the sink, where it gurgled away down the drain. "That," she said, "is spreading the blame too thin."

VETERANS

Some people forget; it can be a failing or a convenient knack, easily acquired. Others remember right to the end, without discriminating as to what they can recall. And there are those whose memory in later years is haunted by an early, careless wrongdoing—an indiscretion, folly, or even a crime.

Franklin Page remembered. He remembered that he hadn't stopped to think. Before he realized what he was doing, or could imagine what it might lead to, he had committed the act that was to change his life as well as that of someone else.

His was a good deed, not a misdeed. At the time of the incident he was fighting in a war. And when the moment came, he figured that he could probably make it into the field, pick up the wounded man, and get back out again. He never gave a thought to what might happen if he didn't succeed. He saw that it was possible and he started to move.

His introduction to military life had been similarly unconsidered. He hadn't waited to be drafted. He'd joined up, choosing armed combat as an alternative to suicide.

Whether he'd run away from home, or had been kicked out, was a point on which his family would never have agreed with him. He'd thought that they had made it clear: he wasn't doing any of the things they expected of him and they didn't want him around until he did. He could go somewhere else till he pulled himself together.

He went to the big city, where he fell in love with a pretty girl several steps above him, who had an ambition to be a ballerina. Her parents liked him, but since their daughter was so young—as he was himself—there was no question of formal approval or disapproval; he looked and sounded right, and wore recognizably good clothes. He appeared to be a boy from a stable background and therefore someone who could be trusted to take their daughter out to movies and meals and the kind of drinking that didn't get out of hand. It was understood from the beginning that the relationship wasn't to be regarded as serious because it wouldn't be subject to the rituals that applied in those days: he'd fallen in love at a time when people still got engaged. Her mother and father wouldn't have thought she'd be sleeping with him; sexual intercourse was reserved for a fiancé. They would have assumed the probability of kissing, cuddling, and even heavy petting, but—naturally—what he and the girl wanted was everything that went with love—the full, physical and sexual encounter without which they couldn't achieve the oneness they longed for.

The fact that his ardor and incompetence had combined to make the girl pregnant was something he didn't know until a series of telephone calls involved him and, eventually, her mother. The mother was the only other person the girl had told and she was also the first to be informed, which should have given him a clue about how matters would progress.

The girl was horrified. He'd kept telling her, she said, that everything was all right and now it wasn't any such thing. Hadn't she said to him that she wanted to be a great dancer? And even if she hadn't had any ambitions, who would want to have a child at the age of nineteen? And to go through nine months and everything afterwards—to undergo all that and then give up a baby for adoption and think she could go on happily with the rest of her life—no: she'd have to get an abortion. Of course she would. If she didn't, what was the rest of her life going to be like? She'd be tied hand and foot for the whole of her twenties. He didn't even have a job; he was doing dishwashing and that kind of thing to put himself through college on a scholarship. And he'd only just started. He didn't expect her parents to support them, did he? Because they couldn't. And what about the child? To grow up resented by a mother who never had time for you because she was busy trying to recapture her lost chances—that wouldn't be so wonderful. And ten or twelve years later, when it was the right time to have her family? For the child that was a mistake—to have to look on and see everybody else being showered with love: that would be torture.

She rattled off everything she had to say, without allowing him to get out a single word. Then she collapsed. She was nice; even on the verge of hysteria she wasn't going to remind him that his grandfather had drunk himself to death and his aunt had gone crazy. After a long pause she just said that this was good-bye. And she hung up.

He called back. He called back forty-three times. Every time, her mother answered; she was polite but unyielding, as was to be expected of the mother of an only child.

He talked about his love. He said that he'd do anything. He hadn't meant to hurt anybody—he'd have done anything rather than that. This just couldn't be good-bye, no matter what they all decided. He reasoned, he whined, he tried not to sound angry. He cried.

When he realized that everything was over, he went out and got drunk. And in the morning he joined up.

His wasn't a world war. It was one of the smaller wars, but just as deadly as any other. "Wars are like snakes," his commanding officer said to him. "Some of the little ones can be even worse than the monsters." It was certainly as bad as anything Franklin had ever imagined, despite all the comforts of modern warfare: danger money, paid leave, medical care, disability compensation, and the G.I. Bill if you came out in one piece.

In a modern battle you didn't often see enemy blood. What you encountered in the way of death and mutilation was mostly from your own side or among the civilian population who weren't supposed to be in the fight; the women and children. Women and children—and, of course, land—were what you were expected to fight for, not against. His war was up to date: air power was an important factor. But it was also like any other war in that after the aircraft had done their work, paratroopers and then the infantry had to go in on the ground. For some troops there was always going to be blood.

In Franklin's case, the most blood he ever saw at one time came out of another man in his outfit. Not even several years later was the birth of his second child—which he would be forced to watch because of a dream his wife had had—to generate so much blood. The soldier outbled anyone or anything Franklin had ever seen and a lot of it ended up over his own uniform because he'd gone to the rescue, while their friends—some of whom hadn't considered the man worth the trouble—covered him.

He was given a citation for bravery, but at the time he hadn't felt any sense of his own courage; he'd still thought it didn't matter if he died, but he was pretty sure that if either of them got hit, it would be the wounded soldier he was carrying over his back, like a protective blanket. There wouldn't have been any better way to get out of the field unless he'd dragged the man, which could have killed him. As it was, every step Franklin took exposed the wounded soldier to further danger. But to abandon him would have meant leaving him to die cruelly, when he might have been saved. Franklin didn't think of himself as heroic. Any other soldier would have done the same if the man to be rescued hadn't quarreled with a bunch of them over something. It was never really clear what that had been about: he suspected it had to do with food supplies or liquor and money, or maybe women.

Afterwards he was surprised at how good he felt. He'd saved somebody. He'd tried to do the right thing and it had worked. It was a shame that the man wasn't particularly worthwhile, but after living a long time with danger, you came to believe it was ridiculous to make those distinctions: everybody was the same. Nobody was worth more than anybody else.

He asked after the soldier and was told that he'd probably live. And that he'd be transported back to the States. Franklin forgot about him.

As soon as he'd served his time in the military, he felt free. He could start a new life. Because of what he'd been through, he knew how precious everything was that he used to hold in contempt or take for granted. He loved his country as he never had before, when it had al‐ ways seemed to belong to other people and to be a place that was never going to be his. In an odd way he was proud of himself. And now he had money in his hand and all the choices in the world. *Do right this time*, he thought.

No serious attempt was made to educate him and his friends back into civilian life. They were given help in other ways. Financially, he was going to be OK and that was pretty good in itself. That was what he needed. Maybe there were others who had different plans. Whoever they were, nobody told them, either: how to deal with the fear and the anger. They were given a few lectures, that was all. The rest was for them to figure out for themselves because it was private. They were warned that perhaps powerful emotions might become hard to con‐ trol, once there was no way of expressing them. They were cautioned against drinking to excess.

"Don't drink?" one of his buddies said. "What is this—Sunday school? Jesus."

But Franklin soon understood. After one or two binges out on the town with a couple of pals and a crowd of strangers, and after waking up from blackouts to find that he had no memory of the night before, there were times when he seemed to be reliving the worst parts of ac‐ tive duty and of the family hatreds that had preceded it. At those mo‐ ments, if he'd had a weapon on him, he would have used it.

He gave up liquor. He gave up smoking. Not smoking was the worst. With the help of the government he went to college. He threw himself into learning.

He studied history; he didn't know exactly why—he had no plans to use what he was being taught. But he felt that everything he read and heard was helping to explain to him what the world was like and how it got that way, and why. He read, hour after hour, and he worked at jobs on the side. He was saving money but still having fun. He didn't know why he was doing the saving; it seemed to be a compulsion, like a squirrel's instinct to bury acorns.

After a time he felt confident enough to start drinking beer again.

When four years had passed, he finally relaxed about everything. He was ready to become reintegrated into civilian life. He went back to see the relatives he'd quarreled with. He made peace with them, but he didn't want to hang around afterwards. While he'd been away they'd shifted their dissatisfaction and malevolence to other members of the family. They were as pleased to see him as if they'd always loved him. But if he stayed, the burden of misery would come back on him, he knew that. It would ruin his life again because he was always going to be fool enough to let them abuse him until he couldn't stand it any longer, and then he'd have to get out again. They talked about how he could take his rightful place now. That meant the will, the land, and so on. That would be something to think about, he told everybody; but it might be a better idea for him—while he was still young—to go back and seek his fortune like the boys in the fairy tales: they always ended up running the kingdom, didn't they?

They clung to him. They told him that it was his duty to stay. His duty to them. He reminded them that they'd thrown him out of the house. Oh, that—that was such a long time ago, they said. And he knew then that he was really well and free because he didn't tell them what it had done to him to be treated like that, nor did he say that he understood now what they were like: like a tribe of cannibals, eating their own children, selling their own people and enslaved by their love of power. He just said that it had been good to see them and he'd send a postcard. And he left.

At about the same time, he lost touch with the other men who had been his friends when he was overseas. He'd kept up with them for a while, but now he wanted to move on to new interests; and to different people, too. He wanted to see them again some day, just not too soon. In several years, maybe.

He switched from place to place, trying out jobs, and always managing to make a modest success as well as to have a good time. He'd stay in a place, start up a business—hardware or dry goods—and turn over a profit, sell up, and move on. He didn't mean to settle down anywhere. That wasn't going to happen for a long time.

He was driving across state, heading nowhere in particular other than from one town to the next, when he came over the brown of a hill in the late afternoon. The light was beginning to sleep in the air. The temperature had started to ease off and a breeze sprang up. It brought him a wave of thick, green fragrance from the alfalfa fields he was passing. And all at once he thought that it had been a beautiful day and that in spite of his intention to do a lot more traveling, this was such a pretty place that he might stop for a while and get to know it.

He didn't realize that at last he was cured and that the restlessness he'd suffered from in the past few years had been part of a healing process.

He left his car next to a pickup truck in a small parking lot off the old main street, stretches of which looked almost the same as they must have been in the last century. There was a dusty but elegant livery stable, a bank like a Roman temple, a drugstore with a tessellated floor. There was also a gas station, a newspaper office, and a grand old wooden building twice the size of a steamship; it contained offices for doctors, a dentist, agricultural consultants, feed merchants, a lawyer, the water board and—downstairs—a beauty parlor, a barbershop, and a fancy dress shop with a milliner's adjoining it.

The first place he entered was the drugstore where, seated up at the counter, he saw the girl he knew he wanted to spend everything on—all the money he'd saved, the time he'd accumulated, the love he'd never been able to give away. Her name was Irene and she was in her last year at high school. Her parents wanted her to go to college like her brothers and sister, but luckily she was more excited by the idea of getting married and having kids. It wasn't that she was unintelligent or anything like that. She was smart enough to have gone through college without any trouble. In all the summer jobs she'd had, she'd been the first to be praised and given promotion. She just wanted the real things instead of studying. And she'd always known that. Even when she was a child, she said to him, she always knew what she wanted.

He told her that finding her was a miracle. Their life together was going to be like the dream he'd had a long time ago: of all the traditional, old-fashioned things that go with a married life, including the part about how they live happily ever after.

He was ready to put down roots that would anchor a solid family life for at least five generations. He was feeling strong enough to last that long himself.

She wanted children as much as he did; she understood procreation to be a sign of success. Everything was decided between them with such speed that many members of her family didn't have time to get to the wedding. Irene didn't care. "We can have all the parties later," she said.

No one had told her how painful childbirth would be nor how exhausting the chores of motherhood could become. Repeated achievement diminished her urge to complain. Instead, she simply demanded extra help.

His idea was that someone else should take care of the children, since they were what had caused all the changes. She said no: she'd look after the kids and he could hire somebody to cook, clean, wash, iron, and vacuum. She wasn't going to become a bad mother just because he couldn't boil water without some woman standing at his elbow, telling him how. The kids were the most important part of the family. If it weren't for them, she'd probably let Raymond Saddler have her great-great-grandfather's land without putting up a fight.

"What land?" he asked.

"Oh, it's such a long story. It started with Aunt Posie—my great-aunt Posie."

That was how—when they'd already been married for over two years and she was expecting her third child—Irene let him know that if she had had her rights, she'd have an inheritance to pass on to their children. A long-dead ancestress named Aunt Posie had been cheated out of her family share by her own brother and by the time her descendants could prove that it should have gone to her, everything had landed up with some cousins named Saddler, who weren't about to give anything back to anybody, not till Hell froze over and probably not even then.

The now distant quarrel in his own family was replaced by the dispute with her cousins. There always had to be something that wasn't right. You couldn't escape from it. The last time he'd tried to get out of a family mess, it wasn't long before he'd ended up in a war.

The man in the bed opened his eyes and couldn't figure out where he was. No sound came to him. The quiet was as deep as if time had stopped. He could see the color of the sky, which seemed to indicate a kind of twilight. It might have been late afternoon or early morning: it was hard to tell. He couldn't be sure of anything. He thought that he might have lost his mind.

"Lost your mind?" his father used to shout at him. "Well, go back and get it." His father had spent a lot of time yelling at him, but he'd also taught him things: how to hunt, how to shoot, and how to kill animals. When the military trained him to kill people, nobody had had to shout at him. The principle was the same and he was already an expert.

He closed his eyes and he disappeared.

Sometime later he was awake, looking at a window and still not knowing what time it was or even what city he was in. Or which country.

Doctors and nurses came to his bed. They stuck needles and thermometers into him. They held his wrist and put the stethoscope on him, took measurements and wrote down the numbers in notebooks or on papers held in a clipboard. Apparently they planned to do something with him. He was washed but not fed. They never gave him anything to eat, yet he wasn't hungry. How could that be?

They'd stuck pins and little tubes all over him. He lay there in the bed like a large devil-doll. The thought came to him that he wasn't the real one: he was standing in for the original, whose name was . . .

He began to feel frightened. A nurse came to the side of his bed.

"Take it easy, hon," she said. "What can I get you?"

Out in the hallway a conversation stopped. Then, a woman's voice said "Hey, he's talking."

"What name are you writing down there?" he asked.

"Your name is Oliver Sherman."

It sounded slightly familiar but not right.

"Are you sure?"

"Sure. It says right here." She gestured toward the information board at the foot of the bed.

When she'd gone, he thought that he'd crawl down to the end of the bed and take a look for himself. But as soon as it dawned on him that he'd have to start untaping all the little plastic pipes they'd put on him, he realized that he was too tired to make it. He went to sleep again instead.

His name wasn't Oliver Sherman. It turned out that—in a combined effort of military and hospital bureaucracies—most of the information about him had been reversed, including his name, which was really Sherman Oliver. But for quite a while he thought of himself the other way around. And sometimes he'd imagine himself with the name Sherman Oaks because that sounded like something he'd heard before, maybe a kind of tree.

He began to think that he'd died and gone to a place where you lived on until they decided to move you to some other form of afterlife: from medical to legal, scientific, chemical, horticultural. One day he thought: *That's it, we're going to be put into pots and grown into something else. That's why they're studying us.*

When they moved a man named Beech into the ward, the idea of trees and gardens became additionally confused. He told Beech, "I think we're all going to be grown in pots, so we can be planted."

Beech said, "That's for sure. That's what's waiting for every one of us. They plant us six feet deep and we don't send up no flowers. We just stay put."

At night the war came back: he went through everything again. And then, after a few months, it left him. He couldn't remember at all for a while. When it began again, the recollections played themselves out in all kinds of different ways. In one version he rescued Franklin instead of the other way around; in the next, a woman called him into the field to help her and then made love to him while the gunfire started up all around them; and in another, his father came into the firing zone to save him and he refused to be moved—he told him to go away and, as he did, his father lifted up his head and was caught by a stray shot. He remembered crawling out to safety by himself, laboriously. And also staying there, burrowing down into the ground.

He would never have believed that he was making these things up. And to have a doctor hint that he might be engineering false memories for himself was infuriating. In fact, when a clean-cut numbskull in a white coat suggested as much, he leaned forward and simply told the man: "Say that again and I'll kill you." Then he asked, "What are you here for, anyway?" And he followed the question with a string of obscenities that wouldn't have upset a child—not even a maiden aunt. But the doctor stopped writing notes and Sherman knew that that was because after his outburst, they only needed one word on the paper: *violent.*

What wasn't violent? Men, women, water, fire, earth; all the seasons of the year, even the ones that seemed the sweetest. Anything that had movement had the potential. Whatever was living was bound into the pattern. It was like what the Bible said: there was a time for everything. When the time for violence came around, violence was what you did.

The doctors and nurses were supposed to be making him well. But what was the point? They were the ones who had the say. He didn't want to survive unless he could come back as the one in charge. For the rest of his life he wanted to feel the way he felt when he was squeezing the trigger.

Nothing else was like it: the perfect moment when you hit the target. At first it was tin cans, then groundhogs, which they called whistling pigs; and in the hunting season, deer, wild turkey, grouse. He'd thought that when he went into the service, life would be like that. Sometimes it was, but mostly you didn't see much. You aimed at a place, not a person. Now he had nothing to aim for, not even a place.

Most of the time, when he was thinking the right way around, memory was like the tide coming back into a stretch of mud flats: stirring everything up again, raising the decaying, rotting material from its bed to where it could flow freely, flooding through every new, clean, and cherished place and making it, too, begin to rot.

When he wasn't thinking the right way around, it was worse. Sometimes he thought that they'd fixed him up the way he should be, but they'd put him back into the wrong person. And he wanted to get out.

He lost a couple of years. It was surprising how fast it could happen; you close your eyes, you blink, and there you are: in another place and it's later. It's later than you think. Who used to say that? Someone he knew once—maybe somebody in his family.

He hung around the bars. One day he drank himself into such a state that the next day the only thing in his head was: *Why am I here? Why do I have to go on with this, year after year? It's going to take so long to get to the end. If somebody could show me where the exit door is, I'd go through it right now.*

Later in the day he recalled the reason why he was there: because some guy had saved his life—Frank somebody. What was his name? And what was he doing now? Where did he live?

He began to ask around. It took him a long time until he got all the information assembled, knew where to go, and bought himself a bus ticket. Before buying the ticket, he took a coin out of his pocket and flipped it into the air for a decision, catching it and slapping it down against the back of his left hand.

When he got off the bus, there was no way to go on to where Franklin lived unless you hired a car. He took out the coin again and spun it high into the air.

He walked. After a couple of hours a farmer stopped to offer him a ride.

They drove up into high land, over a mountain and down, into rich bottom land, across a couple of hills and down again.

The farmer let him off by a big oak tree where the road forked.

He felt good as he walked the rest of the way. He kept thinking: *This is fine-looking country. I wouldn't mind living here.*

He arrived in the late afternoon, not long after Franklin had come home from work.

He went around to the back and pushed the button next to the screen door.

Franklin was standing inside, only a few feet away, and looking out through the screen. He didn't recognize the man on the other side, although he knew that it must be a stranger standing there, otherwise the man would have called out: it was easy to see that the family was at home.

Franklin stepped up to the screen and said, "Hi."

"Hi," Sherman answered.

"Are you looking for me?"

"If your name's Franklin Page. I recognize you, too. I'm Sherman Oliver."

"Oh?"

"The man you rescued. You know. In Korea."

"Jesus," Franklin said. He opened the door.

"I wasn't sure you'd want to see somebody from the past."

"Come on in."

"So I tossed a coin."

"Come on, you'll let the flies in."

Sherman stepped through the doorway and into a space where coats hung from hooks and rubber boots stood in pairs on the linoleum floor. Straight ahead was the kitchen. "So," he mumbled, "just thought I'd look you up."

When two of the children raced into the kitchen, followed by Irene, Sherman stood completely rigid. He'd pictured Franklin living alone, not having moved on to another life or other people. He'd thought of him as being a kind of mirror-image of himself. The first sight of him, through the meshes of the screen and standing in the same attitude as himself, had seemed to correspond to that idea. Now everything was changed.

Franklin made the introductions. He showed Sherman to a bathroom where he told him he could freshen up if he wanted to, and then took him back to the kitchen and sat him down at the table. All the time Franklin was talking, the children kept running everywhere.

"Can we off you a beer, Mr. Oliver?" Irene asked.

"Oh, sure. Maybe just one."

"Make it Sherman, honey," Franklin said. "Sherman and Irene."

One of the children started to wail and grabbed at Irene's legs. She put a beer down on the table and said, "There you are, Sherman."

He thanked her, without looking up. He still couldn't believe that she was there. This wasn't Franklin's house and Franklin's life: it was hers. And here she had all these children and she looked just like a girl—like a high-school sweetheart.

She poured out another glass and handed it to Franklin. "Aren't you having one?" he asked.

"I'll wait till later. Sukie's coming over to get her tomatoes and I've got to feed the kids. Why don't you take Sherman into the living room, where you can hear yourselves think? Pixie, honey, you put that back, now. That isn't good for you."

Franklin stood up and motioned Sherman to follow. They moved to the living room, where Sherman's speech was so slow and stumbling that Franklin—remembering how the last time he'd seen him, Sherman had had part of his head blown in—felt obliged to talk and talk. And he asked Sherman to stay over for "a couple of days," to rest up.

Irene didn't seem to mind. Sherman didn't really look like the kind of person she was used to associating with, but she knew how long it could take before a man was able to digest the kind of experience he was likely to meet with under fire. He looked like an old-time prospector: the beat-up hat, the old boots, the beard that wasn't an intentional, trimmed affair but rather a few weeks' growth that would be shaved off when the thought occurred to him, and then grown again when he forgot about taking care with his appearance. She knew that he'd been wounded and—even before Franklin explained it to her—she knew who Sherman was. She also knew almost immediately what he was like. But she made him welcome for Franklin's sake. After feeding the children, putting them to bed, and serving a meal for the three of them, she joined the conversation. "So," she asked. "How did you get here?"

"Walked," Sherman said.

"Walked? But it's miles."

"Well, I lost my license awhile back. Took the bus to . . . um . . . other side of the mountain, there."

"You must be tired."

"Not specially. I used to walk a lot. Been through all the national parks. That's wild country. I liked that."

"I'd have liked to do that, too," Franklin said. "Maybe later, sometime. We could go camping with the kids. When they're a little older." He smiled at Irene, who said, "You think I can cook and do the laundry for six people out in the Rockies someplace? Oh, that reminds me. Sherman, if you let me have your denim jacket, I can put it into the wash and hang it out on the line with Frank's dungarees."

Sherman nodded, his glance sliding away. "Sure. Thanks," he muttered.

Later that night Franklin took him out for another drink. He'd sized Sherman up as a man who was no good at mixing with other people so, instead of dropping in at one of the places where he might be caught up in talk with acquaintances, he chose a bar he didn't know well.

Without Irene to help, he found it hard to make Sherman loosen up. The man tended to exude a morose withdrawal from the world until the time when a sarcasm or criticism would come out of him. Franklin reported on the general direction his life had taken since the war; then he got down to the details. The catalogue of events went on and on: talking too much was the form his discomfiture had taken. At last he said, "Well, you know about me. I guess just meeting Irene and the kids tells you everything. I had to work like hell to begin with: I went back to school, got through college. I met her after that. She was still in high school, but I knew right away, the first time I saw her, she was the girl I was going to marry."

"I guess you've got it made," Sherman said. "A wife and kids like we used to talk about. Like we used to dream about."

"No, we didn't. We used to sit around and have bull sessions about how we were going to come back and mount a surprise attack on the White House and hold the president ransom for millions. And Captain Pauling was going to call on his cousins' connections and get all the money into Swiss bank accounts for us."

Sherman jerked back his head and laughed with the first sign of genuine enjoyment he'd shown since his arrival. "I remember now," he said. "You're right. That's what we were going to do."

Franklin laughed too, but he was thinking: *This ruined man—did I save him for this? Is he going to be in this condition for the rest of his life?*

What tied them together, Franklin thought—the original act—had been a matter of luck. Circumstances pulled a bold action out of his frightened soul and that had made him strong and lessened his fear of being ultimately unworthy. From then on he had something in reserve that could balance everything to come. Forever afterwards he could point to that moment, telling himself: *That's the kind of man I am.* He no longer worried about making mistakes because they stopped being so important.

But who could tell what the same deed had done to Sherman? He might feel that he was under an obligation. And he might not like that.

"And your wife is named Irene, just like the song: 'Good night, Irene. Good night, Irene. I'll see you in my dreams.'"

"Don't start. It took me five years to get that tune out of my head."

Anything took about five years, he thought—a bereavement, a serious illness, a broken marriage, or love betrayed: anything bad took about five years to come to terms with. That didn't mean you could forgot it, but you could manage.

The next day Franklin showed Sherman around town and told him everybody's life story.

In the afternoon Irene set up the ironing board near the kitchen table where the two men were sitting. When she brought the clothes in off the line, Franklin went to hold the door for her. As she passed him, she whispered, "How long is he staying, honey? I've been trying to talk to him, but it's tough going."

"Not long," he answered. "Take it easy."

The baby was asleep and the other children were out in the yard, where they could be seen and heard.

She sprinkled water over a shirt and started ironing.

Franklin and Sherman began to talk about men who went down into volcanoes to study them and how that was a job neither one of them would envy anybody.

"If you had to, that's different," Franklin said. "But out of choice—no."

"You could do it, sugar," Irene said. "He's so brave, when I had a dream about being in the hospital—"

Franklin groaned. Sherman asked, "What?"

She said, "I had a dream that I was in the hospital, having the baby, and that they wouldn't let Frank in to see me. He was on the other side of the door, calling to me and they wouldn't . . . it was really horrible. In the dream I lost the baby and then I died because he couldn't get to me. So, when the time came—"

"She insisted. She was so sure everything was going to go wrong unless I was there that I thought if I didn't agree, everything probably would happen the way she'd seen it. She was so nervous."

"I don't like dreams," Sherman said.

Irene folded a T-shirt, took up another, and asked, "Why on earth not?"

"They make me feel bad."

"Well, sure. I guess nobody likes having nightmares. Portia's starting to get them. We just have to keep telling her that they're only dreams: they don't mean anything."

"If they don't mean anything, that dream you had about being in the hospital—it would have been the same: only a dream."

"No. That came at a special time. It was like a sign. An omen. If I'd disregarded it, that would have meant . . . well, I don't like to think about that. Children's nightmares are different. They dream about dying, but it's mixed up with growing. They dream that something's chasing them and they can't get away—they can't move fast enough. They're running away from a fire or a big wave from the ocean, or maybe a truck is coming right at them and there's no place to go because they're backed up against a wall. They also have nice dreams about being able to do magical things: being able to fly, and that kind of thing. It's the beginnings of, um, physical feelings. You know. A lot of dreaming is like that. If you need to get up and go to the bathroom, you have a fear dream about being late for something. Or, if you aren't lying in a comfortable position, there's some kind of frustration in the dream's story. Dreams aren't all what those psycho people tell you: all about some sick feeling you've got against your mother. I read this article at the doctor's and it said the brain spends the night sort of putting information into its filing cabinets and getting some of the old stuff out to look at it."

"But some of those drawers," Franklin said, "are labeled s-e-x."

"Well, you know about sex. You had to watch it in the raw, didn't you?"

"I have to admit, it sobers you up. These are some things you don't take for granted anymore."

"Like what?" Sherman asked.

"Like what happens to women. Like what they can go through when some man has said good-bye and shut the door and he thinks that's the end of it."

"Get in, go off, get out, roll over, and go to sleep," Irene said.

Franklin turned his head.

"That's what one of my friends told me," she explained. "We were pretty surprised, too. We always thought her husband was such a nice guy. I guess she could have been describing somebody else, but that would have been even more surprising."

"Well, whichever way you cut it, that isn't me."

"It's plenty of others. So I'm told." She picked up a pair of striped shorts and put them on top of the pile.

"In your dream . . ." Sherman said. "You really died?"

"I was dying and I knew that I was, and that if he couldn't get to me, I would. Not exactly the same, but bad enough."

"They say when you dream you're falling, if you hit the ground in your dream, you die: you die for real, not just in the dream."

"You don't die," Franklin said. "That's just an old wives' tale."

"How do you know?"

"How does anybody know? If you died, who would know that you'd been dreaming? I know because it happened to me. I was up on a skyscraper, walking over the construction girders. Somebody was chasing me."

"And you fell off and hit the ground?"

"You bet."

"What was it like?"

"Right before I was going to hit the ground, I had an orgasm that just about knocked me out of bed and I woke up."

Irene said, "I think this conversation has gone far enough."

"So you didn't hit the ground?"

"I think that's what they mean by dying."

"OK, boys," Irene said to Franklin. "Break it up."

"Yes, sir, Officer O'Brian."

"Who's O'Brian?" Sherman asked.

"The college cop, where I did my studying. We never used his name. We'd just call him 'Break it up, boys,' because that's what he was always saying. He was a nice old guy. In the springtime a lot of the kids used to get drunk and go around in a mob: picking up the back end of cars, and that kind of thing."

"Not very funny for the people in the cars," Irene said.

"Oh, nobody ever got hurt. Nobody even had any paint scratched except just that one time when the guy lost his nerve and gunned the thing, so when they let the wheels down again, he roared ahead at top speed."

Sherman laughed.

Irene sniffed. "Childish," she said.

In the evening the two men went out together again and had a couple of drinks. This time Sherman did the talking.

He was full of bizarre anecdotes and unlikely pieces of information. His favorite reading, he said, had always been "Ripley's Believe It or Not." They couldn't stand or sit or drink in silence for more than a few minutes without Sherman saying, "Did you know that . . . ?" or "I read someplace . . ." or, more often, "A guy I met once told me . . ." Naturally, any such meeting would have taken place in another bar.

As the flow of Sherman's knowledge became a torrent, Franklin understood that he was supposed to admire and not interrupt too often. But it was no good letting his attention wander at any stage because occasionally Sherman would stop in the middle of a narrative and lose track of where he was. Then he'd ask to be prompted.

"A lot of people," he said, "are just here for the ride. You know? Up and down, back and forth. They do a little shopping, they go out for meals, they put on brand-new clothes once a week. What I got to say to those people is: just quit it. If you're only here for the ride, get off the escalator. What you got to do is appreciate the nature of things. See, what's in our minds is dead. In our minds we hold the past and the future: one gone and the other—maybe it's never going to be anything. The present is where we live. It's like a thin line between the dead and the unborn and it doesn't belong to either of them till it happens or it's passed away. Then it can join everything that's dead. I used to think a lot about stuff like that when I was in the veterans' hospital."

"Well, I don't know. I guess I think ideas and philosophy ought to make things clearer, not just get you feeling more mixed up."

"I'm not mixed up. I got it all figured out. Listen. This is what the world is like. Did I tell you about the Canadian fur trappers and the Arctic fox? Some guy I met told me. These foxes are very, very valuable. They're the white ones. But you need a lot of them to make a coat. They've got to be the right size and you have to get yourself several completely pure pelts, unmarked. So what do those trappers do? They don't go out gunning for the things—that way they'd shoot the skins full of holes. No. What they do is: they put a little bit of fresh meat on the tip of a knife and then they bury the knife point up in the snow. The fox smells it from a long ways off and he comes running. He gets to the meat, he licks it, he licks it some more, and he cuts his tongue on the blade. But it's winter and he's half starving, so he keeps going, in spite of the pain. He's tasting all that wonderful, fresh blood and he don't realize that it's his own. That's how they catch them. Not a mark on them; the fox just bleeds to death. It's so simple. And cheap. No cash spent on bullets. You can use the knife again. And you don't have to risk anything—you don't even have to get cold till it's time to go out and collect the corpses."

"Horrible."

"Oh, no. That's what we're like. That's the ingenuity of man."

"They can't still be allowed to do that."

"I guess it's probably outlawed by now but it was a traditional method, specially for a poor man who couldn't afford to waste ammunition. It's so easy and so smart. So, I bet it still goes on. It's a practical method of doing that voodoo thing."

"What's that?"

"You think bad luck onto somebody. If you do anything with real belief, it works."

"Hunting foxes?"

"Killing people without touching them. That kind of thing."

"That's too much. That's like what Irene says her aunt was always telling her: that a cake baked with love tastes better than an ordinary one."

"Well . . ."

"Well, it won't help you if you forget the flour, or the butter or the eggs or anything else that's supposed to go into the mixture. Love isn't one of the necessary ingredients for a cake."

"But I read someplace that all these magnetic and electrical impulses can come out of people depending on how they feel and what mood they're in. They can give off something like a vapor or, ah, something chemical that sort of changes the atmosphere."

"Maybe. But I doubt it."

"Well, I never been to college, like you."

"Oh, you're smart enough, when you want to be."

"Animal cunning, that's what I've got."

Franklin laughed. Every once in a while he found himself enjoying Sherman's company. He'd feel that it was a relief to get out and be in new surroundings, and to escape from the noise of the kids."

"How about another?" Sherman said.

They went on to talk about mountain climbing in different parts of the world and then discussed climate in general and geographical oddities in particular. Sherman liked to describe the places he'd seen since military service and the people he'd met. He enjoyed imparting information on all sorts of subjects.

He'd recently heard some facts about the curative powers of sunlight. Putting a glass of bad water up on the roof of a house would kill the bacteria in it; if you kept the same water down in the cellar, those bacteria stayed alive. But he'd also heard about sunshine causing cancer. He thought it was interesting that the purifying agent was also the one that could kill.

Sooner or later, Franklin thought, they were going to get around to the war. He could feel an unexpressed urgency emanating from every part of Sherman. That was probably why the man had shown up: he wanted to talk.

When Sherman raised his glass and said, "The good old days," Franklin thought: *Here we go*. But it didn't happen. Instead of reminiscing, Sherman said, "Only one thing I recall that was good about wartime: the women treat you better."

"If that's the way you like it."

"Well, you liked it, too, didn't you?"

"Sure. It was worth what we paid for it."

"And how much are you paying for all this?"

"What I've got now is the real thing. It's free. The best things in life, you know. Like the song."

"She made an honest man of you—is that what happened?"

"What happened was: I woke up. I just suddenly saw how every-thing was. I realized that if I was willing to work for it, I could get anything I wanted. But if I didn't get up and do something about it, nothing was going to happen, ever. I'd just live and die like a stone somebody threw into a field."

"Like a lonely flower by the wayside, as Roscoe used to say. Re-member?"

"Sure."

Sherman had arrived just before the weekend. Beginning on Monday, the help started coming in: a cleaning woman called Addie, and friends who took the kids away to play and who—on another day—would drive up to load their own kids onto Irene. A Mrs. Hescott did the serious cooking when there was a party. She'd be assisted by a couple of teenagers who served as waitresses and washed up. Otherwise Addie did most of the housework and fixed lunch on the days when she was there, three times a week. Irene managed the kids. Even with help, for as long as the children were in the house, the noise never seemed to let up; at night they'd cry out in their sleep, causing Irene to excuse herself from the conversation or even to break off what she was saying: she'd move into the hall and partway up the stairs, listening.

Sherman liked some things about the kids. He liked the way they looked, like large toys; and the goofy way they had of talking, which reminded him of the hospital patient named Beech, whose first name he'd never discovered and who hadn't minded when Sherman took to calling him "Nutty." But the constant noise got on his nerves so badly that once or twice he'd really wanted to pick them up and smash them to pieces, especially their heads: all the little screaming heads and faces.

As for Irene, sometimes he thought she was going to come right out and say that he might be moving on. But she never quite broke. She was nice and polite; she was the one in control. And there were times when he was just about ready to hit her across the face, or rip her clothes off, or yell names at her: to see her eyes change. To see her really look back at him, looking into his eyes. He was sure she knew—she had to know what he was thinking, and she was pretending not to. But it was hard to tell about wives. Sometimes when they got that dumb look, they were just thinking about how long to cook the pot roast.

He listened to her breathing at night, asleep. He heard her get up in the dark and go to the children. Her heard her with Franklin, making love.

He got to know their routine: when she'd be surrounded by other young mothers and their children, or when she had time on her own because the kids were with a play group; when she was expecting the grocery delivery, the milk, the mail. In about a month things would be different because the oldest child, Portia, was going to be out of kindergarten and starting the first grade.

He took all of them out to a family restaurant. Everybody had fun and he didn't have to make any effort. The waitresses were laughing and flirting and being nice to the whole group. Everyone was busy keeping the children from acting up. They were seated at a big, round table like a circle. And Sherman at one stage in the evening thought: *The family circle.*

The day after that, they were in the living room when the child named Hagen said, "Do your play, Mama." Irene struck a pose: one hand on heart, the other up in the air as she declaimed, "This by Calpurnia's dream is signified."

"What play?" Sherman asked.

Franklin told him: their daughter, Portia, had been named in honor of a production of *Julius Caesar*, given by Irene's school class when she was fourteen. Portia was the name of a woman character in the play, but Irene herself, owing to the scarcity of boys who could remember the lines, had played a Roman senator called Decius.

They moved to the kitchen, where Irene sat the children down for their supper. The men leaned against the counters, shifting from place to place as she picked up pots and pans and dishes.

"So you could have been a star?" Sherman said.

"Oh, not in the movies. It was the stage. We had such a good drama teacher: Miss Moody. It was really exciting. I think it was the best thing we ever did at school even though we didn't put on the whole play, just part of it. That's the way I remember it, anyway. God, my memory."

"Five cents," Hagen said.

"Yes, honey, thank you. I meant to say, 'Gosh.' No, we'll get the cuss box later. No, Pixie. Now's the time for eating."

"I'll treat you," Franklin said. He reached behind a salt carton, lifted a glass jar, unscrewed the lid, threw a coin in, twisted the lid again, and put the jar back.

Irene blew him a kiss. She wiped Pixie's mouth and picked a piece of potato off the floor. "We had a good cast," she said. "Our Julius Caesar . . . who was it? Who played Caesar? My goodness, I must be losing my mind. Was it Heddy? I think it might have been. But she was in the Greek play we did when we were nine. Anne was the brother, or maybe the brother's friend, and Heddy was the heroine. Or was she? This is awful—it wasn't so long ago. And there isn't anybody I can ask. So many people move away, that's the trouble. I see their parents sometimes. It really is annoying: I used to be able to tell the years apart by thinking about our school grade. Then it was jobs and vacations. And now it's how old the kids are. Honestly, I can't even remember what I did yesterday."

"But you can remember what you ate can't you?" Franklin said. "She can always remember the menu."

"Gee, yes. That was great last night."

Gee, Sherman thought.

Franklin said, "It sure was, but I meant in general. Just as a way of marking the time."

"It's too early to be senility," she went on. "I know what it is: what you see here is a veteran of peace." She laughed wildly and then said, "When I was fourteen, I never missed a word in that part. I could have played any of the other parts, too."

"She could have been the main character."

"I was supposed to tell Caesar's wife that the warning dream she'd had was nothing to worry about. I was one of the conspirators and we all wanted Caesar to go to work that morning so we could stab him—all of us: big assassination scene. We had special plastic daggers loaded with fake blood. When you hit somebody with them, the blade telescoped back into the handle and all this thick, red liquid came pouring out—so realistic. People gasped. During the performance some of the parents in the audience were almost screaming. The dress rehearsal was even better, but we got carried away: we all just kept stabbing and stabbing—it was so much fun. Definitely the highlight of the production. Caesar finally had to say, 'Cut it out. I'm dead enough.'"

"Like a fox in the hen coop," Franklin said.

"Oh, you know that's something. I heard on the radio: they don't do that out of viciousness. A fox is made to strike a flock of birds in the open, while they're getting ready to take off into the air. So, his biology makes him hit as many as he can, just to make sure he gets at least one. He keeps on going until the birds have flown away. But if they're cooped up and can't escape, in that case he kills all of them, even though he can't take away more than a couple. See, it isn't his fault. It's his nature. In a way, you could say it's the farmer who's to blame for putting the chickens into those unnatural surroundings."

"It isn't the fox's fault," Hagen said.

"Yes, sugar. That's what I said. Animals don't have a sense of morals. They only have instincts. Eat up your peas, precious."

"I hate peas."

"Not hate. Dislike intensely."

"Do I have to?"

"You may not like them, but they like you. They're just dying to get into that little tummy to do you some good. Come on, now,"

"Why do I have to?"

"They're so good for you. You want me to spoonfeed you like a baby? OK, open up. And it's down the little red lane they go."

Hagen chewed and then renewed his complaints. "Look," he said. "I ate all the rest of them and everything else, too. Why do I have to finish these?"

She reached over and began to squeeze and tickle him, chanting,

"Why, oh why, oh why, can't I look in my ear with my eye? I'm sure I could do it, if I put my mind to it: you never can tell till you try."

Hagen started to laugh.

Sherman dropped his eyes and stared at the edge of the table. He'd been despising her and now suddenly he knew that he wasn't good enough for her. He also realized that all the child's complaints and her persuasion were part of a game. The boy was now eating whatever food had been left on the plate and he was having a good time. It was the seduction. This was how you learned to do it. This was how far back it had to go, otherwise whenever people disagreed with you, you just did what had been done to you: knocked them across the room.

During the day he went for long walks in order to get out of Irene's way. The cleaning woman, Addie, didn't like him; that was another reason why he couldn't hang around the house. If he'd come at a different time of year, he'd have offered to chop wood or undertake some similar task to show that he was trying to help out and not just freeload. But now he wasn't able to do much of anything except invite Franklin out at night and pay for the drinks. He did that. He was doing it every night.

The summer was almost at an end, which meant that the season of vacation and parties was over, but there were a few dates coming up when Franklin and Irene had issued invitations or were invited out themselves. Big parties were easy; they could ask Sherman along. If they had to go out to anything with a few friends or to have one or two couples in for a sit-down meal, Irene would offer Sherman the choice of meeting some new people and he could say that he thought he'd go see a movie that night.

The one successful celebration at which he was included was their barbecue in the backyard. Even then, Irene said to Franklin afterwards, "Mrs. Anderson asked him, 'And what do you do, Mr. Oliver?' and he said, 'Oh, nothing much. I'm just a vet.' And then she said, 'Oh, maybe you can tell me what I should do for my dachshund, Bismarck. He's having back troubles again and Dr. Dalmers is out of town.' God, I didn't listen to the rest of it. I thought: he got himself into it, he can get himself out. And anyway, she's right. It's years ago now: it's time he moved on to something else. He wasn't even very badly wounded, was he?"

"Head wounds are always bad," Franklin said.

One morning after Franklin had left for work, Sherman lit up a cigarette. From the next room, where she'd moved with a stack of plates, Irene said, "I'd prefer it if you didn't smoke, Sherman. We don't smoke in this house."

"Yeah," he said. "No shit."

"That's a quarter," Hagen said. "A whole quarter."

Portia brought a large glass jar to him. Inside there were a few pennies, nickels, and dimes. He recognized it from the time when Franklin had paid for Irene saying "God."

"What's this?" he asked. "Is this for me?"

"It's the cuss box."

"Well, I never seen one of them before."

Both children refused to smile back. The one called Portia unscrewed the lid and held the jar out to him.

He put his hand into his pocket, found a quarter, and dropped it into the jar. "What are you going to do with all that money?"

Portia said, "We take it to church."

"It's for the children in foreign countries," Hagen added.

Portia breathed in and began to sing: "Remember all God's children, in far-off distant lands." Irene joined in from the next room.

Hagen was too embarrassed to sing in front of a stranger. Sherman said to him, "I guess it might be a good thing for those foreign kids if I did a lot more cussing."

Irene came back into the kitchen. She said, "No thank you, Sherman. We can do without that." Her voice was noncommittal, but she had a set expression on her face. The kids understood straight away. So did Sherman. He cleared his throat and looked around, trying to think of

VETERANS   169

something to say. At last he mumbled, "Well, I sure am impressed at what a good boy old Franklin is. There's hardly any money in there."

"It's like Portia said," Irene told him. "We usually put everything into the collection plate on Sundays."

"Gee," Sherman said.

The morning after that, he lost his hold on a coffee cup. As it fell, it broke. He whispered, "Fuck." Irene heard. She said, "Mr. Oliver, I'm afraid that's two dollars in the cuss box. Unless," she added pointedly, "my husband wants to pay for his friend. We really don't like that kind of language around the children."

Sherman threw Franklin a look. Back in the days when they were under fire, Franklin hadn't worried about what was nice or not. He'd cursed and sworn with the best of them and even gone back to saying ain't, which everyone in his hometown said up to the age of seven or eight, only after that age being straightened out by somebody who was interested in things being nice. Going into battle he'd dropped all the niceties. And then, under the noise and the light, the terror and confusion, the cold and the darkness, he'd have given anything—he'd have given the rest of his life—for one hour of everything being nice, clean, orderly, safe, and just like the commercials.

"I'm sorry," Sherman said. "I guess I just forgot."

He could no longer remember what had been in his mind at the beginning or why he'd decided to go in search of Franklin. Maybe if he hadn't been asked to stay, he'd have started to walk back out of town. Or perhaps he'd have found someplace for the night and then gone on. But now he'd been at the house for so long that he couldn't go. Something had to happen before he could leave.

Sometimes he felt that Franklin had wronged him; that he'd managed to make him a kind of nothing—an object that had had to be lifted from one place to another: out of the field and into the hospital.

Sometimes he thought of him as a man who had made a fatherly and brotherly gesture to him in spite of the fact that they were hardly more than strangers. He would have liked to be that kind of man.

And so, once in a while, he thought of himself becoming Franklin.

꘎

Certain things about Sherman began to worry Franklin: the man's need to seek sanctuary in bars, his capacity for drink and, when drunk, his favorite phrase for summoning the waitress, which was, "Hey you, brainless." Still, they'd been through a bad time together and Franklin soon learned to suggest going only to places he'd never been in and wouldn't mind not going back to. The twilit atmosphere of these saloons began to remind him of the war, where you'd see people's faces lit up from darkness by flares and airport lighting. And the smoky atmosphere was like other bars and nightclubs he'd been in at that time.

They were in a place called "The Highlife Café" when Sherman asked what he could do to repay him for his hospitality. Franklin said, "Relax, Sherman. You're a guest. We don't want anything."

"But I can't keep sponging off of your goodwill like this."

"Cut it out. Do you hear any complaints?"

"It's so strange to see how you've got this whole life, like everything happened someplace else, like it never happened, put it behind you and all. I mean, I know it's been a long time since, um . . . I just don't seem to be able to settle down somehow."

"Do you want to?"

"Well, sure. I guess so. If I could find a girl who'd be interested. But most of the ones I see aren't homemaker types. They're all looking for a lot of money."

"Not all of them. Hell, there are as many different kinds of women as men."

"No. There's only one kind. Because they all do the same thing. They get married and they have kids. When they're young, they're looking forward to it. When they get married, they're in the middle of it, and when they're old, they're those grandmothers: always poking their noses in every place. See, that's all they got."

"A lot of women go out to work."

"Only if they have to. They'd rather be married to a man who's earning enough to let them stay at home. Look after the kids. All that. So on and so forth."

"Maybe," Franklin said.

When they got back to the house, Sherman sensed from the way Irene was standing—as she watched him come in—that if he didn't leave her family in peace for a while, she was going to make her husband kick him out.

He asked Franklin to drop him near the library on his way to work the next day.

"I'm going to need the car," she said. "Remember?"

"Sure. I'll be taking the bus, Sherman. But I can show you which stop. I didn't know you were a reading man."

"I read books about war. I like to hear what everybody has to say on the subject. I found a very interesting book a couple of years ago called *Great Battles of the World*, where they took you through it step by step: the technology, the terrain, the weather, the kings and generals. You know, one of the big problems in olden times was being able to see the enemy and not losing sight of where your commander was heading. That's right. There was one famous battle—I forget which—way back there, where everybody charged forwards for the first few minutes, yelling blue murder and everything and after that they were all blinded by the cloud of dust they'd kicked up. Even the horses couldn't see anything. It was a mess. It was like they was all in the dark and couldn't find their way out."

Irene said, "I guess it's always sensible to choose a good location. And make sure you don't have the sun in your eyes."

"The geography is important. But there's one thing even more vital than that: choosing your time. If you can pick the right time, you can even make it so it's the wrong time for the other guy."

"Strategy," Franklin said.

"Strategy and tactics."

Irene asked, "What's the difference?"

Neither of the men could tell her, but each one thought the other had the wrong idea. The subject shifted to the tactics and strategy needed to be a successful poker player. Irene started to get ready for bed. Franklin dropped the car keys into the brass bowl on the telephone table.

Later in the night Sherman heard the two of them talking:

"He's revolting," she whispered.

"Oh, honey. He's a bit rough and he doesn't know how to behave in polite company, but otherwise he's OK. Come on."

"Keep your voice down," she said. "He's raw, savage, a drunk, and creepy. He's the type that stabs you in the back when you aren't expecting it."

"He just hasn't gotten over it yet."

"Why not? You did. He's only hanging around, feeling sorry for himself."

"Feeling sorry for yourself is the hardest thing of all to fight. You get to thinking that it's natural, because nobody else is going to. There are a lot of people, you know—a lot who don't have anybody to love them. And it isn't easy to live like that: to live without love and to know that the whole of your life is probably going to be that way."

"You were all right."

"Because I finally learned to do without it and to stop wanting. That's the trick. That's when you attract it."

"Your family loved you."

"Let's don't talk about my family. Please."

"Let's not."

"Fine."

"Let's not, not let's don't."

There was silence for a while and then some creaks and rustling and a whisper from one of them, it was impossible to tell which one, saying, "Let's do."

He joined the library, giving Franklin's address as his place of residence. He sat down and looked through at least one book every day he went in, although he didn't often check a book out on his card, as everyone else did, to remove from the building and read at home.

In the evenings he'd be out with Franklin in the bars or maybe going to a movie on his own.

Every day at the library he kept seeing the same people. Most of them were older than he was. He assumed that they were on their own, like him. There were three old-maidish ladies and two men, one of whom—a ferocious old codger—owned a surly police dog he used to leave tied to the railings outside. The dog dozed or lay on its belly as if asleep, unless Sherman was nearby, in which case it would raise its lip to show its teeth, and growl low in its throat. The dislike was mutual: a boy he'd known back in school had been chewed up by the same breed of dog and Sherman had never trusted them since.

He read about the Napoleonic wars. He liked Napoleon. But he also liked the Duke of Wellington. He thought it was interesting that a lot of historical crises threw up great men—one on each side—and that even if you came to the conclusion that one of them was wrong, or had bad ideas, it was usually true that the two were of equal importance. A great man was worthy of a great enemy.

He mentioned some of his reading to Franklin when they went out at night. Irene was happy to get them both out of the house, as for several days in a row she was going to have meetings with women's groups of one kind or another.

"If wars was the way they used to be," Sherman said, "I could have been a general."

"That's what we all think. But it's a special talent. Most of us could be soldiers, or even captains and colonels, but only a few men know how to organize a battle and keep it running when everything starts turning out crazy."

"I bet I could."

"Well, I couldn't. But I think maybe Irene could."

"Is that right?"

"She always gets what she wants."

"Must be a nice feeling."

"Oh, it's nice for me, too. But I'll tell you: they say if you know how to play chess, you could lead an army. I mean, if you're good at it. If you can beat most other people."

"You've changed," Sherman said. "You've been civilized. You've settled down."

"I've adapted. Well, you have to."

"I don't know. Civilian life—you've got to keep telling yourself to behave right. And if you don't, some tight-assed son of a bitch is going to. Peacetime . . . you don't get scared but it's hard on your mind. Everybody's so smug and laced up. You know, once they got something going, they all talk to each other, they go visiting each other, they have their little supper parties together, they go for drives and picnics and cookouts. All that kind of thing. And you have to belong to the club."

"It isn't that bad."

"Don't you remember the way it used to be? Sitting around with the girls? Playing poker. That was better. I miss that. Don't you?"

"What I've got now is better. You'll find out. It'll happen to you some day, too."

"Busted flush, full house, two pairs, royal straight, aces high, deuces wild. Full house—that's your family: three and a pair."

"Four. There's the baby."

"What I always wanted was a royal flush."

"You might get it, but you wouldn't be able to use it."

"Why not?"

"Because that's the way it works."

"The game I used to like best was the one called Midnight Baseball."

"Is that the one where you're betting blind?"

"Right. The one with the psychology."

"If that's what you want to call it. That's a fancy name for throwing your money away."

"Peacetime," Sherman sighed. "It's so quiet, so safe. But sometimes this feeling just comes over me that it isn't real. Look at all this. Once you start it, it works so smooth—and then everybody thinks that this is normal. But you and me, we know it isn't. Listen. Did I ever tell you about the fur trappers in Canada?"

"You told me."

"I just love that. And the baby sharks? No? This one is good." With many gestures, including clawing and biting movements, Sherman related how a marine biologist, back in the late 1940s, had been studying sharks; he'd had a dead female shark on the slab and at one stage during the dissection he'd put his hand into the uterus and had been bitten. Further examination disclosed that although sharks gave birth to one offspring, the original number of embryos in the womb was five; they existed together on the mother's supply of nourishment, which wasn't enough to last up to the time of birth. "When the food runs out," Sherman said, "they have to start eating each other. And it's like the man says: survival of the fittest. Only one gets born."

"Not surprising," Franklin said. "That's what sharks are like."

"But now they're saying how a lot of babies are supposed to be twins but the one kid kind of sucks the other one into itself before they're born. You know about this thing called the afterbirth—it's a big mess of blood—well, that's what's left of the other babies."

"Sherman, the afterbirth is associated with every single birth."

"That's what I'm saying. We're all like that."

"It isn't the remains of other embryos."

"But it is."

"Not according to the medical profession as it's practiced all over the world."

"The medical profession? Jesus, what I could tell you about them."

"It's—"

"Go into a hospital with a headache and—before you know what's hit you—they've stuck you into a straitjacket. Without a boo, biff, or bang."

"Bam."

"What?"

"Without a boo, biff, or bam."

"Bang. My grandmother used to say it."

"So did my mother's cousin, only she said bam."

"Bang. You're thinking of: wham, bam, thank you, ma'am."

"Let's have another," Franklin said. He changed the subject to earth-quakes. And after they'd agreed that earthquakes were even worse than volcanoes, Franklin said, "Too bad you didn't become a gangster. I'd hire you to bump off Raymond Saddler."

"For five thousand bucks I'd shoot my own mother."

"Not really."

"As God is my judge."

"That's the trouble. God said: thou shalt not kill."

"Not my God."

"Yeah, well. We've all done it, but you don't think about it the same way when it's in combat. It's your duty."

"Dead is dead."

"How could you say that about your mother?"

"She's dead."

"I'm sorry. I didn't know."

"It's a way of saying what I'd do. I wouldn't say it like that if she was alive. So, who's Raymond Saddler?"

"Oh, just a mean son of a bitch."

Sherman nodded. "Lot of them around. What I said: that's what we're like."

"Well, I don't know how to answer that except to say that I don't think we're like foxes or sharks."

"OK, you tell me what we're like."

"This is the kind of discussion I don't enjoy getting into."

"Why not?" Sherman waved his hand. The impulse unbalanced him momentarily; he ended the gesture abruptly and grabbed the edge of the bar. "Talk: everybody does it," he said. "What are you scared of?"

"I don't like constantly having to justify myself or talking against something I know is wrong when I don't have the arguments to back up what I want to say. You know—statistics and all that stuff. The truth is, I think people—all people, including myself—are hard to understand. What they teach you in school: two plus two is four, and so on—that's easy. That makes sense. And if somebody tells you their thoughts, they usually make sense. Or their dreams. But emotions: they've always seemed to me to be a kind of mysterious world. Where they come from, why they appear or disappear—I don't understand any of it. And sometimes they scare me. Even when they're good emotions, they strike me as being just about to become uncontrollable. I don't understand why they have to be there at all, if we're capable of thought. Or why they should suddenly run dry when things are the way they've always been."

"Are you talking about marriage?"

"Not necessarily. Love, hatred, desire, jealousy. Greed. Fear. Everything."

"That preacher stuff about sins and virtues?"

"People talk about emotions like they're part of the character, but I don't see how that could be. We all feel things the same way. But our characters are different—as different as fingerprints. I just sometimes think I'm sharing my life with a wild animal that isn't me."

"Frank, that's exactly what I've been saying. Of course it's you. Sure. It ain't nobody else now, is it? Who else would it be?"

"If you had kids, you'd see what I mean. They're so sweet. And then suddenly they go to pieces. They can't open a box or they can't get a toy to work and all their anger and grief and persecution comes out. They howl and break things and, Jesus, it's like Corporal Hicks on payday. And what's it for? That isn't what teaches you things. It isn't even the part of you that recognizes principles of justice or aesthetics or morality. Or anything."

"Sure, it is. Kids don't know anything because they just got off the boat. It takes them awhile to learn. Once you learn, you're fine. But that ain't what you're like. You pat a cat and it purrs. Rub 'em the wrong way and they hate it. Same with us."

"There's more to it than that. But, like I say, I can't talk about it. And I don't understand it. Irene understands. She's so good with the kids. And that's part of the reason why. She understands all that." He slid his beer glass back and forth a couple of times on the tabletop, as if to position himself more accurately against his surroundings. Sherman was sometimes a disquieting companion; there were nights when Franklin could even imagine that he was a figure risen from the dead and that by saving the man's life he'd made him miss his time for leaving the world.

That was where the strangeness lay: that one moment between life and death. In his mind it remained a monument long after the names of his comrades had ceased to repeat themselves as he was falling asleep. All through college he used to hear the names, a nightly roll call in the dark: *Abramowits, Bender, Corey, Dubrowski, Enrico, Garfield, Hicks, Magruder, Oliver, Page, Pettis, Roscoe, Samuelson, Vargas, Viborg, Weiss, Zemlinski.*

And now he and Sherman were sitting down or standing around, drinking beer and shooting the bull. As if nothing had happened.

"Do you ever think about the others?" he asked.

"They're doing all right. Most of the ones I ran into after I got out of the hospital—they're OK. There was only one guy I knew: he was paralyzed from the neck down and he just didn't want to live, so he didn't."

"In the hospital?"

"Oh, it's easy if you really don't want to. You stop cooperating in every way. Pull the plugs out, stop talking, stop trying. Anyway, there was a few of them. But otherwise—"

"I was thinking about the others. The ones who died."

"Well," Sherman said, "they're gone."

At night the whispering went on:

"Why do you keep sticking up for him?"

"Because it could have been me."

"You think he'd lift a finger to save anybody?"

"I mean, it could have been me in his place now: never getting out of the hole he's in because he's lost hope."

"I told you: he feels sorry for himself."

"It's a hard habit to break, once you get down into that mood. Especially if you're on your own."

"He doesn't try. He moans and he disparages and he scorns the ones that do try. And why is he all by himself, anyway? Doesn't he have any family or friends?"

"That's just it. I don't think he does."

The children were fascinated by him. As they called him Sir and asked questions, he fixed them with a look he might have given to a dangerous insect that was about to jump in his direction. Their laughter and rowdy play disconcerted him. Irene kept the older ones in hand with words and the younger ones with action: picking them up, washing their hands, wiping smears off their faces and sticky goo out of their hair. All day long they were yelling, laughing, screaming, running around, falling down, and crying. They drove Sherman crazy.

But she could tame them. He began to realize that little by little, all day long—just by being with them—she was teaching them, like a lioness with her cubs. And they wanted to learn: they were always asking questions. One day the boy, Hagen, walked up to Franklin and asked, "What does it mean when you say the days of yore? The days of your what?"

Even the little girl, Pixie, caught parts of the conversation and tried to make sense of the words. Once, when Franklin said, "That could cause complications," she asked, "Daddy going to sew?"

Irene said, "No, honey. What your granny does is appliqué. Complicated means something else."

"What's it mean?"

"Lots of little parts instead of one big piece."

"Like a tangerine?"

"Yes. Tangerines are complicated, apples are simple."

"What have you started?" Franklin said.

"It's a perfectly good explanation. If you've got a better one, let's hear it."

Franklin turned back to Sherman. Irene didn't waste time gloating. She had too much to do.

All the children liked school; even the baby, Donnie, seemed to respond when the word was spoken. Pixie already went to kindergarten and her older brother and sister had recently finished their time in the classes for four-year-olds and five-year-olds. That wasn't enough for them. They yearned for grown-up pursuits. They wanted to have jobs, to be parents, to drive cars, and to sit at the controls of planes and trains and large ocean liners. They were looking forward to taking their place in the world.

"They're so bossy, too," Irene complained. "Crazy about power. And they're very concerned about how they look. At their age. I mean, they've only just stopped being babies. I don't know where they get it from. Their friends are exactly the same. I heard them talking about playing doctor and Hagen said, 'No, I'm the doctor. You're the nurse.' And Portia said, 'Do I get a uniform?' That was all she was interested in: the clothes."

"Doctors and nurses—sounds pretty hot," Franklin said.

"Oh, let them have fun."

"You'd be surprised what kids can get up to."

"I don't think it's going to do them any harm. I've warned them about infections. They wouldn't try injecting themselves or making a blood pact."

"Doctors and nurses is usually sexy stuff."

"Oh, my goodness—you're right. I just remembered. My friend Carrie's cousin got hold of her parents' enema, or maybe it was even some kind of a douche bag, and there were about seven of us out in the garden shack, lining up to get our thrills."

"What? Married nearly six years and suddenly I hear this?"

"It was wonderful. Carrie's cousin did all of us and we were going to get a second turn and then—to be fair—I said she should have a chance, too. Carrie was chosen to man the machine because she was the next oldest. She said she had a terrible time trying to start it because her cousin was fat and it was so hard to find just where you were supposed to put the end of the hose thing in." She gave a little chuckle and then burst into a loud fit of laughter.

"Revelations," Franklin shouted.

The children ran back into the kitchen, wanting to know what was so funny. In their rush, they piled up at the doorway, jostling in a bunch, and then tumbling all over each other like puppies. "Look at that," Irene said. "Once you're a mother, you're in the front line for the rest of your life."

Sherman said, "So you liked it?"

"Of course. We all did. We loved it. Can't you remember what it was like to be five years old?"

"I can't hardly remember last week."

"That isn't the same thing. I mean your childhood. Once you're grown up, it sort of seals itself off. It's like a closed world or another country. If you're a mother, what you have to do is teach your kids how to have a childhood. They won't get one without your participation. You share yours with them."

"I figure you just try and keep them under control," Franklin said. "That's as much as anybody can do."

"No, honey. You have to make an effort. Otherwise they're at a big disadvantage when they grow up. They may be nice, but they're going to be disliked for their bad habits, their bad manners, and everything else they never learned right. They'll be unpleasant people and they'll make everybody around them unhappy."

There was a silence during which both men observed her intently.

She said, "It's a big responsibility to be a parent. You put new people into the world and it's because of your work that they turn out either good or bad."

Franklin was finally beginning to get so sick of Sherman's company that if it hadn't been for Irene's pestering, he'd have dropped a hint about the length of his stay. That wouldn't have been difficult; he could say something like: if Sherman planned to hang on in that neck of the woods, they'd have to find him a place of his own because, naturally, he'd want to go out and meet people—women, for instance—and bring them back, and so on, which wouldn't be comfortable with kids in the house.

Eventually, he'd get around to that. But in the meantime, he was just vaguely annoyed and sometimes bored on their evenings out. One night, under the influence of the tedium, he came out with the story of Jubal's Field.

Irene's aunt Posie, he said, whose real name was Penelope and who was actually a great-great-something aunt, had been told when still a small child that she was to have three things from her father and mother when they died. Those three things were: the oil painting of the Sioux Indian leading his horse along a mountain path; the Civil War dress sword from her father's side of the family; and the land they called Jubal's Field, including the water rights and whatever building or buildings were still standing on the place at the time of her inheritance.

The sword had been used by Posie's parents to cut their wedding cake. It had sentimental associations for all the family. So did the painting, which had captivated her even as a child. All her life she remembered how her grandfather had lifted her up so that she could see it better.

And Jubal's Field was more than simply a piece of ground. The field was there but beyond it reared the beginning of the woods and the high country, with a pure mountain stream running through it. All of that land was legally attached to the field and it included a springhouse and a tupelo wood. In the fall the leaves of the tupelo trees turned crimson and garnet and wine red. Against blue sky and the pale, grayish bark of the branches, the masses of scarlet foliage were like something out of a stained-glass window.

When Irene's grandmother was already a mother, her aunt Posie told her that once, late in September, she was walking on the carriage trail that passed along the borders of Jubal's land. She was looking into the ruby red leaves against the slope of the hillside, with the bright color of the sky beyond: and all of a sudden a fawn came through the trees. It was a good-sized animal because of the time of year, but still not so big as a full-grown deer, and it went jumping through the fiery wood like a toy on springs. That, Aunt Posie said, was the best thing she'd ever seen in her life except, of course, the faces of the people she loved: the most beautiful scene from nature, anyway—and that included birds, fish, and everything, even the full moon during one really cold Christmas when the whole family had piled into four sleighs and gone riding through the valley with the bells and harness jingling.

How Aunt Posie's oldest brother, Guthrie, managed to trick the other members of his family out of their first, second, and third choice of inherited objects, no one knew. You could only guess that it would have been accomplished with a mixture of bribery and emotional manipulation. Aunt Posie hadn't been married at the time, and for some reason Guthrie assumed that she would remain single and that there was no reason why a person with no descendants should want to inherit anything but money. To whom would she pass things on except to strangers? And heirlooms shouldn't go out of the family.

"I don't know what the rights of it were," Franklin said. "I guess nobody does now. It's gone on too long. Irene's sure. So's her family."

"But?"

"There's usually two sides to most things."

"I guess that's so," Sherman said. "Heads, I win."

❦

Sherman's favorite story was called "The White Mule." It concerned a boy from Arkansas who lived with his widowed mother.

The first time Sherman told him the story, Franklin thought that it was going to be a fantasy like "Jack and the Beanstalk": the mother told her son to take the old white mule to the fair and sell it because there was nothing left in the house to eat. After the beginning, however, the story turned into a realistic anecdote about a swindle perpetrated in childhood by someone Sherman said he'd met: a man named Jeb. According to the plot, Jeb arrived at the fair and found a shed to put the mule in, but the poor animal was so tired by the long walk that

after a few hours it died in its sleep. That was Sherman's favorite moment. His voice rose melodramatically as he asked, "What was he going to do? What was he going to do? His mother was waiting at home,
counting on him to bring her the money for food."

He managed to tell the entire story twice. After that, Franklin
would say that he'd heard it already, but Sherman kept trying to get
through it again. Franklin guessed that the question, "What was he
going to do?" had such dreadful relevance to Sherman's early life that
it made him happy to transpose it to a framework where it could be
answered.

One evening, by breaking off to discuss other things, Sherman contrived to tell the story for an almost complete third time. "Jeb raffled
it," he said. "He sold everybody at the fair a ticket for five dollars and
he said that the winning ticket would get a beautiful white mule and
if the winner had any complaints at all, he'd give him four times his
money back."

"You told me. That's a good story."

"So when the mule turned out to be dead, he gave the winning
man twenty bucks and he went away happy. But Jeb—he had about
five hundred to take home to his mother. That was a lot more than if
he'd just sold it."

"That's right," Franklin said. "That was pretty smart."

Sherman looked into his glass. He turned it around in his hand. As
Franklin was about to suggest that they call it a night, he asked, "Do
you have bad dreams?"

"Well, now that you mention it . . ."

"Yeah?"

"I do have one nightmare that repeats."

"What's it about?"

"It always starts the same way. I'm in a bar someplace, with a friend,
and we get so drunk that we just keep talking all night instead of going
home and getting some sleep."

Sherman blew out a small sound like a cough; it wasn't really a laugh. And after he'd tipped up his glass for the last swallow, Franklin thought: *I shouldn't have said that. He was about to confide in me and I pushed him away. I wouldn't be able to persuade him to open up now, but maybe I should never try. My instincts told me not to get mixed up in this man's bad dreams.*

He missed the freedom to go out whenever he needed to be alone or to see friends on his own. He would have liked to give Irene a night out, too: find a babysitter for the kids and go to that inn over the state line, where there was a dance floor in the restaurant; and a really good band, so everyone kept telling him.

The next time they were out together Sherman said to Franklin, "I don't think it's right that you and your folks had your land stolen by that Raymond fellow. Somebody ought to do something about that."

"Oh, I shouldn't let it get to me. It isn't even my own family."

"That's OK. I'm tolerant. Remember what we said in the service: we kill anyone regardless of race, color, or creed."

"We'd probably stand a good chance of seeing him in a place like this if he wasn't so tightfisted. He does his drinking at home. They say he's so stingy he only owns one lightbulb and whenever he wants to walk from one room to the next in that big house of his, he gets up and unscrews the bulb so he can take it with him."

"Nah. He'd be stumbling around, trying to find—"

"Just a joke. I'm sure that place is flooded with light, day and night. He wasn't always so bad. His wife died four years ago. We all thought she died because of the way he treated her. He was real hard on her. Didn't like for her to talk to anybody. I guess he thought she'd be telling tales on him. Some people are just strange."

"They have kids?"

"No. And none of the rest of the family will go near him, even the ones who could get to him in a day's driving. He's had fights with everybody. So he sits in his big, empty house and he lives like a hermit. He leads a miserable life except for one thing: he's preventing Irene from having what's rightfully hers. Maybe we wouldn't mind so much if he had a family. Or—I don't know. Maybe that would make it worse. Anyway, he's just a dog in the manger."

Some thought nagged at Sherman. It wasn't a memory from the past, but he kept feeling that it was. Every time his mind approached it, the thought dissolved. Trying to pin it down was like trying to remember a lost tune or a forgotten name. It was almost as if he'd had a memory of something in the future.

The next day they were in the car, on the way to "Happy Honolulu," when Franklin said, "By God, there's the old bastard himself. Look, there."

Sherman turned his head to see where. There, on the other side of the street, was the old man from the library; and his dog. *Dog in the manger and dog from the library.*

"Raymond Saddler," Franklin said.

"Is that right? He don't look so tough."

"He's plenty mean and he's a good shot. I've seen him in action during the hunting season. He likes keeping some kind of weapon handy. There you are: that's his shotgun up on the rack there in the pickup."

Irene stood at the kitchen table and sliced tomatoes on the chopping board. She worked quickly but she paid attention. She'd never cut herself badly, not even with the special, razor-sharp knives she'd been given by a sister-in-law for Christmas. The thing to remember about weapons was that everything depended on which way they pointed.

He was going to make a move soon, she thought. If he tried anything, she'd kill him. There, in her own kitchen, each cup and bowl had its place and she knew exactly where everything was. She could be blindfolded and still grab the right handle. But he'd have to look first. As for killing, she'd studied all that from Caesar's assassination. Long before the dress rehearsal, Miss Moody had been very particular about even the smallest detail. She'd told them not to stab downward from above: upward from below was the right way to do it. Miss Moody had shown them where all the vital organs were and how to hit them fast without slicing into bones. She'd taught them more anatomy than they'd ever learned in biology class. "Theater," Miss Moody had said, her voice thrilling with conviction, "is more true than real life. It's above and beyond reality. It reaches for eternal values. So if you don't get the physical part right, it's a disaster—it looks silly. And then the whole audience can start laughing in the scenes that are meant to be serious."

Miss Moody had been an inspiration. And they'd done her proud on that night. Irene always smiled when she remembered. Her parents told her that they'd never seen her so excited: after it was over, she kept asking them, "How was I? Was I really all right? Could you hear me? Was it scary? Did it look real? Did you like it? Was it good? Honest?"

She'd have loved to be an actress. She was sure she would have been good at it. Acting was almost what she was doing now; as long as Sherman was camped on them, she had to act polite. But at night she dropped the good manners and quarreled with Franklin about whether his friend should go or stay.

"That look in his eye—" she said, "like a member of some crazy sect, waiting to take their orders from a flying saucer."

"You don't know what it was like," he said.

"No, I don't know. And you don't know what it was like carrying your four kids and giving birth to then—especially the first time with that disgusting Dr. Graff who gave me the creeps, with his arm all the way up my insides right to the elbow and saying, 'Relax, relax,' like I was a new girl in his whorehouse. Thank God he was on the golf course when I went into labor."

"Every woman—"

"You're damn right. I took it on willingly because I loved you. I'm the one who's supposed to love. But do you care? You're out with Margie Robinson."

"Oh, not that again."

"And I'm stuck here with the servant jobs while you're in a bar with the boys: *Oh, how about that Margie, what I could tell you about her, deal me another, kiddo. Yes siree.*"

"You don't know. You just don't know what it's like to imagine that any minute you're going to be blown to pieces. And picking up the survivors: that wasn't much fun, either."

"Just because—"

"You stick to the shopping and the gingerbread cookies. And shut up about me."

"Jesus God, would I love to kill a few people. Why the hell do you think war is so much more painful and dangerous than what every woman goes through in just ordinary life? All of them standing around, screaming, 'Push, push,' and tearing me to pieces so that after Donnie I was having bowel movements out of my vagina—"

"Christ, Irene. Just quit it, will you? It isn't my fault. I would have done anything to spare you that. But you were the one who kept wanting—"

"I know it isn't your fault. Of course it isn't. I'm not blaming you for anything except thinking that this man is some specially deserving case because you went through all that buddy stuff together. Big deal. Was he your best friend out there?"

"No."

"Well?"

"Well, to tell you the truth, I'd be glad if he moved on. I felt sorry for him. Hell, anybody can go through a rough time. If nobody gives you a helping hand, you can stay there for years."

"He seems to have plenty to spend. Where does he get all that money?'

"His disability compensation, I guess."

"That couldn't be much."

"He's been wandering around the country for a long time: no house, no car, no social life. Maybe his money's been piling up in a bank somewhere."

"He's got a gun."

"We've all got guns."

"A handgun. A pistol. He showed it to Hagen. He said he was going to let him shoot it."

"Oh?" That didn't sound too good. Taking your boy out to practice target shooting with a four-ten was one thing. Handing a four-year-old a loaded revolver was another.

"That's the trouble with bad people," she said. "They touch you with their evil and you can't get rid of it. To defend yourself against them, you have to hate. And that hate begins to distort you."

"Evil? Oh my good Lord. He's a guy who's down on his luck, that's all."

He knew what was going through her mind: that maybe Sherman was the kind of man who might think it was all right to teach a child how to cheat at cards or to shortchange people so that they didn't notice straight away. Maybe he was worse than that.

"He's been through a lot of unhappiness," she said, "and he's looking for someone to pin it on."

Sherman continued to listen. Hearing Franklin say, "Christ, Irene," he remembered the preacher in the hospital: *Christ died for us.* And he was reminded of all the stickers he kept noticing on car bumpers: *Jesus Saves.*

He saves us, Sherman thought, *and he dies doing it. And after that, we're redeemed. He doesn't save us and then go on living.*

He came back early from the library one day. Irene was in the kitchen, but Addie was in the house, too, cleaning the living room. Irene asked if he'd like her to make him a sandwich.

"On, no thanks. I picked up a bite in town. I'll just sit here for a while." He pulled out a chair and sat down. He watched her working. After a few minutes he asked, "You ever play cards?"

"No time," she answered shortly.

"We used to play cards all the time in the service. There's a lot of waiting around. Most of the time it was poker. All the different types of poker games I've played. The one I liked best was called Midnight Baseball, where you're betting blind. We used to play that when we were drunk and out with the girls. We did a lot of cardplaying in the whorehouses. It's something you don't forget: the smell of the per-fume; the long, black hair; the feel of the silk. Him, too—you think he's forgotten?"

"Listen," she said. "I know I should feel sorry for your troubles."

"Oh, you don't have to feel sorry for me. I'm doing OK."

"You have to pity a man who isn't right in the head."

"Uh-huh. I guess I could get away with a lot if I wanted to make that an excuse, couldn't I? Like the women that say: 'I'm a woman, I'm a mother, that's why I'm like this, that's why I did that, that's why these things happen to me.'"

"I see. Well, you may be crazy, but you aren't dumb, are you?"

At last, he thought: a woman who understood him. She didn't like him, but that didn't matter. Whatever was going to happen between him and her was meant to be. "I can tell you something, too," he said. "Old Franklin ain't a very good poker player."

"And you are?"

"That's right."

"But games are for children. And cards are just to pass the time. Frank is a grown man. It took him years to get over the war, but he did it and he's fine now. It can be done. You could do it, too. Talking to people helps, specially if they were in it with you, but trying to drag a cured man down into your sickness isn't going to make you well."

"Oh. Is that what I'm trying to do?"

"And drinking doesn't help, either. It's bad for you and it doesn't make you feel that good, anyway, does it? Alcohol is a depressive, that's what they say. Anyway, it isn't right for the children to see their father drunk."

She wanted for him to get up and go. He was waiting for her to tell him to leave. When the moment had been allowed to pass, he said, "Franklin is a man who's killed."

"But it hasn't changed him."

"How do you know? You didn't know him before."

"I know because he's a good man."

"Except that now he knows it would be easy to do it again. Before you do it, you think it would be impossible. You probably think that."

"What?"

"That you couldn't kill."

"I couldn't."

"I remember—I was so little, it's one of my very first memories: seeing my mother cleaning out a chicken. I thought it was so horrible. We all did. We said: *Ooh, how can she do that?* But you learn that somebody's got to do that or nobody gets to eat roast chicken. You learn. You put your hands inside a dead animal. You kill and you eat what you've killed: birds, fish, deer. And then you stop being so upset. Killing is part of living."

"Killing, maybe. Not murder."

"Well, two girls I went to school with: they got pregnant by mistake and they got rid of it. Wouldn't you do that?"

"That wouldn't happen."

"Accidents can always happen, anywhere. Not just—like they say—accidents in the home. And it's only a question. Some guy that's drunk: he flags down your car and you stop because you think he's in trouble. And then, before you know what he's trying to do . . . would you get rid of it?"

"I certainly would."

"Uh-huh."

"And if one of the kids was in danger. I'd kill anybody for that."

"Even your husband?"

"What?"

"If it came to a choice?"

"There isn't any choice. They're the same thing. Why are you trying to talk me into a corner?"

"Why don't you like thinking about things?"

"This isn't thinking. It's that game of 'What if?' and most of the answers are things nobody knows. You never know for sure till it happens."

"And then?"

"Then you do what you have to. And sometimes that isn't what you thought it was going to be. Sometimes you're tired, you're scared, your concentration is broken, and you forget or you do something dumb or something that's just the opposite of what you meant to do. Sherman, could you move so I can get to the drawer there?"

He pushed the chair back and stopped talking. He enjoyed watching her work. It was like being at home, a long time ago, when everybody was still alive and he was in the kitchen where his mother was doing the baking.

In the evening Irene had a call from one of her sisters-in-law to say that a child in her son's school had come down with some kind of lung infection at summer camp and he'd nearly died.

"That camp's a long way away," Franklin told her.

"It makes you think, though."

It also made both of them think about their life as it used to be, without Sherman, when it was always clear what was important and what didn't have to be taken into consideration because, not being central, it didn't count.

The next day was Saturday. Irene had to get one of the kids dressed for a birthday party and another one ready to go to the swimming pool. While she was setting the kitchen table for breakfast, she said, "It's a beautiful day. Why don't you give Sherman a tour of the district? Show him the local stuff, like it said in the book we had: *items of note*."

"*Not*. Everything in that book was *items of not*. As I recall, we got lost trying to find half of them."

"That was only once. Come on. Otherwise most of the day will go by and you'll just fritter the time away. I can fix you a picnic lunch."

Franklin turned to Sherman for confirmation.

Sherman, who was once again overcome by shyness in Irene's presence, lifted a shoulder and whispered, "Sure." The two little girls stared greedily at him; they kept clutching each other and bursting into giggles for no apparent reason, never taking their eyes off him.

"It's going to be nice," Irene said.

Franklin looked out of the window, up at the sky, and from one side to the other. He said, "Right."

They'd had the sweltering days from the end of July and the hurricanes at the beginning of August. The first frost was to come and after that the leaves on the dogwood would redden, the old trees first, and gradually all the colors would come: the maples gold and orange and scarlet, even some of the oaks turning pink. The foods of the earth would reach perfection: apples and pumpkins, nuts and pears. The time of abundance was just ahead. But now it was still summer and they were coming to the end of it.

Franklin drove Sherman on a circuit around town and out onto the road that ran down by the river, to where the logging camp used to be. He talked about who used to live where and how the landscape had changed or stayed the same.

After a while Sherman said, "This whole place used to be Indian country, coast to coast. If the early settlers had intermarried instead of fighting, you and me would be Indians right now."

"That's a thought."

"Would it be so different?"

"It would for me. I can't imagine an existence with that kind of social structure: all that tribal business with elders and so on."

"It wouldn't make any difference to me. I'd be just the same."

"You'd be married with ten kids because that's what the society would demand. Even in this area, in this state—in this country, for that matter—after a few years people are going to feel they should know why you don't want or can't get what everybody else thinks is of value."

"I'd be a brave."

"Braves are young. Beautiful maidens are young. You get through one stage and you go on to the next. If you don't go on to the next, everybody's going to think you aren't up to it. Unless you've got something better to do. And that doesn't often happen. If you want to dedicate your life to some important work, say. Or some worthy cause."

They were headed for an open-air agricultural museum, the Buckhorn

Farm, when Franklin changed his mind. He said, "Hey, I know what I can show you. The family inheritance that never was: Raymond Saddler's place that ought to belong to Irene."

They turned off the highway, went down a dirt road, traveled a good way along it, and stopped.

There in the distance was a house, set back, with three big trees growing nearby but not so close that they could be a danger to the roof.

"And that's where the old buzzard lives," Franklin said.

The family had to attend an anniversary celebration over in the next state. They'd be gone all day—Franklin, Irene, and the four kids. And they wouldn't be back till late.

Franklin handed Sherman the keys. Irene didn't look too happy at that, but she didn't say anything.

While they were away, Sherman went into town. He bought a piece of steak, took it back to the house, carried it upstairs to the bathroom, and laced it with the sleeping pills he'd seen in the medicine cabinet. Then he packed it up in waxed paper and started off for Raymond Saddler's place. He rode part of the way by bus and then walked.

He got into the house through a window at the back. Once he was inside, he went to the room he'd chosen, and stayed there.

From any part of an empty house the overall dimensions could be guessed—and, Sherman thought, you could also tell what kind of character the place had. The longer he waited, the more he liked it.

Saddler didn't show up till midafternoon. The dog came rushing ahead of him—out of the pickup and scrabbling across the threshold as soon as the door was unlocked. Saddler had the gun broken over his arm. For a bad-tempered man he didn't act very suspicious.

The dog threw himself around the corner and Sherman tossed him the meat fast. Then he withdrew into a back room.

While Saddler was busy locking up, his dog bolted back every bit of the steak and lay down on the rug to sleep.

Sherman heard Saddler going into the kitchen. He moved from cover. He approached the hallway, where he saw the shotgun, no longer broken, standing up against the wall. That made everything easier. Before that moment, he'd intended to use his knife.

The next day, at noon, the rumors went around that Raymond Saddler had committed suicide. He'd shot his dog first, but he'd been really fond of that dog: he'd fed it some sleeping pills before he did it.

Irene made two telephone calls to establish what part of the story was fact. Then she was on the phone for another hour, talking to friends and relatives.

The Page family expressed a decent regret at the news but they were jubilant. There was no doubt about what was to come: the property, the house, the money, and all that it represented.

With the thought in mind of his wife's certain inheritance, Franklin took Sherman out for a drink and told him that he saw how things were and he wanted to help Sherman to do what he'd done himself: pick a town somewhere, start up a business, and make himself at home. He couldn't spare much, butt since Irene was going to come into Aunt Posie's legacy at last, he could let Sherman have five hundred dollars. He handed over the check then and there.

Sherman took a swallow of beer and started to think. He thought until he convinced himself that Franklin had demanded a sacrifice of him that was equal to the moment in the war that neither of them could get away from. And when he'd cleared the debt by agreeing to carry out Franklin's dearest wish for him, he was given an insulting five hundred bucks in exchange.

Was five hundred dollars enough to wipe away the memory of Raymond Saddler's face or to allow him to sleep without seeing it again? From now on Franklin would be laughing: leading his normal life as if he didn't have any connection with a single thing that was low or underhand. Five hundred dollars was certainly not enough. Especially when you considered what that land was probably worth. If Franklin were any kind of a decent man—the kind that stuck by his friends—he'd have had the idea on his own that Sherman deserved a little extra. A supplement.

People who have money, Sherman thought, *will always rather give you money than a piece of their time. Franklin doesn't have all that much, which means that . . . he's willing to go without, as long as he can get rid of me. It wasn't just what she wanted. He paid me off.*

It would have to be five thousand at least, to make up for having to carry the burden. And also, for being treated like that: hired and fired—used, like some kind of menial servant.

That wife of his, too: Irene. All polite on top, and underneath she couldn't stand you. That was something else that would have to be changed.

"That's mighty good of you, Frank," he said. "I appreciate it."

"For old time's sake," Franklin told him.

Back at the house, Irene got her speech in, too. She told Sherman the latest gossip: according to the investigations, there was nothing suspicious about Raymond Saddler's death—it was his own gun. She couldn't feel sorry: he'd brought it on himself, leading that hermit life all alone in a big house, just so he could keep it from somebody else. No wonder he went crazy. But the thing was: she and Franklin were going to need the guest room now, because of the funeral. There were all kinds of cousins coming.

They'd hated Raymond Saddler, but of course they'd go to the funeral. And collect the money.

"You get his house?" he asked.

"Well, I don't know. Why?"

"That's a nice house."

"Sort of broken down, maybe. He was the kind of man who'd never fix anything—he'd wait for it to fall down before he'd shell out on new paint."

But it was a good house. With a house like that, you could get a wife easy. She'd clean it up, make it pretty, have lots of kids, and they'd bring him his comfortable shoes in front of the fire. He'd have his dog and his gun, like Raymond Saddler, but not the same kind of dog—not one of those European police dogs. A good old American hunting hound. Get it when it was a pup and raise it to be his alone. He'd always wanted one. And the house.

The house was better than Franklin's: larger, and with wider and taller windows that looked out onto big trees—the kind of place a gentleman would have owned in the old days. The days of yore. *The days of your and the days of mine.*

During the night there was a light rain, just enough to make the next day fresh. In the morning, after breakfast and as Franklin was about to suggest taking him for a drive on the way to work, Sherman said, "Guess I should be moving on."

Franklin was caught so that he could only say, "Oh?" He'd been intending to talk to Sherman in the car and in a reasonable way to put forward exactly that suggestion, reiterating the need to use the guest room for cousins.

Irene said, "I think that would be a good idea, Sherman. You don't want to sit around, going stale, when you could get out and make a life for yourself. And we can't give anybody much hospitality with the kids running around all the time."

"Oh, I got no complaints," he said.

Franklin thought he meant it. Irene wasn't sure, and she became convinced to the contrary when—as he was finally stepping over the threshold to go out of the house—Sherman stopped dead, slapped his hands over his pockets, and explained, "Don't want to forget anything. I might have to come back."

They got into the car and started off. Neither of them felt much like talking. Sherman was busy thinking: *This is my chance. I'm only going to have one crack at it and that's all. Because otherwise I'd have to work up to everything he's got. But if I just step into it, she won't mind. She'll still have the kids and the house and what her cousin tried to gyp her out of. And the other house . . . the nice one. And it was thanks to me that she's got it back. He wouldn't have done anything himself. He had to pay somebody else to do his dirty work.*

Farther along the drive, he thought: *No, I can't do that. He saved me.* When he remembered that, he was—as always—struck into a kind of amazement by the strangeness of the fact. It was so simple, just something that had happened; yet it was a mystery. He'd think: *He saved me. Why? I was nothing to him, or he to me. But he did that. And he could have been killed doing it.*

The event had become one of the large questions, like: *Why was I born?* or *What am I here for?* It perplexed him. Sometimes it filled him with despair.

They left the fields and drove through the hills. Sherman thought about Franklin's life, so full of people and work and activity. What made Franklin so much better, that he deserved all that? When they'd come out of the service they were both the same. And now Franklin was on the inside, looking out. And he was on the outside, looking in. That wasn't fair. Franklin had the house and the wife and the kids; that was what put him on the inside—not his character, which was no better than his own.

He could wait awhile and then go back; go to Franklin and say: *I want some more money, or I'll tell.*

Or, even better: *I'll tell her. And she'll believe it and she won't want to stay married to you.*

Or he could just go ahead and tell her, the two of them alone in the kitchen: *He said the place would be empty except for the dog and that it was some kind of insurance thing with the store. I didn't think I was going to hurt anybody. I wanted to repay him for saving my life.*

She'd believe that. Wouldn't she?

I could say that he told me he wanted the money for a woman named Margie Somebody.

Sherman remembered the hushed, nighttime conversation, but not the woman's last name. As he tried to recall the sound of it, he became unsure about the first name, too: whether it was Maggie or Maisie or Molly. Or it might not have begun with an M at all; it might have begun with a W. He'd have to drop that idea.

They went over the mountains and back into the valleys again, passing fields and farmhouses. Franklin drove him to the next town, where there was a bus depot—the same one where Sherman had been set down on his way to find Franklin's address.

After he'd let him out, Franklin shook his hand. He wished him luck, got back into the car and—waving once, casually—drove away.

Sherman boarded a bus. As soon as it headed out of town he realized that he'd chosen one going in the wrong direction. He'd stepped down at the first stop.

He'd been deposited a few yards from an ancient filling station where the gasoline tanks had been removed and the service shack was falling to pieces. A toilet, with the seat off, sat in front of the door; somebody had filled it up with dirt. Down the road were two paint-peeled houses and a broken-down tarpaper hen coop.

He started to walk. As he moved along, he tried to figure things out. He'd left, but he hadn't left. He kept thinking about Irene. *She's so good with the kids. She understands all that.*

He could go back. If he did, he'd have to do it at night. Except—if he went back in the daytime, Franklin wouldn't be at home. And if he picked the right time, Addie wouldn't be there either, or the kids. *I was pretty careful, but even if I forgot some things, he's in the clear. Unless I tell somebody. Then it's going to look like it was his idea all along, because why would I want to shoot a stranger? And I've got his check. I could say that money he gave me was for the killing. And I'd get away without a jail sentence because . . . they consider me not right in the head, so it wouldn't be my fault. I'd say I thought he was showing me a way I could pay back what he'd done for me. That's what I could say. I did kind of think that, too.*

He'd seen no more than two cars in all the time he'd been walking. One of the drivers asked if he needed a lift, but Sherman waved and called out, "No, thanks." The road he was on seemed to be heading back, but it wasn't the same one he'd walked before or been driven over by the farmer who had let him hitch a ride. He'd have to keep going before he knew which direction he should take next.

She liked that house. Maybe she'd come visiting. If I said that he'd paid me to do it, would he contest it? He's got a lot to lose. I don't have that com-plication. Tangerines are complicated, apples are simple. She did eat of the apple and she offered it to him. She offered it. Because they always do. And if you aren't quick enough, they take it away again.

Maybe Franklin would say: "I'll think about it."

And after he'd thought, maybe he'd come gunning for me. That would make everything easy from his point of view. If you own a lot of woodland, you can bury a man anywhere and feel safe.

It would be best to start on Irene.

Maybe she'd just say no. In that case . . . but she wouldn't, would she? *She understands all that.* He had his pistol, but a shotgun would be better. Suppose he went back at night and got hold of that gun Franklin had? Do it like the last time. They'd say Franklin had shot her and then Inky, Dinky, Pinky, and Twinky—one after the other: bam, bam, bam. And then himself, like Raymond Saddler. Only no dog to worry about.

He was thirsty and he was hungry, but he kept walking.

At sometime in the afternoon he came to a crossroad. There were trees bordering the road; everything else was fields. If you'd been stand-ing in the center of one of them, you could imagine that the whole place was one huge field, even bigger than the one where he'd been trapped and destroyed years ago.

He stood where the roads intersected: at the crosspoint. For a long time he wondered which way to go, then he sat down under one of the trees. He fell asleep.

He had a dream about being killed in the war. When he woke up, he was breathing fast. He took the coin out of his pocket, tossed it up, and caught it. As he threw and caught and fingered the coin, he whispered, "One good turn." In a little while it would be too dark to see what side came up, but he could still feel the picture with his thumb. He could keep turning it around, without throwing it. One good turn deserved another.

He had his knife and his revolver. There was the coin to tell him

what to do: two sides to every question; and the bit field where everything always ended up. He could take his time.

The crickets were chirring in the field. The light was dying from the
air. Shadows came in like water on the tide. He hung in the twilight,
undecided: breathing in and out, and waiting for the long, languid
swell of night to carry him into the darkness.

THE ICON

Everybody except the old man was still at breakfast when Stratis came into the room. He'd hoped that most of the family would have eaten already and that he'd be able to pour himself a cup of coffee in peace. Out of the whole bunch (Elvira, Lucian, Lydia, Zenon, Aristides, Theo, Olga, Dimitrios, and Nestor), the old man—his great-grandfather—was the only one he could stand at the moment.

If the early spring hadn't been so wet and gloomy that year, none of the others would be there. They'd be down in the country during the week and up in town only for visits. But April had been cold and rainy. And now that the weather had improved, most of the family was still in town for the week and Stratis had decided to stay at the house for a while, too, although he had his own apartment.

Several months earlier, in October, he'd fallen in love with a New England girl named Julia, who was unlike any woman he'd been out with before. She came from a traditional Yankee family and she was as pretty and as blond as a Christmas angel always neatly dressed in an expensive, preppy style: with her hair brushed back and held in a ribbon or—when she went out in the evenings—worn up. She looked like a nice, decent girl from a good family. That was what she was. She was also—or so he'd thought at the time—fairly chaste compared to most and certainly more so than could naturally be expected of a girl whose parents didn't go to church.

His parents went to church. His whole, gigantic family went, except for the old man. And as far as Stratis could see, not one of them believed, although they retained a respect for the institution. He lost even that after Julia said good-bye sometime in February, just as he was about to propose. From the moment he'd seen her, even before their first date, he was certain that she was the girl he was going to marry, but, because he hadn't wanted to face the whole, formal family thing and all the questions and hinting that would go on afterwards, he hadn't asked her home for a meal. He'd assumed that that would come in time.

As soon as they were sleeping together, he knew that the family introduction would be easy. But he didn't want to share her. They were isolated and perfect together. He was even amused by the fact that she couldn't get his name right. He once asked her, "Why do you keep calling me Stratos? I'm good, but I'm not that good."

"Good?" she said.

"It means an army. My name is spelled with an *i*, not an *o*. And the accent goes on the last syllable: Stratis, like MacNiece."

But she kept forgetting. It didn't really irritate him until the night of their big quarrel. Given his cue by some trivial remark, he told her loudly, and with plenty of colorful phrases, that he must have been crazy to think of getting married to her: she had all kinds of faults, a lot more than he did, and she might as well hear the whole list.

She listened in silence, hurt at first, and then grim. He'd expected her to come back at him with a list of her own. But she didn't do anything for a long time: she only continued to look at him contemptuously. And at last she said, "Never mind, Stratos. I'm sure you'll find the right girl eventually." And she moved past him, over the threshold and down the hallway, without closing the door behind her. He thought that she was going to walk off her anger or go find a friend to complain to. But she didn't behave in any of the ways he'd imagined. She just went.

He took his dismissal badly. He'd never had to put up with being told no. Everything had always gone smoothly for him.

For months the family teased him about her. Uncle Theo was the worst. At breakfast one day back at the beginning of April, Uncle Theo had said in a loud aside to Aunt Ariana, "Oh, poor Stratis, she must have said no in a big way. Look at his face."

Like many of the men he called uncle, Uncle Theo should have been addressed as "Great Uncle." The house usually contained four generations and, for the moment, a fifth had been added: Cousin Sylvie had come up from the country, bringing her new baby, Melinda. She'd decided to spend the night because nobody wanted to let go of the baby—a placid, good-tempered child who didn't throw things across the room, scream, or make sudden, awkward movements that might cause her to injure herself. Stratis was glad to have the focus of family concern shifted to someone else. Uncle Theo's remarks across the table were becoming outrageous.

Now that it was May and nearing the time when the relatives would prepare for their summer habits, the house down in the country had been given its spring cleaning and repainting. The two hundred and three windows had all been cleaned, the French windows leading into the courtyard had been sprayed against termites, and seven cracked flagstones on the terrace had been replaced. In the bedrooms elderly great-aunts and -uncles, cousins, and widowed in-laws supervised the unpacking and packing of winter, spring, and summer clothes. As soon as the old man moved out of town, new schedules and their time-tables would go into operation. Life would continue, with weekend trips back to the city or—for some—longer vacations. Later still, the house on the beach would also be full, and the boats in use. Not every year was precisely the same; the old man's moods had to be taken into consideration.

Stratis would be hanging around in town for as long as his grandfather stayed there. And Julia was still around, so he'd heard. He might run into her. He'd also picked up the information that she was going out with some actor who was working between parts as a waiter. Stratis had made a point of taking a look at him from a distance. The guy was a jerk. He even had a ponytail.

"A ponytail, for God's sake," Stratis said, looking at an ad in the papers.

"They're all the rage," Aunt Lydia told him. "The height of fashion."

"Only among phonies."

"Oh, no—even the movie stars have them. It's considered glamorous."

He wouldn't waste his breath on an answer to that. Aunt Lydia satisfied her sexual longings—if they could be called that—by poring over magazine pictures of young people of both sexes.

"Not by me," he said.

"And another style is firmly established among young men—a lot of stubble on the chin and a shaved head like a Victorian convict. And a very expensive Italian suit, often pinstriped. A most peculiar combination. But the middle-aged do find young people's fashions extraordinary."

Aunt Lydia could not seriously be thought of as middle-aged. She was old, like all the others. She had simply made up her mind at a certain point that anything from sixty to seventy-five was middle-aged.

"And waiters are quite chic nowadays," she went on. "All so young and good-looking. It's a quick way to earn a living while they're aspiring to do something else. A lot of artists make money waiting on tables: painters, singers, actors, film directors. Before they're established, you know."

He grunted. Uncle Theo said, "Don't take it too hard, my boy."

Aunt Lydia continued, "I suppose you're right in general, in a big city like this. From the crowds I saw yesterday, you'd think everyone under forty was colorblind and not in possession of a mirror. The young have not yet developed a sense of taste. They try everything out. As they should. They're sometimes drawn toward the unsuitable, the cheap, the fake, the pretentious, the sentimental."

"Do you mean me?" he asked.

"Certainly not. With no disrespect intended, I was referring to the fact that your wayward young lady has chosen to move on to another and less deserving young man. I'm sorry to hear it, but I'm afraid it happens a lot. It always did. In fact, sometimes girls and boys will deliberately seek out the worthless because they aren't ready to make a commitment—they know that they can break off that kind of thing at a moment's notice, without any trouble."

"Maybe," he said, looking away. "Who knows?" Julia had broken it off with him even faster than that: no notice at all, just quits. He stretched out a hand for part of Uncle Zenon's newspaper.

Uncle Zenon snatched up the section he'd been saving for when he finished with his first choice; he slid it across the table to the other side of his place, where Stratis wouldn't be able to reach it without getting up.

Stratis didn't notice. He took what was left and began to read. The others, too, lapsed into silence, scanning their papers until Uncle Lucian began to talk about a play that was on in town: absolutely disgusting, and unfortunately it was impossible to obtain tickets to it; everyone said that even the scalpers couldn't get in.

"And this exhibition of icons looks interesting," Aunt Ariana said.

"Oh, not that old stuff," Aunt Lydia told her.

"They say it's fascinating: *untypical exhibits, unusual, free painting style, in contrast to the stereotypical idea of Byzantine stiffness and* . . . I've got to get some new glasses . . . wait: here it is. *The most important show of hitherto unknown—*"

"But it's just icons," Aunt Lydia said. "All those dreary saints and Madonnas and so primitive and wooden-looking."

"So Greek."

"Well, you have to admit that the Italians did it better."

"Not better. Different. It says here—"

Uncle Theo chuckled. He found his relatives particularly diverting when they were disagreeing.

Stratis removed his conscious attention from the talk, the room, the place in general. Maybe what Aunt Lydia had really been saying was that when Julia went out with him, she was slumming, just as she was doing now with the guy who had the ponytail.

He got up without excusing himself and left the table. He was heading for the door when he heard the small, muffled thump of the rubber protector on the tip of his great-grandfather's cane. The sound was coming from around the corner.

Stratis was the only one in the family who wasn't afraid of the old man, whom he called grandfather, although there was an extra generation between them and—owing to the introduction of divorce and remarriage among some of his relatives—a confusing half generation: the family had one nephew older than his uncle and two aunts younger than their niece. And the whole family: all of them—whether doing well in business or retired on a solid annuity—owed their success to the old man, who thought that every one of them, except Stratis, was useless; and he occasionally told them so in a way that could be lighthearted, but with a twist. He usually didn't bother to point it out. It was too obvious. Among the enormous family he belonged to, his was the dominant personality, and his control over the others was absolute. Even so, occasionally he'd make a play for sympathy, always with some purpose in mind. "I'm an old man," he'd say, and then pause. "I won't be here much longer." After that, he'd add, "Indulge me this time," or, "Let me have my way about this. It isn't asking much for someone who has so few years left," or, "It's a small thing—what can it matter: such an insignificant request from an old man?"

At least he never went on about his will. Others in the family had done that. One, a great-great-aunt, had changed her will nearly every week for the last five years of her life. During that time she hadn't paid any bills; when she finally died, the lawyers' fees as well as the debts were taken from her estate and they were considerable. The other will-fanatic had been a man; his changeableness proceeded not from whim, nor fears of being cheated, nor as an effort to upset his descendants, but as the result of forgetfulness. His preoccupation with his will was frustrating rather than infuriating. As soon as he managed to get himself over to his lawyer's office, he'd seem confused for a few minutes until they showed him their copy of the will. "I just wanted to make sure that you still had it," he'd say. Then, to be polite after causing everyone so much trouble, he'd have some minor item altered before he went home. No one considered his vacillations tiresome, as he was so evidently worried about them himself. Sometimes he'd fly into rages, but just as often he'd cry. He remembered enough to realize what was happening to him. His last year was sad for all the family.

There was nothing sad about Stratis's grandfather, the old man, Eustratirios. He was a tough old bird who had worked his way up in business until he had several million dollars, four houses, many cars and boats, two light aircraft, and three rooms full of Impressionist paintings that were as good as any you could see in the museums, although they didn't constitute a collection that could be thought large in comparison to those of the big private buyers like the Greek shipping magnates.

He owned a few other pictures, too: three Dutch landscapes and two tiny, dark Guardis, no bigger than framed snapshots; he kept those two on his desk in the country, as if they'd been a couple of family photographs. There was also an American seascape that hung on the wall of the first landing in his house on the Cape; and an icon. The icon was usually in the house in town, where it stayed hidden behind a curtain in back of the chair at his study desk. But since the painting measured only about seven by five inches, he sometimes took it with him in his briefcase if he had to stay anywhere else for the night. His study in the country, and in the house at the beach, had the same construction as the one in town: with a covered place behind the desk. When the window curtains were drawn, the line of material ran from side to side as if made of one piece.

Once, as a child, Stratis had come into his grandfather's study when the old man had gone out for a moment. The curtains were open and he'd seen the icon. He'd been amazed to find out that there was anything there at all. He'd always assumed that the curtained space between the two windows was a decoration. He'd never guessed that anything might be behind it other than the wall. To see that a religious painting was hidden there, housed and protected, made him wonder whether there might be some secondary reason for keeping the sacred object where it would remain concealed: perhaps it was much more valuable than it looked. Maybe it was even one of the special Madonnas said to be able to grant wishes and to cure people.

As soon as he found out about the icon, Stratis began to speculate about his grandfather's beliefs. The old man railed against priests and against the idea of God, yet he kept an icon. He seemed to be so attached to it that he wouldn't be parted from it for more than a day. Most of the time it stayed behind its curtains. Very rarely, on special feast days—at Easter, for example—it was to be seen looking out from the parted drapery, and then one could observe that it was not merely small but distinctly lacking in artistic merit.

Because of the icon, Stratis was still very young when he began to think that there might be many things—events or institutions or people and their emotions—about which the surface presented to the world was no truer nor more important than what was kept from sight. Later, when he was in his early teens, his grandfather—in the middle of a conversation—swiveled his chair around, saying, "Let me show you something." He pulled the curtains apart. "Didn't know this was there, did you? It's so simple, no one would ever bother to look."

"You had it on show six years ago," Stratis said. "Christmas and Easter, remember? And I saw it once, a long time ago, when you must have stepped out of the room for a minute."

"You didn't say anything."

"Like what?"

"You didn't ask me about her."

"I guess I must have been afraid you'd think I was snooping."

"She's brought me luck. I took her with me after the war." He meant after the First World War, after Athens but before Marseilles, Paris, Manchester, and Cairo. "I've always liked her face," he said.

Stratis made up something about the attractiveness of the Madonna, the spiritual but loving, warm look in her large eyes. He was good at that kind of off-the-cuff speech; just short of glib. And in his grandfather's company he hardly had to think about the wording in order to please. He was the favorite. The old man loved even his bad qualities, many of which sprang from character faults that he himself had suffered from before he learned to take life calmly.

He'd done terrible things: unfair, childish, cruel, and spiteful. He'd

hurt the people who had loved him. He'd done it like a man in a fight—
to show them that they didn't love him enough or in the right way. What
had been wrong with him? What was wrong with Stratis? Whatever
it was, it was the same malady. Most of it could be ascribed to youth,
which you wouldn't really want to wish away. He sympathized.

As for Stratis, like everyone else, he revered the old man; but he
also felt an affection for him that was stronger than his love for any
other member of his family. He'd once come upon a photograph of his
grandfather dating from a holiday in the south of France, sometime in
the 1920s: in bathing costume and smiling for the camera. There was
the athletic build, the dark hair and eyes, the smile full of beautiful
teeth. And Stratis had thought: *Who is this? He looks exactly like me.*

Hearing his grandfather approach, he stepped back and coughed to
announce himself.

"Stratis?" the old man said. "Come see me."

He heard his grandfather turning around. He followed. They went
to the study.

Most of their talks were informal. Stratis would drop in twice a
day to gossip and chat. He was seldom summoned; the serious matters would be mixed in with everything else. Just recently, the same
question kept coming up in their talks: what profession Stratis should
train for.

His grandfather broached the subject with relaxed approval. It was
clear to him that his grandson was going to be exceptional, but there
was still some question about the direction he'd take. Back in October,
when he'd met the girl, Stratis had wanted to be a poet; in March he'd
agreed that maybe being a poet wasn't a career that could support a
wife and children, not that he'd want either at the moment. Besides,
he'd just begun to realize that poetry was too difficult. He had to concede that it shouldn't be his choice or, rather, that it hadn't chosen him.
But he had no desire to go into business. He couldn't believe that, feeling no interest, he had an ability for it.

"You could be a lawyer," his grandfather suggested.

"A good lawyer should be able to argue a case either way. I couldn't do that. Some things strike me as really wrong. And others aren't important. And all that paperwork. I wouldn't mind being a doctor if I didn't have to watch people being cut open."

"There are all kinds of doctors."

"But most of them are practical, aren't they? I'd only be good on the theoretical side. I'd like to help people but—not if it means having to stitch up wounds and hammer back pieces of bones and stuff. I really don't have what it takes to deal with fixing up people who've been crushed and burned and torn up."

"Well, there are specialists: lungs, heart, ears—"

"No, no. I can't imagine that I'd be any good at it."

"You're good at everything, Stratis. Then you get bored. I was the same. But an occupation isn't like a girlfriend: you don't pick it up and pursue it till you lose interest."

"So it's like falling in love?"

"On the contrary. You have to have some interest, yes. But the important thing is to learn the profession. Training. It doesn't matter what it is. And I think that while you're making up your mind, it would be a good idea for you to go to business school."

"Why?"

"They teach you a lot of useful things: economics, the stock market, corporations. It might help me, too. We could talk about your studies together. You could tell me how things have changed in the business world. And maybe I could give you a few tips. Think about it. You can't just dither, year after year. I realize that it isn't easy to choose; there's no reason why you can't qualify for one thing and then go on to another. There's time for more than one decision. Some people are lucky—they know very early what they want to do in life. I didn't know. I only knew that no one was ever going to beat me. And I was willing to try anything. Why not try, Stratis? I think maybe your talents have to be awakened by use. You have brains. You can get your qualification in some discipline and then find your own way to practice it: make it better, more modern, more yours. Why not? You'll like it. The world is very interesting, you know. You don't have to have the shining object that's hanging just out of your reach. Look at what's already in your hand. Use that."

Stratis always felt better after one of their talks. He still didn't know what to do with his life, but he felt sure that someone else had faith in him. In his grandfather's company he believed that his future was clear: if he couldn't see it, at least his grandfather could.

The old man enjoyed their talks even when Stratis spouted wildly about the artistic life, the crooked businessmen, the corrupt legal and political systems. "Yes, yes," he'd say, "but let me tell you about my friend, Nikos." And he'd illustrate some point with a story from his youth. All the time he'd be thinking: *Who can know the love I feel for this boy? He's myself when young, but better. He's the one who is going to live for me after I'm gone. I'm proud of him, but also nervous. He's more than I deserve.*

One of Julia's friends, a girl named Nina, telephoned Stratis. She wasn't a very good friend. Sometimes he wondered if Julia knew what Nina was like; at others he suspected that she had actually told Nina to look after him in order to keep him away from her—as if giving him another woman would erase her from his mind.

He'd already found two girls for himself. Sex wasn't the problem. They were both fun but they weren't Julia. It wasn't love. Nina wasn't love, either. And she wasn't even fun.

"Want to see a movie?" she asked.

"On a spring day, when the sun's shining?"

"I thought you said anytime was good for seeing a good movie."

"I'd rather try a museum. Or just go for a walk."

"I know what: there's an exhibition of icons . . . where was it?"

"Oh, right. There was something about it in the papers. You really want to see that stuff?"

"Sure," she said. "You can translate."

"Don't bank on it. I can barely transliterate."

"What's that?"

"The alphabet. They have different letters. What are you majoring in?"

"Soc. Rel."

"Uh-huh."

Social Relations, he thought. Was he going to be cultural research as well as the object of her desires? That could be another kind of slumming: *From Greece to the USA: A Case Study of Four Generations*. He didn't think Nina was smart enough for anything like that.

He took a taxi to the gallery. She was waiting at the door and she handed him one of the free leaflets. He started to skim the text on the way in, but as soon as they got through the doors, the light fell away and sounds were hushed. If anyone spoke, it was in a whisper. The place felt like a church or even a tomb. It wasn't just the presence of the icons, nor the half-darkened surroundings, that produced the atmosphere of awe. Something in the attitude of the onlookers contributed to the impression of sanctity. The dimness was merely a practical necessity, as the paintings could be damaged by strong light.

The show turned out to be huge. The most beautiful icons, and apparently the most unusual, were from Crete. Stratis knew nothing about the historical side of the painting—the monasteries, the tradition of the workshops, the composition of the materials used—but he could tell that the artistry itself was of a higher caliber than in other icons he'd seen. The excellence of the workmanship drew him to the characters portrayed and to the stories as well as the look of the people. He suddenly understood the strangeness and glory of sainthood as a naturally occurring complexity of spirit and emotion, unchangingly present in a world where religion was imposed from without. He'd always thought of the saints' legends the way his grandfather described them: the product of ignorance and poverty. "Once people have running water and central heating, comfort and plenty," his grandfather used to tell him, "their belief changes. Religion may still mean something to them, but it's no longer personal. That's what all that belief is for—to compensate for the things you don't have in this world."

Nina asked about a couple of words written at the top of a paint-

ing. After he'd spelled out the names of the saints for her, she recipro-
cated by making some remarks about the icons and the era from which
each of them came. There was a typed information card on the wall at
the side of every exhibit, but Stratis paid no attention to them. Nina
started a system: she'd take a brief look at the work itself and then go
to the card and read aloud in a low voice while he continued to concentrate on the painting. Almost immediately she'd join him and whisper
a comment. Gradually he began to ask questions and her answers became longer, as did his questions.

Why did they make everything in those weird shapes, he wanted
to know; what was the purpose of arranging the city buildings in the
background to look like a bouquet of flowers? And the rocks or mountain crags, or whatever they were: why did they look like pieces of
planking? And that orange color? And the black leaves over there?

She talked about the light and what it meant and which part of
the icon it came from. She told him that certain colors were traditional and that, in addition, some pigments faded or became unstable.
And as for the shape of things, the general design: she said, "These
paintings aren't realistic. But they aren't supposed to be. They had the
technique to paint realistically, so this is what they wanted. They liked
it this way. It's a style. It's meant to be beautiful and inspirational, not
photographic. There are times when artists and their patrons begin to
distrust work that's highly accomplished in a kind of slick way, so that
it seems to be lacking in feeling. Then the fashion changes to portraits
that are more sort of blunt. And that can change, too, until it develops
into a style where, let's say, the use of color is subtle but the line is deliberately . . . if you look over here: the general effect is polished, but
the perspective—have you ever seen any Persian miniatures?"

"As far as painting goes, I'm a hick. You know, I like movies."

"Everybody likes movies."

"But this is interesting. You really care about this kind of thing,
don't you?"

She cared because she didn't have the rest. She wasn't good-looking,
not even faintly pretty, and she loved handsome men.

She said, "Most of that stuff is from a course I took last summer. I just thought it would be great to go to Europe with a group of other students, but we were studying for three weeks before we even got on the plane and I guess a lot of it stuck."

He could imagine it: everybody else would be going out at night and getting laid, while Nina was rereading her books. He said, "It never grabbed me before. I think I'll get the catalogue." He'd buy the catalogue for the pictures and because some of the relatives might want to see it. He probably wouldn't open it more than once himself.

They moved to other rooms. After the Cretan paintings, the rest were disappointing. Stratis was still interested, but he'd begun to feel that he'd seen a lot of icons for one day.

Nina pointed to a far wall, saying, "That must be where the missing ones were supposed to be." A row of three spaces led to the corner; one was blank, the next had a photograph pinned at the center of it, and the last displayed a piece of paper.

She approached the empty space. It would have held a famous, miracle-working painting if the people of its island had been willing to let it go. They hadn't even sanctioned a reproduction.

The black-and-white snapshot to its right was of an icon out of a private collection; the object was too fragile to be transported. The photograph showed many places of wear and a missing edge.

"It's still good," she said.

"Too bad it isn't in color."

"Color never reproduces right. Sometimes it's better to have black and white. But probably the reason is that the owner doesn't want anybody trying to copy it. Art forgery is a big industry."

He walked ahead and stood in front of the piece of paper. Now that they were closer, it was obvious that it was a photograph of a lightly penciled sketch. Stratis looked, while Nina read the information card.

"This is a stolen one," she whispered. "It was taken from its island and ever since then the place has had bad luck—the harvests fail, the children die, there are outbreaks of disease, the water goes bad, and all they pray for is that the Madonna will come back to them." She moved closer, peering at the sketch. "Well, we didn't miss much there," she decided. "It must have been one of those purely religious objects. But it's sad that they've lost everything. They should stop hoping to get it back. They should paint a new one and start again."

The Madonna of New Beginnings, Stratis thought: *holding a micro-wave and a concrete mixer.* Or was she talking about his continued longing for Julia?

"If there's only one," he told her, "you can't replace it."

"You actually like this thing?"

"Well, it isn't very good, but the eyes are nice."

Nina stiffened to attention, like a jealous woman who hears another woman's looks praised by the man she loves. She pushed her head forward to examine the picture. Stratis stepped back. He'd already seen more than enough to know that inch for inch, and line for line, the sketch was copied from his grandfather's icon.

Nina wanted to go on somewhere for a cup of coffee or a meal or maybe a film. As they walked to the subway entrance, she made sure of his interest by saying that she'd seen Julia recently, with the new boyfriend. "I don't think he's anything to worry about," she told him. "That won't last."

How long did it last with me? he thought. And was there still a chance that she'd come back? If the situation had been reversed, he wouldn't have gone back. He'd never return to someone he'd left. Apparently, other people did. He'd finally accepted the fact that she'd gone, but he still couldn't believe that she preferred the total loser she was going out with now.

Nina said, "I think it's her way of getting to know people. A way of being democratic. She had this very sheltered upbringing and she wants to know about the world. For a man, that's easy. But for some women—the only way you ever get to know a cross section of society is to sleep around."

He shouldn't listen. She wanted him herself; she'd speak against

Julia in order to put herself in a better light. And maybe she'd already been telling him lies. He was so eager to hear any news, even to hear Julia's name spoken, that he'd accept all information, true or made up. He'd never understood stories in the papers about men who set out to pursue women after being rejected, and who would then kidnap them or shoot them. Now he understood completely.

"I have an aunt," he said, "who tells me that sometimes 'young people,' as she puts it, use their sexuality to go slumming: to see how the other half loves."

"Slumming? I don't see the connection."

"You attach yourself to the person without really having to enter the life, but that's the way you find out about it."

"I still don't see it," Nina said. "Slumming?"

"Isn't that what you were saying? Anyway, it's just a theory. She has a lot of them."

Later that day he began to feel unsure about the similarity of his grandfather's icon to the sketch in the show. He went into the old man's study—a thing no one else would dream of doing, and which he'd never done without permission except for that once in his childhood. His heart began to beat loudly and heavily, all the way up to his throat, as he pulled aside the curtain and looked at the painting. But, while he studied it, he forgot what the sketch had been like.

The next day he went back to the gallery. Standing in front of the sketch again, he felt the same, odd sense of recognition. But now he had to laugh at the though that—unless he could see the two together—he was never going to be able to tell for sure how closely his grandfather's icon resembled the picture on the paper.

Going out of the ground-level forecourt, he noticed a man sitting on the stairs to the building's side door. The man looked like a beggar: he was old and emaciated and he wore a frayed suit, a stained shirt, and a battered, antiquated hat; Stratis thought at first that he had stopped to rest before attempting the main staircase in the warm, sunny weather.

As he came closer, he saw that the man had propped a shabby briefcase against the steps and a little sign that said, LOST, underneath which was pasted a copy of the museum sketch: the one of the stolen icon.

When he got right up to the man, he was able to read what had been printed from the sketch: *Please help to relieve the suffering of our people until the Virgin returns to the island.* Next to the briefcase was a stack of photocopies of the picture.

"How much?" Stratis asked.

The old man held up a finger, his grave demeanor making the motion seem like a warning. Stratis gave him a dollar and took one of the copies. Then, on impulse, he added a five-dollar bill.

He moved on, deciding that it was such a good day to be outdoors—despite the traffic and the crowds—that he'd walk back to his grandfather's house.

The picture seller or beggar, or whatever he was, must have been close behind him, following an impulse of his own; or perhaps he'd read beyond the young man's gesture of sympathy to a deeper interest that could be tapped. At any rate, the next morning, there he was on the front steps of the house.

Stratis spoke to him and was answered in a Greek that was difficult to understand. Greek changed to halting, broken English that described the painting and installation of the icon in the sixteenth century, and the events leading up to its theft. That part of the speech must have been memorized as, immediately afterwards, the man reverted to his own language: he held up one of his photocopies and he kept touching the face of the Madonna as he talked. Stratis nodded. He handed over some more money but, as the words became more emotional and at the same time entirely unintelligible, he imitated one of his grandfather's gestures—the one that meant "No more"—and walked away down the street.

On his return early that afternoon the man was still there, wanting to talk. Stratis turned his face away.

He knocked on the study door as soon as his grandfather had finished his afternoon nap. He took the catalogue with him, and the piece of paper, which he opened so that the sketch showed. He tapped his finger on a corner of it.

"That old man outside says it was stolen."

"They aren't the same," his grandfather told him. "Even if they look alike, they aren't. Maybe mine was stolen once upon a time, but it isn't stolen now. It belongs to me. I bought it in good faith."

"He says it was taken out of the church."

"It was probably sold by a priest or one of the monks. To get money for wine. They drink up all the wine and then they need more."

"It's your island, isn't it? And you've never been back."

"There's nothing to go back for. It was always one of those places out of the Dark Ages and it's even worse now. The people are like animals: they stare, they grunt; no thought ever enters their heads."

"That's because they're poor. That's what poverty does to people."

"They aren't poor. You don't know what poverty is. Look at the poverty of the past and what all those people created in spite of it."

"Only a few did the creating. They were the ones with the money."

"No. They got the money because they deserved to have it. The others were all busy staring into the distance and grunting. It's the same nowadays: they've got food and clothes and a roof over their heads and all the time in the world. So, what do they do with it? They go to those disco places. And when they're not doing that, they've got the earphones on. You see their heads bobbing and their feet stamping. That isn't music. What is that? It's a constant rhythm over and over. No melody, no change. It's a masturbation for the ears. That's what they all need—some simple pattern that they can keep repeating. Then they're happy. It's like hypnotizing a chicken. And as if that isn't enough, they take drugs."

"He says the picture was stolen out of the church by a choirboy."

"I bought that icon in Athens, in good faith. I don't have the receipt because I lost it in the war. You think I was worrying about a piece of paper when we lost houses and people? And countries?"

"You were right here in town during the war."

"The first war. I fought in the first war on the Albanian frontier. And after that we had the influenza: the Asian flu. We thought it came from the east, but they're saying now that it was like the Spanish flu. You could go down the streets in Athens and they were deserted. Everybody had it. The only reason I escaped was that I'd had malaria in the army. If you'd had malaria, you didn't catch it."

"Grandfather, this man says that they've prayed for over seventy years to get their picture back. The luck of the island depends on it."

"Oh, really? Was that island so lucky in the days when they had it? Don't forget what my name means."

"'The one who walks straight.'"

"And your name, too. That means you should have your head screwed on right, not that you should listen to lies and fables. I remember that church, all falling down, all rotting. And the priests in their long hair, like a bunch of dirty old women with beards. They could tell anybody what to do, because God told them, you know. I think it's a good thing that somebody took that painting away. It's another story like the Elgin marbles; what would they be now if the British hadn't put them in a museum? The Turks used the Acropolis as a powder magazine: they could all have blown up. And that painting—that icon would be just shreds by now. But anyway, it isn't the same one. I remember what it looked like and it isn't the same."

"It looks exactly like the sketch. Here, I'll show you."

"No. All those things were done to a standard. They kept on with the same face and pose for centuries. The experts say they can tell one from the other, if you want to believe them. But I don't think so."

"You could have an expert look at yours."

"What for? I know what it is. Even if it's a copy, I like it. And it isn't insured. Nobody knows that it's here. Some professor of art walks into this house and by the end of the week everybody has a note in a book that says these paintings can be found at this address. How do things get stolen? Because stupid people insure them and any crook can get a job in one of those companies, where he can look up the list of what you've got that's worth stealing."

"Everything else you've got is insured."

"I don't want to talk about this, Stratis. It doesn't concern you or anybody else. So don't go telling everybody what's in your grandfather's house, OK? You hear what I'm telling you?"

"OK, OK. Of course I wouldn't. I just feel sorry for that island, where everything's going wrong. And that old man outside—"

"That old man is a sneaky old crook who sees another Greek with a big house. You forget him. I've known these people all my life. They're not worth wiping your feet on."

"But I've got a photocopy of the sketch. We could compare them right now."

"I told you, all those damn Christ pictures look alike."

"It isn't Christ. It's the Madonna."

"Same difference. And it's all lies, anyway."

"Not for the people who believe."

"What are you talking about? An icon doesn't mean anything. It's a representation of meaning. You know: a picture. The real thing . . . the real thing can't be shown. It isn't visible. A religious picture simply represents. Everything used to be that way once. Now people want to have a painting for what it is." He gestured toward the little Daumier and the Hobbema that Stratis had never appreciated until one day he'd looked at it again and began to like it, as if he'd never seen it before.

"But he's here. And he's here about the icon—as far as I can figure out. How did he know what yours looks like?"

"He doesn't. That thing on the paper isn't mine. It's the one in the show."

"He wouldn't know about that one, either. How could he get a sketch of the icon at the gallery?"

"Easy. You say the story about the lost picture was in the papers before this show opened? Well, he paid the price of admission once:

saw that sketch, drew his own copy of it on some paper that looked the same size, and made a hundred Photostats. Then he sells them with this line he's got about collecting for the island. Oh, he's collecting, all right."

"It belongs to the monastery there," Stratis said. "The whole island has had bad luck since it was taken away." He didn't dare to repeat the word "stolen."

"You wait till you've worked for twenty years. Then you'll know the value of things."

"But Grandfather, don't you agree that a religious work of art is different from other kinds? I mean, it isn't just a lot of nice colors, like one of those French pictures of lily pads. To the people who believe in religion, it has a special meaning above and beyond the way it looks."

The old man continued to regard him with a kindly expression. Then he laughed. He waved his hand several times as if he were an overfed diner, disdaining additional offerings. The subject was closed.

Stratis threw up his hands, saying, "It doesn't matter."

"It doesn't matter?"

"It doesn't matter whether it was stolen or not. The important thing is to put it back."

"I have never," his grandfather said, "never stolen anything in my life."

"Aunt Lydia and Uncle Maurice would agree with me."

"Your aunt Lydia would send this entire family to Park Burnett if she thought she could raise some cash by selling us. Nothing is sacred to her except her gallbladder and her collection of Italian shoes. And as for your uncle Maurice—"

"But the people who live on that island—"

"Enough," the old man murmured. He pointed to the door.

"It should go back to the island," Stratis said.

His grandfather rocked slowly to his feet and stood, balancing himself against the front of the desk. He leaned forward. "Don't tell me what I should do," he said.

"Their need is so great."

"No one's need is as great as mine," his grandfather said emphatically. "You will not speak of this again, Stratis."

"Can't you see—?"

"Out!" the old man shouted.

Stratis bowed his head. He could feel his grandfather's anger, as if it were heat or noise, still coming across the desk at him. He sighed. He shrugged. He looked up and muttered, "All right," as if agreeing that he'd lost the attempt to convince. He stood up, turned around, and left the room.

When he went out for the evening, the beggar was still there, and when he came back.

In the morning after breakfast he dropped in to the study and mentioned the fact to his grandfather, who simply nodded, and asked, "What makes you think he's from the island, anyway?"

"He has the accent."

"How would you know? You can hardly understand a word of ordinary Greek, much less the dialects. Even I have trouble with them."

"It has the same sound. It's like hearing you talk to your friend, Costa, over the phone."

"If he's anything, I bet he's an art dealer. A lot of robberies still start by word of mouth. Somebody says, 'Oh, they have a solid silver tea set,' or 'a painting by so-and-so': and eventually that information gets to the ones who are in a position to do something about it."

"Not according to what I've heard. Most theft is opportunistic: somebody sees an open window or they go down the street, trying the car doors."

"Professional crime, specialized. Art theft. And, as I said, big-time operators are always tied in with the insurance companies. China and jewelry, too. Rugs, furniture. That's how they knew about Mrs. Solomon's silver. They didn't touch the silver plate. They just look up your name, see what you've got. And then they ask around, to get an offer before they go to the trouble of stealing the stuff."

"How much have you insured it for?"

"I told you: it isn't insured."

"Really?"

"Of course not. It's irreplaceable. Once you insure it, they know you've got it. They know, the tax man knows—everybody. Anyway, I don't want money. I want what I've got." He threw himself from side to side in his chair and resettled himself more comfortably. "I paid for it," he said.

When Stratis went out of the front door a few minutes later, he wouldn't look at the beggar, nor when he returned. He reported back to his grandfather, saying, "He's out there whenever I leave the house. He must be staying on the doorstep all night. If it isn't so important, what does he want?"

"Money, a home. He's a Greek and I'm a Greek. That isn't enough. I haven't worked my guts out for nearly a century so that some freeloader from the old country can milk me. Stratis, my boy, it's a good thing to have a soft heart at the right time, but it can also be a danger. It can lead you into cruelties you would never contemplate if you weren't thinking of the immediate pleasure of flattering yourself. That's what all this sentimentality is: you think for one glorious moment that you're the Good Samaritan, or Jesus Christ or God. And then people take you up on it. You've given them a promise, so they expect you to fulfill it. They want to know why you can't carry them on your shoulders for the rest of their lives, seeing how much you have and how little they do. Ask yourself: what kind of a man gets into a state like that?"

"A man who's had bad luck."

"Bad luck comes to people who don't make plans for sidestepping it when it's there."

"That isn't always possible, especially for a poor man."

"But why is he poor? Children can be poor. A woman with children can be poor. But a man? In the modern world?"

"Things aren't the way they used to be. Jobs—"

"A man who remains poor all his life in a country like this is a man who deserves to be poor: a drunkard, a drug addict, a gambler, a man who's extremely stupid or lazy or mentally deficient or insane, who can't or won't adapt to the normal requirements of authority, who can't get along with other people, and so on. Why do you want to lift someone up out of his misery, just to drop him down into it again?"

"It doesn't work like that. Fate—"

"Yes, it does."

"It can happen to anybody. Maybe he had a family and they all died. Maybe—"

"Stratis, I want to talk to you about your future."

"I really couldn't stand to be a lawyer. I couldn't even do the studying. It's completely deadening."

"Yes. Probably just as well not to begin, if you feel that way. And you can't even outargue me."

"Nobody does that, Grandfather."

The old man cackled. He said, "Well, you have a few more months before anything should be decided. We can talk about it again. Do some thinking. And then we'll go for a walk on the golf course and plan it out. Let's hope I don't get any stiffer or you may have to push me in a wheelchair."

"That's never going to happen, Grandfather. You're going to stay on your feet. You could have walked to the sea with Xenophon."

"How do you know about Xenophon?"

"High school. History 2A."

"You see? Education is important."

"Sure. It doesn't make you happy. It doesn't help you to get your girl back."

"Oh, Stratis. Some things you have to do for yourself."

"Grandfather, I can see that you're trying not to laugh, but—"

"I'm smiling. I'm fond of you and I know that you're going to come through this discouraging time."

Stratis felt better. He remembered all the dangerous times his grandfather had lived through: yet the old man was kind to him, never suggesting that he might be spoiled because he had too much freedom and too many of the good things in life. He didn't forget about the other old man, but he told himself that his responsibilities lay near to home, so that whatever injustice had been perpetrated, it wasn't going to be up to him to redress it. And that was just as well because his grandfather wasn't a man who could be persuaded—his first instincts were strong, unquestioning and unquestioned. He didn't care if that meant that he was sometimes wrong. He'd made millions out of the times when he was right.

Ancient though he was, he'd also somehow managed, during their talks, to avoid allowing a direct comparison of icon and copy, and—whether by mistake or intent—had kept the Photostat, which was the only one Stratis had bought.

He went out for an evening meal with two friends. On their way home, he took them to the café where Julia's new lover worked.

He and his friends sat down for a cup of coffee. They behaved themselves impeccably because a different waiter came to their table. *He's a coward, too,* Stratis thought. *He was supposed to work the table we chose, but when he saw us coming, he asked somebody to swap with him.*

On their way out, all three of them saw Julia walk across the other side of the terrace, probably going to meet the ponytail. Stratis turned his head. One of his friends, who had had a lot to drink, started to say something, but the other one hushed him and pulled Stratis by the arm. "Time to go," he said. "This way."

They were out on the sidewalk and saying good night without Julia's name having been mentioned once. The sober friend said that he'd call in a couple of days. The drunken one waved and lurched away.

Stratis walked. He hadn't realized at the time how much he'd wanted to get into a fight, but now he was glad that other people had allowed him to avoid one. He was lucky to have friends who wouldn't let him make a fool of himself. And he'd seen Julia again—that was the main thing.

After a while he hailed a cab. By then his thoughts had drawn him back to the mystery of his grandfather's icon. All during the ride, he wondered about it.

It had to be the same one. His grandfather would have taken it with him when he left the island. He could imagine the old brigand, even when young, going about things in that high-handed way; just appropriating what he'd decided he ought to have. His grandfather had taken a beautiful, interesting, useful object and made it dead. That wasn't right. No wonder all the people on the island thought that they had lost their way. Such an act couldn't help but bring bad luck.

The beggar was still on the doorstep and remained there all night, as if holding vigil. And he was there the next day. By that time all the relatives knew about him, although not about his need to recover a lost icon. No one else but Stratis had given him any money or stopped to listen to what he was trying to say.

The day after that, he was gone. According to the rest of the family, Aunt Ariana found him still on the front steps when she went out to do some early shopping. She screamed at him in Greek, calling him a dirty beggar, and when he didn't move, rushed back indoors, beyond the kitchen to the back pantry: to find a broom. She re-emerged, broom in hand, and proceeded to beat him furiously, all the while screeching without a pause. One of the things she kept saying was that she was going to call the police and let them take care of him. Her vehemence didn't impress the man, but the sight of a patrol car in the distance seemed to make him apprehensive. He gathered his papers and brief-case and hobbled away. He didn't come back.

Down in the country, visitors would soon be arriving. There were many springtime and summer distractions: tennis, trail riding or—the most popular—going out to dinner with other families in the neighbor-hood. Across the road from the old man's land—and just before the hills began—was a golf course much in demand by city men who left the concrete and plate glass behind them every weekend, looking for a slower pace, fresher air, and relatively uncrowded peace.

After the golfers finished playing their rounds, the old man used to walk over the fairway with Stratis and they'd talk. Whether his grandson joined him or not, he invariably took some exercise every day; he called it his "constitutional." Stratis had been tagging along with him ever since childhood, starting with the years when his parents were traveling through other countries, having left him in his grandfather's care.

They'd cover all kinds of topics during their rambles, at times going off into laughing fits together and then becoming serious or impassioned, straightening out many of the world's most difficult problems.

The large and comfortable house was easily able to accommodate regular visitors or unexpected guests. It was built around a small, partially covered courtyard, in the center of which was a fountain. The old man preferred that to air conditioning. The ancients, he used to say, knew a lot of things. And they did most of them better than we did now. Courtyards and running water were the old ways of regulating temperature; and positioning your house on the rise of a small hill so that it caught the breezes but not the full force of wind and cold. By such simple methods you could ensure that summer days cooled down at night and winter evenings escaped the penetrating chill of the nearby mountainside. Trees were important, too: to shade and protect, to shelter the birds, and to lend beauty to your surroundings.

He never referred to early civilizations as things of the past or to their rulers as men and women who had lived a long time ago; they were always "ancients" and their historical period was "in ancient times." When he mentioned them, it was as if he were relating family gossip about his cousins from a few generations past, who just happened to be kings and queens and the heroes of legend: no ordinary people.

"That tree is sick," Uncle Zenon said. Stratis walked over to see. The tree appeared to be perfectly all right, but he didn't know about such things. Uncle Zenon did, or said that he did. Not only did the tree seem all right: it was lovely. It was one of Stratis's favorites. If he looked out of his bedroom window from inside the house, its branches led his eye along a graceful curve of feathery leaves and—through minutely differentiated levels of green—to the landscape beyond. It gave the vision a way to proceed by stages and to enjoy near and distant sights as if the view were a musical experience. What would life be like when the tree was gone—when he had to look out at an empty space and a far horizon for which there was no preparatory flourish, no introduction of line and shape? The outer world would sit there in the distance, unconnected and uninteresting.

"Are you sure?" he asked.

"Oh, yes. Look at the back, there."

He looked more closely. Everything still appeared normal to him. Nothing had happened yet but already the death of the tree and its future absence had darkened his mood. The future wasn't always going to be new and bright and at the same time full of everything from the past out of which it grew. That wasn't the way it worked. Things disappeared all the time.

All that night he wondered about the future. If only he hadn't had the quarrel with Julia, his path would be clear. They'd have married, he'd have qualified in some skill or other; maybe, to please his grandfather, he'd have chosen business school, and possibly even have started to raise a family shortly after marriage. That would have pleased the old man enormously. And Melinda would have friends to play with when Sylvie brought her to visit.

The wind blew hard from nightfall till dawn, tugging and releasing one of the window hooks in its catch, so that the room began to seem like a boat that was straining against its moorings.

In the morning the weather and news programs reported a storm moving up the coast. Gales had already caused widespread devastation to the south and drivers were being warned to be prepared: if they were commuters, they ought to consider leaving their cars in town and taking public transport home, or even spending the night.

The sky was white, brightening occasionally to let a sunny luster show itself for a few moments. The wind blew relentlessly. Gradually the day dimmed. By lunchtime the sun was gone, and an hour after lunch Stratis said that he couldn't stand being cooped up indoors for another minute. He went for a walk in the hills.

Everyone called after him that he shouldn't go out. He took one of the umbrellas from the hall stand and left without answering.

Thunder muttered at the back of the sky. It began low and muffled, far away. He thought that he'd have plenty of time to take his walk— maybe a little faster than he'd figured at first—and be home again without getting wet.

As he pushed forward, the thunder retreated. He entered the more densely wooded, higher ground with the feeling that he could relax.

Less than ten minutes later, the thunder started again. This time it was nearer, coming in long, rumbling swells. It was accompanied by a palpable drop in the air pressure. He hurried to the place in the trail where a lookout had been cut through the trees.

Across the intervening hills he could see down to the gap. The sky was a shade of black that appeared green. The storm was coming up and it seemed inevitable. He began to walk fast, hoping to outrun the rain.

There were bright flickerings at the horizon. Behind him the deep, full, angry voice of the thunder issued from a sky like night and it carried a tone of personal, vengeful intent. Other people, his family, the houses he'd left only half an hour before, the city beyond—all the world had vanished, leaving only him and the pursuing storm.

As soon as the big, branched lightning began, he threw away the umbrella and ran.

The wind came driving through the boughs, ripping branches away, scattering the leaves: whistling and rattling. Everything whipped and writhed around him and then—more frightening than the commotion— all noise and movement stopped, leaving him racing ahead through silence.

Suddenly, with a tearing crack, the world exploded and a tree burst right in front of him, the raw inside smoking as the bark was peeled away: sliced like a carrot from top to bottom. And instantly the bolt of electricity slammed into three neighboring trees in quick succession, splintering them into pieces as small as matches. He threw himself on the ground.

The rain let loose, battering down everywhere. Mud and water poured over him in streams, drenching him so thoroughly that he might have been under the sea. He stayed where he was until the worst of the storm passed by. When he got to his feet and dragged himself back to the house, half the relatives were as worried as if he'd been a missing child. The others laughed.

He took off his shoes in the back hall, carried some coffee up to his room, and left his sodden clothes on the floor of his bathroom. He stood under a hot shower until he warmed up.

What his grandfather called "the ancients" were right: the elements were gods—how could anyone doubt that?

His grandfather was a terrible old scoundrel, an old pirate, but he loved him. Nevertheless, the storm was a sign. It had shown him how insignificant every life was and how vulnerable, even to a momentary change in the weather. It was as if he'd been told to hold onto what was true: to make sure that he didn't forget again.

The icon had to go back to the island it had been stolen from. Since his grandfather would rather be boiled in oil before he'd make restitution to anyone for anything, it was up to someone else to do it.

In the night he went downstairs to his grandfather's study, found the briefcase in which the icon was usually transported, pried open the hinges at the back, and took out the painting. As soon as he held it in his hands, he sensed that he was doing the right thing. He also felt a delayed fear at the thought of what a mess everything would be if—as well as the icon—there had been important papers in the case. What would he have done then? He might have found himself having to destroy legal documents, share certificates, and private letters.

As it was, he could simply take the briefcase with him and ditch it. When the loss was discovered, his grandfather might begin to doubt that he'd brought the icon down to the country. He was an old man: his memory wasn't faultless. No matter how strong his recollection, he'd phone back to town and have a search started. And then the incident would become like the loss of his gold pen. The pen had rolled off the night table and been kicked under the four-poster, to remain in the one spot the maid, Stamata, missed in her vacuuming. She'd found it after five months. And the old man had had to admit that the pen hadn't been in the other house, as he'd thought, and hadn't been lost somewhere in his study: it was a mystery. But his treasure had been restored to him and he wouldn't hear anything against Stamata's housecleaning methods; hadn't she been the one to find the lost object?

There had never been a mystery, of course. The disappearance of the pen had taken place while the old man wasn't paying attention and so he couldn't remember.

That was what would happen now, Stratis thought. By the time he was home again, the hunt for the briefcase would be in full swing. And, meanwhile, he'd have taken a plane to Greece, restored the icon to its church on the island and, if the news ever came out, he could simply lie. He could say to his grandfather: *You were right—all those things look alike. I went out and bought a fake in a souvenir shop. And that's what I gave them. To jolt them out of their depression. I thought it was worth a try.*

Maybe his grandfather wouldn't quite believe or disbelieve him. The fate of the icon would become something unacknowledged between them, neither certain fact nor doubt. It might even happen that after a year or so, if any suspicion remained, his grandfather would entertain the idea of a theft with less horror, perhaps with a touch of admiration. After all, hadn't he been the first to steal? His anger would pass, as would the outrage: the sense of having been robbed.

Stratis left a note to say that he was going to stay with a friend while he worked on an idea he'd had for a poem. He phoned the friend and told him that he was taking a trip with a married woman the family disapproved of; he'd be gone for a couple of days so if anyone called up and asked to speak to him, the friend should say that Stratis had been there but that he'd left to go someplace else and he hadn't told anyone where.

In the morning, as soon as the old man looked for his briefcase to take out the icon and hang it up in its place, he realized that—having failed to get anywhere by talk—his grandson had resorted to force, and had taken what he wanted.

His disappointment was so bitter that for two days it took away his appetite. *He stole it from me,* he thought. *He, to whom I would have given anything; and I'd made plans to leave him everything, including what he stole.*

He sat in his study and refused to join the others for meals. But he did nothing about the theft, and said nothing. It was for Stratis to come back to him with apologies, explanations, and pleas for forgiveness.

On the third day he heard from the police.

They telephoned first, saying that they wanted to speak to him about his grandson, who had had an accident; the authorities in Greece had been in touch with them. A man would call at the house.

Stratis was dead. The body was going to be shipped home as soon as the formalities were completed. He'd been carrying his passport, but identification would still be necessary. The police had tried, but failed, to contact the boy's parents.

The man in charge arrived with a Greek Orthodox priest and a translator. He didn't look like a policeman; and he was wearing a suit, not a uniform. But that was what he was, even if his department extended to international territory. The priest and interpreter accepted chairs at the side of the room while the policeman explained that Stratis had been found on his grandfather's island. He was first seen asking two priests the way to the church; he appeared to be in great distress. The priests tried to find out what was wrong with him, but his command of Greek wasn't up to dealing with their local version of the language, even though they took care to speak slowly. They attempted to persuade him to rest, but he pushed them away and kept walking. They thought that he was sick; he was staggering and gasping. Every once in a while he'd stop and bow his head, stumble around a little, and continue. At last, as he was in sight of the church, he fell. They rushed forward to help.

When they opened his coat—an unnecessary garment at that time of year—they saw that he was soaked with blood. He was trying to talk. He touched the piece of wood that was buttoned inside his shirt. He said something about it that they didn't understand. However, a search of his pockets afterwards disclosed a list of Greek words and phrases: the word for "church," "water," and "car"; and questions such as, "Where is . . . ?", "How much is it?", "How far is it?" and, right at the end, "This is the lost icon belonging to the church and the people of this island. The good luck has returned."

The two priests removed the piece of wood and recognized it as an icon of the Madonna. It, too, was bloodstained, all the way up to the Virgin's neck, but her face was untouched and—even before they became aware of the importance of that particular icon—they noticed how lovingly her eyes rested on the island that was her home. Stratis at that stage was dying. He kept trying to repeat the phrase about returning the icon, but the priests didn't understand that until the discovery of the paper with its penciled list of phrases. Knowing that death was near, they asked him if he was firm in his belief and ready to meet the Lord of Creation. He couldn't say anything for a while, although his lips moved. Then a tear ran down his face and he smiled. And he said yes.

"I don't believe it," his grandfather said.

The interpreter whispered something to the priest. They both stood up. "Later," the policeman told them. The two resumed their places, but they continued to talk hurriedly to each other in soft hisses. "If you wouldn't mind," the policeman said.

The interpreter insisted, "This is the reason why we are here. To assure the family that the young man died in the faith of his ancestors. He said yes and the spirit left him. It was his final word."

"Half the family is Catholic in any case," the old man told him. "But what language was he speaking when he was supposed to be saying yes?"

"Greek, naturally."

"All right. I understand. I'm not doubting your word. Let's proceed with the officer's account."

They were mistaken, of course. There had been a misinterpreta-
tion. Stratis's command of Greek was pathetic; he'd probably forgotten
that *né* meant yes: because it sounded so close to "nay." He must have
believed he was saying no. And that would be why he'd smiled.

The ignorance of the others was already foisting upon the world
a false notion of Stratis's character—someone they didn't even know.
Those two priests, who had shared his last moments, were like witnesses at a traffic accident, not even clear about what they'd seen with
their own eyes.

"He was stabbed," the policeman said. "We've traced the wounding
to the men's lavatory at the airport in Athens, where a gang of four
dealers was splitting up a drug shipment for cash. Did you ever suspect
that your grandson was involved with drugs?"

"Absolutely not. He liked to drink when he went out in the evening; sometimes a lot, and like anyone young, but most of the time
just three or four drinks with a meal, sharing a couple of bottles with
some friends. That's all."

"You're sure of that?"

"Definitely."

"Can you explain why he might have taken part in a fight between
drug dealers?"

"I can only think that he was an innocent bystander and they
thought he was a spy: someone from the narcotics squad. If this fight
took place in a public lavatory, well . . . why do you think he'd be there?
To relieve himself."

"We were wondering whether the icon might have been part of the
exchange?"

"So that he could give it away?"

"No, it doesn't make sense."

"And I think I can tell you about that. He'd seen an exhibition of
icons at an art gallery last month. He spoke to me about a lost icon
that came from an island where everything had gone wrong since it
disappeared. I told him . . . I told him that if the islanders were really
superstitious enough to believe that, they'd probably be happy with

one of those cheap copies you can buy in any junk shop all over the world—they all look alike."

"But where would the icon have come from?"

"Oh, anywhere. Here, probably. From someplace that sells religious bric-a-brac."

"I suppose it isn't possible that the painting was genuine?"

"Of course not. He'd never have dared to take it through customs."

"It was small and the airport is notoriously lax."

"Nevertheless. Art theft? A jail sentence? Why would he risk that?"

"Was he very religious?"

"On the contrary."

"The priest seems to think that he was."

"Well, he's wrong. Maybe Stratis saw the restoration of the icon as an adventure, or even a joke: he'd take it to the island and if they accepted it as genuine, that would help them out of their troubles. Just as I said."

And of course the island would accept it now. Blood had been spilled. That made everything true. You wouldn't die for something that was fake, would you?

The island would prosper and Stratis, who had made such an extraordinary gesture—giving his life for the sake of strangers—would become famous. His story would be told all over the island and, in the telling, the facts would be worn down as the sea wears away the stones on the shore, so that eventually his recounted history would resemble the life of a saint: a rich young man who—rebelling against his family—cast away all worldly vanities and entered a sacred state.

"I'm tired," the old man said. "This news is hard to bear. I would like to rest."

"I don't think we'll need to ask you anything more. Are the boy's parents—?"

"They're traveling. I've telephoned. They're flying to Athens and then back here."

Everyone stood. As the policeman left the room, the priest began to talk about the island's great joy at having the treasure restored. The true treasure was faith, which they had lost with the disappearance of their protectress. Now they could never doubt again. His grandson had shown the world that heaven meant them to be blessed. All the people of the island joined him and his fellow clerics in extending their condolences to the family for the loss of this splendid young man who had sacrificed himself, so nobly, for others.

The old man put a hand to his temple for the last part of the speech, and closed his eyes. When both priest and interpreter had finished, he said to the priest in Greek, "I thank you for your sympathy and for coming all this way in person. I must retire now, but the family would be happy if you could join them for a meal before you leave. My cousins will attend to everything." He rang the bell on his desk. Later he heard that, after many protestations, the two did stay for dinner and managed to exact contributions for a memorial to Stratis.

Vultures, he thought; even at the graveside, hustling for money to keep them in business. And now their miserable island was going to be on the map: a genuine tourist attraction with a legend to go with it.

The newspaper accounts didn't mention the fact that one of Stratis's relatives had come from the island. The surname was different, but the old man's name—even in the shortened, most easily pronounceable form he had adopted on arrival in America—would have been recognized by an islander. And the priest had sat down to dinner at the house. Had nobody admitted that there was a family connection with the place of the icon's church? Apparently not. Nor did anyone in the family remark on the peculiar circumstances of Stratis's death. The icon was never mentioned at all, although they knew that there was one in the house. They might even have realized that that one was now gone. Perhaps they simply weren't curious, or possibly the fact of death had taken away their interest in peripheral matters.

Maybe they believed, as Stratis had, that his grandfather had stolen the painting when young. Perhaps they didn't want to investigate what they saw as a crime of long ago that had finally been put right.

The funeral was attended by all the relatives and some friends. A girl no one in the family knew—probably the one who had caused all the trouble—was there. She was pretty enough, but unremarkable, looking serious and rather melancholy. She came with an ugly friend, who cried a lot.

The old man didn't cry. He exerted all his strength to stay standing, with the help of his cane. And after that, he went to bed.

The young were natural betrayers, of course—particularly young men: that was a fact of life. They were always moving forward too fast to keep up with old ties. They had to find their place in the world and not simply copy the ways of older generations. You made them the inheritors of your future self and then they threw it away.

But Stratis had had a good heart. How could he have failed to stop and think about what he was doing? How could he have so misbelieved and misunderstood?

It must have been the girl: the utterly unsuitable, superficially attractive girl who was just like thousands of others he could have found any day—all of whom would have fallen at his feet as long as he didn't allow them to imagine that they were more important than the next woman.

Stratis had been too impatient. He'd continued to want something he couldn't have. He hadn't been content to wait. He would certainly have found another girl, better and more to his liking, and one who loved him back.

He, too, had suffered early disappointment and betrayal in love. That was when the painting had come to him, at the moment when he'd made the decision to step out of one life and into another, taking nothing with him—except, as it turned out, that one thing.

A week before leaving Athens for good, he'd seen an icon for sale. He'd spotted it from the street outside; it was right at the back of the shop. He'd gone in. And he was inspecting the painting closely, thinking how much it reminded him of the one on his island, when the owner had come up to him, saying, "You like it?"

"I like it," he'd replied, "although it's a copy." He hadn't known that for sure, but he'd assumed it. Nearly all art for sale was a copy if it purported to be old. You were safe only if you bought new paintings; sometimes not even then.

"A copy, naturally," the owner had agreed. "But a good one." And then he'd said that he couldn't hold it; he'd already had a very attractive offer for it.

Of course he had. From someone who was going to try to resell it as the real thing. Or perhaps from a richer man, who had never seen the original and would be buying it in the hope that it would turn out to be genuine. The owner was slick enough to absolve himself from the responsibility of guaranteeing the genuineness of his wares. Copyists were so skillful nowadays—well, they always had been and always would be. It was a good idea, when purchasing a work of art, never to hope for an investment but, rather, to buy what you liked and wanted to live with: like choosing a friend or a partner in marriage.

He said that he'd think about it.

The day after that, he'd seen another icon in a junk shop, as he was passing through a less fashionable part of town. The picture was approximately the same size—perhaps a little smaller but even more appealing than the first one. He'd bought it after enough conversation and haggling to please the owner. He'd been sure at the time that it was a bargain and that the half-blind old shopkeeper, possibly without the knowledge of his younger relatives, had sold him an authentic work by mistake. He'd intended to have it valued. But the day before he was due to take it in to the dealers, the famous Icon of Miracles was stolen from the church on his island and, looking at the reproduction of it in his newspaper, he saw how like—how almost identical—it was to the one he'd bought. He remembered, too, that undoubtedly, whatever else he'd felt at the time, that resemblance had played a part in the purchase and in the joy of possession. *Crafty old man,* he thought: to pretend ignorance in order to get a higher price for something that was an imitation. It made sense that when someone was planning to steal a painting, the market should be flooded with reproductions beforehand, so that detection of the original would be more difficult.

But even the experts could be fooled and he didn't think it would be a good idea to show his copy to a valuer when the papers were full of the recent theft. The fact that he had a dated receipt wouldn't stop an investigation; papers were even easier to forge than artworks. His emigration plans might have to be canceled, his mental readiness dispelled.

He never took the picture in to be assessed. As soon as he felt sure that his icon was a forgery, he was almost pleased. That seemed to fit in with his reasons for going: the false promises and broken faith. And even if it was a reproduction, the copyist was an artist, otherwise the picture wouldn't have been able to draw from him the kind of emotion he felt for it. It brought him luck, too, although he knew that that idea was nonsense: the success of his business life was founded on his own ability. One of the reasons why he was so phenomenally successful was that he understood the nature of fakes and of everyone's attitude toward them. People could live quite happily with a fake until its fraudulence was pointed out to them. That was what they minded: having it pointed out. And afterwards an effort was required: to come to terms with deception that didn't pretend to be anything else. That meant keeping certain thoughts in separate compartments.

He missed the icon. It had always reminded him of his mother— not the way she looked, but the way she was. He had photographs of her, but they didn't resemble her so closely as the painting, just as the photograph of his father was not such a good likeness as the boy, Stratis, had been.

The summer passed, and the fall and the long winter months. He saw the next spring, the summer and on into the end of September. Still no one would speak to him about Stratis. If the members of his family had any thoughts about the removal of the icon, they kept quiet about them. If they had known about the theft, they'd probably believe that he was unforgiving. But the truth was the reverse: he'd forgiven Stratis completely. He thought of him as having gone somewhere—again, to some other country—where he would remain, waiting.

He was ready to go now himself. But the days went by and still he didn't leave. His visits to the Cape became shorter, like his stays in town. He preferred the house in the country, where Stratis had spent so much time as a child.

He continued to take his daily outdoor exercise, even in wet weather, unless it was raining heavily. At the height of the summer he'd stay indoors during the day, venturing out to the golf course in the early evening. When the ground was muddy and slippery, he'd traipse through the upstairs hallways of the house, back and forth, counting the steps to keep himself going when he felt tired or bored. He was frail now, all in the space of a year and a few months. At one stage he'd been fat. His progress then had been like that of an old elephant: a dignified, swaying shuffle. But when the flesh had fallen away, he'd shrunk in height, too. He bowed his head. Sometimes he walked sideways, like a crab. He relied more and more on his stick. And his eyes were no longer good. But the passing of the seasons moved him and he enjoyed his walk, no matter how often he felt like putting it off, or how difficult he found the beginning.

It was necessary, he told himself, to endure. There were people who lost one thing, or one person, and because they had invested so much of themselves in that, the loss destroyed them. There were others who lost everything—every family member, every stone of the house they'd lived in, even their country. They arrived like orphans among strangers, in a place where they couldn't even speak the language. And they started again. Out of nothing they made friends, family, work: a full life.

It was important to keep going. He had had it hard at the start, even though he'd never gone through the real immigrant nightmare, as so many in the country had: like the poor young farmers out in the middle west—barely a century ago—who would struggle for twelve years against disease and locusts, crop rot and the weather: losing three sets of children to diphtheria and finally going crazy, committing suicide or ending up in jail after burning the barn down for the insurance money.

He hadn't had to contend with the land. He'd lived in cities. And he'd been a success.

At the end of September, about sixteen months after the police had called at the house, he woke one morning feeling that something special was going to happen; it was like being a child again, on his birthday. The weather was sunny, the skies clear. He looked forward all day to his walk.

Even in the afternoon, the air was still warm but—as always, now—down by the golf-course clubhouse and the stone bridge the going was slow and painful He pushed himself, not wanting to stop until he reached one of the places he had designated as a spot where he was allowed to rest. He'd chosen each lookout point carefully. The contemplation of every view added shape to his journey and eased the effort, singling out moments around which he could arrange his thoughts.

The first station on his way was the one that overlooked the practice green, the grove of trees beyond the bridge and the eighteenth hole with the hills beyond it. He enjoyed standing there, watching the ripe afternoon sun on the trees. In winter you could make out nearly all of the white house up in the woods; now it was almost invisible, concealed by greenery. Sometimes he'd see Dr. Jeffries, who would drive down from the clinic to play a few practice shots when he was on call. His sports car would be waiting with the door open and the key in the ignition, the front wheels headed away from the course so that he could make it to any bedside in the clinic in under two minutes, all the while listening to the rescue squad, who would be able to tell him about the condition of the patients they were bringing in.

The car was missing today. That meant that if one of the doctor's patients fell down on the golf course or had a stroke or a heart attack, the ground crew wouldn't know until the morning. No one had to come out to the fairway to stop the sprinklers, which were connected to a system worked by a central switch.

What Stratis was a child, he used to love taking off his shoes and socks and walking across the putting greens in bare feet. He'd once tried to describe the sensation by saying, "It's like Aunt Lydia's little purse." He'd meant that the grass was as smooth as suede. No one else in the family had such thoughts.

The next lap of the walk went downhill, over the road and across the next tee. From that point it was possible to look back and see the oxygen mist from the mountains: a fog through which the shapes of trees loomed like ships in a harbor. Today it was hard to tell what color anything was in the distance. The trees, ridges, and hills became an indistinguishable gray as they receded.

The last golfers had completed the eighteenth hole and were heading for the clubhouse. Only the old man remained, and the sprinkler systems with their tirelessly wheeling jets of spinning water. Spray surrounded each whirling source with a halo of whiteness that drifted at the edges. In places the finer water beads hung in the air like smoke, to meet the flash of droplets circling around again, repeating the previous sweep. As the metal arms moved, the water arched—dazzling, traveling, shining, falling, vanishing.

All the laws were fresh and springy. As he started down the hill, he thought that if there were such a thing as Paradise, this would be the perfect time to arrive there: at the end of the late afternoon, when they were watering the grass.

NO LOVE LOST 🕊

They walked in silence, seeing a corner of the house in the distance, then a larger part, and finally enough to hope. Neither of them said anything until they were inside.

It was dark, dirty, and squalid. Every corner stank.

"Well, at least it's still there," his wife said. "And they left the roof on."

Some regions weren't so lucky: everything had been burned to the ground. He'd already heard that his parents' house—on the other side of town—was gone; it was like knowing that a friend had died. And now every time he remembered, the loss grieved him. He never wanted to go back: to look at the hole in the ground where the house had stood or, worse still, to see some other building put up to replace it. The old schoolhouse was burned out, too.

The churches remained, although the windows were broken and fires had been lit in the interiors. But it isn't easy to burn stone. The houses and temples of God are usually built to withstand anything but a direct hit; the house of stone and the heart of stone.

His wife looked everywhere: the walls, floor, ceilings, the staircase, and the rooms upstairs. Her eyes moved over the slashed, gouged, and cracked surfaces, the smashed and waterlogged pieces of carpet. All the time that she was going up or down—moving restlessly past shattered window frames and over filthy floorboards—she kept hold of the baby. At last she returned to the front room downstairs, wrapped the baby in her shawl, and put him in a torn cardboard box on the ground. She told one of the older children to stay and keep watch, in case there were rats. Then she walked through the doorway and out.

He didn't notice at first. He was still circling through the rooms, remembering that this dilapidated, sorry hovel had once been home and telling himself that—like so much else over the past four years—it had died. What particularly distressed him was the little room next to their bedroom. It had been the safe nest where they'd put the first child when she was old enough to sleep alone but within earshot. Obscene words had been carved deep into the walls and the place had the reek of a sewer.

In a daze he turned back to the bedroom and looked out into the paved yard. Once upon a time they had had fruit trees, vegetables, and flowers.

He saw his wife, hands free, striding away from the house. He thought that she was finally walking out on them for good.

He reached the front door faster than he could think what he was doing. Later on he'd thank his good instincts that he hadn't hurt himself going down the uneven, pitted stairs.

"Where are you going?" he yelled at her. She disregarded the question. Ever since he'd been discharged from the army with a missing hand, she'd ignored his threats. When he'd shout at her, she wouldn't respond and she sometimes didn't even seem to hear: she'd simply stop listening whenever she felt like it.

"Go next door on the other side," she told him. "If anybody's there, say you're looking for food and go to the next house. If nobody's at home, take anything you can find: floorboards, anything metal we can use. Look for where they hid the ax. If there's only one person left, use your judgment."

He had no idea what she meant, although it came to him not long afterwards that she was giving him a command to kill whoever might be living or hiding in a neighboring house; as long as it looked as if he could get away with it. His own children would be all right: she would have entrusted a knife to the oldest boy.

At least there wouldn't be any mines, she said that evening. You could never tell, of course, how stupid men could be. Usually they planted mines only if they were sure they wouldn't be retracing their steps or coming back another time from a different direction. Mining the landscape was a thing you did to destroy an oncoming enemy in a country where you hadn't grown up and where your friends and relatives wouldn't be spending the next quarter of a century having their limbs blown off as they tried to work the fields.

There wouldn't be mines planted near their house because, having taken it once, the enemy had intended to come back and take it again, even though this time they'd lost.

But, as his wife also said, anything was possible.

She talked quite a lot like one of his commanding officers—a good soldier and a decent man but someone who at a certain depth was unfeeling. It was as if ordinary rules of behavior—and emotions normally considered natural—were kept at the shallower levels of his consciousness: beyond that point you couldn't find them and he'd operate on purely practical principles, without squeamishness. He was a man who would do what had to be done, no matter what that was. If it could help your survival to kill someone, you did; it would be stupid not to. If you had children to think about, it would be criminal not to.

His wife was now his commanding officer. He didn't mind. She was good at it.

He'd been a soldier for nearly three years. At first he'd liked the life. And since for a long while he and his friends were seeing everything from a distance and had no casualties in their unit, he wasn't afraid. They joked. They drank. They had all sorts of luxuries not available to the civilian population. And they despised civilians. They thought of them as sheep who would run this way and that once the gates were open or one of them feel through a gap in the hedge: instantly a whole field of sheep would be pushing and shoving, trying to get through the same opening, do the same thing—to copy, to follow. Soldiers were the ones who told them where to move, how to protect themselves, what to do. Civilians had no personalities; they were simply part of a vast herd: women, children, old people. They were dull and slow beyond belief, and helplessness had become a way of life to them. That was why, as long as he was in the army, he felt no pity for anyone who complained of being stolen from, raped or tortured. What did they expect? Nothing that happened to any of them could be so bad as what might happen to him and his friends. Capture could sometimes be worse than injury. They all knew stories about soldiers who killed themselves with their own weapons rather than risk being imprisoned, beaten, tortured, mutilated: there was nothing people wouldn't do to each other, given the opportunity. Even without the expediency of war, cruelty could become a habit.

For a while everything had been fine, even in bad weather. It was a schoolboy's dream of what life could be when you were grown up: you and your friends would go around in a gang all day long, picking up girls when you felt like it and moving on to new places, and new girls.

No civilian had had any meat for months, but in his company they had food, alcohol: anything they wanted. And if they didn't have it, they'd find out where it was and then go and take it. One of the few good things about being in the army was that although you were under orders, in your own outfit there was freedom. You could do what you liked, and if anything went wrong, your friends were there to back you up. And there were times when life was fun. He'd laughed a lot.

He'd even sung. To keep themselves from being bored, he and his friends made up a silly song they'd sing to one another whenever they were in a good mood or drunk, or when one of them had managed to invent another addition. The song was about a poor boy—the youngest of three brothers—who was offered a chance to attend the royal celebrations at a king's palace, where he'd be given as much food and drink as he wanted and would also take part in a competition: he'd be allowed to kiss the princess, and she'd select her husband from among the competitors. She'd choose the one who gave her the kiss of true love. There were many passages in the song of alliteration and polysyllabic words, with whole verses composed of things listed alphabetically; and by tradition certain phrases were always shouted in unison.

One of their company came up with a completely new version one night during an epic spree. It went on for what seemed like hours—stanza after stanza, all rhyming and in a strange combination of the hilarious, the beautiful, and the scatological. Everyone wanted a copy afterwards, especially since they'd been too drunk to remember more than a couple of consecutive lines. The poet hadn't had any copies, not even a written one for himself. It was all in his head, he told them. And he was killed the next afternoon. That was their first death.

Their good luck lasted a long while, but as soon as it broke, everything went at once. They were in the thick of things day after day, all the time. And he was terrified. He lived with the knowledge that in a split second he could lose both legs and an arm and his eyesight. He stayed mildly drunk whenever he could: never enough to make him incapable of saving himself, but the right amount to blunt his sense of danger and to keep him ready to fight, turning all his fear into rage.

As his friends were picked off around him, he retained the ability to laugh. What else could you do? One morning a man in their outfit woke up speaking sounds without any meaning. They tried to talk to him, but he didn't seem to understand a word—he'd just given an idiotic smile at whatever was said to him. They thought that he must be suffering from some kind of brain damage brought on by the constant firing; or even the result of a stroke. But they didn't know and they never found out. They had to leave him behind with a rescue team that was blown off the road a week later.

Once, for three days, he thought that he'd gone deaf, but his hearing returned; it came back when they pulled out of the action. And then he felt the pain: to hear again suddenly, with such acuteness, was maddening.

His wife and children were out of the fighting at that stage, evacuated to a different sector. When he was given leave, he'd go back to a place that looked normal. The silence was unnerving after the constant, overwhelming noise. He couldn't sleep.

His wife didn't want to sleep. She wanted to make love all the time or, rather, she needed to be pregnant.

She was pregnant again, and he was back in the unit with his friends when he was in the explosion. He never found out what had caused it: grenade, gunfire, a hit from the air, even a sniper's lucky shot at the fuel tank. The noise, the light and burning and pain all seemed to come at the same time. If he and the others hadn't been relaxed and inattentive after their leave, they might have noticed some warning sign. Then again, they might have missed it if things had been the other way around: if their senses had been dulled and confused by fatigue or boredom—too many months without a break.

He was lying on the ground and twitching uncontrollably. All around there was screaming and a terrible smell. Then they were carrying him. He saw the fire. As they put him into the jeep one of his friends came running up behind the others, reached forward and dropped something into his lap. "Here," he said. "They can do anything nowadays. You never know."

It was a hand, perfect almost to the wrist and then like something on a butcher's slab. He looked down at his left arm and the bloody pulp pulled into a bandage at the end of it. He passed out.

He came to in a field hospital where the doctor bent over each man in turn, making a quick decision about the order of operation.

He held out the detached, dead hand.

"What's this?" the doctor asked.

"They thought you might be able to sew it back."

"Me and the lace-makers' guild," the doctor snorted. He took the hand. He said, "It isn't yours. Look. It's a right hand. That's the one you've still got." He started to move away. Over his shoulder he asked, "Are you right-handed?"

"Yes."

"You've been lucky," the doctor told him, and turned to the next man.

Everything had become a matter of luck over the past few years. And luck was crazy. Being caught behind the fighting could sometimes be as dangerous as being sent into action. When the lines moved, everything else changed, too.

First came the bombardment. Everyone ran away. People died or got lost on the run. They couldn't find anywhere to stay because the ones in front of them were running, too. Finally they reached the city, where some were taken in and others were put into camps. The fear was that as soon as the enemy was near enough, all the people in the camps would force their way into the city, would have to be accommodated, and then, in the ensuing siege, would ensure that everyone starved.

But while he was still recovering, the tide reversed. A third force joined the soldiers behind the fleeing civilians. Together they turned around and routed the enemy, taking back the land that had been lost.

He was discharged to go and live with his family. At that time his wife was housed in a place where she shared with three other families. Humanitarian aid societies doled out a bread portion to all of them. She was about to give birth. One of the children was sick and running a high fever. The authorities wanted to take the child—a baby girl—to an isolation ward. His wife wouldn't hear of it. She nursed the girl herself until all at once it became clear that there was no hope. Then she put the child in a corner and told everybody to stay away from that part of the room. She sent him to find a doctor. Everyone he asked said the same thing: he was on a futile search. No one with any medical knowledge could be found outside the hospitals, where the staff stayed and worked as if condemned. The hospitals had become the end and the beginning: childbirth, medicines, narcotics, the black market, the dying.

His wife gave birth in their quarter of a single, crowded room, where she was seen by a male aid worker the next day; he took her temperature and pronounced her fit. From its corner in the room the body of the sick child, now dead, was removed. They were given a receipt. Within a few days they received notice to collect the remains. His wife tore up the paper as soon as it arrived.

"How are we going to find her now?" he asked. "All the reference numbers were on that."

"Leave it," she ordered. "They make you pay to reclaim anything."

"We can't just leave her. Our own daughter?"

"It isn't going to do her any good, is it?" she snapped. "We need everything we can save. For food and medicine. Suppose the baby gets sick—what would you do?"

Since he was still recuperating, he put up with everything from her. He was so conscious of his own wound that it didn't occur to him that she, too, might be suffering the effects of war.

The children were nervous of him. They behaved as if he were a stranger. At some moments they'd look fixedly at the place where his left hand out to have been, at others they'd turn their heads quickly in order to escape being caught in the act of staring at a disability.

He gave them the creeps. The realization pained him as much as would the loss of their love. And perhaps it came to the same thing: they didn't quite shrink away, but whenever he approached too near, he could feel their dread. He told his wife, whispering into her ear at night. She answered softly, "Give them time. They'll get used to you eventually. You're their father, but they don't know you yet. It's all going to take time."

It made him feel better to talk to her. What made her feel better was to make love, even so soon after the last birth. Once or twice he asked if she thought they really should: what if she got pregnant again?

She finally said to him, "I can't do without it and if I don't get it from you, I'll get it any way I can."

As soon as she was pregnant again, she calmed down and he understood: that unless she was carrying a child or nursing a newborn baby, she couldn't feel that there was any point in going on. There had to be something in her life that hadn't yet been ruined.

He also understood that she had allowed their daughter to die because the child was a girl, not a boy, and not the favorite daughter and because—if the aid workers had taken the child away in time to save its life—the family would have had to accept a cut in the bread rationing. His wife had made all those decisions while he was unaware of what she was doing.

When he saw the extent to which their lives had been determined and directed by her, he was amazed. The slight edge he felt of queasiness, even horror, actually increased her desirability. But he knew that with such a wife he couldn't afford to lose his strength.

He did exercises to keep the muscles limber in his shoulder and arm. He walked. Whenever he lifted a weight, he remembered to balance it and not to favor one side. He learned to use the left arm again. The doctors had promised him an array of implements that would fit onto a socket at the end of his healed stump: various builder's tools, a plastic hand without moving parts, and the traditional pirate's hook. He hadn't really believed in the hook, but just as he healed well enough to be ready for the ingenious tool kit with its many ultramodern gadgets, he was offered an artificial hand and a hook. Nothing else, he was told, was available; the other choices had now been discontinued. He refused the hand. It was unshaped: no indication on it of joints or knuckles, and it had a dead color like a plastic toilet seat. He chose the hook, with all its historical connotations of violence and romance. And after more exercises, he found that it was useful.

During those initial days of homecoming, their scavenging wasn't very organized. They wasted time by not conferring and by forgetting to take essential equipment with them. But as soon as they felt established, they began to fear the arrival of others. They'd have to hurry if they wanted to furnish the house, gather food and other supplies, and remove from the neighborhood anything that could be used as building material.

The first things they took were beds and mattresses. After that, anything: in no particular order of importance. Most of the nearby houses were in the same condition as theirs, but they did find a child's wheelbarrow that had been hidden, or possibly lost, under the foundations of a collapsed terrace by the old market gardens. Every single pane of glass had been shivered out of the greenhouses, but there were still seeds, roots, and bulbs.

They stripped enough wood from the walls and floors of neighboring houses to rebuild their own place and also to amass a good stock of firewood. Nothing would last through the winter, of course. To feel at all hopeful they needed the gas and electricity back, the running water, the telephones. But they had enough fuel to cook with.

They unbricked the well down behind the abandoned orchard, and he volunteered to drink the first cupful. They had heard so many stories about booby traps and poisoned wells that he expected to die, but the water was still pure. Some of the old trees, gnarled and decrepit as they were, had been scarred and split, and some had been chopped down. The stumps were left but there was no sign of the wood. Others had just been hacked up—splintered and torn and probably shot at for target practice or for fun. But most of the trees had been left. A few bore small, bitter apples. One or two rows contained trees on which all the fruit, though minute, was edible and even sweet. To pick one of the tiny apples and hold it close to his face, breathing in the smell—and then to bite into the fruit and taste the sour sweetness—was a delight and, while it lasted, an astonishment.

Later in the next year, catching a whiff of fragrance blowing from the blossoming old trees, he'd think he was back in his boyhood again, loving and in love, with a soul unbroken: before he'd lost his hand, before he'd killed or done the other things he'd done, or seen everything that he'd seen.

He tried not to remember the trees that used to stand directly behind the house; they had brought the loveliness of spring up to the windows and its honey breath into all the rooms. In the autumn they had supplied large, luscious fruit that could be stored through the winter or made into bottled preserves. They had had apples and plums. Those were the trees that the enemy troops had used for firewood, simply out of laziness, because they were the ones nearest to the back door.

They had flour, some dried meat, salt, and three precious bags of potatoes. Before they set out on their first well-planned plundering expedition, he went to the place where he'd buried an ax before joining up. It was still there. That was a triumph: the moment when he felt that, no matter how bad things were, he'd come home.

His wife inspected all the gardens in the area. She came back carrying a sack full of roots and leaves. One of the children proudly steered the wheelbarrow at her side; it was heaped with dusty bulbs: that was what they'd be eating and they'd be very pleased with it. Anything that fell under their eyes was like a forest creature caught in the cross-sights. They were like wild animals themselves: always hungry, always looking at everything with greedy eyes; criminals and murderers, he thought. How could you teach your children anything when they'd been through this?

And what did he tell them, anyway? *Don't get caught. Don't lose what you're carrying. Don't let them find the stuff on you. If anybody stops you, fight like hell, and if they try to tell their side of the story, lie your head off.*

He still knew how to handle the kids, but sometimes he didn't understand them. You couldn't teach them not to touch each other, not to touch themselves, not to touch insects or animals if they could find any in the destroyed landscape. They chased whatever hopped or crawled. They wanted to eat everything growing and anything they could pick up off the floor. You couldn't even prevent them, after all that had happened, from doing things that were dangerous: trying to grab a pan of scalding water off the edge of a table, swallowing a bottle of something without thinking that it might be harmful. You had to keep an eye on them all the time. That was bad enough. The children who were in real trouble were the ones who stopped whining. They'd sit in a corner all day, silent. They wouldn't eat. They'd say, "I feel sick," and not long after that they'd come down with the same infection everyone else had, but they'd be the ones to die.

One day he put down the load he was carrying and straightened up to rest for a moment. He listened. The silence was enormous: a gigantic emptiness. You could have heard a cough or a hammer blow for miles. There couldn't have been a bird left alive in the country. And the pets they'd had: cats, dogs—where were they? Somebody had pushed them into a cooking pot and made gloves out of the skins, undoubtedly. Vermin, on the other hand, were plentiful, both big and small.

After years of living with shelling so unremitting that he had come to believe his full hearing would never return, his ears now strained for sound. He loved the slight pattering of leaves moving in a breeze. And he missed the song of all the many different kinds of birds he remembered. Now that the troops were gone, the birds would come back; but until they did, their absence remained another sign in the landscape of recent and comprehensive disaster.

The silence at night was entire, completing the darkness.

As they were settling back in, others were being moved and uprooted again. Some had official approval to go back to what had once been home, where—like him—they'd find the house gutted, the furniture gone, the inner walls defaced and in places knocked down or with holes punched through them. But they'd be lucky.

In many areas families found their houses occupied by people who would wave a set of papers at them, saying that they'd been granted the property by a provisional committee for something-or-other.

In their own district, enemy occupation was recent; the civilians had been moved out in a hurry to the nearest safe place, which meant that nobody else had been allocated their land. Not all the houses were left, of course. A number of families returned to an empty space; they were taken to the center of town and put up in deserted shops, old warehouses, churches, and any other large construction that still had a roof.

The government officials in charge of housing installed families and went away, taking their papers with them and saying that food and clothing would follow. But what was on paper had ceased to mean much. Most people made themselves as comfortable as they could: begging for what they could get and taking more when your back was turned.

For weeks he was the only man in the area over twelve and under sixty-eight. When the others arrived they were on stretchers or on crutches.

Soon the time might come when the most nearly able-bodied men would band together to form a guard or sentry unit for protecting the weaker households from theft and damage. But at the moment nobody could be spared. Just as there was no extra food, there was no free time.

The quiet held—the limitless, eerie silence after years of fighting and months of being walled up under bombardment. It was as still as the moment after snow stops falling.

You could imagine that the world had gone backward a few centuries to a time when everything depended on harvests, and you walked to the next village to buy and sell on market days.

They weren't really in a village, just out in the country on the outskirts of a small town. The town had been hit by air power, but not badly, since there had never been much there. A few kilometers away a larger town had had the paper mill and the gasworks bombed, neither of which had been of military importance, although from the air they might have seemed good targets. The troops who had been dropped there had stayed for a few days and moved on.

Everyone was afraid of the armies coming back, even of their own soldiers returning. Now that he was a civilian, he had thoughts and feelings like the people he'd once held in contempt. When he remembered some of the things he'd done, he didn't mind. Everybody else had done the same: just as bad and—most of them—worse. None of that was important. It was important to be alive. And to stay alive. He'd been doubly and especially fortunate: to be alive and to be out of the whole dirty business; because, as far as any of them knew, there was still fighting going on in other parts of what had once been their country. The official reports didn't say it was fighting. They called it negotiating.

About a month after other people started to reclaim houses in the nearby town, an old woman stopped him at the end of the lane and asked if she could have some apples from the orchard. He said, "You'll have to ask my wife about that."

"Your wife is a hard woman."

"My wife is a fair woman. That's why we're still alive. Her first duty is to her own family."

"What can I do?" the woman complained. "We're starving."

"I don't know and I don't care," he told her. "I've done my stint for other people, and I've learned that as soon as they've got what they want, they forget what you gave up to help them. You're the same. You want something and you don't mind where you get it from. Look around you. Where am I going to find a single thing extra? And if I do find it, it's going to be for us. We're all in trouble. And we've been in trouble for a long time."

She stood there, too dejected to speak. What he said was true, and she still didn't have anywhere else to go. He wasn't sure that she was even from around there. He didn't recognize her, which didn't mean much: hardship could obliterate faces and personalities. His arm shot out, pointing to the distance. He said, "You can take some apples from the far end of the orchard, but make it fast and don't do it again. And next time, ask somebody else." He turned his back. He heard her running away to fill her shawl and her skirt. She hadn't thanked him: she'd asked God to reward him.

God was asked to do so many things, especially at times when He didn't seem to be there. One of the army's men of God used to say to them, "No, boys, just because our Lord is on vacation at the moment, that doesn't mean that He's forgotten about us." He'd been a well-meaning man. They'd all thought he was a fool. He'd continued to pray over one dying soldier until the man began to scream, "Oh shut up, just shut up and let me die in peace." And when he'd tried to skip to the end, to get the important words said at least, the man's brother had stood up and belted him.

After he'd seen death once, he began to expect it. It was all around, just waiting for its time. Even in years of peace, when it was usually hidden away, it was natural: a part of life. Other losses began to strike him as equally shocking but not natural: the loss of mental and spiritual power in everyone, including himself, and in the country at large—a draining away of honesty and fair dealing: an overall abandonment of principles, a general debasement.

Few of the changes were immediate. There were stages and developments, as in the growth of plants or the progress of a disease. The moral decay he saw had been going on for years, but because he had been part of it, he hadn't been particularly aware of it. The fact that it dismayed him meant that apparently he still had some virtue left: just enough to cause him pain without doing good to anyone else.

He remembered a time during his recuperation: they were all in a shelter, waiting for the bombardment. There were so many people that his main worry was of the air giving out, although as soon as he thought about that he began to sense the claustrophobia and impending panic in everyone around him. That reminded him that an outbreak of hysteria could be worse than mild suffocation. The hands and hair, the bodies and clothing of strangers were pressed tightly to him—sometimes even in his face. A child suddenly complained, "Something bit me," and a few people laughed, which broke the tension. But shortly after that a woman screamed, "My necklace—it's gone!" She started to call out, "Thief, thief," but a crowd of other voices told her to quit. Before the fighting, a lot of people would have murmured, "Poor woman." And even a year after it had begun, they would have thought: *Stupid bitch, why didn't she hide it better? Necklaces aren't to wear, they're to sell.* But finally most of them, like him, envied the thief and asked themselves why they hadn't been lucky enough to spot the necklace so that they could have stolen it themselves.

His wife was good at sneaking away with things: food, clothing, small objects—anything that caught her eye. He never commented. He'd notice what she'd managed to steal, or get the kids to steal, and he'd be glad of his share.

Their neighbors were back; first one family, then two more, and at last all of them who were still alive or not caught between borders and behind lines. He and his wife lied about how long they'd been at home. They made it seem that they'd arrived a few hours ahead of the others, and had spent all their time cleaning and scrubbing and unbricking the well. "No fuel?" they said; "No, we're in the same state. We're all in the same boat." "Yes," the children agreed, lying expertly. Telling lies was a peacetime skill as well as a wartime necessity.

He had beds and mattresses. Other people were lucky if they owned one blanket to share among the whole family. Everything was obvious, of course. The neighbors knew. And he knew what they thought of him. But everyone realized that nobody else—and certainly none of them—would have acted differently. The laws of the lawless were in operation: *First come, first served; finders keepers, losers weepers.*

After the neighbors came the refugees: twenty thousand of them in a procession that looked like a picture of the damned let out of Hell. This time the aid workers were at the head of the column instead of the tail end. They'd learned that if they didn't introduce and explain the distribution system, householders would simply beat up anyone who came to the door. As for a slowly moving line of unarmed people, most of them related to the enemy—that presented an opportunity for reprisal without injury. Even the smallest children turned up with sticks and stones.

Two immense refugee groups were herded across their territory. After that, the numbers were fewer, although his wife said that the neighboring district had had fifty thousand march through.

When the count dropped, the so-called friendly refugees joined the human flood, and the housing system began. In the first settlement they had eight orphaned children billeted on them. He'd managed to rebuild the big bed so that all the refugees could sleep in it, jammed up against each other like sardines in a can. His wife was allocated food rations for the orphans and—as long as her family was taking care of refugees—for herself and her husband and children, too. They were given bread. There was nothing else. For six weeks they had bread. And they were grateful.

One late evening he headed for home with a pile of lumber on his back. The light down by the horizon was a strange, bruised purple. All he could hear was his breathing and his feet moving. As he thought about how his children were growing up in a world without school and books and religion, he heard the howling of a dog. He stopped and heard it again. It had seemed immeasurably far away at first, but while he was listening to the repetition, he placed it: the sound must be coming from the quarry, which meant that it had to be human.

He told his wife about it and she said, "Forget you heard it. Don't interfere. Nobody falls in by mistake nowadays."

Since there was no longer any local or national economy as people had once known it, he set up a business of exchange and reciprocal favors, which he ran together with a man he happened on while out walking or, as he called it, foraging. He was always looking for anything that could be used in some way.

The man was middle-aged and husky, yet despite his look of strength there was a sadness about him. He didn't talk much. When he did, there was a melancholy in his voice, too. Before the war he'd been a cellist in a symphony orchestra, so he said. Below the knee his left leg ended in a wooden peg that he'd made himself while he was in the hospital, waiting to be released. He introduced himself as "Peg-leg." He said that everybody was going to remember him by his disability in any case, so he might as well get used to it. And nothing was going to be the same again after all this mess, so it wasn't such a bad idea to begin with a new name to go with the new life; otherwise it could break your heart to keep thinking about how things used to be. "Is there any work around here," he asked, "for an ex-soldier?"

"That depends. What can you do?"

"Anything."

"You can work with me," he suggested. "I'm a carpenter: beds, tables, chairs, doors, window frames. Even roofing."

"I could learn all that."

"Where are you living?"

"I'm not anywhere," Peg-leg told him. "I was passing through, but now I'll find someplace. I can stay and work with you till spring. Then I'll move on."

They'd meet in the morning and start off to town together to look for jobs to do. There was plenty of work for carpenters. He liked Peg-leg because he was serious, a good worker and, like himself, injured. In the hospital, and whenever he'd met people around that time, he couldn't understand the tactlessness that made them all say the same thing: *Lucky it wasn't the right hand.* But now he knew that that was the truth. Without his right hand, everything would have been difficult, every movement unnatural and perhaps never possible to relearn.

At home his wife struggled with the children and with the orphans, whom she resented. He was glad to get out of the house every morning, even in the worst weather. And when it was a fine day, his spirits would rise as he breathed the clear air and looked at the trees and, off in the distance, saw Peg-leg waiting at the gate where they met. One day he felt that he'd woken from darkness into light; he was well again. He might be missing one hand, but he was alive and healthy and still young and still a man who could find work and feed his family. And he was out of the fighting. And he had a friend.

❧

They got through the worst of the winter and his mind was filled with the thought of a new pair of boots. His wife dreamt of the moment when life would become so normal that a dentist would move to a nearby town, and she'd be able to find the time and the money to make an appointment.

There wasn't a day when somebody in the house didn't have a bad cold. Sometimes they were all down with colds and fevers, except his wife: she couldn't afford to be sick, she said.

The birds started to come back, and there was a hint of spring in the softer winds: it wasn't quite there but it was anticipated. He began to notice—in the mud and melting snow—the tracks and droppings of small animals. One day after a long thaw he saw two cats and a dog. He warned everyone in the family: a tame animal, reverting to the wild, could be as dangerous as any genuinely wild creature never on friendly terms with man. Occasionally it could be worse because it would be fearful and full of mistrust. It could attack, unprovoked. It would almost certainly carry diseases; a bite or scratch might be fatal. It wouldn't be a bad idea, he said, to carry a stick.

Just as what was left of the flower bed began to produce green shoots under the retreating snows, the orphan children were moved on. He saw them waiting outside the front door for the truck that would take them away. They were skinny and hollow-eyed, their clothing in tatters. His own children were beginning to look well tended and fatter in comparison. And, following the example of their elders, they had been using every opportunity to persecute their weaker companions. He'd never said anything, because the house—together with the food and the children—was his wife's business. But now he was touched by pity at their malnourished, hopeless look. He went to where she hid the food. The child on guard asked, "What are you doing?"

"You shut up," he answered. He took the refugee children a few scraps—enough so that they'd have something to get them through a long journey. They ate the food straight away. "I hope they find you someplace better than this," he told them.

There was no better place. The whole country was exactly like his own neighborhood, except that in the cities it was easier for your neighbors to steal from you and there was a greater danger of sudden bombardment and siege.

"I'm sorry we didn't have more to give you," he added. The children listened with a dead look on their faces. *You did have more*, they were thinking, *and you gave it to your own children.*

When the aid workers arrived, one of the orphans—an undersized little boy, who had been in the habit of following him around—ran back, snatched up his right hand, and pressed his face to it.

He felt the small hands and a warm wetness, as if the child had licked his knuckles. The boy turned and ran off.

His wife was standing in the doorway, holding the baby who was screaming. "Did he bite you?" she asked.

He'd have felt better if he'd been bitten. The gesture had probably been meant as a kiss.

"I thought the little bastard was going to bite you," she said. "That's all we need. Make sure he didn't break the skin."

He didn't bother to look. Who could afford medicine? And black-market medicine was likely to be adulterated with so many substances that it could kill you all on its own.

"Imagine if they were ours," he said.

Their children would be all right. They were adept at every dirty trick of the petty criminal. If they had to, they'd kill and eat any family chosen to take them in.

She looked at him in a way that told him his weakness was disgusting. "We've lost the bread ration, too," she said.

"There'll be more."

"No. They're moving all the kids out."

"They'll bring us some others."

"How do you know? Maybe they will, maybe not. You don't know. I've seen people starve to death. Nobody starves in the army. You only find out about that when you're captured."

Or sent back, wounded. "We'll see," he said.

The refugee children were counted and loaded into the trucks and then counted again. One of the aid workers said that the orphans' place would soon be taken by others—in fact, someone should call about the transaction in the afternoon. His wife looked up at that. "How many? She asked. "No idea," the man answered, in the way many people with a little power had acquired over the past years: you could tell from the tone of voice how good it made them feel to be able to give you—truthfully or untruthfully—information you didn't want or no information at all when you really had to know.

As soon as the trucks were out of sight, one of the children mentioned food: could they have something to eat? As a present, like the orphans.

It wasn't exactly tattling, so he couldn't feel angry. He told them again that the orphans didn't have anything. Another one of the children piped up, "Those aid people have to give them so much food every day, or else they're arrested for keeping the money."

"But they may have a long trip before they get to where they're going. I told you."

"You gave them our food?" his wife screamed. She came at him from the doorway and hit him across the face. The blow made a loud noise. His cheek, ear, and eye burned with the impact. She called him a stupid son of a bitch. Ordinarily he would have let things go until she calmed down, especially in front of the kids and while she was holding the baby against her hip, but this time he knew that it was important for him to keep his authority. When she came at him again for a second try, he punched her in the breast and then slapped her hard on the side of the face. She landed several feet away, gasping and on her knees, with the baby setting up a piercing cry. The children crouched against the wall.

"It's all right," he told them. "Your mother needs some time to rest. Let's go for a walk." He held out his good hand. "Come on," he coaxed. For a terrible moment he was afraid that they might run away. But the smallest girl finally moved toward him in short, tottering steps, holding out her arms for him to lift her up. And after her, the others followed.

He led them out of the house and began to tell them a story as they walked. Their need for stories was almost as great as their hunger for food. They were always begging to be told a story, usually one that they'd already heard.

He knew that he had won. When they returned to the house, his wife would regret what she'd done; she'd think that she had deserved to be punished. And he'd appear to be apologetic too, although he'd taken care not to strike her too hard. If he hadn't been injured, he'd be able to handle her with a softer touch: he didn't like hurting her. But if she was going to hit him in front of his own kids, she'd better be prepared to be laid out flat. He was the man of the house, after all. The children had to respect him. If he'd still had both hands, he'd have slung her over his back, carried her to the old millpond, and dumped her in from the wooden bridge—that was what they'd done centuries ago to the witches and the gossips and the whores.

The children began to ask questions about the story he was telling. He answered and went on. He threw in a few extra jokes. They all began to enjoy the walk, the fresh air, and being together. He turned the story into the nonsense tale he and his army friends used to recite when they'd been drinking: about the poor boy and the contest to win the hand of the princess and give her the kiss of true love.

The version he used for them was always heavily censored. Some sections were his own invention. For instance, as he told it, the boy started to have good luck when he paid attention at school and his studious efforts brought results at the end of a year—a year and a day: the teachers at the school awarded him one of the entrance tickets to the palace dinner. Many tickets had been distributed throughout the length and breadth of the land, but they weren't given to just anybody, because you had to earn prizes and treasures in this life. If you didn't earn them, you didn't deserve them.

He could have chosen other stories, but since this was the one all the children liked best, he knew he could slip in some moralizing and get away with it. He was surprised to find that many of his interpolations, and even the offshoots into the sententious, produced requests for more, just as if they'd been part of the original fabric.

The food list was especially good; the main portion represented the combined efforts of his combat unit over a period of years. But the best sections had been made up one winter's night by a friend of his to whom rhyme came easily—a lighthearted young man who'd been blown to pieces in the same explosion that had taken away his own left hand.

The children would listen, entranced, sometimes joining in. And then they'd insist on having everything repeated. One of the best-loved sections described the clothes everyone at the palace wore to the ball before the kissing contest began. They loved the clothes and the food, the names of the characters, the music of the words, the fact that it was all unreal and sounded silly and that there was also a beautiful princess in the story. And, of course, that the hero won and everything ended happily.

Only the children who were seriously ill failed to respond to the poor boy and the princess.

In the army the favored verses were the ones that dealt with the "kissing," which involved the princess trying out all the men, and vice versa, until the hero—the poor boy—won.

"For true love is sweetest," he told his children," and true love is best, and whoever finds true love is happy and blest."

When they returned from their walk, his wife was standing in the doorway, breathing out a narrow cloud like a banner. The air was cold enough to see your breath, but he'd smelled the nicotine from a distance. He stopped in front of her and held out his hand. From behind her back she produced the cigarette. He took a drag and handed it to her again. He half closed his eyes as he exhaled. That was when it was best: on the way out, where you could look at it in the air, while you were still tasting it.

They stood like that, sharing the cigarette until it was finished. He let her have the end. She stuck a toothpick through the last of it. When there was almost nothing left, she squeezed off the fire, stepped on it, and saved the few unburned strands to be collected with others and made into a fresh cigarette.

That was their conversation, their apology and explanation.

Neither of them mentioned the beating. They showed each other no sign that they wanted to hold onto the memory of violence nor to the knowledge that everything had taken place in front of their children. The kids would find out about marriage soon enough, just as they were discovering everything else; not that every marriage was the same. In this one, he knew, the day when he allowed his wife to get away with striking him in the face, whether she did it in public or in private, was the day when she'd make up her mind to replace him with a different husband. She had vigorous ideas about what a man should do and be. Some things she wouldn't stand for at all. At other times she'd pretty much ask to be kept in her place. Sometimes what she wanted from him was to know what he expected from her. He still thought that they'd be all right as long as he trusted his instincts, and they didn't talk about any of it.

Where on earth had she managed to find a cigarette? From one of the aid workers, of course. But what did she have to offer in exchange? Nothing, while he was there. A promise—that was all she'd have to bargain with: a look in the eye, which she could deny afterwards. Unless she didn't want to.

He admired her quickness of wit, her suspiciousness and cynicism. Before the fighting started she was so different that he could hardly remember what she'd been like. He could only recall a vague picture of the way she'd looked: fresh, eager, delicately slender. But he'd been different, too. He had no idea what he'd been like—a nice, decent young man, probably. Now he was like everyone else—like a ragged, mean-looking cur that snuffles around the garbage piles at the back of a village.

They waited for the aid workers to bring supplies and another consign-ment of orphans—perhaps a batch of them hardly old enough to feed themselves: children who had to be closely supervised. Maybe there would be even more than in the first distribution.

The term "aid worker" was relatively new. They used to be called charity workers. People no longer knew what the word charity meant. They didn't know the meaning of love or pity or how similar or differ-ent they were; they saw no strict divisions between compassion, con-descension, and contempt. The weak went under. If you didn't want it to happen to you, it was to your advantage to make it happen to somebody else. That would give you a better chance.

Sometimes at night he thought he could hear the howling of dogs. If real, and not simply a thing he imagined while he was waiting for sleep, the sound would be like the first howling he'd heard, and proba-bly coming from the quarry. Abandoned mines and quarries were good places to keep prisoners or to bury them. You could fit a lot of people into a mine: put them in, station armed guards on the heights, and blow up the entrance. And even more could be thrown into a disused quarry, although usually the intention there would be to free them at some stage because they'd remain visible.

Nobody talked about the quarry and everybody knew. It had a long history. Since his return, the only time he'd heard it mentioned openly by anyone except his wife was when a stranger had laughed about it, saying in a whisper, "They divorce court where you don't need to bother with lawyers."

When he was a child, life was orderly. Parents were strict; indoors they told their children: *Don't keep rushing everywhere. Don't jump around like that. Why are you laughing in that silly way? Be quiet.* Outside the house they said: *You're making a spectacle of yourself. Everybody's looking at you. Stop showing off.*

The teachers at school were also fairly uncompromising. They specialized in verbal castigation. Some of his friends preferred that. They knew how to defend themselves against it. He would rather have been strapped on the hands or whipped. That happened, too, but none of it was too bad.

He had two close friends who followed or led him into escapades that ranged from the hilarious to the terrifying. Because they were such a small group, and because they never did anything really bad, they had no worries about betrayal from within. His brothers and sisters didn't know what he was up to and anyway they had secrets of their own that could be used against them if they told on him. So at the age when he was ready for adventure and adulthood, he and his two friends were climbing out of their houses at night and heading for the one place in the neighborhood where there were no rules: the abandoned quarry beyond the far side of town.

Once, when still a boy, he'd been persuaded to spend a night there on his own. It was almost like the more usual dare to stay overnight in a haunted house, except that there was a big difference between fear of unknown other worlds and fear of unknown genuine trouble. At the time so many stories were in circulation about the place and what went on in it that the quarry exerted an attraction nicely balanced between dread and longing. They all knew, even as children, that it was where people went to meet each other unobserved, to plan robberies, to hand over stolen goods, to see men and women who were disapproved of, and "to do it." It was the latter activity that had become irresistibly fascinating to their imaginations. They wanted information. A prize had been selected: a ticket to something they also wanted desperately. He remembered that part only vaguely.

He and his two friends turned up at their usual meeting place and began the long walk to the quarry. In those days there were several sets of stairs leading down to the bottom, where by daylight the ground looked like a riverbed in time of drought: gravelly, full of dried bushes, sand and patches of mud and water. The place was huge, with divisions of landscape like the ones you might see in a large park gone back to the wild: the narrow offshoot like a tree-lined canyon, the uneven ravine bulged with sloping rock faces that were tilted and stepped like the overlapping waves of a sideways-moving sea; the clearings surrounded by scrubby undergrowth, the big open plains.

By luck they had chosen a cloudy night when the moon was full enough to allow some vision but not bright enough to make hiding impossible—just the sort of time and weather everyone wanted. And the ground was dry. He'd agreed to meet them at dawn in the abandoned farm shack they used as a clubhouse.

He started down the steps, remembering as he moved not to trust the rotting handrails nor to look for complete safety in the stone below and by his side. Where the walls and stairs were worn, they could be slippery, glassily polished; and the stone had a method—peculiar to itself and treacherous—of retaining or breathing out moisture.

While he was undergoing his ordeal, his friends indulged in a midnight feast at their clubhouse. He expected that they'd be asleep when he got out but, because he'd promised, he did what they'd arranged: at three in the morning he climbed up the quarry stairs again and took the long walk back.

The others hadn't slept; they'd finished up the food and after that, all night long, they'd been telling stories. They wanted to hear every-thing. Without proof, naturally, they wouldn't hand over the prize.

He tried to tell them. As he talked, he grew less shocked, although there were some descriptions he didn't even attempt, nor could he convey the absolute terror he'd felt—not just at the idea of being caught, but at the sight of what was happening in front of him. He'd witnessed all sorts of activity, much of which he didn't even identify as sexual. He had looked on at gambling, knife fights, nakedness: men, women, and children. There had been hundreds of people down there. Some groups had been peacefully eating and drinking around a fire—large parties, some of whose members would go off together into the straggly bushes and then drift back to the crowd. There had also been smaller gatherings where whatever went on was being forced on one or more people by others. No one interfered in any of the quarrels, which were loud. Yelling and screaming was ignored by the rest. Most people were drinking. As he talked about his adventure, it came to him that some of the bodies he'd stepped over and fallen against in an effort to remain hidden hadn't been dead but simply drunk, or asleep, or both.

His friends didn't believe half of what he told them. But since there was no question that he'd been down in the quarry and had seen quite a lot of what they imagined must be going on there anyway, they let him have the prize, whatever it was.

The days were warmer, but the real spring wouldn't come for over a month at the soonest and probably later than that. You could smell it in the air and feel it in the ground; that meant nothing. They could still have storms and weeks of freezing rain afterwards. Nevertheless, Peg-leg decided that the moment had come for him to move on. He announced his departure early one morning and said good-bye the same afternoon.

All at once it seemed as if a period of disappointment had begun. He refused to imagine that they might be heading for a stretch of bad luck: after what they'd gone through already, that would be ridiculous, although the thought of it was always near.

Until the aid workers brought new refugees and food-ration credits, they'd be living right at the edge. Without the extra bread, everyone felt nervous. Despite what they'd hoarded, most of their provisions were near exhaustion. Once the weather changed, transportation and travel in general would be easier. It was possible that that was what the authorities were waiting for.

Good weather was also needed for planting and putting the house in order. All he'd really been able to do before the cold months was to make the place watertight and as warm as possible: to block the holes and board up the windows. A coat of fresh paint, whitewash, and new windows would make the house look more normal again, less like a half-derelict construction behind which a family was barricaded.

If you'd approached the district at night, it would have been like coming to a place that had the reputation of being haunted. All the houses still standing were like his, and some much worse.

That was the prize, he remembered: for spending a night in the quarry—the reward was a ticket to a traveling fair. And he'd gone to the show they had all called the Haunted House, which was actually named the House of Horrors. It was a collection of optical illusions and things that jumped out at you while you rode in the open car of a miniature train. The train carried a full load: children, parents, lovers, all laughing and shrieking. When you heard them calling out around the bend, you knew that there was something you should be prepared for. He'd whooped and cheered with the rest. He'd loved it. At no time was he so frightened as when he'd had to sit still and watch and be silent down in the quarry.

His first experience of women had also taken place in the quarry. He was interested in two girls at school and another who worked in a bakery. He used to have daydreams about going out with them and about how much they'd let him do. His two friends were similarly plagued by futile dreaming. They were still trading lies and secrets when an older girl asked him if he'd like to come out on a picnic. He'd almost said no, not understanding that she'd used a code phrase. She'd been nice and hadn't laughed at him. "At night," she'd explained. "You know. In the quarry. Have a couple of beers and cook some sausages over a fire." Then she'd smiled, seeing that he'd understood. He'd said yes. And that was the beginning: going back to the place of terror to become an initiate, learning to feel at ease and to belong to the crowd of people who went there.

It didn't change the way he thought about the two other girls at school and the one at the bakery. But after a while it began to influence the way they thought about him. Only after he'd acquired the reputation of taking a girl to the quarry did he become someone to whom younger girls felt they could entrust themselves, while their parents were sure that they could not.

He was still in his teens when the quarry was declared out of bounds. First of all, several women were found murdered. Two were pregnant girls. Suspicion naturally fell on the man or men who might have fathered the unborn children. While investigations were still going on—and one man was already under arrest—more deaths occurred. The combination of methods used—strangling and knifing—suggested that more than one man was behind the crimes. The arrested suspect argued that despite his acquaintance with the dead girl he was supposed to have murdered, he hadn't seen her in some time, and it wasn't likely that she'd been out at the quarry to meet another man who was the real father—or many men, who would pay cash for sexual intercourse, as a lot of people there did?

More bodies were discovered, including those of two young boys. The arrested man was released. No one ever found out who was responsible for any of the deaths.

After the killing of women and boys came the big fights between men. Family, religion, race, and former nationality all helped to give the participants an incentive, as did the occasional winning or losing of some regional sports team at an important competition. Or the cause might simply have been the need to get into a fight.

As soon as the first men were killed and others badly injured, the friends and families came out in force. More men died; some of the women formed a protest group and went out to try to stop the fighting. They were beaten up by both sides. Three of them were hauled off to the far end of the quarry and raped. After that, the police stepped in. They entered with guns against a mob that knew the lie of the land better than they did and, greatly outnumbering them, took their weapons and beat them to a pulp.

The next stage was closure. The army took charge. Soldiers went down into the quarry, scoured every corner of it for human remains, broke and blasted the steps, railings, and footholds from the rock face, and removed the ladders. They used so much dynamite that no entrances remained, only a sheer drop from every point. The bad feeling they left behind quickly transferred itself back to the original sources of conflict. People thought, and said, that—as far as they were concerned—enemies didn't live in foreign countries: they lived right down the road and on the other side of town.

When the war began, there was plenty of hatred to call on. And once things were rolling, the few who had been neutral were sucked into the action. They became part of it. And then they hated, too.

⚜

They had three weeks of colds in the house. His theory was that the aid workers had brought sickness when they'd come to take the orphans away. One night the children got into a fight about something. There was screaming, shouting, and crying—a general outpouring of misery and complaint that overwhelmed them all, including him and his wife. Afterwards he was tired to death. He woke up in the middle of the night and got out of bed. His wife turned over, murmuring, "What's wrong?"

He said, "I need some air." He moved to the window and pulled the cloth aside. A wild, ghostly pallor flooded down from a full moon high in the sky. His hook was on the sill, where he left it every night before going to bed. The light touched it, making it gleam. She hated the hook. It wasn't that she was afraid of having him hurt her without meaning to if he rolled over in bed or flung out an arm in sleep. She just hated it anyway.

He felt his way downstairs and stepped out into the night. Everything was caught up in the moon's estranging glamour. He walked into the old orchard and roamed through the twisted alleyways. Long ago there had been a stone fountain near the center of the place, at least he thought he remembered something of the kind from his childhood, when the trees had belonged to a neighboring farm.

He couldn't find the fountain, nor any trace or stone or pipeline. He stopped walking. It seemed to him that everything was gone. The wonderful light threw a momentary allure over the dreary muddle of ruined landscape and buildings. But there was nothing worth looking at in daylight. Beauty had gone from the world and from their lives. The long delay of spring, the vanishing of the hope they had been given earlier in the year, made their poverty worse than before. What was left to offer a child like the one who had kissed his hand? When he thought of that sweet, inept gesture, he wanted to weep. But no tears came from him. That was gone, too.

If only they could get through the war—that was what he used to think: if only they could get through it, everything would be all right. But it was beginning to seem to him that nothing would ever be right again.

He kept going to work every morning, as usual. The days were empty, companionless.

Every crumb was counted as they waited for the next handout.

The aid workers didn't come back for another two weeks. When they did, they brought bedding, socks, mittens, and food. A soldier who was traveling with them handed over a secret package of coffee, which he and his wife saved as if it were the gold of the fairy tales. Genuine gold was worth hardly anything anymore and money was just paper. But coffee could get you out of trouble or buy you a favor. Sometimes coffee could even buy medicine. Cigarettes were also valuable, but not nearly so precious. All the soldiers still had cigarettes and matches. Coffee—even dried out, even ancient—was exquisite luxury.

The next morning their refugee arrived—only one: an old woman whose name and age they were never told because no one knew anything about her. She was simply being preserved as an example of the aid workers' goodness and proof that they were acting according to humanitarian principles. They'd given her a number.

She was carried into the house and placed in the center of the only decent downstairs bed they still had.

"Not there," his wife objected. "I know these old people. Their bladders work day and night. Put her over there. We'll rearrange things as soon as we can."

The woman was shifted to a corner of the room where three of the children had been hanging around, full of curiosity about the aid people. As the workers lowered their burden to the floor, a stream of urine gushed from her; a steamy, stale odor filled the room. The children became hysterical, holding their noses and making sounds that imitated farts. One of the men who had helped to carry her muttered, "Christ, not again."

"See?" his wife said. "I told you." She signed the paper held out to her. As she handed it back, she asked, "What can you tell me about her?"

"Nothing. She doesn't move but she isn't paralyzed. She's old. Maybe she's sick, maybe not."

"Does she talk?"

"She makes noises. That's all."

"We should get extra rations for this. Somebody's got to keep cleaning her up all the time."

"You get what's written down there."

"Well, we'll do our best, but just look at her. I mean, she isn't going to last long, no matter what we do for her. It looks like she's had a stroke, anyway. Did a doctor see her before you loaded her into that cattle truck?"

"Doctor?" both the aid workers repeated. They laughed. One of them said, "When was the last time you saw a doctor, Professor?"

The other one said, "I expect that would be Dr. Houdini you're referring to—we haven't seen him around for quite a while."

The first one said, "I guess he's done a disappearing act."

After the two of them had left the house, they could still be heard, faintly: laughing as they got back into their open-sided van, banged the doors, and started the engine.

That evening he helped to move the beds. They had to keep the old woman downstairs, where the smell immediately began to infiltrate everything around her. His wife said, "We'll never be able to get rid of her."

He answered in a low voice, "They're sure to move her along soon. We aren't qualified to deal with her."

"How qualified do you need to be to clean up piss and shit?"

"In a hospital they might be able to get her speech back."

"Oh my God, what for? Who's got the time for that sentimental garbage? Look around you. It's the children who need what this old biddy's using up. She's had her chance. And she had more than most—she must be a hundred if she's a day. She'd better stop making that noise."

"She probably doesn't know she's doing it."

"It makes me feel like hitting her over the head."

"Don't forget: we're lucky to have a refugee with us."

"You don't have to do the washing. Listen. There she goes again. Well, she can just lie in it. I'm not doing anything more till the kids are in bed."

As he had feared, they went into a cold snap. It lasted nearly a week. All doors and windows had to be shut tight against the bitter daytime winds and the freezing nights. The old woman whined and groaned and the house reeked of her uncontrollable bodily emissions. Her mind might have been blocked by some unknown inner disaster, but the rest was without restraint. Whatever went in, came out. The stink reached every part of the house. After a while they began to taste it in the food they ate and even in the water they drank.

"She's as strong as a horse," his wife said. "She'll last forever."

"Hush," he whispered.

"What for?"

He'd been told that people who were immobile and unable to talk—even people who were in a coma—could sometimes still hear. If the woman knew what they'd been saying from her arrival onward, she'd be in a state of anguish.

Outside the house the air was clear. He stayed away from home, going into town or moving father out into the country and working as long as he could, despite the cold.

Spring came at last, the real spring. Children who had hidden indoors for the past months came out to play. They formed gangs. Sometimes they took part in the ancient circle games and dances he'd grown up with. When he heard their voices from far away, he was reminded of his own childhood, his parents, and the world that had been safe and happy before everything was smashed to pieces. But more often the games became like rehearsals for military activity. The gangs had leaders and bullies; the girls were excluded or beaten into submission. He could see the time coming when the older girls would be turned into whores until they became pregnant, after which their parents would throw them out of the house. And by that time the boys would have armed themselves with weapons to use against rival gangs; they'd already found tunes for the words they shouted as they strode back and forth, acting important. He didn't like to see them marching: it made him think that everything was going to happen all over again. But, of course, it would.

He concentrated on the vegetable garden, using the children as guards. They understood that their presence next to the newly dug and planted rows was essential. They never left the house except in a group, knowing that if anything were found to be missing at home, he or his wife would punish them for it after their return.

Everyone stole. His main worry, especially during the night, was the food. No matter how they tried to disguise it, anyone could tell that they had plenty now: enough to eat and to save, as well as seeds, bulbs, and roots in the ground. Three of their neighbors had similar gardens, but you could never have too much and—as his wife pointed out—those were just the people who would be the first to try out a midnight raid on somebody else because they could always say that the stolen produce had come from their own place.

The trees came into bud. People forgot their desire to have just one object that wasn't chipped, cracked, worn, torn, broken, mended, or secondhand. They'd been given a fresh beginning and their world felt transformed.

The young ones longed for love and adventure while at the same time dealing in corruption and copying all the brutalities of their elders. They were busy trying things out. He took care to remain alert to what his own kids were getting up to, but it was impossible to keep all of them under control.

He couldn't even hold them down when they were at home. He used to step into the house to hear whispers and smothered, explosive giggles coming from the direction of the old woman's bed. She'd be whimpering and moaning as usual. And he'd find them pushing things into her mouth, pinching her, driving pins into her arms, pretending to stab her in the eyes with a stick. "What are you doing?" he'd roar at them, and they'd scatter. But they were always drawn back. In their minds she wasn't human or even animal; she was an object—an object of amusement. Their favorite trick was to make her mew and cry in patterns, as if she were singing a song.

He'd tried to explain things to them until he realized the true horror: they understood perfectly well that the old woman could still feel pain and that their actions were hurting and frightening her. That was what they liked. That was the essence of the enjoyment.

If they behaved that way when they were young, what was their generation going to be like later? How would they treat ailing parents and grandparents or—when they had them—their own children?

They had no respect for the weak and helpless: the old, the newly born, the sick, injured, crazed, or blind. They accepted no responsibility for any of that. The young had been shown that even the strongest could die. They could see no point in prolonging the lives of the second-rate.

The spring was as lovely as in any year of peace. On some days it seemed like a season from an ancient age when all the world was beautiful, peopled by gods and goddesses.

They thought for a while that things might be getting better. It was even possible, they imagined, that the fighting might come to a stop.

They carried the old woman outdoors so that she could enjoy the fresh air. But her piteous whines and fearful gasps, her grunts and sighs, ruined the fine weather for them, just as when they were indoors she made the house unbearable. Feeble and miserable as she was, she seemed indomitable, whereas they were being worn down.

"She'll live forever," his wife said. "She'll probably outlive us."

One day he returned to the house for a bag of nails and a couple of hinges that were stored in the shed. On his way past the front door, he heard the old woman moaning. He stepped inside, where he found the children persecuting her again. He chased them out of the house and then went to the back to collect what he'd come for. He crashed around in the cramped space, so angry for a moment that he had to stop and cover his eyes with his hands, thinking: *Be careful. This is how people have accidents. Calm down.*

They were just young, he told himself; they would learn. They'd change, like everything else. As soon as there was a genuine political settlement, the economy would stabilize and there would be enough for everyone. There would be celebrations, feasts, the ritual marking of days and years. Children would enjoy being innocent again and cruelty would recede from their minds. That was his hope, although he now saw little evidence for continuing to believe it.

In the distance he heard three of his children singing the alphabet song:

The Queen of Dalmatia, whose name was Aspatia, arrived in a grand coach for four. She had footmen and flunkies and uniformed monkeys and pink pearls right down to the floor.

They all sat down early and ate until late: pomegranates, pickles, and pears; pasta, pies, parsnips, and plump purple plums; peaches, pineapples, and peas. Peacocks and partridges, pancakes and plaice; peppers and pretzels and palm trees. Prime poached, puce piglets, and purest champagne that poured from the bottles like rain.

The Prince of Pomander ate a live salamander. He grimaced and gargled and gagged. He'd done it by accident but it set a court precedent much admired in Shiraz and Baghdad.

Oh, what delectable dishes they ate, from the lowliest up to the mighty and great. What speeches rang out through the old dining hall, what flirting and drinking and laughter went on. Oh, what a fine time they had, eating and talking and dancing away. All through the evening and into the dawn, everyone happy and glad. And the party went on the next day.

The sound of their voices drew away his fury. But he thought that it wouldn't be long now before they changed the nonsense rhymes to jingles that came close to the original obscenities of the old army version.

A military workforce came through with builders and engineers, leaving a restricted and unreliable telephone system and a low-level electricity supply that cut out just when you didn't expect it to. They were becoming a part of the modern world again. They had bottled gas, kerosene, and intermittent running water that wasn't always safe to drink. They could get eggs, but not chickens, except on the black market. You could get anything there, so people said.

Occasionally you could catch sight of the big dealers going by, usually in the evening. There were always two cars: the bodyguards up in the front of the first one, with the boss in the backseat, sometimes accompanied by a henchman, and—in the second car—the women, in fur coats and diamonds and face paint you could see from a distance. They and their friends continued to do business without bothering most people; their fights were all with others of their own kind. Among the ordinary populace the general feeling was that they were providing a service no government was yet able to offer. Of course it was also true that if you went against them, they shot you; but everyone knew that. They were predictable and therefore less of a threat than, say, a roving band of deserters—that was the sort of thing that made everyone nervous, even the crooks.

By the time the leaves were out on the trees, his wife was saying that she'd rather live in a work camp than keep the old woman with them.

"What are we going to do without the extra rations?" he asked.

"I don't know. And I don't care. If you want her here, you can take care of her."

"I'm working already."

"Who isn't?"

"I don't understand why she doesn't die. She's in such a bad state."

"She's alive because she's being treated like royalty in this house."

"I guess if she died, we'd be issued with another refugee. One that would be easier to look after."

"Don't you believe it. People like us have taken over the work of the hospitals. But this is beyond anything. If I ever set eyes on another one like this, I'll just let her lie there. We don't even have hygienic surroundings. They couldn't have expected her to last more than a couple of days. She should have died a long time ago."

They stopped talking and stared at the woman, who no longer had even the look of someone who should be pitied. She was repulsive. She was the only one in the house who had a bed to herself although, God knew, nobody would want to use it after her. When she finally died, they'd have to burn it. Except that they wouldn't. They'd put the next refugee into it.

"You do it," his wife said. "It's your job."

Over the next few days he found himself thinking at odd moments that it would benefit everyone, including the old woman, if he got rid of her; such a killing would be what was called "humane," "an act of compassion," or "putting her out of her misery."

It was even possible that the blubbering, whining noises she made were an attempt to ask someone to dispatch her rather than let her continue in bondage to her irreparably damaged body.

And maybe not. Perhaps she was just saying: *Feed me, love me, pity me, make me well again: help me.* But he'd seen plenty of hospitals where there were patients who just kept repeating, "Oh God, let me die." And they'd meant it. Lots of people felt like that. He could imagine feeling that way himself.

He didn't want to hurt her. That wouldn't be right. None of their troubles, including her own condition, could be considered her fault and certainly not the war, nor the system of refugee housing.

He didn't want to get caught, either. How could he dispose of her safely and painlessly? He thought about that during the next week and over the following months as the summer came and then reached its height and even with all the boards taken off the windows and the doors standing open, the oily tang of urine and the fulsome, barnyard stench of excrement reached every corner and expanded, ballooned, pulsated in the air. You could choke on it from the next room.

One day he realized that all day he'd been thinking: *I hope I don't die like that.* Pretending to himself that his feelings were nobler than they were, he asked himself how she could want to go on living. It would be doing her a kindness to put an end to her.

He remembered his friends, so young and full of exuberance, who were now dead while a rotting piece of senility like this lived on. The mere fact of it enraged him. And the next moment, it filled him with sorrow. This thing had had a mother once. Once upon a time, a young woman had cradled a baby in her arms and looked lovingly down into its face; and it was to become this pitiable wreck.

Somebody should just hit her on the head with a shovel. He didn't want to do it himself. But if his wife did it, he'd accept it.

His wife wouldn't do it. She'd told him straight to his face that it was his responsibility. It was something he was just going to have to carry out without thinking: like breaking the neck of an injured animal.

The summer went by and the warm days of September. The crops were better than they had hoped for. They were able to save up toward the coming months. They were eating well for the first time that year; but their good fortune was spoiled by the old woman's presence.

It was bad enough in the warm weather when they could open the windows. What was it going to be like if she had to spend a whole winter with them?

Of course someone in her condition couldn't last much longer. He didn't think so, anyway. But his wife said, "That old bag is just the kind who'll go on for another ten years, sucking it in at one end and pumping it out at the other." He didn't like to hear her talk like that, but he knew that her derision was a sign that she was looking for a fight. It was better to let her talk and not to make any comment.

"We've got to get rid of her," she told him. "We could get her out of the house and keep on drawing the rations."

"Suppose they want to see her?"

"We could produce somebody. I heard of a case where five families lived off one old crone like this. They just moved her from house to house when the aid workers came around. It would be even easier here. You just give one of the officials a percentage."

"And wind up in jail."

"Not if you know the right ones. I could fix it. Just get her out of here."

The rains began, followed by the first frost and then, near the end of October, a week of mild weather that was springlike, almost summery. And suddenly, with the warmth, there was an outbreak of killing. As usual, there were some strangled girls, either pregnant or raped, but a lot more of the victims were children. He and his wife reminded the kids to be wary of strangers and overfriendly people. From the snake-eyed silence with which the advice was received, he began to suspect that many of the perpetrators were also children. That was certainly possible: war had awakened in the general population a readiness to kill. In any place where troops had gone through, there were always more corpses than seemed normal. Wherever there might have been hand-to-hand combat you could get away with it. People settled their quarrels as soon as they saw the first uniform go by.

His wife would do it if she had to. Even if she didn't have to. If she thought she could escape detection, she'd do it for a cup of sugar. It meant nothing to her.

How much did he mean to her himself? She still needed him, but he was damaged. As soon as other, able-bodied and younger men arrived back—on leave after a temporary cease-fire or with the occupying and peacekeeping forces or, should it ever be possible, at the end of the fighting—she might start looking around for something better. He had no idea now what she was like except that he feared she might be turning into someone who was stronger than he was and who eventually wouldn't have any use for him.

"I'm not going through a winter with that lump of disease in the house," she told him.

"She isn't sick. She's old."

"She's sick. I don't want the children to catch it."

It was the children who brought everything in: colds, influenza, fevers, lice, bugs, fleas, skin diseases."

"We've got to get rid of her."

"All right," he said. "I agree. But we can't make it look like an accident if she can't move, can we? And if it doesn't look natural, they'll get us for it."

"She just has to stop breathing, that's all."

"It'll show."

"Then it's got to be the quarry."

"What does that mean?"

"That's what everybody else has been doing. Not just our neighborhood. Everyone in the district."

"Oh? Where did you hear that?"

"I keep my ears open."

So do I, he thought. He still hadn't heard anything definite about the quarry other than the occasional hushed joke. And he'd assumed that the black-market traders would have been using it for payoffs and assignations if there had been any way to get in and out. There were rumors, but all of them seemed to refer to what had gone on before the fighting.

"They've been taking their refugees to the quarry, throwing them in, and saying that they ran away. Nobody can get out down there. It's sealed."

"And if somebody finds them? If the aid workers get to know about it?"

"Listen. This is the way it works: you take your refugees out there and throw them in. If you hit them on the head first, they don't last long and they can't tell anybody their names. You go back home and say they moved off, looking for more food or trying to trace their cousins, or something like that. Then you get new ones. All the aid agencies have is their names—they don't have time to make a record of anything else. Nobody official is going to remember what any of them look like. We aren't supposed to have them more than a couple of months, anyway."

"But we aren't supposed to kill them."

"You don't have to kill anybody. Once they're in the quarry, the rest of the bunch in there take care of things. They'd probably eat anybody healthy who just fell in. That's what I think happened to that missing boy—I think some of his friends pushed him in for fun and the quarry people ate him."

"That's ridiculous."

"Well, there isn't any food down there."

"But they aren't animals."

"They're starving, injured, and sick. They see a nice, clean, well-fed young child alone and unprotected among hundreds of them—are you serious? They'd roast him on a spit."

"Hundreds?"

"That's what I hear. Well, to start out with. Dozens, maybe. The rest will be corpses now. And bones. So. You get her out there and I tell everybody; her health improved so much that she just walked out on us."

"The kids would be spilling the beans to everybody and his grandmother. They'd think it was funny."

"I'll handle the kids," she said. "That's my department."

He set off to walk to the quarry. He hadn't been there since before the war, when he'd lived in his parents' house on the other side of town. From his own place it wasn't far. It wouldn't take long.

As he walked, he thought about his wife. Where had she really heard those things? Women sometimes kept a piece of news away from the men of a community just as the men did from the women, but the problem of refugees was one that affected everyone. And surely the children would be talking about the quarry, if the story were true.

He could understand that something of the kind might happen. The time for pity and humanity was during and right after the shooting and bombardment; after the savagery of fighting. As soon as a year or so had gone by, the injured became a burden. But despite the lack of policing and the makeshift nature of organizations in the district, people wouldn't feel safe committing such atrocities unless they thought they couldn't get caught. And the only reason they might feel that was if the aid agencies were in on some sort of swindle with them: handing the regular food ration to the families and dumping the refugees into the quarry to rot.

That made sense. And in that case, it would mean that she'd heard it from the man who kept giving her the cigarettes. So, had she been seeing him on the side? She was pregnant again, too. Was she pregnant by the other man? Was she in love?

The wind was behind him as it usually was if you were heading out of town from that point. That was why the quarry, the slaughterhouse, and the tannery were all in the same general area. And it was another reason why his parents' house, now gone, had been in a better location than his and why his first long trek to the quarry had seemed such an adventure.

Despite the direction of the wind, as soon as he was close enough to see the outcrops of rock that marked the quarry boundary, he became aware of the smell: it was sporadically evident, moving in single, fugitive wafts and then the occasional full gust.

He circled the place, looking down. All the people he could see at the far end were entirely without clothes or shoes. They lay separately and most of them appeared to be dead, but during his inspection one figure gave signs of consciousness. As he continued to walk, he caught sight of another: a man, wrapped in a few strips of cloth, who raised his head, crawled forward a few feet, and lay down again. A crowd of noisy birds circled overhead. They landed near the bodies and flew back up, to come down at a different spot. A few desultory groans reached him: it was impossible to tell where they came from.

All at once he heard the children's voices. Ahead of him, among the brushwood and scrub running up to the lip of the quarry, stood a girl and a boy: the girl no older than six and the boy possibly about four. They were throwing something down to one of the people below. He caught the girl's words: "bread" and later—triumphantly—"blanket." A dark shape rose into the air and disappeared from view.

He wrapped his handkerchief around his hook and crept closer. The children were so preoccupied that they didn't notice. He was right on top of them before they saw him. The boy screamed. The girl whirled around and stared, ready to run.

In an easy, conversational tone he said, "Do you know somebody down there?"

"Anna," the boy answered.

"Is she your mother?"

"She's our friend. She takes care of us."

The girl pointed off into the bushes, and said, "We found a ladder, but it's too heavy."

"He could lift it," the boy told her.

He said, "I know those ladders. They're old. They've rotted. You'd hurt yourself on them. Haven't your parents told you to stay away from here?"

Both children looked down. The girl mumbled, "We hear them crying."

"Well," he said vaguely, "I'll see what I can do. But you'd better go home now. Nobody's safe here. And remember to keep away from the ladders. You could fall in there yourselves, you know. Go on." He moved his good hand in an outward sweep. They stood still for a few moments, looked at each other, and then ran.

He stepped forward to the quarry itself and peered over the drop. A middle-aged woman was standing directly below him, looking up. She was wrapped in the blanket the children had thrown down. "Please," she called up. "For God's sake."

Behind her stood a young woman, the only person he'd yet seen in the place who had on any clothes other than rags. She was not simply fully dressed: she was magnificently attired for the evening in sumptuous garments, the like of which hadn't been seen since before the war—a long, silky gown and a little velvet jacket with elbow-length sleeves. Her shoes, one of which was just visible beneath the hem of her dress, were of satiny black with an arrow-shaped stripe of some glittering substance at the front: metal or beads. Like the older woman, she was eating food from a piece of paper. There was no indication that anything had been taken by force; the two were evidently friends or had become allies through circumstance.

The older woman limped a step nearer. As she tightened her hand on the blanket he could see that she wore some kind of dark shift, possibly underclothing borrowed from her friend. "Please," she called out again, more desperately Behind her the young woman crumpled up and threw away the piece of paper that had held the food. She made a graceful, swinging move forward, like the first step of a dance. "Please," she reported. Her voice was stronger and fuller but also smoother and sweeter than the other woman's. As she spoke, she put her hands to the front of the dress underneath her jacket and pulled the material apart, showing him her breasts. "Please," she insisted, so softly that he could hardly catch the sound. It was as if he stood right next to her, close enough to touch, transfixed by her large, dark eyes, the kissing shape of her mouth after speech had left it, the beautiful breasts that she covered again.

"What's your name?" he asked.

"Maria."

"And you're Anna?" he said to the older woman. She nodded. "What's wrong with your leg?"

"It happened when they threw me in."

"Could you climb a ladder?"

"Yes. But soon, please. Every hour we're weaker. We don't dare to fall asleep at the same time."

He looked at Maria again. Her eyes held his, but she didn't add any words to what her gesture had already promised in return for rescue. He said, "I'll try," and turned away.

He followed the direction the little girl had indicated. After beating the undergrowth and shrubbery for a while, he found the ladder. It was old but long enough to reach to the bottom of the pit from one of the lower sides. Several rungs were missing, although the long sections looked all right; in some places they had been reinforced with metal. He kicked the wood. He tried its weight. He thought that he'd be able to get Maria out if he came back and put three more rungs in. He'd bring a rope, too, in case they had to tie Anna to the lower rungs and haul her up that way. It would be easy if they had a car or a tractor or a horse—or any of several other things nobody had anymore.

He didn't go back to look at them. Anything could happen between then and the next day. The ladder, for instance, might belong to a gang that was still using the place for smuggling or secret meetings, in spite of the gruesome recent addition of the living graveyard. He might return and find the ladder gone. The children's parents could be there, lying in wait for him, ready to deal with anyone who knew what they had done to the pleasant, gray-haired refugee who had been working as a nursemaid to their children.

He'd do what he had promised: he'd try. And they'd wait where they were, knowing that he'd expect them to be in the same spot when he came back.

A few drops of rain spattered down as he made his way home. At first he thought that he'd misjudged the hour and that the darkening sky meant an early evening, but the rain convinced him that he still had time to do everything: collect his toolbox, pick up some clothes, and find the ropes he kept coiled in the corner cupboard to the right of the sink. The longest rope would certainly be enough. And there were two shorter ones.

As he walked, he scanned the houses in the distance. One of them would be the place where the two children lived. He wondered how the women in the quarry would be able to stand the cold and wet in a downpour. Thinking about the older woman reminded him of the old woman at home. What was he going to do with her now? If he hadn't met the children and Anna and Maria, he'd have taken a quick look, come back at night, and just shoved her over. But he'd have needed to borrow a car from somewhere, so maybe he'd have postponed any action till then.

The rain passed by. He came to the lane that led to his house. He'd have to think up something to tell his wife. He'd say that he'd decided to do what she'd been asking and get rid of the old woman. So, he'd gone to the quarry. But there was a woman and . . . her daughter . . . who had been tricked, robbed, and thrown in there with the others. And he was going to get them out. They could work in the house. They could take care of the children. And if she didn't like it, she could get out, because she sure as hell didn't do much herself nowadays. All she did was smoke black-market cigarettes one after the other.

He stepped over the threshold. The whimpers of the old woman started up as if renewing themselves in increasing frequency. And the smell was there. But his wife wasn't at home. And the children were out; they ought to have been back in the house at that hour. Maybe they were at a neighborhood party or walking home from a soccer game or doing work somewhere in order to earn extra money. But now it really was beginning to get dark and he didn't like the girls to stay out late unless they were with friends. Had his wife taken them all somewhere without telling him beforehand—had she left him? She wouldn't be able to manage on her own. And what man would take on a woman who had all those kids?

He heard another noise above the sounds of the old woman: the cries of someone in pain. They came from one of the back rooms where some of the children slept. He hurried toward the noise. Long before he reached the door, he must have recognized the grunts and moans for what they were. And as soon as he knew, he should have stopped, gone away to think, and laid a trap. But he didn't miss a step. He didn't seem to think at all, although something must have been taking place in his mind because he speeded up, going faster toward the door and not bothering to walk quietly. So, even though he had surprise on his side, they would have heard his approach before he came through the door.

He pulled the aid worker off his wife, swiped him across the side of his head with his hook, and when the man produced the knife he'd reached for, jumped on the bed and started to kick him in the belly. His wife scrabbled around for the fallen knife. He slammed her in the face. Blood gushed from her nose and she fainted. He turned back to the man, but not fast enough.

He saw the fist coming at him, right in front of his face.

He woke with a headache worse than any hangover he'd ever had. The night sky was above him, irradiated by a half moon. Someone was bending over him: a woman—a beautiful woman. Maria.

He was in the quarry. As soon as he understood where he was, he could smell the pungent reek: coming from all around him, especially from a large, lumpy shape lying on the ground ahead of him.

"Are you badly hurt?" Maria asked. "Can you understand what I'm saying?"

He felt his jaw and tested the action of his limbs. He was still in his clothes and boots, but his hook was gone. He wondered if it had been lost during the fall. Of course not; it had to be unscrewed. He was lucky that they hadn't beaten the other half out of the bone; that could help to identify him, if anyone ever wanted to take the trouble.

He was sore, but that was all. No bones were broken, not even his jaw, and he still had his teeth. All the pain—except for his head—came from bruising, nothing more.

"They were in a hurry," she told them. "They threw the old woman over first. You fell right on top of her, with your arm under your head. Otherwise, you'd probably be dead."

"This is the sandy side," he said. "Everybody knows that. They must have been scared. Or lazy. They must have known the fall might not kill me."

A shadow moved behind Maria: Anna, still wrapped in her blanket. She sat down on the ground next to him, and sighed, saying, "What difference does it make? We can't get out. You might be better off if you'd broken your neck."

"They had a car," Maria said. "We heard it. I came over here to look. Anna stayed where we'd seen you in the afternoon."

"How long ago did this happen?"

"Ten minutes, no longer."

He sat up, thinking: *Thank God I haven't been here for a week and lost my strength.* The clothes and boots were a help, but not necessary. The missing hook was more important; without it he felt somehow unsure of his balance.

He told them about the stone steps that used to lead from the top. The stairs that went down to gravel and the ones that ended on solid stone had been left with projections and rough edges. The ones that led from stone still contained a long middle section of steps. Going up from gravel the stairs were more destroyed and higher, but less dangerous if you fell. It was a question of weighing advantage against disadvantage. He chose the stone. The women disagreed with him. He said, "We'll see what it's like first."

They walked across the quarry in the moonlight, Maria stepping daintily in her party shoes, Anna limping behind. Halfway over to the other side, someone began to follow them. He stopped to chase the intruder away. Anna said, "Most of them are quiet till near the end, when they start to go crazy. That gives them a burst of energy every once in a while." When the same form scuttled back, he turned around and kicked out at it. No one bothered them after that.

He put his hand on the rock face; it was cold but not wet. He wiped his hand on his trousers. He considered taking his boots off and decided against it. He longed for his hook.

"Stand back while I'm climbing," he told the women. "If I get out, I'll come back to where they threw me over the side. And I'll try to find the car. If I don't come back, I'll be dead."

The first part of the climb was easy. At the still almost complete mid-section, he went up the steps without hesitation. Only after that did the ordeal begin, as he moved across jutting spars and ledges that broke under his weight, or leaned close to the rock wall to catch his breath and slow his heartbeat, only to find that the stone now seemed moist and slippery. He was running with sweat and gasping for air. His head felt ready to burst and he began to tremble. In the half-light his sense of distance was distorted so that he mistook shadow for solid ground. Pieces of rock crumbled away beneath him as he tried to find a safe place to stand and rest. But the longer he struggled, the clearer it became that there wasn't going to be any rest. He couldn't go back: he would never be able to repeat any stretch of the climb, much less do it again from the beginning; the trail was collapsing—erasing itself as he moved. This was the test that was like life: you went through it once and that was your only chance.

He was afraid that his muscles were going to go into spasm or to lock without warning, but he couldn't turn the other way because there wasn't room. *Don't do anything sudden out of desperation,* he thought. *Just keep going.*

He couldn't believe that he was going to make it to the top. He would have lost hope if he hadn't remembered that there were other people counting on him. Trying to remain calm, he forced himself to go on. For a while it seemed to him that he was gaining and losing, only to stay in the same place. Then he made some progress. The idea of stopping, and of looking down, began to pull at him. He wanted to look back even though he knew that that would be the end. He kept on.

As he reached for the top, he lunged ahead and up, getting his hand, his good arm, and a leg over the edge of the stone shelf. He rolled forward, pressing himself to the security of free ground. Behind him another section of rock slipped downward and fell with a crash to the quarry floor.

This time he looked back, to see if the others were all right. They were both standing where he'd told them to. Maria was clapping her hands. He waved.

Everything was clear and dreamlike in the moonlight. He moved with a steady pace. If he hadn't felt strange, he would have liked to run. Anyone who saw him would have thought there was nothing wrong, but he knew that something peculiar was happening to him. Being knocked out, and then landing in the quarry, might have shaken up his head. Maybe he had a concussion. He'd have to worry about that later.

He had a strong sense of the unreality of everything he looked at. He was also uncannily aware of being protected. Later he'd imagine that there had been a giant hand above him. At the moment it was simply a presence.

This time, he thought, he wouldn't make the mistake of charging through the front door and on into the back room, if that was still where they were. If his wife had sent the children away for the afternoon, they'd be at home again now. And the man might have moved on; with the opportunities of a job like his, he probably had several women in the district. Or maybe not. Perhaps his wife's pregnancy was a sign that the man was committed to her.

As he neared the house he inspected all the overgrown fences, the broken-down walls, the disused paths. He was looking for the car. He had to wait until he was closer.

The car was parked outside the house. It had been positioned at the back, so that no passerby would be tempted to steal it, but it was right next to the door, to save its owner time and to keep him from getting wet if it rained.

He crept along the side of the house to the toolshed, pulled the loose plank away, and reached in under the shelf where he kept an ex-tra knife. It was still there, in its sheath. The ax was in its place, too, up under the slope of the shed roof over the woodpile. He stuck the knife down his boot and carried the ax in his hand.

Which part of the house would they be in? Not in the back room this time; the children would be in that bed. And not where the old woman's bed had stood; he could see the mattress sagging against one of the trees. They'd be upstairs, in his own bed.

He got in through a window, climbed the stairs stealthily, tiptoed beyond the other room where the children would be sleeping, and stopped outside the bedroom. He tried the door. It moved forward under his hand; they hadn't turned the key because they'd thought that he was safely disposed of.

He could hear them inside, breathing in sleep.

He pushed the door wide, snapped on the light with his elbow, stepped forward and swung the ax down on the back of the man's head. Then he pulled out the knife. The sight of the woman—her face partly covered by a white mask—brought him to a halt. He didn't know who she was. For an instant he wondered if he'd gone out of his mind, or if he'd entered the wrong house by mistake and just imagined all the rooms to be familiar in the half-dark and moonlight. Had a strange couple been invited over for the night?

She made a sound and opened her eyes. He realized that what she was wearing was a large bandage. He must have broken her nose when he'd hit her earlier in the evening.

He dropped the knife on the bed, pulled her by the hair, and got her neck into the crook of his arm. He picked up the knife again. She hadn't even had time to scream. "Where's the hook?" he demanded. She tried to speak. He released his grip slightly.

She said, "It wasn't my idea. I didn't want to—"

"Where is it?" he repeated. "Quick. Or I'll take one of your eyes out." He pushed the knife forward at her."

"It's gone."

"Where?"

"I threw it out. He said to."

"Where?"

"In the garbage?"

"Outside?"

"No. Still in the bag. Under the sink."

He said that they'd go there together and not to make any noise. She wanted to talk. He tightened his grip, pulled her out of the bed, and forced her to walk in front of him. As he dragged her from under the covers he saw her eyes go to the man and the ax. She began to moan. He told her to shut up. She started to cry. "Quiet," he said. "If you wake the kids, I'll kill you."

"I won't do anything," she whispered. She breathed fast, choking. He loosened his hold on her.

"I didn't want anything to happen to you," she said. "I did it for the food and cigarettes, I—"

"Move," he hissed, shoving her forward.

When they arrived in the kitchen, he made her point out the bag that contained the hook. With the knife still in his hand he lifted the bag out of the pail and dumped it into the sink. "Find it," he told her.

That was the moment where he almost relented: when, pressing her forward and still gripping her neck in his arm, he saw her hands shake uncontrollably as they searched through the eggshells and the rotten ends of cabbage leaves. He felt such pity at the sight that he almost let her go. The next instant, she had the hook, and she was trying to twist around, to reach up and stick it into his face, at the same time kicking backward at him. The trembling had been caused by hope, not fear.

He lifted her off her feet, threw the knife away, and brought his hand forward to press more tightly into her neck. He squeezed as hard as he could until her body relaxed and—as far as he could tell—her breathing stopped, but she could be pretending. He waited. And afterwards, to make sure, he chopped the back of her neck with the side of his hand. He wasn't going to leave anyone half dead. *No prisoners, no survivors, no ghosts*: that was what his friends used to say.

He moved her to a chair and ran some water over the hook, cleaned it with the towel by the sink, and screwed it back into his socket.

From then on, he worked as if he had actually planned everything, knowing how much time he could save by doing which thing first. He went through the neatly folded clothes that had been placed on the bedroom chair. He found car keys, identification, a notebook, and jewelry. He removed a watch, a heavy gold bracelet and neck chain, a large gold ring with an eagle stamped on it. He put the keys in his pocket. The shoes and knife were under the side of the bed.

He retrieved the ax from the body, wiped it on the man's trousers, looked at the shoes to determine whether or not they'd fit anyone he knew, and decided to sell them. He threw them—with the knife, the papers and notebook and jewelry—into the man's shirt, tied the arms to make a bundle, and stuck it under the bed. Then he wrapped the trousers around the man's head and carried him out to the car. On the way back to the front of the house, he collected a hammer, saw, screwdriver, nails, screws and bolts, and a lamp. He left them all on the front seat and returned to the house for two of the ropes and the ax, which he'd stood in a corner.

He pulled the nightdress off his wife, looked it over for bloodstains, and dropped it into the laundry pile. He carried her outside and slung her into the backseat of the car, on top of the man. The ax and ropes went into the front with the rest of the tools. He wanted to stop but he didn't dare. As soon as the wish for sleep crossed his mind, he knew how close he was to complete exhaustion.

He looked around the kitchen to see if he'd forgotten anything that should be hidden or cleaned. His eye fell on the man's coat—an extremely beautiful and expensive-looking leather coat hanging on the back of the door. In an inside pocket there was a pistol. How had that gone unnoticed by the children?

He went through the other pockets quickly, pulling out an unused handkerchief, an open pack of cigarettes, a wad of money, a spare magazine for the gun, a map, and an address book. He himself would never have gone to another room and left such treasures unguarded.

A couple of empty bottles and two glasses on the table might have explained such carelessness. They'd been drunk. After what they'd been through earlier in the evening, they'd undoubtedly taken to the bottle, starting as they bandaged his wife's nose, continuing during the struggle to drag him and the old woman into the car, and then pausing while they had to deal with the return of the children to the house. Perhaps they'd made the kids drunk, too, to be sure that there would be no interruption, and no awakenings when they were away from the house. They'd both go, of course; each to see that the other did what should be done.

He kept the pistol on him. The rest of the things he put under the bed upstairs, except for the coat, which he took out to the car. He threw it over the two in the backseat. It was too dangerous to keep, no matter how much it was worth. To sell the car—and the shoes and jewelry—would be easy. A dead man's coat was another matter.

He released the brake and pushed the car away from the house. He didn't think a short distance would be much use in disguising the noise of the engine starting up, but after having made so many mistakes earlier, he didn't want to ruin everything now. He was already so tired that he was forgetting things: he was behind the wheel, the car moving, when he remembered that he'd meant to bring the two women another blanket and his wife's coat.

He drove to the quarry without seeing anyone and, he hoped, without being seen.

Before anything else, he heaved the two bodies over the side. He tore the bandage from his wife's face and threw the sticky ball of gauze and adhesive into the bushes before he let her drop down. The man went after that, with the trousers still knotted around his head.

He leaned over the edge. "Are you down there?" he called softly.

Maria's voice came back: "Is that you?"

"I've got a car and some ropes. The ladder's got to be a last resort. You're going to have to do most of the work."

They washed, changed their clothes, and sat down to a meal. The children were sleeping so soundly that he was sure his guess was right: they'd been given something to keep them quiet. In the morning he'd give them another kind of sedative: he'd tell them a story. This time the fiction would be about their mother and a strange, bad man and—unlike the tales of kings and princesses—no one would ask to hear it a second time.

Maria had a story, too. She said right at the beginning—that first night—that she was going to tell him all the information he'd ever want to know about her; he'd never have to question her again and he shouldn't try to interrupt, otherwise she wouldn't be able to get through to the end. In the half-dark before dawn she spoke in a hoarse whisper so hurried that he couldn't have stopped her anyway.

She was at school when the town she lived in had been caught in a daylight attack. Her first thought was to find her sister. Her sister was in one of the upper grades composed entirely of girls because the boys had been taken into combat.

She'd fled from her classroom only to encounter soldiers raising their guns at her. Grenades came through the windows. One of her friends, standing next to her, was shot in the face and fell to the floor without making a sound, the back of her head blown out against the wall. There was panic in all the corridors. Soon everyone was screaming and pushing. She ran into the gymnasium, where she climbed up an exercise rope that hung from one of the beams, then pulled the rope up after her and hid in the rafters. When the rest of the school took refuge in the gym, followed by the soldiers, she was perfectly placed to see the massacre that followed and, after she turned her head away, to hear it. That was what she said she kept remembering—not anything she'd seen, but what she'd heard: all the different sounds of fear and pain and the laughter: the sound of men laughing at suffering. Her position wasn't so safe a few hours later when the retreating troops set fire to the building. And when she got out alive—even without injury—and reached home, all her mother had had to say to her was, "Where's your sister?" Much later, at the height of an argument about

Maria's racketeer boyfriend, her mother had shouted, "If only you'd been the one to die and not your sister. Why couldn't it have been you?" That was the reason, Maria said, why she'd left home.

He still thought that once they'd concocted a good story, he should have gone straight to the house where the two children lived: to install Anna there, drive the parents back to the quarry, and throw them in. When the girl and boy woke in the morning, Anna could have told them that the fairies had come to take the parents away and that they'd left her in their place. But Anna had said no and anyway, by the time they'd managed to get her to the top of the rock face, all three of them were at the end of their strength.

He'd wanted to go after Maria's lover, too—the man who had seduced her, taken her out on wild sprees with his black-market friends, indirectly caused her family to disown her and—undoubtedly—had been planning to turn her into a whore: he'd driven her out to the quarry at night; she knew what it was, but he'd told her that the place represented a part of their country's history that no one was ever going to record, so she ought to see it. It shouldn't upset her: the people down there deserved to be there; they had all transgressed in some way. Maria had found herself having to live up to her reputation—based on her looks—for being tempestuous as well as sensual. She'd said: sure, she wasn't scared. He'd parked the car near the edge, pulled her out, made her look over, and asked her if she could see the rats. And then he'd said: what the hell had she wanted to go and get herself pregnant for? What use was she going to be to him now, and anyway didn't she know he was married? Of course he had a wife; everybody did. You got married the first time so she'd say yes and all the other times afterwards, you just promised it. Why didn't she know that? Everybody else knew. And now he'd had all the trouble of breaking her in without getting his money's worth because she was just a dumb farm girl after all.

He'd slapped her. She'd taken a step back. He'd called her obscene names. He'd hit her again, this time on the other side of her face, and then advanced on her. As she took the next step back, she turned to see how close to the edge she was, and while she was still trying to protect herself rather than thinking of attacking him, he made a rush at her and pushed her quickly several times, until she went over.

The moment when she realized she was falling—she wouldn't describe it except to say that it was worse than the moment when she knew that she'd never get out. From above her he'd shouted, "And you can stay there."

It would have been simple to find the man. Maria could remain unseen and point him out; it would be easy to kill him.

"Let's see if he comes around saying it was all a joke," she said. "Then I'll kill him myself. But those people he runs around with are pretty rough. They'll probably take care of him."

"Unless they come after me."

"No. I don't think we'll have to worry about that. As far as they're concerned, there isn't any connection. And he'll probably think he was so drunk that he dreamt it."

After a few days went by, it was too late: he no longer had the readiness, nor the high sense of righteousness, to take revenge. He wanted peace; and to begin life again, with Maria. She wasn't in love with him, but that was something he didn't have to think about at the moment. He loved. And that was enough. As long as Anna stayed with them, Maria would probably be satisfied. Anna had replaced mother and sister; he was a substitute for the lover and possibly also the father.

As it turned out, they couldn't find anyone who had seen Maria's lover since the night he'd been out at the quarry with her. But they decided that if any questions came up, Anna would say she'd heard a rumor that the man had killed an aid worker and the married woman he was sleeping with: because the two men were in some kind of smuggling racket together and the woman was sleeping with them both and didn't know which one was the father of her unborn child.

Their enemies were in plain view. One day Anna and Maria went shopping in town while the younger children were being looked after in a nursery group. The older ones were away at the first educational classes they'd seen since the evacuation: a kind of school that had just been started up by a group of mothers and grandmothers, one of whom—before her retirement—had been a teacher of mathematics.

Maria was rummaging through bins of patched and worn children's clothing when Anna saw one of her tormentors: the mother from the family with whom she'd been housed. The woman was reaching into a pile of clothes. "Still grabbing," Anna said. The woman didn't react at first, but after a moment she looked up.

Maria later perfected an imitation of the woman's horrified understanding and her recoil. When she and Anna recounted the story of the meeting, Maria would act it out while Anna described it, declaring solemnly, "She just stood there, as if turned to stone."

Anna said to the woman, "We'll call in to see the children in a few days. I'm still very fond of them. And I'll pick up my refugee rations, of course. I won't put you to the trouble of giving me a roof over my head, even if it is your duty. We'll speak to the authorities and see what we can do about having me transferred to the family I'm with now. I'm not vindictive." The woman closed her eyes with relief and possibly from faintness. Anna continued in an ordinary tone of voice, saying, "On the other hand, you're going to have to pay my medical bills. I've had quite a lot of trouble with my leg after the fall I had. You owe me that. And you know how long I'm going to have to wait to find a doctor. So maybe you'd better leave those clothes alone. You aren't going to be able to afford them." The woman nodded slowly and moved away, putting out a hand to support herself against the wall as she left.

"It was wonderful," Maria told him. But Anna said, "As soon as they pay up for the doctor, that's the end. I don't want them to get so scared that they try it again. I think if they ever see the chance, they'll move."

Maria disagreed. "I don't see why. It's their word against yours. I wouldn't." She turned to him and asked, "Would you?"

"No," he said. "This is home."

One night he went out into the orchard and dug a false grave and filled it in again. Every time he pushed the blade of the shovel into the ground he thought what bad luck it was that after climbing free from the quarry he'd been too used up to think straight; because, if he'd been fully alert, he'd have buried his wife instead of taking her in the car. That way, they'd have had a body. As it was, he'd have to pretend—if anyone wanted to investigate—that he couldn't remember exactly which spot he'd chosen, that he'd done the grave digging at night in order to keep the children from being upset, and he was as mystified as anyone else to find that what certainly looked like the place now turned out to be wrong. The authorities weren't going to start digging up the entire orchard. However, if by some extraordinary chance they did, he'd be forced to admit in the end that he'd lied. But that wasn't so serious. Anyone would understand that he'd want to tell a lie: to keep drawing the rations. He'd say that there wasn't any corpse—the old battle-ax had fooled them all and gone off with one of the aid workers who had claimed that he could house her someplace closer to where she used to live.

Nevertheless, he kept digging. And soon afterwards he went to town and reported the death of the old woman. No one did anything except put the information on paper. He was told that he was now eligible to receive another refugee.

"We buried her in the orchard," he began to explain.

"Yes, yes," the official said. "No possessions?"

"I'm afraid we had to burn the nightdress. It was too—"

"Of course. They have her age down here as 'from eighty-five to a hundred.' It's a miracle that she lasted so long."

"We already have a new refugee," he said. "She had some trouble with the family she was with. I can give you their name. They've agreed to let you transfer her. We've been taking care of her for a few weeks, but we need the extra rations."

"I'll see what I can do," the official told him.

The new school was a success. Within days everyone had heard about it. It attracted more pupils every week and, luckily, a few extra teachers, too.

The next bit of good luck turned up when a huge shipment of

flour, sugar, and salt came through legally and was distributed by the authorities.

Some of the old occupations came back, even if not as they had been practiced before the fighting. So few professionals survived anywhere that amateurs were considered better than nothing: as long as they did the work, who cared? Two girls, whose father had been a plumber, set themselves up in business using the knowledge he'd passed on to them and the tools and material he'd left behind. Even children joined the scramble for employment. A boy who had inherited his uncle's optical equipment—and had discovered all of it, unbroken, behind a trick panel in the cellar—was now reading the medical books he'd been left. He planned to begin work as soon as he had some answers to the letters he'd sent out.

"But that's silly," Anna commented. "You need lenses and somebody's got to grind them. That's specialized work. They're made in factories, in dust-free conditions. That belongs to another world. That's all over now. I suppose you have to admire his initiative."

"And his optimism," Maria said. "He'll probably be just the right age to be drafted when the next wave of fighting begins."

"Don't even say it. Everybody's talking about it again."

"They're always talking about it," he said. "You can't get a newspaper unless you know the right people and have the right stuff to trade, but if you do, you can read any publication you like from other countries. The only trouble is: what they print about us won't do you any good because they don't know what's going on here any more than we do."

Local news traveled—as usual—by the grapevine, which was extremely effective, although the information relayed was occasionally completely unfounded. If you wanted customers, or were looking for a particular thing you needed for your work, the best way to get results was still to put out the word among friends, neighbors, acquaintances, and strangers. A woman on the other side of town had done just that after she'd had a dream that she could cure her rheumatism by dancing. She'd talked an official into lending her a hall and some chairs and then she'd simply accosted people on the street to let them know that she was in business. One of the first men to turn up became her second-in-command by offering to bring his accordion and to supply the music. The woman rapidly collected a dedicated group of enthusiasts who were willing to pay. Her dream hadn't mentioned remuneration; that was a natural development and a pleasant surprise. Even more unexpected was the fact that after she'd molded her idea into a reality and had given it the name of "The Tuesday and Thursday Tango Tea," she was besieged by racketeers' girlfriends who had time on their hands and wanted to pick up some refinement. Within a few weeks she'd become one of the luminaries of what—temporarily, at least—passed for society in their part of the world. It wasn't long before the root tea and watery soup grew to resemble real tea and alcohol. To the accordionist's dismay, the music also improved when the woman entered into a contract with a professional band that traveled from town to town all week long. They played on Thursdays, which became the popular day and helped to divide the clientele into rich and poor as well as dubious or respectable. Most dancers became Tuesday people or Thursday people. After a while no one went on both nights, except the woman who had thought the thing up and who, despite a life formerly marked by bouts of invalidism, managed to remain at the helm.

Before the school began, there had been a local mail service run as a cooperative effort by children. Each child had had to complete a certain number of hours stamping and sorting and out on the rounds. An exception had been made for one of the founder members who was born lame and another two who had been injured in infancy by enemy action. The school cut into the children's working time, but added to the number of recruits. Since paper was scarce, their next project was going to be a paper factory and a shop where old paper could be exchanged for credits. That was for the future, as were most other similar ideas. But the town was getting organized, pulling the outlying regions into its returning life. A neighboring district had set up hospital facilities that were said to include emergency transportation to the nearest big city; no one had investigated the claim yet, as there was a strict list of conditions that had to be met by patients: all cases not considered critical were refused. However, the possibility was there and that meant hope for development: more medicine, equipment, doctors and nurses.

Some of the schemes people dreamt up were crazy, some illegal, and some—often both crazy and illegal—worked, like the convoluted system of barter and banking started up by an old man who said he was ninety but was probably in his seventies and who, after a few days' trading, became known as Major Money.

It seemed for a while as if life might continue along its peaceful course: getting back to normal and also heading toward a future of unbroken peace. But just as things were improving, the winter brought hardship again. No matter how happy they were, it was impossible to forget the cold and hunger. A series of fevers and children's diseases ran through the entire sector. There were deaths as well as children who survived with damaged hearing, eyesight, and lungs. Food was scarce, and once more it was a long winter.

The next time the aid workers turned up, they brought two nine-year-old children: a twin brother and sister, who were almost completely silent for a few days. They didn't even trust the other children, preferring Anna's company. But they helped with any work that had to be done. After a while, slowly, they joined in the conversation. Soon they were enrolled in the school and sharing sentry duty on the first planting in the garden.

"They're nice kids," Anna told him. "I think they're going to be fine as long as nobody asks them any stupid questions, like, 'Where are your parents?'"

The days were warmer, longer, lighter. It was nearly spring.

With the good weather came better food and more of it. One or two luxuries turned up as a result of haggling at the weekly market. It began to seem as if, for that year at least, they could be leaving the bad days behind. There was work and building material. He'd even been able to get hold of some cans of paint that hadn't dried out.

And then, after so many years, the fair came back to town. Everyone took its appearance as a sign that someone was sure about an eventual peaceful settlement to the hostilities. The traveling musicians had been the first professional entertainment to return to the region, but they hadn't been the real thing: they could pick up their instruments and run if they had to. A whole fairground was different; you needed tents and ladders, transport trucks and food for the animals.

Every day his children told him news of the marvels to be seen at the fair. He heard the same descriptions repeated by adults in town: that there was a big tent with a cage full of animals and even room for a trapeze act as well as tightrope walkers. The animals weren't the wonderful striped, spotted, or maned big cats; they were the more or-dinary bears and seals, but the bears at any rate were dangerous, so the children could derive some pleasure from them. One of the bears in particular was gigantic. It was the only one kept muzzled and chained. Word of its size and fierceness spread through the neighborhood be-fore anyone had seen it.

Everybody wanted to go to the fair. It was traveling around the country, which meant that it would set down near them only for a short while. It would be the big treat of the year. Of course he'd have to take everyone in the house—the whole crowd of them.

He produced his wallet and counted out bills. A few of the children were so impatient that they danced up and down in front of him. He paid the money to the woman in the ticket booth. She handed him a long ribbon of paper, still unbroken. He passed it to Anna, who began to tear the single strip into separate pieces, giving a ticket to each child. "Remember now," she told them, "don't get lost. Come back here just inside the gate when the whistle blows, and don't speak to strangers, even if they tell you they're from school or the district hospital or the police."

"Especially not if they tell you something like that," he said. "If they try to get you to go with them for any reason at all, you just run away. And if they grab you: kick, bite, and yell as loud as you can."

The children nodded. They remembered what had happened to their mother: a man had come to their house and he'd made her say that their father had walked out on them, taking the old woman with him for the sake of the aid money. The real truth was that the man had killed the old woman and burned her in the stove. Then he'd beaten up their mother so badly that her face was covered with bandages; he'd said that their father had done it, but they didn't believe that. Their mother had given them a hot drink and put them to bed. She'd told them that everything would be all right in the morning. And that was true, because in the morning their father was back. The man had tried to kill him, and then he'd taken their mother away as a prisoner, probably to a different country so that she could never return. But their father was going to bring them up himself, with the help of Anna and her daughter, Maria, so at least they'd have somebody to look after them: somebody who loved them. And they were never to tell anybody about that other man killing the old woman. They should say that she died of old age and they'd buried her in the orchard; because if they didn't, the aid people weren't going to give them their food allowance and the authorities might even accuse their father of getting rid of her himself.

Maria counted out the spending money for each child. "If you buy any food," she said, "try not to eat it too fast. And be careful of that ride over there—the one that goes up and down and tilts while it spins. It makes you feel horrible. I remember that one from my first trip to the fair. You feel awful for days."

Anna said, "I'll take the little ones to see the baby animals." The smaller children shouted: yes, baby animals.

"What are the baby animals?" he asked.

Anna shrugged. "Lambs, piglets, baby chicks."

"Yum-yum," Maria whispered.

He laughed. Maybe that was what had happened to the tigers.

"Remember, everybody," Anna repeated. "When you hear the whistle." The children ran, breaking into groups before they were out of sight.

"They'll all be sick this evening," he predicted.

"Sick, but happy. And with nice memories. We'll see you later." Anna moved away, the three smaller children clinging to her.

"Isn't she wonderful?" Maria said. "If only my mother had been like that. God, it's strange. All the best things in my life happened within twenty-four hours of being shoved into the pit of hell. What a comedy."

"Happy endings. That's what I like. To survive and to live well, knowing that you've deserved it."

They set off hand in hand to investigate the shows. He looked around at the other parents and their children, all of them trying, and failing, to do simple tricks that had once been so easy for him: throwing a hoop over a wooden stake, hitting a moving toy bird with a ball, shooting down a target. He still had a good eye, but that wasn't enough.

Maria said, "I was always told those places were rigged: the stake is angled away from you and it's just a little too big for the hoop to fit it. And the ducks over there are on a supporting piece that never moves unless you complain, and then they flip a switch that releases the spring and they show you that you can knock the entire thing over easily: you're just missing it every time."

"I guess so. They get away with what they can. On some of these things they probably have a way of letting a few people win, so the others can see it."

"Their friends and relatives."

"But if you don't win at one, you try the next. Or you can ride on one of the cars, or have your future told."

"Oh. Do you want to do that?"

"Not for anything. It's hard enough dealing with the past and the present. Come on."

They saw Anna a long way ahead. She was kneeling in the middle of her bevy of children and using a handkerchief to take a speck of dirt out of a child's eye.

He looked up at the big wheel and at the smaller, slower merry-go-round with its painted horses. "How about that?" he suggested. "It wouldn't be too fast."

"No, thanks. I seem to remember that it starts slow and speeds up. And then it's too late to jump off."

"All right. Where to?"

"How about the House of Horrors? That's pretty tame."

"The House of Horrors. Definitely. Unless you don't think it's a good idea."

She put a hand on her belly, and said, "If this child can thrive on everything it's been through already, I don't think a haunted house or two is going to hurt it."

They couldn't find the House of Horrors. They trailed around the stands and cages, wondering what they could do with their time until the whistle blew to mark the hour. They passed the seals and the bears, the table where there was a glass jar full of pebbles whose number could be guessed. Maria wanted to sit down. "Here," she said.

They entered a tent inscribed with the name *Professor Miracolo*. The show was about to begin. There wasn't time to bother with tickets; as soon as he'd paid at the desk, they were waved ahead into a small, semicircular theater already crowded with other customers. They were barely in their seats when the side lights dimmed and the stage was flooded by a dazzling glare from above.

Two men stepped into the field of brightness. One told the members of the audience what they were going to see: "The world's greatest ... the most renowned ... expert in the arts of contortion ... the foremost practitioner of magic transformations learned through years of study in the fabled schools of the mystic East ... the one and only Professor Miracolo will now perform his internationally celebrated repertoire of astounding magical acts, concluding with the incredible, supernatural finger-balancing exercise, a feat so hazardous that only the Professor himself has been able to master it."

They watched the Professor—who was dressed in a top hat and tails—remove his hat and go through the colored ribbon trick, the flags, and the rabbit. Further well-known mystifications called for audience participation: children were chosen from the crowd to cut a piece of paper with scissors that had been functioning perfectly well for the Professor but, as soon as he handed them over, wouldn't open for the child. Much laughter ensued at the expense of the young volunteers, who were utterly confounded by the business. "That's so mean," Maria murmured. "It's just a knob he flicks to the side every time he takes the scissors back to look at them. It locks the blades, like a safety catch." She applauded loudly as a child stepped back and rejoined its parents.

Professor Miracolo set up a display that included four candles. He was helped by a woman in her forties who was dressed in a spangled costume with a skirt like a dancer's tutu. Her hair was piled up in a glistening mound, her shoes were high-heeled gold sandals. As she retired behind the curtains with the announcer, the Professor lit the candles by pointing a wand at them, one by one.

Maria turned her face away at the sight of the flames. She looked for the way out. He pulled her closer and ran his hand over her hair.

Professor Miracolo waved his wand again. The row of lights sank from sight. He repeated the action and they all came back. He singled out the candle at the end, the one at the beginning. It was easy to see that the flames were live fire; how did he do it? The audience applauded, even Maria.

For the last, culminating show of skill, the barker rolled a large, heavy-looking ball into the spotlight. He told everyone that this magical demonstration was the best of all, saved to the last, and only the professor—the highest genius in the world of magic—could carry out this extraordinary proof of mind over matter.

Professor Miracolo emerged from between the dark curtains. He approached the ball, which reached above his knees. He bent over it, put his hands on it, and then lifted himself up into a handstand. An outbreak of clapping stopped as he began to take one hand away. There was silence while everyone watched. He brought back the hand, placed it so that only one finger touched the ball and—in a move that looked both naturally easy and strangely untrue—put all his weight on that one finger and took away the other hand. He was balancing upside-down on top of a round rubber ball and using only a single finger of one hand. The audience was so astonished that for a while everyone simply sat and looked. Then people began to realize that no matter how impossible it seemed, the trick was worth a show of appreciation. They went wild.

At the height of the cheering and stamping, the lights blinked out and came back almost immediately. The ball had disappeared and the professor was revealed standing between the announcer and the female assistant. All three of them bowed.

They came out into the sunlight, and he repeated what he'd already said several times: "It's impossible."

"I don't understand it, either," Maria said, "but I had it explained to me once. Apparently you can give the illusion of practically anything if you cut off the real thing by a reflection from a mirror."

"But he was right in front of us."

"I know. It's amazing."

"I really liked that," he said. "If I were ten years old, it would drive me crazy, but I think I've reached just the perfect age for magic."

"Look," she said. "The House of Horrors. We were going in the wrong direction."

"And some of our bunch coming out of it." He whistled. The children turned their heads. He called to them. They came running to tell him about their adventures. Two of the girls admitted that they'd been scared in the House of Horrors, but the two older boys said it was nothing—just kid stuff: not a single good thing; you could see the wires everywhere, like a puppet show.

One of the younger boys didn't say anything. He stayed behind when the others went on to the next entertainment.

"Did you see Professor Miracolo?" Maria asked him.

"Oh, that was the best." He flushed with eagerness to talk about the magic. They walked together to the entrance of the House of Horrors.

Another thing he'd liked, he told them, was the princess in the thimble, who could dance to the music of a guitar even though she was so tiny that you had to look at her through a magnifying glass.

"You didn't like the haunted house?" she asked.

"Not as much. Everybody was screaming and it was dark."

"Want to try it again?" he asked. "You can come with us. If you've already been through once, you'll remember when things are going to jump out, so you'll know what to expect. And you can tell us about the really bad ones ahead of time. I don't want Maria to be upset."

The boy nodded. It was impossible to tell whether he was reluctant or overjoyed, but the answer came a few minutes later, after they'd taken their seats in the open carriage—the boy behind and he and Maria in front. His son's voice filled with confidence as he began his commentary.

I've got a rival, he thought. *The boy's hardly more than a child, and he's fallen in love with his father's woman.*

The track was full of curves, sudden twists, and bumps. As they creaked around the corner, ghosts wavered into their faces from the sides of the tunnel. All around them people burst into shouts and laughter.

"There's a very noisy skeleton next," the boy informed them.

He was glad of the warning. The sound took him back to the days when he was in uniform. With almost the same boom and crunch, followed by a loud crack, a skeleton shot toward them, seeming at the last moment to fly over their heads. Shortly afterwards a shoal of smaller skeletons danced in a moving archway, giggling and gibbering above and beside the train; one of them had part of a skeletal arm in its mouth, with blood dripping down the sides of its bony jaws and blood smeared across the captive hand.

He laughed, but his son didn't. *Out of consideration for me. Because of my lost hand. But one hand is like another once it's bare of flesh; one corpse is like the others when it's turned to bones.*

Every day he had to resist the urge to go out to the quarry. The temptation was almost unbearable, but he knew that that was the way people wrecked their lives: by picking at the details, over and over again, trying to cover their tracks and get everything right. It was better, even if you'd made mistakes, to leave it and not go back—to let the world move on. Time would overtake the past.

He had to keep repeating the good advice he'd decided to abide by: not to go back there for at least a year and not to admit anything, ever. He'd report the disappearance after it was too late to tell one person from another; and then they'd have the incident officially closed. His wife had run off with an aid worker: that was all, unless somebody went down there and started to identify people, in which case it would appear that the man had probably tried to kill her but in the act of pushing her into the quarry, he'd fallen in, too. Or maybe her assailant had succeeded in killing her and somebody from his gang of crooks had pushed him over the side later; the state of his head could be attributed to that, or even to something done to him by other people down there in the pit. That was as much as anyone would be able to guess.

The train ran through cackling monsters, witches, cauldrons of boiling oil, and bright, crawling things that appeared to be falling from the tunnel roof and landing all over the passengers: those were the most effective of all. Everyone tried frantically to brush the things off.

The boy crowed with delight. He said, "There isn't anything there. It's like pictures. They don't stay there when you're in the light."

Laughter overcame the sounds of distress. What had they been worried about? Maria, too, laughed heartily, secure against the arm he held around her. As the horrors came faster and with an ever greater excess of grotesque detail, the enjoyment increased. Everybody loved the ride, even the small children who had been brought in with parents. He remembered that his initial acquaintance with the place had been different, but it seemed to him that what made the difference was probably his own subsequent experience rather than any of the elaborate props and tricks of lighting added by the owners. Some of the dusty and faded monsters that worked on wheels or springs might have been the very same ones he'd met years ago. Yet they still had an effect on their audience. And on him. He was charmed. At the same time he was aware of how strange it was that—having lived through so many horrors—anyone should want to subject himself to this gallery of artificial terror. Was it a kind of protection, like a prophylactic medicine? The answer wasn't that no one knew the difference between the true and the false; they knew. But they still needed magic. The delights of illusion were similar to the pleasure of imagining a thing true when you knew that it couldn't be, or hoping for a marvelous event when you didn't really think it could happen. The workings of memory, too, like the magician's sleight of hand, made you believe. You couldn't go on living if you didn't believe that through the power of heart and mind you could keep whatever you lost: that the part of you that was good could transform and outlast even the chaos of war—that there could still be love and that love didn't die.

They had to shade their eyes against the light when they came out. Maria said, "That was fun. That was really nice."

He caught sight of Anna up by the gates. "See where Anna is?" he said to his son. "Go tell her to stay there till we catch up." The boy ran off. Maria called after him, "Thanks for the guided tour."

"That kid is wildly in love with you," he said.

"I hope so. In my condition I can use all the encouragement I can get."

He squeezed her to him and she turned up a smiling face. She breathed in deeply and then let the air out in a long sigh. "This is what I'm going to tell my grandchildren about," she said. "Days like today."

RACHEL INGALLS grew up in Cambridge, Massachusetts. She has had various jobs, from theatre dresser and librarian to publisher's reader. She is a confirmed radio and film addict and has lived in London since 1965. She is the author of several novels and short stories.

The text of *Times Like These* has been set in Adobe Jenson Pro, a typeface designed by Robert Slimbach that captures the essence of Nicolas Jenson's roman and Ludovico degli Arrighi's italic typeface designs. Book design by Wendy Holdman. Composition by Stanton Publication Services, Inc. Manufactured by Friesens on acid-free paper.